P.D. CACEK

SECOND LIVES

This is a **FLAME TREE PRESS** book

FLAME TREE PRESS
6 Melbray Mews, London, SW6 3NS, UK
flametreepress.com

Distribution and warehouse:
Baker & Taylor Publisher Services (BTPS)
30 Amberwood Parkway, Ashland, OH 44805
btpubservices.com

Publisher's Note: This is a work of fiction. Names, characters, places, and
incidents are a product of the author's imagination. Locales and public names
are sometimes used for atmospheric purposes. Any resemblance to actual
people, living or dead, or to businesses, companies, events, institutions, or
locales is completely coincidental.

Thanks to the Flame Tree Press team, including:
Taylor Bentley, Frances Bodiam, Federica Ciaravella, Don D'Auria,
Chris Herbert, Matteo Middlemiss, Josie Mitchell, Mike Spender,
Cat Taylor, Maria Tissot, Nick Wells, Gillian Whitaker.

The cover is created by Flame Tree Studio with
thanks to Nik Keevil and Shutterstock.com.
The font families used are Avenir and Bembo.

Flame Tree Press is an imprint of Flame Tree Publishing Ltd
flametreepublishing.com

A copy of the CIP data for this book is available from the British Library
and the Library of Congress.

HB ISBN: 978-1-78758-159-3
PB ISBN: 978-1-78758-157-9
ebook ISBN: 978-1-78758-160-9
Also available in FLAME TREE AUDIO

Printed in the US at Bookmasters, Ashland, Ohio

P.D. CACEK

SECOND LIVES

FLAME TREE PRESS
London & New York

To my sons Mike and Peter, never stop believing.
And to Edward W. Bryant, Jr. and Dallas Mayr, hurry back.

PART ONE
JUNE

CHAPTER ONE

Henry

"Wanna go. Now!"

"I know, Henry—"

"Hank! My name's Hank! Henry's a sissy name."

"I'm sorry. Hank."

Nora gathered up her purse and car keys before turning toward the stranger who'd taken the place of the man she'd married fifty-eight years ago. Anger etched the creases of his face.

He wanted to hit her.

Again.

The last time she told everyone she'd bumped into a cupboard door.

"Did you hear me? Wanna go!"

The stranger took a step forward, his right fist rising above his head.

"Yes, Hank...I heard you."

Without breaking eye contact, Nora opened her purse and slowly reached inside. If she moved too quickly it could startle him into doing something he'd regret; and he would, because there was still enough Henry left that when he came back he'd know what Hank had done to her. Then he'd beg her to forgive him.

And she would.

"Look what I have, Hank." Nora pulled out the cellophane-wrapped sucker and handed it to him. It was the kind of lollipop she used to buy their daughter Marjorie when she was still a toddler.

"CHERRY! Gimme!"

"Okay, let me unwrap it first."

He waited as patiently as any child could for a treat – shifting from one foot to the other, eager, hand reaching, fingers spread.

"Here you go."

His fingers touched hers as they took the lollipop and Nora smiled as she released it.

"Are you ready to go, Hank?"

He looked at her, eyes big while his mouth worked the cherry flavor down his throat. "Umm?"

"We're going for a ride, remember? You like rides."

He gave her a red-tinted smile. "I like rides."

"Yes, you do. Okay, let's go."

"Let's go!"

★ ★ ★

Henry was back in time for his doctor's appointment.

"So, how have things been this week, Henry?"

Henry took Nora's hand and squeezed it. Nora squeezed back.

"Think you're asking the wrong Rollins, doc."

The doctor, who Nora thought looked like a young Sidney Poitier, nodded and flashed a million-watt smile. Her stomach did a little flip. Silly old woman, he's young enough to be your grandchild.

She cleared her throat and gave Henry's hand another squeeze.

"Things have been pretty good."

Dr. Cross gave her another kind of look. "And how pretty would that be, Miss Nora?"

He always added the 'Miss' when talking to her. So respectful.

"Well, he has his ups and downs, but who doesn't? Still eats like a horse and he's good about taking his pills – of course he's better for the visiting nurse than he is for me. Still a flirt when it comes to the ladies, I'm afraid."

Both Henry and the doctor chuckled at that, even though it was a lie about him being a flirt. He was better when the nurse came on her biweekly visits, almost himself even when he wasn't.

It was the same when their daughter visited. It seemed as if she was the only one Hank didn't like.

Dr. Cross smiled. "Well, you can't fault a man for flirting, can you? But other than that, how's it been?"

"About the same."

The doctor nodded and turned his attention to Henry. "You ready to join the day group? I think it's art day."

"Ah…Basket Weaving 101," Henry said.

A nurse would put him into a wheelchair the moment they stepped into the hall. It was for insurance purposes they always told him, but Nora knew better – it was easier to move him from the doctor's office to the Alzheimer's unit two floors down then, afterward, back to the main lobby and out the door.

Just plain easier.

"See, Nora," Henry said as he nudged her, "I always told you I'd be weaving baskets and drooling one day."

The doctor chuckled and Nora thought it sounded as phony as her laugh.

"Oh, Henry!" she said. "You hush up, now."

"Okay, but don't say I didn't warn you."

"Ready, Mr. Rollins?" a young feminine voice asked from the doorway.

"Always," Henry said as he sat down. "Let's get this show on the road."

The nurse's giggle sounded genuine as she pushed him from view. Nora smiled at the doctor.

"How is he really?"

Nora straightened her shoulders. "About the same."

"Mood swings getting worse?"

"Some."

"How about the physical violence…has he hit you again?"

"It was an accident. I told you that. He didn't mean to."

The doctor leaned back in his chair. "Of course he didn't, but that's not what I asked you. Miss Nora, I don't want to sound like a broken record, but we've talked about your options before—"

Nora took a deep breath. Yes, they had, almost from the first moment they'd met.

But he hadn't been the first.

Even before there'd been a diagnosis and Henry could laugh off his lapses in memory and coordination as 'gittin' old', their family doctor had hinted it might be something more serious. But Henry had been so sure it was just his age – "same thing happened to my daddy" – that Nora made up her mind to believe him.

He was still Henry…more or less.

He still liked to putter around the garden, even though she'd sometimes find him hunched over crying because he'd forgotten the name of a flower or what you called those long green things on the poles. "Beans, honey, they're called beans," and then she'd help him pick some for dinner and he'd be all right again.

He still recognized their daughter and grandsons – most of the time – and if he happened to call the boys the names of childhood friends long dead and buried, one of Nora's oatmeal cookies and a whispered reminder that "Granddaddy's just getting old, baby" made it all better.

Those were the good days.

Other times he'd wander around the house muttering or sit down in the chair by the window and not move until the sun went down. Not even to go to the bathroom.

Those days weren't as good.

Then Hank showed up….

"Miss Nora?"

Nora blinked.

"Did you hear me?"

Nora could lie to herself and to Henry, even lie to Hank sometimes, but she found it impossible to lie to a man who looked like Sidney Poitier. "No…. I'm sorry. Maybe I'm getting like Henry."

"I don't think you have to worry about that just yet." He took a deep breath and released it. "I said I think it's time, Miss Nora."

Nora glanced toward the office's window bright with California sunshine until the burning in her eyes stopped. Everyone, their daughter, the doctors, their friends, the neighbors, even Henry himself, when he was himself, had said the time would come…and here it was.

Finally and officially.

When she turned back her eyes were dry. "Are you sure?"

He nodded. Of course he was sure, but Nora wanted to be able to tell Henry that she'd asked.

If he remembered.

"When?"

Dr. Cross seemed surprised, as if he'd expected her to put up more of a fight. It'd surprised Nora too, but only a little bit.

"I believe you and Henry have already taken the tour of our assisted living unit?"

Nora nodded. They had been given a tour after Henry's second visit/evaluation – just to have a look, should they want to consider it, when the time came. Henry had jokingly asked if he could bring Nora with him because 'it was such a nice place'.

And it was, for what it was: a sprawling, beautifully appointed one-story building that was separated from the main medical center by a parking lot and parklike 'Memory Walk' green belt. A miniature hospital in itself, the unit had its own medical staff, art and therapy classrooms, a twenty-four-hour emergency shuttle to the main hospital complex and a one-hundred-and-ten-bed 'permanent care' facility.

Each room was private with its own handicap-accessible bath, a twin bed (that could, their docent/tour guide told them, be replaced with a hospital bed when needed), end table, reclining chair, dresser, desk and chair, and wall-mounted flat-screen TV. If it hadn't been for the two ready-access oxygen outlets and three emergency call buttons in the room – one next to the bed, one in the bathroom and one in the TV remote – it could have been a college dorm room.

"Our guests are never more than a few feet away from being able to summon medical help," the tour coordinator told them with pride, "which their caregivers find most reassuring."

They'd talked about it when they got home and both agreed that it was certainly an option…when the time came.

Nora licked her lips and tasted the sweet/chemical tang of the lipstick she'd put on that morning.

"Okay." Dr. Cross nodded. "I think the faster we get Henry settled in the better it will be for both of you. Don't you agree, Miss Nora?"

She nodded again because she couldn't bring herself to say it out loud.

"Good. I know how hard this must be on you, but I promise it is the best thing for Henry." Picking up his cell phone, he swiped the screen, punched a number then looked up and smiled at her the same way Sidney Poitier had smiled at the old Mother Superior in *Lilies of the Field*. "Yes," he said to whomever he'd called. "This is Dr. Cross. We will be admitting Mr. Henry Rollins to the memory unit. Yes. Fine. Thank you." He swiped the phone again and set it down on his desk. "It's done."

"That fast?"

"That fast."

Standing up, the handsome young doctor walked around the desk to Nora's chair and offered his hand. She took it and, as she always did when shaking his hand in greeting or in parting, marveled at the softness of his skin as she got to her feet.

"Thank you. Well, I guess I'd better collect Henry and head for home. We have some packing to do."

Dr. Cross cupped her hand in both of his.

"Miss Nora. I think it would be best for everyone if you went home and he stayed here." When Nora tried to pull away the pressure on her hand increased. "I know, but it will be less traumatic for both of you in the long run."

"But— Please. He'll think I abandoned him."

"We'll make sure he understands that you didn't."

"But...." Her thoughts raced around the inside of her head like a hamster in a wheel. "But...he doesn't have his pajamas or toothbrush."

The doctor laughed and gave her hand a little squeeze. "I'm sure we can find something for him tonight and tomorrow I'll arrange for the visiting nurse to stop by and pick up a few of his things. Now, go home and get some rest, doctor's orders."

They walked out of his office and down the brightly lit hall hand in hand, and he didn't let go until they reached the entrance in the main lobby. Her hand felt cold after his touch.

"One more thing, Miss Nora. It would be best if you didn't come back for a few days."

Nora's cold hand touched the hollow of her throat. "Why? Henry'll wonder what happened to me. And I'll have to bring him his favorite slippers — he has these ratty old slippers and I...."

Then she ran out of breath and couldn't say another word.

"I know how hard this seems," Dr. Cross said, "but it will make Henry's adjustment a lot easier if you aren't here. And I'm only talking a couple of days…although a week would be best. Think you can give us a week, Miss Nora?"

Nora took a deep breath. "All right."

Dr. Cross touched her shoulder. "Thank you. Now before you think you're off the hook or anything, I expect at least a dozen of those wonderful oatmeal cookies on my desk when you do come back. Dare I hope?"

Nora let herself chuckle and nodded. "I'll have enough time to bake cookies for everybody."

She hadn't thought about that before, but, finally she would have enough time to bake and sleep and watch whatever TV show she wanted to and not have to worry and wander the house checking up on Henry and placating Hank and making sure he hadn't started a fire or gone outside without telling her or fallen down the stairs or….

She'd have enough time to sit and think about what she'd just done.

"Mmm-*mmm!* Can't wait." His smile softened. "It's going to be okay, Miss Nora, it really will. I know this is going to sound impossible, but try not to worry. I'll talk to Henry myself and explain things and I'm sure he'll understand this is all for the best."

Nora looked out through the entrance doors to the bright summer day and nodded. "Thank you."

"You are more than welcome, Miss Nora. Get some rest."

"I will," Nora promised, "and then I'll get to baking."

Dr. Cross pressed both hands to the front of his lab coat, just above his heart, and rolled his eyes. Nora smiled as she walked out into the bright summer sunshine and kept smiling until she heard the automatic door whoosh shut behind her.

CHAPTER TWO

Timmy

(1956)

HONK-HONK!

"Honk!" Timmy answered, then fell back into one of the sofa pillows he'd put on the floor. "Honk! Honk! Honk!"

HONK! HONK! SSSSSSSSSSSSSSS!

Timmy lifted his head just in time to watch Clarabell the Clown squirt Buffalo Bob with seltzer and laughed so hard he almost couldn't breathe. He'd caught what Grandpa Jake called a 'bad case-a the chuckles' and couldn't stop...

...until he heard his second favorite song in the whole world.

It made him so happy he just had to sing along.

So he did.

"Clarabell! Clarabell! CLARABELL!"

"Timothy Patrick O'Neal!"

Even though Buffalo Bob was saying something and Clarabell was honking his answer, Timmy quickly put the pillow back on the sofa *where it belonged,* then jumped up to join it and sat like a human being: hands in his lap, back straight, and sneakers nowhere near the coffee table. He might only have been five (and a half), but he knew what the rules were and how they were supposed to be followed.

When he remembered.

Always say please and thank you.

Eat everything on your plate because there are starving children in China.

No elbows on the table.

No running or yelling in the house.

No sitting too close to the TV.

And especially *no noise in the morning if Mommy and Daddy had gone out the night before.*

Like they did last night.

"Timothy. Did you hear me calling you, young man?" his mother asked.

He sat straighter. "Yes, Mama?"

Timmy could hear – and feel – the heavy *thump*-swish, *thump*-swish of her slippers as she walked out of the kitchen. Mama was mad.

When she finally reached the living room and turned off the TV, he could tell she wasn't feeling good either. She was still wearing her robe and PJs and her eyes were all red and funny-looking.

But he didn't laugh.

"Timothy Patrick, what have we told you about—?"

"You gotta cold, mama? You look like you gotta cold."

For a minute his mama's face stayed angry, then it changed and she smiled. "What am I going to do with you?"

Timmy shrugged because he didn't know.

His mama sighed. "What have we told you about yelling in the house?"

"But I wasn't yelling, I was singing."

Timmy didn't know why, but that made his mama smile even more.

"Yes, but you were singing very loudly and your mommy and daddy were up very late last night and…we have headaches."

"Sarr-reee."

His mama walked over to the sofa and sat down next to him, pulling him into a big hug. Timmy buried his face into her side and took a deep breath. Her robe smelled like sunshine and soap and flowers and her, all good things.

"I know you're sorry and you're a good boy. I just forget how little you are sometimes."

Timmy lifted his head and felt his lower lip pooch out. "I'm not little. I'm five and a half. I'm gonna be six in this many days."

He held up five fingers.

"Yes, I'm sorry," his mama said and put down one of his fingers, "you're not little. You're a big boy, a very big boy…and I have something to tell you."

"Okay."

His mama lifted him onto her lap. And even though Timmy was a big boy and would be six in four more days, he liked being there. Liked the smell and warm and safe of her.

"You know how your daddy and I went out last night and Grandpa Jake stayed with you?"

"Uh-huh. We watched *Rin Tin Tin* and *'Ventures of Jim Bowie!*"

"Now, the reason your daddy and I went out last night is because we were celebrating. You see, there's going to be a little stranger in the house soon."

"Strangers are bad," Timmy reminded her. "Don't talk to strangers."

She laughed and her belly went up and down. Timmy liked that.

"No, not like that. This is a good stranger." Then she stopped laughing and brushed a hand through his hair. "You're going to be a big brother. Do you know what a big brother is?"

Timmy thought about it. His bestest friend Danny had a BIG BROTHER, and so did his second bestest friend Ronny. And BIG BROTHERS were COOL. They got to ride their bikes in the street, and wear denim jeans and drink soda right out of the bottle and got to stay up late and all sorts of COOL stuff.

Timmy nodded. "Uh-huh."

"Well, that's what you're going to be. You're going to be a big brother because Mommy's going to have a baby. Do you understand?"

Mama was going to have a baby and he'd already been a baby. He knew that because he'd seen the pictures Mama kept in a big white photo album.

"Uh-huh."

But then he got worried. Timmy turned around to look out the living room door to the hallway – there wasn't any room for a baby. His mama and daddy had a room and he had a room and his Grandpa Jake slept in the 'verted garage.

"Where's he gonna sleep?"

His mama put a finger under his chin and turned his face back toward her.

"Well, we won't have to worry about that for another – " his mama put up six fingers, " – this many months. And it might not be a 'he'…you might have a little sister."

Timmy frowned. "Don't you know?"

"No, honey, I don't, we have to wait until the baby's born. And we were thinking, your daddy and I, that when it was born, it would be really nice if the new baby could sleep in your room."

And Timmy suddenly remembered something else that BIG BROTHERS had. Something that was even COOLER than riding bikes in the street or drinking soda out of the bottle.

"Bunk beds?"

His mama blinked her eyes and smiled. "Maybe when the baby's a bit older."

"Cool!"

His mama started to laugh, then must have remembered about her headache because she stopped and squeezed her eyes shut tight.

"You okay, Mama?"

"Yes," she said, very softly, "I will be." Then she opened her eyes. "You're a good boy."

"And a big brother."

"Yes, you'll be the big brother and protect the baby and help keep it safe." His mama pushed him away a little. "You don't mind about the new baby, do you?"

"No. What's the baby's name?"

His mama cleared her throat. "Well, it doesn't really have a name yet, but your daddy and I were thinking Linda for a girl—"

Timmy wrinkled his nose.

"Um…and maybe Michael…or Peter for a boy?" His mama cleared her throat. "What name do you like?"

Timmy thought about it. "Clarabell Howdy O'Neal."

His mama hiccupped. "O…kay, but what if the baby's a girl?"

Timmy didn't have to think about that at all. "Summerfall Winterspring O'Neal."

"I'll talk to your daddy about it. You go play now."

"'Kay! 'Bye."

His mama swatted him lightly on the rump as he darted for the back door. "No running in the house!"

"'Kay," he shouted but didn't slow down. He was too excited and only a little bit sad that his mama had turned off the TV before all the kids in the Peanut Gallery got to sing his favoritest song in the whole world.

But that was kind of okay because he was going to be a BIG BROTHER. And BIG BROTHERS could sing anytime they wanted to.

Timmy started singing before he reached his bike and was still singing when he coasted down the driveway and into the street. He was a BIG BROTHER and BIG BROTHERS got to ride their bikes in the street.

"It's Howdy Doody Time. It's Howdy Doody Time."

He couldn't wait to tell all his friends.

Timmy didn't see the car until it crumpled the front of his bike.

The driver never saw Timmy at all.

TIMOTHY PATRICK O'NEAL
June 10, 1950 – June 6, 1956

CHAPTER THREE

Sara

"What do you think you're doing?"

Caught.

Looking up, Sara opened her eyes wide and tried her best 'who me?' smile. It didn't work. Danny just stood there in the doorway, coffee mug in hand, and glared down at her.

With what she hoped would sound like a long-suffering sigh, Sara dropped the sponge into the bucket of warm soapy water and sat back, pulling off the rubber gloves as discreetly as a sweating seven-months-one-week pregnant woman in shorts and a faded 2XL L.A. Rams tee-shirt could.

"I'm not doing anything," she said and hoped he'd believe her words instead of his own eyes. But after five years together she knew better.

Danny set the mug down on the top of the counter, which Sara had so diligently scrubbed, hard enough to make her jump.

"Hey! Careful with the crockery. That's a K-Mart special, you know."

Danny leaned down and grabbed the gloves out of her hand before he picked up the bucket and poured it into the sink behind her.

"Why should *I* be careful?" Walking around her, he squatted and slipped his hands under her arms, taking most of her now-considerable weight as she struggled to get her bare feet under her. "When it's obvious I'm the only one around here who is."

"You...aren't the...only one. Wait!"

Sara felt Danny's body go rigid, his fingers digging into her skin, and knew he was probably thinking of the time during her second trimester when she'd stood up too quickly and passed out. She woke up a few hours later in the hospital with Danny and her OB/GYN staring down at her like anxious vultures. The baby was fine, Dr. Palmer had told her, but she was suffering from hypertension…which was nothing to worry about IF she took it easy. She'd crossed her heart and promised she would…and she had…more or less. There were just so many things that needed to get done.

"What's wrong?" he asked. The panic in his voice almost scared her.

"Nothing." Reaching behind her to give his leg a reassuring pat, Sara braced her feet against the floor and pushed. "I just didn't…have any…leverage. There…."

It took three deep breaths before the miniature fireworks display in front of her eyes stopped and another before she felt steady enough to slap his hands away and turn around.

"See, I'm fine. It just takes longer for pregnant elephants to get up."

Danny glared down at her. That was the problem with marrying a man seven inches taller than her own five feet five inches, you were always looked…or glared…down at.

Even so she still hoped the baby – William Dennis or Emily Melinda or A-Couple-Others-Still-Under-Consideration – would get some of that height along with his blue-green eyes to go with her strawberry-blond hair.

Sara offered him a cute little pout. He shook his head, not buying it.

"The only time a pregnant elephant has a problem is when she doesn't listen when her doctors tell her to take it easy."

"I was taking it easy. I was sitting down."

"Halfway under the kitchen sink? What were you doing under there anyway?"

"Washing the pipes."

"The pi— Why?"

"It's called 'nesting'. And it's very popular among pregnant elephants."

For a minute he seemed at a loss for words and she almost applauded. After the hospital scare Danny never seemed to stop talking about what could happen to her or to the baby if she DIDN'T REST. *"Take it easy, take it easy,"* had become his daily mantra.

So it was kind of nice to hear nothing.

"Look," she said, breaking the silence, "I know what can go wrong and I am tak—" The room shifted and she had to grab the front of his tee-shirt to keep her balance. "Whoa."

Danny's face went white. "What?"

"I...don't...hmm."

Sara shook her head and listened to what sounded like waves pounding against the inside of her ears. It was like hearing the ocean in a shell – distant, but peaceful. What wasn't peaceful was the way Danny's face swam past her in the opposite direction from the way the kitchen was leaning. The ocean inside her head was getting choppy. And hot. God, it was hot!

"The air-conditioning go off?" she asked and watched his mouth move as he pitched and rolled in front of her.

She couldn't hear him over the wave sounds, but that was probably just as well, because she really didn't feel like listening right now. Sweat erupted from her forehead, sliding down her face just as her legs began to melt.

Then he grabbed her and instantly the air cooled and the waves inside her head began to ebb.

"SARA!" Danny's face was red and he was yelling. "WHAT IS IT? TALK TO ME?"

"Phew!" Sara backed away to wave a hand through the air between them. "You had onions for lunch again, didn't you?"

"What?"

"Onions. You know I can't handle the smell of raw onions now. Cooked is okay, but raw really makes me want to hurl."

"Onions?" He leaned back against the sink but didn't let go of her arms. "What the hell are you talking about? Are you okay? You looked like you were about to pass out."

"You know the old saying – 'The more pregnant the woman, the more stuff makes her sick.'"

He let her go then crossed his arms across the CSULB logo on the front of his tee-shirt. "I never heard of that particular old saying."

"Then you don't watch enough TV."

Danny looked over the top of her head and sighed. The raw onion smell really was terrible. Since the scare it seemed as though his skin had grown thinner while hers thickened...but maybe that was normal. Daddies-to-be could afford to get all emotional while mamas-to-be couldn't. A whole new generation depended on 'Mom' to keep everything together.

Sara pulled his arms apart and waddled into them, snuggling her face against his chest to prevent any of the lingering onion scent from pushing her out to sea again.

"I'm sorry. I'm just being a fat bitch. Forgive me?"

She felt his arms tighten around her.

"You're not fat," he said and stopped.

She punched his arm.

"Hey! I said you weren't fat."

"But you didn't say anything about me not being a bitch."

He ignored the trap. "What really happened?"

"Nothing, I just got up too fast. Really...and the onions. It wasn't like the other time – honest. I'm fine." Pause. "You believe me, don't you?"

When he didn't answer, Sara pushed him away with an exasperated sigh and lumbered over to the breakfast nook to sit down in one of the whitewashed, ladder-back chairs. It had been comfortable when they first bought the set, but now her girth had exceeded the manufacturer's specifications.

And there were still almost two months to go.

Blowing damp bangs off her forehead, she looked down at her belly.

"I *am* fat."

"You're pregnant," Danny corrected, his back to her as he rinsed out the pail. "And it'd be great if you'd realize that every now and then."

Sara looked down at the anatomical equivalent of a beach ball. "Believe me, I realize it."

"Really? Look, the doctor told you to rest and take—"

"It easy," Sara finished. "I know and I am. It's just that, sometimes, I get this...urge."

"To crawl under the sink and wash the pipes."

"And get rid of stuff like bleach and cleanser and...furniture polish – the old kind in the bottle your mom gave us that we never use, not the spray kind." She watched the back of Danny's head swivel from side to side. "What if the baby got under there and got sick?"

"I think we have a few months to worry about that before she's able to get into anything."

She.

Sara smiled. Except for Danny, all the other fathers-to-be in their

Lamaze class used the masculine pronoun when referring to their bulge-about-to-be-baby. Danny wanted a daughter – little Emily or….

"How do you like Roselyn and Hudson?"

"Who are they?"

"No, I mean names for the baby."

"You're kidding, right? Besides, I thought we finally decided on Emily Melinda or Victoria Regina."

"Or Daniel William, Junior – D.J. for short – or Gerard Butler."

He looked at her over his shoulder. "I am not naming my kid after an actor."

"No, but you're okay with naming a kid after a prissy ultra-conservative queen. Guess that's what I get for marrying a high school history teacher."

"Yes, it is, oh, graphic arts designer." He sighed. "Okay. Fine. Add the names to the list. Now, everything's washed and…I guess the pipes are clean, so can we talk about taking it easy, now?"

"Good idea, why don't you? You do look kind of tired."

"Sa-RA."

"Dan-NEE."

He closed his eyes and Sara knew he was silently counting down from ten to one. He'd been doing a lot of counting since her earlier impromptu visit to the ER and she loved him for it. He'd make as good a father as he was a husband.

"Okay," she said, "I'm sorry." Danny opened his eyes and looked at her. "And I promise I'll try…no, I *will* take it easy until Emily or Vicki or…whoever shows up. But all bets are off after that. Got it?"

Danny nodded, wiping his hands on a dishtowel as he walked toward her. "Yes, ma'am, anything you want, ma'am. But for now…."

Sara crossed both her heart and the top half of her mountainous belly. "Rest. And I will. Right after we get back from Buy Buy Baby."

He stopped wiping. "But we were just there."

"They called yesterday and said the car seat we ordered came in. Remember?"

"Oh, right. But we don't have to get it right now, do we?"

"Yes, we do. We can't bring the baby home from the hospital without a car seat."

Danny tossed the dishtowel onto the table and squatted at her feet.

Sara envied him his ability to do that without turning red and huffing like a broken airbrush.

"We still have a couple months."

"So? Look, I *need* to have everything done and perfect before I *really* have to take it easy. Please, Danny, everything has to be perfect before—"

And then the baby – little Emily or Vicki or D.J. or Gerard or whoever – added her or his two cents' worth.

"Ow!"

Danny's back straightened and his head came up, giving a great imitation of a meerkat on alert. "What is it?"

"Just the newest member of the Cortland family doing a pirouette on my kidneys. Which reminds me." She held out her hands, wiggling her fingers. "Help me up and I'll hit the head before we go."

Danny stood and only mumbled a little to himself as he took her hands. "I can go myself, you know. All I have to do is pick up the car seat and come home. Shouldn't take more than thirty minutes, tops."

Sara squeezed his hands and smiled. "I want to pick up a couple more receiving blankets and maybe some onesies and stuff."

"You should rest."

"I'll rest when we get home. Promise. Now, pull."

Danny's sigh scented the air with onions again, but Sara held her breath as she tightened the muscles in her legs and leaned forward, preparing to push off. And maybe she shouldn't have because suddenly the bright Saturday morning light was obscured by thousands of swirling dots – red to green, yellow to purple, blue to orange – that flashed and flared and exploded in front of her eyes.

"Okay," he said and his voice sounded so far away, so far above her, "but this time I'm holding you to that promise."

She blinked and the last thing she saw was his face.

He was smiling.

"Danny? I don't feel so—"

CHAPTER FOUR

Elisabeth

(1914)

"Why are you hovering at the threshold, Elisabeth? Either come in or leave."

Since leaving was not an option, she entered the parlor and tried not to tremble when the dog lifted its massive gargoyle head and growled.

"Julius, hush now," her mother reproached with more kindness than Elisabeth herself had ever received, "you know how you frighten her. Now then, Elisabeth, I understand that you feel obliged to go out this evening, is that correct?"

"Yes, Mother."

"I see no reason for that, Elisabeth. You've already been out twice this week. Surely your...friend will understand your cancellation."

Elisabeth tugged at the vertical plane of her shirtwaist, following the ribs of the corset beneath, as if straightening a flaw in the material.

"Stop that fidgeting at once. How do you ever hope to attract a husband?"

As if that was still a possibility.

She was thirty-nine, as her mother kept reminding her, well past the time when any man might be interested in making her acquaintance, and decidedly plain...another flaw her mother was fond of reaffirming. Whereas her mother had been a noted beauty of her time, petite, wasp-waisted, with golden hair and sapphire eyes, Elisabeth had taken after her father: sturdy and tall with a ruddy complexion, mouse-colored hair and mud-green eyes that weren't shortsighted enough to avoid the many mirrors that were prominently displayed about the house.

"How many times must I remind you that men do not like women who cannot keep still?"

Elisabeth clasped her hands together.

"Now, take one of my blue note cards and send your friend your regrets."

"No."

"I beg your pardon?"

Elisabeth lowered her eyes. "I'm sorry, Mother, but I must keep my appointment."

The mantle clock ticked off several seconds.

"What do you mean, *you must?*"

Elisabeth kept her chin lowered as she looked up. "You taught me it is simply good manners to keep one's appointments. Frances is undoubtedly already waiting for me. To send a note now would do her a great disservice. She may have had other plans that she canceled for my benefit."

Elisabeth watched her mother sit back against the burgundy moiré fabric of the parlor chair and lift the embroidery hoop from her lap. "I suppose I must allow it if only for form's sake, but I must tell you I do not approve of your friend. She is overly headstrong and no doubt would descend upon us if you didn't keep your appointment. Does this appointment have anything to do with her forthcoming escapade?"

A wave of heat inched its way along the high collar of Elisabeth's starched blouse. The escapade, as her mother phrased it, was a two-week summer session of ladies' courses at Oberlin College in Ohio – which Frances would be attending unescorted and unchaperoned.

It had been the subject of much discussion by her mother's social acquaintances.

"No, Mother. We are simply going to the library. She wishes to show me a series of history books."

The embroidery hoop quivered slightly. "Books I advise you never to bring into this house."

"No, Mother." Elisabeth turned and walked to the wrought-iron coat stand next to the front door. She had just finished removing the hatpin from her unadorned straw boater when she heard a cough and returned to the parlor. "Yes, Mother?"

"As long as you're going out − " her mother paused to assure Elisabeth's full attention, " − I wonder if you wouldn't mind stopping in at the pharmacist."

"Are you not feeling well, Mother?"

Lowering the hoop, her mother lifted one hand daintily to the starched lace of her bodice and took a ragged breath.

"It's just a small pain, here." Her mother tapped the lace. "But I'm sure it's nothing for you to be concerned with. It will pass, in time…it always does."

"What do you need from the pharmacist, Mother?"

A small smile played upon her mother's lips. "Oil of peppermint and tell them to put it on my account."

Elisabeth nodded as she placed the hat squarely on her head and secured it with the pin. "Of course, Mother. I won't be long."

"See to it that you aren't."

Her mother coughed once more as Elisabeth left the house.

After the dark, cloying chill of her mother's parlor the June heat was almost staggering, and the day was so bright Elisabeth raised one hand to the brim of her hat in hopes of extending its limited shade.

Just the minimal exertion of stepping from the front stoop to the stairs immediately made her regret her choice of not bringing a parasol.

Elisabeth almost fled back to the indifference and cold when she heard her name called.

"Bessie! Finally!"

Dressed all in white from hat to hem, Frances stood just beyond the property's wrought-iron gate. It was, Elisabeth thought, a most appropriate color for so warm a day, but the appropriateness ended when her friend pushed open the gate to reveal both the shortness of her skirt, which showed a glimpse of leg above her high-top boots, and the object trailing from her hand. Elisabeth backed away.

"Frances…no."

"Bessie, yes," her friend said as she snapped open the patriotically colored sash and strung it crosswise over herself from right shoulder to left hip.

VOTES FOR WOMEN

Elisabeth pressed one hand against the rigid corset beneath her shirtwaist and looked back toward the carved front door. If her mother happened to look out from one of the narrow side windows that braced that door....

Elisabeth hurried across the walk and stepped through the gate, slamming it shut behind her. Arm in arm, Elisabeth kept her head down and face averted to the cobblestones as her friend led her through the streets.

When they finally stopped Elisabeth lifted her face only to step back in horror when Frances produced another sash identical to her own and held it out.

"Oh for heaven's sake, Bessie," her friend laughed, "it's not a snake, it won't bite you."

"But it could very well bite *you*."

"Never!" Frances said, "but I warrant it will bite many others before it's laid to rest. Put it on!"

Elisabeth shook her head.

"Oh, very well then." Frances slipped it back into the pocket of her skirt. "There, the snake's put away. Come on, we're going to be late."

"But you can't possibly think of going to the library wearing... that, can you? They'll bar us at the door."

Frances lifted her dimpled chin. "I would like to see them try, but the library will have to wait. We're not going to look at history in books, Bessie, we're going to watch it unfold." Her hand clamped around Elisabeth's wrist like a vise. "We're going to be part of it!"

Without giving Elisabeth a moment to think, Frances tightened her grip and pulled her in a the opposite direction to the library. Taken by surprise, it was all Elisabeth could do to keep pace.

They hurried thus for two more blocks before Frances turned onto the broad thoroughfare that led to City Hall. A dozen steps more and Elisabeth stopped, shocked by the spectacle before them.

"Oh, Bessie," Frances gushed, loosening her grip on Elisabeth's arm. "It's just as I said – history in the making. Look...do you see?"

Elisabeth could most definitely see, and what she saw made her tremble.

A ceremony had been planned for that evening at the City Hall to commemorate a statue honoring those men from the area who had helped work on the soon-to-be-opened Panama Canal, but it was almost impossible to see the patriotic bunting and flags that draped the building's marble façade due to the size of the crowd gathered before it.

"...tramping out the vintage where the grapes of..."

Given the number of angry red-faced men who shouted and cursed and belittled, it should have been impossible to hear the choir of raised voices from the women who stood and sang, side by side, along the iron fence that encircled the edifice. It should have been impossible to hear the hymn, but Elisabeth did and the sound only accentuated the horror unfolding before her.

A small contingency of uniformed police officers stood on the steps of City Hall, safe behind the closed gates, batons in hand, but silent and passive.

Watching while the women sang.

Some of the women were dressed in white like Frances, others more suitably attired, but each wore the same incriminating sash that marked them, and her friend, as a Suffragette. A number of women held standards demanding the Right to Vote, others American flags, but each stood tall, heads high, and sang, ignoring the shouts and threats and anger until the first blows fell.

Then the song stopped and their voices rose in screams.

While the police officers watched and maintained their silent vigil.

Elisabeth stumbled back a step, hands pressed against her lips as she watched crimson flowers bloom on starched white clothing.

"NO!"

She turned as a patch of white brushed against her and fluttered away. By the time Elisabeth realized what it was her friend was already halfway across the street and well into the melee, pummeling both tiny fists against the back of a gentleman in a well-cut business suit until he turned and struck her down.

"Frances!"

Elisabeth's only thought as she rushed forward was to get her friend to safety, but when she touched the gentleman's arm – "Please," she shouted only to be heard. *"Please!"* – a snarl disfigured what might have been a genteel or even refined face.

He struck so quickly that Elisabeth neither felt the pain of the walking stick splitting her skull nor the heat from the cobbled roadway when her body collapsed like a rag doll. It had all happened so quickly she hadn't even time to....

ELISABETH REGINA WYMAN
November 22, 1874 – June 4, 1914

CHAPTER FIVE

Jamie

Ryan held the wineglass against his lips and watched Jamie play with the baby, goo-gooing and ga-gaing while the baby's parents – Jiro and Oren – puffed out their chests and recorded each moment on one or the other's cell phone. It was all so fucking sweet Ryan wanted to vomit.

Sachiko-Rachel Takahashi-Nachman, for whom the dinner party was being thrown, gurgled and spit up. Jiro moved in for a close-up while Jamie used a cocktail napkin to clean the coagulated formula off her chin. The birth-mother, a friend of a friend of a friend who'd played 'eenie, meenie, miney, moe' with two vials of frozen sperm before picking the one she wanted for insemination, had been at the party just long enough to take one picture before handing over the bundle o' joy and collecting her fee for the nine months' rent of her womb.

Ryan lowered the glass and took a long swallow.

"Just look at that face," Jamie murmured to the bundle in his arms. "Isn't she the prettiest little thing you've ever seen?"

Ryan knew it had to be a rhetorical question, because to him the baby looked like a cross between Toshiro Mifune and Winston Churchill, the epicanthic folds clearly showing that Jiro's juice had been the winner in the baby-making contest.

The baby spit up again and Ryan felt his own stomach quiver.

"Oh-oh, your tummy not feeling so good?" Jamie cooed while baby-slime soaked into the weave of his IZOD polo. "Well, don't you mind, sweet girl, these things happen."

"God, Jamie, wipe that off," Ryan said. "The smell's never going to come out."

Jamie looked up and offered him the benevolent smile of the truly blessed. "It's okay…it's baby smell."

"No, it's curdled milk smell."

A half dozen faces turned away from the precious little spit-up machine and scowled in his direction.

"That's only a part of the baby smell, Ry, and it's precious. You wanna hold her?"

Ryan downed the rest of the wine in one gulp.

"Need a refill first," he said and headed for the bar. Across the room the goo-gooing resumed.

He didn't mind kids, they were fine…in small to medium doses… but he'd never given any thought to becoming a father. His brother had provided enough ankle-biters to carry on the family name so—

"Looks like you'll be next."

"What?"

Oren took Ryan's empty glass and replaced it with a full one, clinking his own against it. "L'chaim!"

He nodded back. "Likewise." And took a sip.

"So when are you and Jamie going to do it?"

That was a two-meaning question – 1) When are you two going to 'make it legal', and 2) start a family? – neither of which Ryan wanted to think about or answer. Not here, not now, not yet.

So he shrugged and smiled.

"You two," Oren laughed, "always thinking about today and not tomorrow."

Ryan let the smile drop.

"What's that supposed to mean?"

"Only that you two aren't getting any younger." Oren's glance shifted from Ryan to the Jamie-and-Child tableau. "He's so good with her."

"Yeah, he's always been good with kids and puppies…but that doesn't mean I want to start breeding dogs either."

Oren's pale blue eyes turned back to him. "Babies aren't dogs, Ry."

Ooh, he'd hit a nerve. "No, they require much more care. When a puppy's one, it's an adult. Kids take longer. Sorry, I didn't mean to sound nasty."

"That's okay. Jamie said you've been pretty stressed at work. Hope the merger works out."

Ryan took another mouthful of the sweet white wine. Jamie had been flapping his lips again. Ryan couldn't remember how many times he'd told him not to do it – but it never helped. Jamie was a talker, a giver, a 'let's get everything out in the open'-er.

"Yeah," Ryan said. "Fingers crossed."

"Well, that still doesn't mean you should put your life on hold. Babies are the future, Ry, the only real piece of immortality we get on this crazy ol' planet."

"For Jiro maybe."

Oren's smile widened. "We're already talking about a second one...this time with only one donor. Me. How old are you guys again? Twenty-seven and thirty-nine, right?"

As if he didn't know. "Right. I'm the senior spokesman."

"Well, that's still not too old." Oren leaned in slightly. "Just don't wait too long – tick, tick, tick. Excuses...gotta go get my baby before Jamie decides to take her home." He took three steps and turned, winking. "Remember – tick, tick, tick."

"Tock."

Hah. Hah. Hah.

He still had a hard time realizing that he'd be forty in two months. How in God's name did that happen?

Ryan stayed by the bar just long enough to see Jamie's reluctance as he handed the baby to Oren – after a few moments of comedic 'no you can't have her, she's mine' routine – before walking out the French doors and into a little piece of rural Japan tucked into a modest, middle-class Los Angeles suburb. Live bamboo masked both the chain-link fence that surrounded the property and the neighboring houses, and clustered around the small gazebo-like 'teahouse' at the back of the garden.

Ryan lifted the glass to his lips.

"How many is that?"

Ryan turned to find Jamie frowning at him.

"How many swallows? Maybe five. Sips...I lost count. Glasses?" He had to stop and think about that. "Two. No, three."

"You're drunk."

"On three glasses of very cheap, very sweet wine? No, honey, I'm far from drunk, although that sounds like an excellent suggestion."

"You had a couple beers before we left home."

"Lite beers," Ryan reminded him.

"Don't you think you've had enough?"

"Not even close, besides I called 'Designated Drunk', remember? See, I'm fine. Now, if you'll excuse me."

Ryan started to sidestep his partner of five-going-on-six years only to have it countered. Which was laughable. Jamie might be younger, possibly even stronger if put to the test and decidedly in much better condition – jogging Nazi that he was – but he was also a good deal shorter than Ryan's own six feet two inches frame.

He did, however, manage to grab the glass out of Ryan's hand. "You don't need any more."

"Need has nothing to do with it, sweetheart. I'm beginning to enjoy the flavor of fortified grape juice." He tried to snatch it back only to knock it out of Jamie's hand. The glass shattered against the edge of the patio.

"Jesus, Ry…."

"It's their fault for not using plastic."

"I'll go get a broom." Jamie started to turn toward the house, then stopped. "Why did you tell Oren we didn't want children?"

"What? I didn't say anything about—"

"Oren said you're very hostile to the idea of children."

"I didn't…I'm not. Oh, Jesus, you know how he gets sometimes."

Fortunately, they did. Jamie nodded and slid both hands into the back pockets of his jeans.

"Sorry. It's just that…I don't know. She is just so freakin' cute, isn't she?"

"Yeah, I guess so."

"So, you do want kids?"

Oh, God. Ryan looked down at the shattered wineglass and sighed. This was not the time for that conversation. They weren't home, they weren't alone, and he was nowhere near drunk enough.

"Ry?"

He looked up. "I told you not to talk about me."

"What?"

"Oren said you told him about the merger. Jamie, I told you not to say anything."

"I just mentioned...." He reached out but Ryan slapped his hand away. "Jesus, you are drunk."

"No, believe me, I'm not."

"Then why are you acting like this?"

Ryan looked over Jamie's shoulder to the small clutch of partygoers who'd joined them on the patio, trying ever so hard to appear as if they weren't actively eavesdropping.

"I really don't want to have this conversation right now."

Turning, Ryan stepped off the patio and onto the pathway of smooth white stones. He almost made it all the way to the teahouse before Jamie caught up to him.

"And what conversation would that be? The one where you don't think you're drunk? Or the one where you're paranoid about me talking to our friends? Or how you're not ready to commit to me or a baby because you're not sure you're, quote, totally into this relationship, unquote, because you don't think you've, quote, found yourself yet, unquote?"

Of all the things Jamie did that got under Ryan's skin, the two he absolutely hated were Jamie's liberal use of air quotes and when he turned into the stereotypical flamer: loud, hysterical, red of face and squeaky of voice.

Jamie knew how he felt, since they'd talked/fought about it enough times, so when Ryan turned his back and walked away it should have ended right there and then.

It didn't, of course, but it should have.

This time Ryan only got a couple of feet away before Jamie descended upon him like an avenging god, and the two other couples who were already in the teahouse went on alert. Fight, fight!

"Don't you dare walk away from me, Ryan!" Jamie yelled. "This time you're going to stand here and *talk to me*!"

The four men in the teahouse grabbed their drinks and hightailed it back to the house.

"Did you hear me?"

Ryan took a deep breath. "Dogs three blocks away can hear

you, Jamie. You want to lower the volume control from hysterical to frantic?"

"You bastard."

Ryan smiled, knowing Jamie could see it. "Never claimed to be anything else, if you remember."

"You always have to make a joke about everything, don't you?"

He shrugged. "That's what we bastards do. Now, come on, let's calm down and go inside. I really could use another dr—"

"No!" The volume was back up to hysterical bordering on screeching. "Not until we finish this."

Ryan noticed that the patio was full to capacity.

"Do you really want to finish this here, like this? With everyone watching?"

Jamie looked back over his shoulder and the crowd quickly dispersed. Ryan was impressed.

"Wish I could do that."

"Make people disappear?" Jamie asked without turning around. "I thought you were the expert on that already."

Ryan felt a solid hit to his Past-Relationships-That-Had-Failed region.

"Good one."

"No, no it wasn't." Ryan caught a quick sparkle of tears on his partner's cheeks as Jamie finally turned around. "I'm done."

Thank God. "Good. Let's grab our stuff and say our goodbyes and—"

"No, I mean I can't do this anymore, Ryan. I'm *done*. Goodbye."

Jamie turned and walked away.

"Jesus. Come on, Jamie, stop acting like a broken blossom."

Jamie held up one finger and kept walking.

"Hey! Did you forget we took my car?"

The shadow-form kept walking and never looked back.

Typical Jamie modus operandi – play the martyr so Ryan had to be the one to apologize and then promise everything would be okay, just like he always did.

"Come *on*, Jamie!"

Ryan took a deep breath and that turned out to be a big mistake. It let his brain realize what his partner had already known: he really was drunk and needed to go home.

Now.

Right this minute.

One foot in front of the other, repeat as necessary.

And it worked all the way down the path – which he'd only managed to miss twice – and across the patio, but stepping up into the house he stumbled into one of the French doors.

"Oops."

Faces turned toward him and all conversation stopped. Even the baby, secure in her Daddy Jiro's arms, seemed concerned. Jamie's was the only face missing.

Oren took a step toward him, but Ryan shook his head.

"I'm fine. Oh…I dropped a wineglass out there. On the patio thing…edge. Sorry."

"That's okay, no problem." Oren was still moving toward him, his voice soft and reassuring. "Hey, we just put on some coffee – how 'bout a cup?"

Ryan shook his head, which was another mistake, but to cover it, he focused on pulling the car keys from his pocket. "Naw, s'kay. Gotta get home, stuff to do. Great party. Cute kid. Thanks anyway, I'm fine."

"Give me the keys, Ryan."

Jamie made his way through the crowd. He looked like he'd aged ten years. His face was pale and haggard, his gray eyes rimmed in red.

"I'm fine," Ryan repeated.

"No, you're not." Jamie's voice was flat and calm. Would wonders never cease? "You're drunk. Just give me the keys."

Ryan took another step.

"I said I was fine."

Jamie held out his hand. "Give me the damn keys and stop acting like an idiot."

Ryan slapped the hand away.

"You're not here," he said, "you're quote, done, unquote… remember?"

Jamie made a grab for the car keys, acting like he was suddenly the mature one in the relationship, so Ryan pushed him away, just a little give-me-some-room shove. But it must have been harder than he thought because Jamie went down like a statue knocked off its pedestal.

And broke.

They all heard it, the wet celery snap when Jamie hit the floor and lay there like a crumpled doll, his head turned at an impossible angle.

The room was suddenly filled with words *"—okay?—"* *"— 9-1-1—"*

"—breathing—" *"—ambulance—"* *"—dead?—"* *"—accident—"* *"—neck—"* *"—broken.—"* *"—hurry—"* that floated around Ryan but didn't make sense…

…until Jamie moaned.

"Don't move him; the ambulance is on the way."

"Jamie?" Ryan took a step closer. "Open your eyes, Jamie."

Jamie moaned again but didn't open his eyes.

God, what did I do? "Jamie? JAMIE!"

Someone grabbed Ryan's arm and led him to a chair, sat him down and stayed next to him. It was going to be okay, the someone told him, Jamie was alive and the ambulance was on its way.

Somewhere in the distance the baby started crying.

CHAPTER SIX

Aryeh

(1926)

"Esther, *kumen?*"

"Yes, Mama. I'm coming."

"She comes." Rena, his wife and the mother of his three children, shook her head. "She comes like ice from a pump in winter she comes."

"*Sha*, wife," he scolded gently, "she comes, that's what matters."

His wife sniffed loudly and went back to making sure their other children – Jaffa, his firstborn angel, and Leben, only five but already strong enough to help sweep up in the shop – were presentable.

As if she would let any of them set one foot from their apartment if they weren't. She reminded him so much of his own dear mameh, may she rest in peace.

"ESTHER! You come now or we go without you!"

So very much like his mameh.

From upstairs came a series of thumps but only one clang as something small and metallic crashed to the floor. A moment later Esther, their middle child, came running down the stairs. Where Jaffa and Leben were more like him in looks – thin and angular with dark brown hair and brown eyes – Esther was more like her mother: a plump little pigeon with hair the color of summer wheat and eyes like warm honey.

"What fell?" he asked.

"It didn't break."

Aryeh Rosenberg looked at his wife who could only shake her head and sigh. "I'm so glad. And what was it didn't break?"

Esther stopped on the bottom stair, the look of fear in her eyes.

"It was only the silver plate, Papa."

"Only the good silver plate I keep for company to make everything nice?" his wife shouted. "The one for Jaffa when she gets married silver plate? That silver plate that didn't break?"

Aryeh watched the terror deepen in his little pigeon's eyes.

"Yes, Mameh, but it's not broken…only a little bent."

"Bent!?" His wife's voice echoed up the stairs to their apartment and down the narrow hall to his watch shop. "Bent! Did you hear that, husband – bent! It's not enough that she runs around like a three-legged calf bumping into everything, now she destroys her own sister's bridal gifts! How did I give birth to such a klutz, will someone tell me? *Velkh am ikh geun keyn ton mit du?*"

What am I going to do with you?

If it had just been the two of them alone Aryeh would have answered, "Love her as you love all our children," but they were not alone and, as their mother, she had the final say in such matters.

"Wife, speak American. We are Americans now and we must speak like Americans. *Yoh?* Now, to answer, you will not do nothing now because if you do something now you will be late and keep everyone waiting and how would that look, eh? Worse I think than a dent in a plate."

His wife's eyes narrowed just enough to let Aryeh know she wasn't happy about his interference and would be speaking to him later about it, after the children were in bed.

"But it's Jaffa's plate…."

"Then I will look and see and fix, then I will come and all will be gut."

"Good," she corrected and there was a twinkle in her eyes when she said it. "Fine, we go and I make your excuse. But not too long… you know Mrs. Katz."

Aryeh nodded. He knew Mrs. Katz; more than he wanted, he knew Mrs. Katz. Everyone in the neighborhood knew Mrs. Katz the Matchmaker, and if you didn't, not to worry because she would come find you.

She'd found them a week after they'd gotten off the boat and were still living with Rena's married brother and his family in a cramped apartment near Tompkins Square Park. Jaffa had only been a baby and the other two children not even dreams in God's eye. They met

Mrs. Katz while they were pushing Jaffa around the park one bright spring morning.

"Such a beautiful baby!" was the first thing from the woman's mouth, and "Have you made a match for her yet?" was the second.

They were not even Americans yet, nor had Aryeh a job, but this was a taste of home that, until it was said, neither he nor Rena realized they'd been starving for. Mrs. Katz made a match for Jaffa within a month of their meeting – "A good boy from a good family" – and, when she learned Aryeh was good with his hands, found him a place as a watchmaker's apprentice. And when the watchmaker died, it was Mrs. Katz who suggested Aryeh buy the shop with its apartment upstairs and become a businessman like the American he was.

That had been thirteen years ago but without Mrs. Katz, who knew what would have become of them? Maybe still living with Rena's brother with him hauling rags for pennies instead of sitting straight in his own shop with windows filled with sunlight. Now he had two fine matches for his daughters and maybe tonight there would be another made for his son.

His life was good, a bent plate could be fixed, and Mrs. Katz should not be kept waiting.

"Why are you still standing? You want I should engrave you an invitation to go?" Aryeh flicked his hands toward his family the same way he'd seen his mother and grandmother shoo chickens. "Go. And tell her I come soon."

"Soon." His wife repeated the word to let him know that she'd heard and would keep him to that promise before turning her attention to their children. "Hurry, you heard your papa...we go now so we should not be late for Mrs. Katz, he comes later." She looked back over her shoulder. "Maybe with a box of that nice salted water taffy she likes so much, yes?"

Aryeh nodded. Bringing gifts when one went to visit, even when one went to visit a *shadchen*, was one of those American customs, like people not even married dancing marathons until they passed out (*Cholileh!*) that he still had trouble with. But who was he to argue with the way things were done in his new homeland? Nothing but a watchmaker on Essex Street Neuyork Neuyork.

And that was enough.

"*Yoh.* Yes, I buy, but for that I will show up a little less soon."

"But she'll like. All right, children – come."

Taking their son's hand, Rena marched to the front door, then stood to one side and watched like a general on a hilltop as their daughters walked into the late-afternoon warmth. There were only a few hours before sunset, but that was of little worry. Mrs. Katz's dead husband, may his soul be forever blessed, had left her a wealthy widow. Mrs. Katz wanted for nothing, and had a cook and maid who were Irish goyim so that even on Shabbos the lights could be turned on and fires lit and dinner served after the sun went down.

Such was America.

The *goldeneh medinah*, the golden country.

Still, to show up late would not be such a nice thing, especially for the 'light tea and cakes' Mrs. Katz was offering along with the first meeting of Leben's future wife and her family. A box of taffy would make his lateness maybe less *shlekht* manners.

"You hurry," his wife said then, smoothing down the *sheitel* he'd bought for her from a store on Houston Street, pulled their son from the house and closed the door behind them.

The hallway felt colder with them gone. It was always like that when they left – the house silent of the small sounds he knew as well as the beating of his own heart, the rooms empty, leaving him a ghost to haunt alone.

"*Narishkeit,*" Aryeh chided himself as he turned and walked up the stairs to their apartment. "Foolishness. *Shoyn genug*, that's enough. All right, first, best to see what damage and maybe leave it until later."

The dent was nothing. A few minutes tapping it out, then polish and it would be as good as new. And it could wait. But, knowing his beloved would ask about it and fret and worry and make narrow eyes at Esther, Aryeh took the plate down to the shop.

Five minutes to fix, six maybe and it would be done and he could—

"Mr. Rosenberg?"

Aryeh stopped with his hand still on the doorknob and with one foot still poised to take the next step. He'd closed the shop early because of their appointment with the Matchmaker, had turned the sign around and locked the door and turned off the lights, but there they were – two men in well-cut suits holding their hats in their hands like regular gentlemen.

"You are Mr. Rosenberg, yes?"

Aryeh nodded and let his foot finally settle on the floor, but his hand refused to let go of the doorknob.

"*Yoh.* Yes, I am Rosenberg."

"Very pleased to make your acquaintance, Mr. Rosenberg," the taller of the two men said. His suit was tan, the other man's a light gray. "Please to excuse the intrusion, but the door was open so we came in."

"It was?"

Aryeh dipped his head in respect as he hurried past the men to the door. He was sure he'd locked it.

The Closed sign was still hanging in the window facing the street, and when Aryeh got closer he saw that the brass door lock had been broken inward.

"Shame about the lock," the tall man said, "those things can get expensive to replace. Ask any shopkeeper on this block. They know and will tell you."

When Aryeh turned the shorter man smiled.

"Hoodlums and vandals*, vos-in-der-kort*," he said, "such bad men around, but what you gonna do, right? You put a new lock, they break again, then you get another new lock and another and another and then, who knows, maybe the next time it's a broken window and then, maybe something more valuable gets broken. Maybe something you can't replace, eh, like an arm or leg?"

Aryeh felt a chill colder than the one he imagined when his wife and children left.

"What are you saying to me?"

It was the tall man's turn to smile. "Only that the city isn't what it used to be, Mr. Rosenberg. More and more people are moving in every day and, well—" He shrugged his shoulders and Aryeh saw the edge of a brick peek out from his coat pocket. "Maybe they ain't such nice people."

"No," Aryeh agreed. "Not so nice."

"Then we understand each other, Mr. Rosenberg?" the tall man asked. "Mr. Joseph Toblinsky will be happy to hear."

Joseph Toblinsky. Aryeh knew the name from the Yiddish print American newspapers. He was a gangster they said, stories told to him in whispers from his neighbors who had to pay, each and every week so their shops – and families – would be left in peace. Joseph Toblinsky was a *parech*, a bad man.

"You want I should pay."

Both men, tall and short, smiled.

"For protection, yes."

"No," Aryeh said. "This is America, Land of the Free."

The shorter man laughed. "Only here in this shop is America? Mr. Toblinsky will be interested to know that."

Aryeh reached behind him and opened the door. The broken lock rattled.

"Go and tell him no, not from me one penny will you get."

The shorter man walked to the door and pushed it closed, brushing Aryeh aside.

"A penny," the man shook his head, leaning back to block the door. "Did you hear, the man should tell jokes for a living. A penny."

"I heard," the taller man said. "But no, from you we want more than a penny, Mr. Rosenberg…or things could happen."

Still smiling, the tall man took the brick from his pocket and began walking around the shop, looking down into the showcases.

"Beautiful things you got here, Mr. Rosenberg." He stopped in front of the glass-topped counter and leaned down. "You do all the fixing yourself?"

Aryeh nodded, his tongue suddenly too dry to make words.

The tall man nodded as if he'd seen. "Old-world craftsmanship, you don't find that too much anymore."

Almost too fast for Aryeh to see, the tall man raised the brick and smashed it down against the countertop. He remembered the sound. He was only thirteen during the pogrom in Yekaterinoslav, but the sound of shattering glass brought it all back and he reacted without thinking. In his mind he saw his father dead with blood coming from the wound on his head, and the men pushing his mother and sisters down to the floor. In his mind he felt again the pain of the truncheons against the back of his skull.

In his mind he forgot he was American.

"*NEIN!*"

Aryeh took one step and fell. The shorter man had tripped him and now stood over him like a hunter over a fallen bear.

"This one has some spunk," the short man said and sounded impressed. The taller man only shook his head.

"Not such a good thing to have spunk, Mr. Rosenberg, this I tell you as a friend, and friends we will become, because in this life a man without friends is like a fish without water…he don't breathe for long. *Farshtain?* Understand?"

Blood filled Aryeh's mouth from where he'd bitten his tongue, but he would not swallow it.

"I understand," he said and let the blood run down his chin. "I understand the boss of you is a *groyser tzuleyger*, big shot of nothing and you are nothings."

The hard sole of a shoe pressed down on his back. "What I tell you…spunk!"

The tall man shook his head again and, putting the brick back into his pocket, reached down into the case and took out the yellow-gold pocket watch with the rose-gold inlay. The man held it by its golden chain and let it dangle from his fingers.

"How much you want for this?" he asked and when Aryeh didn't answer he felt the pain deepen in his spine.

"Twenty dollars."

The tall man's eyes widened. "Twenty dollars? That's highway robbery! I can get a suit with a vest and two pairs of pants for twenty dollars."

"And a nice tie thrown in," the shorter man added.

"That's right, and a nice tie thrown in. You sell many watches at that price?"

Aryeh swallowed the blood and nodded. "Some."

"Good. That means you're a good businessman and can afford this." The tall man swung the gold watch until the chain was wrapped around his fingers and put it into the inside breast pocket of his coat. Then he pulled out another twenty-dollar watch and reached for a third. "You want one, right?"

"*Yoh*, pick one that goes good with this suit."

The tall man looked at his partner, then selected the one with fancy scrollwork on the front.

"No. Please," Aryeh whispered. "My family...."

The pressure on his back doubled. "Your family will be proud you gave us such nice gifts."

"That's right," the taller man said, "a man is known by the gifts he gives. That's what Mr. Toblinsky always says. And he will be pleased with the gift you give. Now, as to the matter of insurance."

"Wh-what?"

"You pay us insurance for protection from crooks and hoodlums, like all the other shop owners, and Mr. Toblinsky makes sure no one bothers you or takes gifts that aren't freely given. Now you understand, *yoh*?"

The pressure left his back so that Aryeh was able to watch the tall man with the three stolen watches move to the cash register and crank it open. "For a man who sells twenty-dollar watches, I think ten dollars a week is—"

"Papa?"

Esther stood in the hall doorway looking at them. Her face was pale, her eyes filled with something beyond terror. It was the same look he'd seen in his sisters' eyes when the men began tearing away their clothes....

He wouldn't let it happen again.

"*NEIN!*"

The shorter man stumbled to one side as Aryeh stood up. He had never, never in his life hit a man. To strike another was an affront to God, *averah*, a transgression, a sin that would stay upon his soul for all eternity, but when he remembered his sisters' screams....

Aryeh struck the shorter man across the face with his closed fist. He fell heavy like a sack of potatoes.

"Esther—*gaien*, go! Run! Get *politsai*! Robbery...get police! *Gai*—"

But Esther just stood there with her big eyes and pale face until the moment she screamed. The taller man didn't use the brick, he had a gun.

ARYEH ROSENBERG
December 20, 1892 – June 4, 1926

CHAPTER SEVEN
Helen

Helen used the hair dryer to clear the steam off the bathroom mirror then dropped the towel and gave herself a good once-over-not-so-lightly look in the glass. Setting the dryer down, she raised her arms over her head. Good. Next she dropped her hands to her hips, lowered her chin and looked up through her lashes, lips in full pout. Not bad at all. Finally she took a deep breath and….

Nothing.

She took a deeper breath….

"Come on, dammit – lift!"

Her size 38Ds quivered but didn't move.

Helen exhaled. Her body was still in the upper ten per cent, but her breasts weren't as high as they'd been when she was twenty and there was already the hint of a 'muffin top' beginning to form along her waistline.

She'd been a perpetual dieter since her teens, avoided starches, carbs and sugar as if they were small disease-carrying rodentia, ran track in both high school and college, had a gold card membership at a local fitness club and still jogged four times a week.

Not that any of her discipline and self-denial made a difference. She'd seen enough family photos to know she came from 'hearty, big-boned farming stock'.

Helen turned, looking for and finding all the imperfections her DNA foisted on her.

Yee-haw, let's hear it for genetics.

Helen unplugged the dryer and dropped it into the vanity cabinet. She could dye her hair to cover the gray and there was always Botox, when and if she needed it, but unless she wanted to spend most of her savings on medical 'body sculpting' – which she *might* consider one day – diet and exercise would continue to be her boon companions.

Forever and ever.

Amen.

Her cell chirped while she was slipping into her running bra and shorts.

"Y'ello?"

"Me," the voice said. "ETA three minutes, more or less. Just pulling into the visitors' parking lot now."

"Which one?"

"Blue Heron."

Helen did a quick calculation. Blue Heron was on the far southern end of the massive parking lot, three full units down from her own, but generally empty which was why her friend and partner-in-pain, Kate, always used it. Three minutes plus another two to get on her cross-trainers plus two flights down and....

"Okay, meet you at the front gate in ten. And this time stretch before I get there."

"Yes, ma'am."

Turning off her cell, Helen set it on the desk next to the file she'd brought home to check and double-check before the next morning's deposition. On the surface, a simple divorce, but under the calm façade was the little matter of an iron-clad pre-nup that her client, a soon-to-be ex-wife, wanted to challenge.

The pre-nup had been made when her client and the co-respondent were both young and in love, and his father's money (soon to be inherited, as it turned out) didn't matter. Now, after twenty-eight years it did matter, and the not-so-young and obviously not-so-much-in-love lady wanted her fair share.

And Helen L. Harmon, Esq. was going to get it for her with the same energy, assurance and legal prestidigitation that she'd used to acquire the condo, the good car, the health club membership and a nice little monthly stipend from her own former true love.

Helen was very good at her job and looked even better on the firm's prime time television commercials.

So far.

That thought produced a faint puckering of skin between her eyes as she left the condo and stalked the concrete path to the parking lot, a pucker that deepened into the beginnings of a real frown when she saw her friend leaning up against the side of her SUV smoking as she watched the ocean rise and fall on the other side of the complex's chain-link security fence.

Helen jogged the last twenty feet across the blacktop, feeling the heat off the blacktop through the cross-trainer's thick soles. It was past six, a little less than an hour before sunset, but the air was still thick and muggy. Sweat had begun to rise along her shoulders and gather between her breasts the moment she'd left her lovely air-conditioned cocoon. It had been another scorcher, the seventh in a row, and it was only early June.

God help her and her fellow Californians by the time August rolled around.

"Hey!"

Kate's reaction was as comical as it was expected. Plucking the cigarette from her lips, she threw it to the ground and crushed it under the toe of her running shoe. She smiled, but there was guilt shimmering in her eyes.

"I stretched at home."

"Of course you did. Well, don't cry to me when you cramp up. I thought we'd do Ocean Front Walk up to the Santa Monica Pier."

Her friend's face went from its natural mahogany to a shade somewhere between red oak and walnut. "Santa Monica? That's…a million miles away."

Helen leaned to the left, pulling her left arm over her head with her right, then reversed directions – stretching to show her friend how it was done.

"It's not far, Kate, and we've jogged three times that distance lots of times."

"Yeah, maybe…around the marina, but—"

Helen dipped into a squat/lunge. "That's right…butt. Gluteus going to the maximus if we don't watch out. Come on and I'll treat you to a ride on the carousel."

Her friend made a face. "But I thought we could jog over to that seafood place at the marina for the margarita shrimp we like so much."

Helen turned and looked toward the line of heat-shimmering buildings and boats. It was maybe a fifteen to twenty minute run…

if that. Obviously their ideas of what constituted physical exercise differed greatly.

"You mean that marina?"

Her friend smiled.

"Okay, but we'll have to do, oh, let's say two loops around the marina before we eat." Her friend stopped smiling. "Or…we can do a nice easy jog down along Ocean Front Walk and stop in at this great little place I heard about at work today. It's supposed to make the best gluten-free pasta in town."

"Gluten-free pasta? What do they give you…air?"

Helen ignored the comment and leaned into the first of her quad stretches when a familiar, and utterly annoying, chirping sounded.

"Oh, you are kidding…."

"I know, I know—" Kate simultaneously nodded and pulled the cell phone from the zippered side pocket in her Munvot running shorts. "But we've got a deal in the works that could generate a lot of publicity."

Helen looked skyward as she pulled in her left leg and lunged forward with her right. Kate worked for an art gallery in Beverly Hills, for God's sake. It wasn't like she was a brain surgeon and needed to be on call 24/7.

"It's a Henderson," her friend said, eyes gleaming.

Helen brought both arms over her head – hands together, fingers laced – and leaned back over her hips.

"Fantastic!" Kate squealed into the phone and actually jumped up and down. "We got it!" she told Helen and did a little happy dance. "It's ours!"

"Whoo-hoo. Now, shut that thing off. You know the rules…no outside distractions during exercise."

"Unless it's tall and cute."

"Yes," Helen agreed, "but your phone isn't. Off."

Helen made sure her friend turned the smartphone off, and didn't just put it on vibrate.

"Any particular reason you're being a hard-ass tonight?" Kate asked as she slipped the phone back into her pocket.

Helen slapped her ass with both hands as an answer. "Leave the phone."

"Why? It's off."

Helen rolled gracefully from forward lunges to side stretches. "Yes, but we've been…friends too long…I know you you'll be checking it every…five minutes. And then calling back…everyone who left…a… message." She came to center and began bouncing on the balls of her feet.

Kate looked like she was about to argue, but only nodded instead. "Okay."

Helen watched with a justified sense of accomplishment as her friend unlocked her car and placed the phone under the driver's seat before slamming – and locking – the door. That had been for Helen's benefit – hiding the phone – as if they were leaving the car on some back alley off Twenty-Eighth and Hoover instead of an upscale, security-monitored and patrolled gated condominium complex in the heart of Marina del Rey.

"Thank you. And I promise to come in next week and buy whatever overpriced painting you want to sell me."

Her friend's smile was back. "Really?"

"As long as it matches the living room furniture," Helen said and took off at a dead run.

They'd only gone a mile or so down Ocean Front Walk before the first alarm was sounded.

"HMB, three o'clock."

Helen shifted her gaze to the Hard Male Bod coming toward them on her right and did a quick appraisal. Tall, lean, tan, minus shirt to show off the washboard abs and semi-loose nylon shorts riding low on the hips. Pricey sunglasses and high-quality running shoes. Sockless. The right side of thirty. A bronze god and he knew it.

"G or S?" Kate huffed next to her.

Helen moved her gaze back to the near-empty walkway. "G."

She could feel her friend's disappointment against her side like a chilly breeze. "You think so?"

"Yup."

"Couldn't he be an S but just extremely shallow?"

"Nope."

"Shit."

"Yup."

"B?"

Helen did another glance back over her shoulder, watching the twenty-something jog away. Oh yeah – now there was an ass you could flip quarters off.

"Maybe," she said and returned her full attention to the path. "So many guys are metrosexual now it's hard to tell."

"Yeah, but there's always hope." Kate's voice was getting thin and raspy, a good indication that she hadn't hydrated on the drive over. "I mean...you never know...right?"

"Did you drink anything before we started?"

"Yeah...a venti iced...coffee."

"I mean water."

"There's water...in...coffee."

Helen cursed under her breath.

Once she'd gotten her stride, she didn't like to stop for anything short of a natural disaster until she reached her appointed destination. Unfortunately that evening's said destination was still a good mile away and even though she was sure Kate would make it, the thought of trying to enjoy a big platter of guilt-free pasta while her friend secreted bodily fluids and panted like a sick dog was more than her imagination could handle.

Helen slowed from jog to walk. "Let's pull up for a minute."

"'Kay." Kate stopped dead and leaned over her legs. "Good." Pant. Pant. "Idea."

"Come on, keep moving or you'll cramp up. You know the—"

"Rules." Kate straightened, nodding. "Right. Okay."

Helen made sure Kate was up and breathing more or less evenly before steering her into one of the many tourist shops. Kate selected a blue-tinted 'sports' drink from the prominently displayed refrigerated case. Helen asked for, and received, a tepid bottle of spring water.

Kate was back to almost her old self by the time they left the shop.

"Why can't you let yourself live a little?" she asked, taking a sip. Her bottle was still almost full while Helen's was down by three-quarters.

"I do, but water is to hydrate, not enjoy."

Kate held out her sports drink. "But you can do both. Here, try it."

Helen took the bottle and sniffed it. It smelled exactly how it looked – not related to anything in nature. She handed the bottle back and finished her water, tossing the empty into one of the many recycling bins that lined the path. "You about ready?"

Kate looked at the blue fluid and took a deep breath, which was followed by a half dozen equally deep swallows.

Helen stretched. "Put the top back on and stick it in your waistband. The restaurant's going to fill up if we don't hurry."

Kate did as she was told. "For gluten-free pasta? Somehow I doubt that."

"You'll love it."

Helen took off and was just looking over her shoulder to make sure Kate was following when someone hit her in the middle of the chest with an invisible bowling ball.

Jesus H. Ch—

CHAPTER EIGHT

Crissy

(1992)

It had to be a mistake.

Crissy took a deep breath and closed her eyes. Maybe she'd read it wrong; her teachers were always telling her she missed things because she read too fast.

Exhaling slowly the way her vocal coach showed her, Crissy opened her eyes and used one blossom-pink fingernail to slowly go down the list of names again.

John Proctor – Anthony Carr
Abigail Williams – Trisha Blaine
Elisabeth Proctor – Wanda Peterson
Rev. Samuel Parrish – Carlos Hawsley
Tituba – Mia Montgomery
Ann Putnam – Andrea Roth

Her nail picked up speed, stopping when she found her name, third from the bottom:

Mary Warren – Christine Moore

A bit part.

It was a mistake, all right.

She'd been either the lead or secondary lead in every school production, drama and musical, since her freshman year, plus she'd given a killer audition. *The Crucible* was one of her favorite plays and she'd done exactly what Mr. Byrd always told them to do: she'd 'gotten into the skin' of Abigail, the temptress/lover of John Proctor who later condemned him.

For those few minutes, even reading cold from the script, she *was* Abigail Williams.

Mr. Byrd had even applauded.

So it had to be a mistake, someone had put her name in the wrong place…and she knew exactly who that someone was: Blankie Frankie, Mr. Byrd's stupid, stuttering, blank-as-a-plank TA. He was always messing up…like the time he misspelled her name on the program for the spring musical – Christine More instead of Moore.

Jerk.

Crissy ripped the cast list off the bulletin board and shoved it into her notebook.

"Hi, Crissy."

Crissy closed the notebook as she turned. "Hey, Trisha."

Trisha Blaine had only been at Sherwood Academy for half a semester and already the staff – primarily Mr. Byrd, the head of the drama department – was falling all over themselves over her.

Trisha smiled and looked past Crissy to the empty bulletin board.

"They said the cast list was up for *Crucible.*"

"*THE Crucible*?" Crissy corrected. Real actresses never shortened a play's name. She shrugged. "Guess not."

"That's weird. Andrea told me it was."

Andrea was supposed to be Crissy's best friend. "Well, I guess *Andrea's* wrong."

"Yeah, but…." A tiny shy smile touched Trisha's naturally pink lips. Crissy almost threw up. "She said I got Abigail."

Crissy felt a prickling rush of heat against the back of her neck as she walked away.

"No one *gets* Abigail, Abigail has to be *earned.*"

It took Crissy only a few minutes to walk from the theater arts office to Mr. Byrd's classroom on the second floor.

"C-Cr-Crissy. H-h-h-hi!"

Oh shit.

Blankie Frankie Stanton was sitting at Mr. Byrd's desk and smiled so wide, Crissy could see the mashed remains of whatever he'd had for lunch in his braces. Tall, thin and resembling nothing much in particular, he always got the non-speaking, hold-the-spear parts no one wanted.

Frankie stood up and waved a stapler at her. "Hi, Crissy. I've been stapling."

Jesus Louisesus.

"Duh," Crissy said and became Lady Macbeth. "Where. Is. He?"

Frankie's narrow eyes blinked. "Who?"

What a loser. "Who do you think, Frankie?"

Blink, blink, blink, like it was Morse code or something. "Oh. You mean Mr. B.?"

"Of course I mean Mr. *Byrd*." Crissy stormed the desk, smiling when Blankie Frankie stumbled back against the wall. "I'm going to tell him what you did!"

"What did I did...do?"

Crissy stopped being Lady Macbeth – it was wasted on Frankie – as she pulled the cast list out of her notebook and slammed it down on top of the 'theater vocabulary' test sheets Frankie had been stapling together.

"Yeah," he said, "okay."

Crissy stamped her foot. "What do you mean yeah okay? Fix it."

"Oh, gosh...did I spell your name wrong again?" He leaned closer. "No...no, it's okay." He picked up the list, holding it out to her as he stood up. "I spelled it right, see."

She snatched the paper out of his hand and tore it into pieces. "That's not what I mean and you know it!"

Blankie Frankie owl-blinked again. "Why did you do that?"

"Miss Moore," a soft cultured voice said from the doorway. "Mr. Stanton."

Crissy took a deep breath and reformed herself into the character of poor, fragile Blanche DuBois, minus the accent, of course, because that would have been too obvious.

"Oh...Mr. Byrd." She turned, fluttering her lashes, a sad pout touching her lips. "I didn't see you there."

"So I gathered. Generally, my students save their histrionics for the stage...unless you two are rehearsing something for extra credit."

Crissy tittered lightly, the way Vivien Leigh did in the movie.

Mr. Byrd smiled and became the most handsome man on Earth. All of the girls in school and most of the female staff had a crush on Mr. Byrd, Crissy included…but not because he was in his early thirties and English and sounded like Rupert Everett. *She appreciated him for his talent.* He'd been on stage in England and done a couple 'independent films' here in what he called 'the States'.

He was a real actor and only teaching because, he told them the first day of class, he liked helping talented young people achieve their goals.

Crissy lowered her chin and looked up at Mr. Byrd through her lashes. "I'm sorry I tore it up."

"I'm sure you had your reasons," he said. "Would you mind telling me what it was you tore up?"

God, she loved listening to his voice.

"It was *The Crucible*'s cast list." Sigh.

"Ah." Mr. Byrd nodded and looked at Blankie Frankie. "Mr. Stanton, would you mind making another copy and put it back up onto the bulletin board?"

Frankie scurried out from behind the desk and headed for the door. "S-s-sure. Glad t-t-to. D-d-d-do it right n-n-n—"

"Wait!"

Blankie Frankie's outstretched hand slammed into the doorknob, but Mr. Byrd just looked at her, one eyebrow raised like Mr. Spock in the *Star Trek* reruns her dad watched.

"Yes?" he asked.

"He has to fix it first."

"Fix it?"

"Blan— Frank made a mistake when he was typing out the list. I'm sure he wasn't trying to hurt me on purpose…."

"I'd-I'd-I'd never d-d-do that!"

Mr. Byrd looked up at Frankie and smiled.

"I'm sure you wouldn't, Mr. Stanton."

"But he did!" Crissy shouted. "He put my name in the wrong place."

"Oh?"

Crissy took a deep breath. She couldn't think of an actress to imitate, so she just played herself. It wasn't her best character.

"Well, yeah. I'm *supposed* to be Abigail and he put me down as Mary Warren."

Blankie Frankie made a strangling noise. "I— Ah-ah-ah. N-n-n-n-no. I m-m-m-m-mean...."

"Ah, I see the problem." Mr. Byrd nodded at Frankie. "Would you mind making that new copy? I'd like it posted before last period."

"S-s-s-sure."

"Wait a minute!"

But Blankie Frankie was already out the door and probably halfway down the hall by the time the door slammed shut. Mr. Byrd swept the paper bits into the wastepaper basket next to his desk and sat down.

"I'd ask you to sit down, Miss Moore," he said in his beautiful accent, "but I'm afraid I left all the office chairs down in the audition room and I really don't have much time right now as it is. I just came in to drop off my briefcase before heading down to set up the stage for our first read-through tomorrow morning. I can give you your parental permission slip now, if you like." Mr. Byrd picked up a sheet of paper off his desk and held it out to her. "If you get it signed tonight you'll be that much more ahead of—"

"I auditioned for Abigail. Only Abigail."

"Yes, I know." He nodded. "And you were good."

"Better than Trisha Blaine."

"In some ways, yes."

"Then you have to change the cast list."

Mr. Byrd put the permission slip on his desk and leaned back. His chair squeaked. "As a matter of fact, Miss Moore, I don't."

"But...I'm supposed to be Abigail."

"No, you're *supposed* to be Mary Warren. I know it might be hard for you to understand, Crissy, considering you're a very talented young actress."

"I know that."

He laughed softly. "But that is exactly why I chose you to play Mary Warren."

"But Mary Warren's a...nothing."

"On the contrary, Mary Warren can be a pivotal character if portrayed correctly, which is why I want you in the part. As written, Mary Warren is a gullible child, a weak-willed follower. She is a pathetic and totally forgettable creature...but you can make her into something else. You have the talent to turn Mary Warren into something rare and brilliant."

Crissy lowered her chin. "Are you fucking Trisha Blaine?"

Mr. Byrd's face went white. "Wh-what?"

"Everybody says you give special acting lessons to certain girls after school."

"Did I ever attempt such a...thing with you?"

"You didn't have to – I don't *need* any acting lessons."

"No, but it would appear that you certainly need something. Now, if you'll excuse me, Miss Moore...."

Although he kept his voice low, Mr. Byrd's face stayed pale as he stood up and walked out of his office.

Crissy stood staring at the empty desk until the sound of the double doors at the far end of the hall slamming shut snapped her out of it. The doors led to the auditorium/theater's balcony level where Mr. Byrd...the high and mighty Mr. Byrd...sat like God Almighty to watch his puppets perform.

Well, not this puppet...not anymore!

Crissy ran down the hall and hit the right side of the double doors with enough force that it sounded like a bomb going off in her ears. It must have sounded the same to Mr. Byrd, because he stopped at the first row of balcony seats and looked back.

"Miss Moore, I believe we have already discussed the matter—"

"You wanna fuck me?"

Mr. Byrd took a step back. "Dear God."

"Because I'm not going to."

"I wasn't expecting you to."

Crissy smiled. "Then why did you bring me in here?"

"I didn't bring you here, you followed me. But perhaps it's a good thing since you're obviously either hysterical or badly overacting. Either way, you've chosen the right place. Soundproof and with good internal acoustics. Enjoy."

He turned and started toward the staircase at the end of the balcony. He was leaving and he was going to give the part of Abigail to Trisha Blaine.

"I'll tell!"

He stopped at the top of the stairs but didn't turn around.

"Tell what?"

"That you…raped me."

"Seriously?"

Crissy waited for him to turn around, hungry to see the fear in his eyes. When he didn't she felt something cold twitch in her belly.

"And who exactly do you think will believe you?"

"Everyone!" she yelled. "Frankie would."

"Ah." When he turned there was no fear on his face, just a bemused expression. "And would this be the same Frankie whom you accused of tampering with the cast list when you discovered you weren't given the lead? Do you really think anyone will believe this is not simply your attempt to get back at me for giving you a *bit* part?"

He couldn't have said a meaner thing if he'd tried.

"If it's any consolation, this is why I want you to play the part of Mary Warren. This kind of raw, unrelenting, untrainable passion, although a bit overdone at the moment, is just what the character needs. You *are* Mary Warren, Miss Moore, accept that." Turning, he walked down the stairs to the main floor. "Don't miss your next class."

"No," she whispered. Then louder, "No." And louder, "No! No! No!" And finally screaming, "NO!"

He was right about the acoustics.

"Please stop." He turned when he reached the orchestra pit and looked up at her. "If this is really the way you feel, perhaps it's best that you decline the role. I'll extend your regrets to the rest of the cast and—"

When she ran to the balcony railing all she wanted to do was to stop him from saying anything else. She didn't realize how fast she was going or how heavy her notebook was, but, mostly, she forgot about gravity.

Crissy hit the railing at waist level and the last thing she saw as she pitched over it was the large spotlight mounted to the outside of the balcony. It had been her best friend when she was on stage and she played to it.

But she never actually noticed the thick electric cable that looped under it.

Until it snapped her neck.

CHRISTINE (CRISSY) TAYLOR MOORE
April 20, 1976 – June 4, 1992

PART TWO
JULY

CHAPTER NINE
Henry

"And that's the pond…not very deep, but it's got a fountain and I like to come out after supper and sit by it and, you know, watch the lights come up in the city. Reminds me of the stream that ran behind the cabin we rented up in Big Bear that summer when Marjorie was little. You remember that?"

Nora nodded. "I remember the mosquitoes."

Henry laughed and clapped his hands together. "Oh, that's right… they just loved you, didn't they? Didn't bother with me or Margie all that much, but, man, did they take after you. I remember…you were all covered with that pink stuff."

"Calamine lotion."

"Right." He wiped the laugh-tears from his eyes. "All lumpy and pink. Funny."

Nora chuckled, not at the memory – it had been the worst summer vacation she could remember – but because Henry was having one of his Really Good Days. He'd known who she was when she walked in that morning and knew her all through lunch and his physical therapy, and he still remembered her and their life together.

On days like this Nora almost allowed herself to believe in miracles.

"Turn here," he said, "I want to show you something."

Henry pounded the wheelchair's armrest with his right hand and lifted his left hand, waving like a policeman directing traffic. They were on the 'Memory Walk', a tree-lined meandering path dotted with benches and covered in a rubberized asphalt. The fountain, bordered by carefully tended flower beds, was at the center of the Walk and drew not only patients and their caregivers, but also the doctors and nurses. It wasn't a big space, maybe not even as big as their front and back yards together, but it was a peaceful little oasis just a dozen or so blocks from downtown Los Angeles. Nora waved to an orderly she recognized.

"There! There!" Henry's arm was waving like a flag. "Look!"

Nora hauled back on the wheelchair handles and squinted. She wasn't sure exactly what Henry was pointing at.

"I'm looking, Henry, I'm looking."

And because he was still Henry, he knew she wasn't sure.

"Oh, for heaven's sake, woman…right there!" And his arm waved again. "You were exactly that color."

It took another minute for her to figure out that he was pointing to the miniature pink rosebush next to an engraved marble plaque.

Remember these things for me.
Remember our talks and our silences.
Remember the nights and the days
and the shadows in between.
Remember what I was and what we were.
Remember these things for me.
 – Anonymous

"You were exactly that color."

"Oh, I was, was I?"

"Yup. I don't think there was one square inch of you that wasn't pink." He laughed. "You remember what Marjorie said."

Nora felt a chill work its way beneath the July heat searing her arms. What had Marjorie said? She couldn't remember. Oh God. Was this how it started with Henry?

"She said, 'Mama, make me a clown too.'" Henry pounded his legs with both hands and laughed so hard the wheelchair shook. "Funniest thing I ever heard. Man, she was bright, wasn't she?"

"She still is."

"True. She takes after her daddy."

Nora forced a laugh. *Please God, don't let her take after her daddy.*

They looked at the roses and watched the little golden Skipper butterflies dart from flower to flower until Henry sighed.

"You hated that trip."

"Oh," Nora said, "it wasn't that bad."

Henry's shoulders slumped. "No, it was. It was that bad and you hated it, I know you did...but you never complained, not once. Margie was so little and you had to take care of her. All I wanted to do was fish and that's what I did. I went fishing and left you alone and then the bugs got after you and you were all pink from that goop...but you never complained. You never asked to go home, you just cleaned the fish I caught and fried them. I ruined your summer."

"No, Henry, it was fun."

"No, it wasn't! I ruined your summer and the baby's all because I wanted to go fishing. I didn't care about you or the bugs. I just wanted to...I wanted to...." Henry slipped down in the chair. "Wanted to go...to...you know...with the pole and things and...water, there was water and I...you know...and...and...the bugs."

And just like that, Henry was gone.

"You know I don't like bugs! Why did you bring me out here with all these bugs?"

"But you wanted to come out and—" Nora pressed her lips together. It was useless to argue with Hank about anything. "Sorry, we'll go back."

"Yeah, go back! Now!"

Nora pulled the wheelchair backward and to the left. She could already feel the muscles in her arms and shoulders begin to tremble, but Hank wanted to go back and what Hank wanted he got.

But he still wasn't happy.

"It's hot and there's too many bugs. I hate bugs. They should get rid of all the bugs, get that.... You, know, the stuff t'kill bugs but they won't. They don't care. I hate this place. Too hot and too many bugs. Hate this place, you know that?"

Nora kept her eyes focused on the path directly in front of them. "Yes."

"Well, say it."

"You hate this place."

"That's right. Hate! I see them workin' out here, oh, I see them. Got a whole bunch of them workin' all the time but they don't do nothin' 'bout the bugs. What you lookin' at?"

Nora watched a person-shaped shadow step into her field of vision and become a pair of white shoes and pale blue pants legs.

"Hey there Mr. R., Mrs. R. Is there a problem?"

Nora looked up at Stan, the young orderly she'd waved to and who worked at the facility during the day and took classes at night to become an RN. Stan was kind and helpful and funny and a bit of a chatterer – and best of all, Henry liked him.

Hank didn't.

"No problem 'cept you!" Hank grumbled.

Stan met Nora's eyes and nodded, then squatted down in front of the chair so Henry...Hank wouldn't have to look up into the sun.

"Sorry, Mr. H., didn't mean to be a problem. Is there anything I can do for you?"

"Get out of the way, too many bugs out here."

Stan stood up and took a step back. "That there is. Sorry, Mr. H."

"You should be. Hate this place! Gotta do something about the bugs."

"I'll do that, sir." Stan looked at Nora. "Are you okay, Mrs. Rollins?"

"Don't talk to her! Who said you could talk to her? Come on." He grabbed the chair's armrests and shook back and forth. "Go in. Now!"

Stan stepped to the side to let them pass.

"I'm sorry," Nora whispered.

"It's okay, Mrs. Rollins. Here, why don't you let me push for a while?"

There was a part of her that wanted to tell him not to, that it might upset Hank, but it felt good to just let go and step away, if only for a moment.

"Thank you."

Henry...Hank turned around.

"Why are you thanking him?" he asked. "You don't have to thank him, he's just one of the kids they hire for the summer to help out with the boats and things. You don't have to thank him."

"He's thinking about the fishing camp we used to go to," Nora explained. "Hen— Hank, this is Stan. You remember Stan."

"Well, of course I remember Stan!" When he turned around again, his face was shiny with sweat but he was smiling. "Stan the Man. Plays a mean game of dominoes, don't you, Stan?"

"That I do, Mr. H….but you still always beat my butt."

"Beat your butt," Henry or Hank or whoever it was now threw back his head and howled with laughter. "Beat your butt! Gonna beat your butt!"

He was getting too excited.

"Shh, it's okay. Shh," Nora said softly. "Just calm down and relax."

Henry/Hank stopped shouting and glared at her. "Don't you tell me to relax, woman. Who the hell you think you're talking to? I don't know you."

This was the new one: tense, suspicious and, as yet, without a name. He'd only been around a couple of weeks and, thankfully, most of his 'visits' were short. Dr. Cross said it was a normal progression of the disease.

As if anything was normal now.

Stan stopped the wheelchair and touched Nora's arm before turning his attention to Henry.

"Now, Mr. H., you stop that. This is a very nice lady and you shouldn't yell at her like that."

The tension drained from Henry's body as it crumpled in on itself.

"Oh. Yeah, I…I'm sorry, missus, I shouldn't have…said, you know, that. My mama taught me better'n that."

"That's okay," Nora said and fell in step next to the wheelchair as the three of them headed back to the facility.

"No." Henry shook his head. "No, it isn't. My mama would'a smacked me silly if she'd heard me talk like that to anyone, let alone a nice lady like you."

Stan chuckled. "And what do you think your wife would say?"

Henry tipped his head back and laughed. "Wife? I don't have a wife! My mama'd skin me bald if I didn't finish high school first!"

And he laughed and laughed and laughed until he yawned and fell asleep.

"Well," Stan said softly.

Nora nodded. "Well."

"It's just the illness."

"I know."

Stan pushed the wheelchair to one side of the path to let an elderly lady with a walker and her companion, a nurse's aide named Cindy, go by.

"Good afternoon, Miss Carter," Stan said to the woman. "Have a nice walk."

"Oh, we will," Cindy answered and looked down at Henry before meeting Nora's eyes. "Hi, Mrs. Rollins. He's sleeping, that's nice."

It was nice when Henry was asleep, but when he woke up there'd be a little more of him missing. And she knew that one day he'd go to sleep and when he woke up, if he woke up, there'd be nothing of him left.

"Why don't I just take him back to his room," Stan said, already pushing him toward the facility's back entrance, "I think he's pretty much done for the day."

Sundowner Syndrome, they called it…but it wasn't even mid-afternoon. "Tell him I'll be back in the morning."

"I will," Stan promised as he wheeled Henry away, "and I'll tell him you said good night."

Nora watched them until they disappeared into the building and wondered if Henry would even remember she'd been there.

CHAPTER TEN

Sara

"…and I swear I had nothing to do with it." Danny crossed his heart. "But our dads put up this giant swing set in the backyard…and I mean massive. Here, I took pictures, let me show you."

Danny held his smartphone up and quickly scrolled through the images. He'd upgraded when Sara told him they were pregnant and most of the pictures in the online album were of her showing off her belly bulge as it grew from month to month.

She'd always been smiling in the pictures and even now, with the breathing tube taped to her cheek, it looked like the corners of her mouth tilted upward.

Danny swiped another image onto the screen.

"See…what did I tell you? Look at that thing? It's got everything… two regular swings and one of those seesaw kind of things and a slide and climbing tower. Pretty cool, huh?"

Danny closed the app and put the phone away, then poured himself a tumbler of water from the pitcher on her bedside table. The water was warm and flat and tasted like plastic.

"It was really hot last weekend and I told them it could wait, but you know our dads." He finished the water and put the tumbler back on the table. "Oh, shoot, there's something else I need to show you."

Hauling out his phone again, Danny swiped through the images until he found the ones he wanted and turned the phone toward her.

"Look what our moms did."

It was a picture of the baby's room, finished and furnished and looking like something out of a magazine ad.

They hadn't done much to the room except pick a gender-neutral color for the wall (gray) and agree on white for the trim, windows and door. But while they had cleaned out and packed away the items in the room they'd used for storage since moving in, they'd never actually started painting.

They'd planned to – him painting and her kibitzing – but then she'd gone into the hospital and the paint cans just sat in a corner gathering dust.

Until their mothers decided not to be outdone by their husbands.

"Whadda ya think?"

The first picture showed the white-framed prints of storybook animals that decorated the gray (*Offshore Mist*) wall above the dresser and changing table. The next picture was of the trompe l'oeil window that opened onto a magical kingdom. The crib, decked out in pastel colors, sat beneath the painted window.

Danny imagined Sara's eyes going wide as he enlarged the picture. He'd gotten good at imagining things like that.

"Wow, huh?" He nodded as if she'd answered him. "My mom knows the artist, a guy named Hugh from back east. Anyway, Mom asked him to do a mural in the baby's room and...voila."

Danny reduced the image and imagined Sara laughing.

"You don't think the mural's too much, do you?"

No, it's perfect.

"Really?"

It's beautiful.

Danny nodded. "How about the gray walls?"

I knew it would work, really makes the trim stand out.

Danny took a deep breath and nodded. "Yeah, I think you're right, it's perfect for the baby."

"What is?"

Danny looked up to see Jessie, one of the ICU nurses come through the doorway. He held out the phone to show her.

"The baby's room, I was just showing Sara."

"Ooo, let's have a closer look." Medium-height and compact of frame, she crossed the floor with the easy grace of a long-distance runner. Danny guessed she was middle-aged, late fifties to mid-sixties if the crown of tightly coiled gray ringlets that bounced with each step and crow's feet around her eyes were any indication. Sara would have known.

"Wow."

"Yeah, our moms put it all together."

Whistling her approval, the nurse pushed the healthcare computer on wheels — affectionately called 'Bessie' — around to the opposite side of the bed and replaced the empty IV bag with the full one.

"Happy Hour," she said. "I brought you a nice Malbec tonight… very mellow with just a hint of spice at the end." Jessie looked at Danny and winked. "It's amazing what we can do with nutritional supplements nowadays. How about you? You want me to have them bring you a tray or will you be braving the culinary wilds of the cafeteria? It's Tuesday."

Tuesday — Taco Night. Last night, Monday, was Build Your Own Burgers. Tomorrow, Wednesday, would be Mac-n-Cheese followed by Meatloaf Thursday and Fish Fry Friday. Weekends it was safer to stick with pizza or the soup and salad bar.

In seven weeks of daily visits Danny had memorized the menu, the names of the ICU nurses, morning and night shifts, and knew who was on a diet and who was allergic to what. He knew how many ceiling tiles there were in the family waiting room and how many electric candles flickered on the altar in the small hospital chapel.

After seven weeks he even knew which stairwells he could escape to when he needed to cry.

"Yay, tacos," Danny said and slipped the smartphone back into his pocket. "But I'm not hungry right now."

"You have to eat something," Jessie said as she fed Sara's current stats into Bessie.

"I will."

"Can I make a suggestion?"

"Sure."

Jessie looked up. "Go home, kick off your shoes and *make* something to eat. It can even be a peanut butter and jelly sandwich, just make sure it's something you like, no, not just like…something you love."

"Why?"

"Because you need to remember there are still good things outside this hospital, kiddo. And you need some time off."

Jessie turned her attention back to the computer. "Besides, you're going to need all the rest you can get. Pretty soon you're going to be a new dad and from that moment on life, as you know it, will never be the same."

It's not the same now.

"I guess."

"Well, I *know*. So, go home, have a PB&J, crack open a beer and watch ESPN."

Danny reached through the bed rail and took Sara's hand. It was warm and soft and smooth, a living hand attached to a living arm attached to a body that was only being kept alive for the sake of the baby growing inside it.

Dr. Palmer, Sara's primary physician, told them – him, their parents – that Sara had died that morning on the kitchen floor.

"I'll go home early tomorrow," he said. "Promise."

"Tomorrow." Jessie sighed and brushed a wisp of hair off Sara's forehead. They washed her hair every three days. "What are we going to do with this man of yours, hmm? "

It was a game they played, him and the ICU nurses, talking to Sara as if she could still hear them…just a game.

"There, we're done." Picking up the depleted IV bag, Jessie wheeled Bessie to the door. "You really should take a night off, Danny."

Danny nodded. "I know."

When she was gone, Danny scooted the chair closer to the edge of Sara's hospital bed.

"I'm probably driving her crazy," he whispered, "but between you and me, I think she loves it. Just don't tell her I said that, okay?"

Never.

Picking up the bed's integrated control, Danny leaned back in his chair and turned on the wall-mounted TV. The hospital got HBO and SHOWTIME, but Sara had always been an old movie buff, so Danny kept it on TCM.

"So, let's see what's on tonight. All right! We hit the jackpot. *The Misfits*…that's one of your favorites. It already started. Is it loud enough? I'll just turn it a little louder, how's that?"

Perfect.

God bless you, Ted Turner.

The last thing Danny remembered was seeing Marilyn Monroe smile, and woke to the sound of footsteps in the corridor, blinking the TV screen back into view. Either *The Misfits* was over, or else he'd forgotten the part with Yul Brynner and the Nazis. He turned the set off.

The footsteps in the corridor got louder as Danny raised his arms over his head and stretched.

"Don't you ever go home?"

Danny lowered his arms and smiled. "We were watching a movie."

"Ah."

Dr. Palmer was probably his age, but the streaks of gray in his jet-black hair and deepening lines in his face made him look older. In the seven weeks they'd been there Danny had never seen the man wear anything but dark blue scrubs. Tonight he had on a white lab coat over the scrubs.

"Going formal tonight, I see."

The doctor smoothed the lapels of the coat. "I try. I came by earlier, but didn't want to wake you."

Danny sat up straighter. "You were here?"

"Only for a minute," Dr. Palmer said as he walked to the foot of the bed. "Jessie tells me that she's been scolding you."

"She has."

"Good, so…"

Danny forced himself to relax. The first few times he'd listened to the doctor talk about Sara's blood pressure and respiration rate and blood oxygen saturation levels and fetal placental circulation and pressure sores, the muscles in Danny's neck and shoulders had cramped.

"…she's one tough little lady."

Danny reached out and took his wife's hand. "Sara always was."

"I know," Dr. Palmer said, "but I'm talking about your daughter."

"My daughter?" Danny squeezed his wife's hand and forgot, really forgot, that she wasn't there. "Did you hear that, Sara? We're going to have a daughter." Still holding her hand, he leaned forward and talked directly to her swollen belly. "Hi, Emily."

"That's a nice name."

"Yeah. Emily…." A cold wave washed over him. "I forgot what her middle name's supposed to be."

"You have some time, don't worry about it yet."

"Yeah." Danny took a deep breath. "Yeah, okay."

"I didn't know if you wanted to know or not, but— Well, it's a rather unique case and I thought…." The doctor's voice trailed off into nothing.

"No. No, it's fine. Thank you." He looked up, nodding like a bobblehead. They were going to have a daughter. He could call his folks and Sara's and tell them they were going to have a granddaughter. "Really, thank you. Wow…a daughter. I knew it. I kept teasing Sara that we'd have a girl."

"Daddy's little girl," the doctor said. "Congratulations."

The doctor was right. Emily would be her daddy's little girl, because that's the only parent she'd have. *They* weren't having a daughter, he was. His daughter, Emily, would never know her mother except from pictures and old videos because once she was delivered the plan was to turn off the machines that were keeping her mother alive.

Danny took a deep breath. "When?"

"We're aiming for August 24th."

"That soon? I thought the baby…Sara's due date was mid-September."

The doctor nodded. "That was the original plan, but it would be better for the baby—"

"For Emily," Danny corrected. "It's not that much longer, couldn't we wait?"

"It would be better for Emily."

Danny put his hand on his wife's belly and felt his daughter move beneath her skin.

"This is where she's supposed to be. It's the best place for her."

"Under normal circumstances it would be, but we can only do so much to keep Sara viable. If her lungs were more developed I'd deliver your daughter now, but they aren't and, you're right, for the moment this *is* the best place for her."

A tiny bump, a hand or foot, traced the lifeline on Danny's palm. She was strong. "August 24th…that's Leo, right? Our little lioness."

"No, it's Virgo," the doctor said, "but it's close enough."

CHAPTER ELEVEN

Jamie

"Just sit down, will you, Ry?"

Ryan stood just beyond the room's privacy curtain, his back to the hallway, the pastry bag he'd managed to sneak past the nurses' station in hand, and glared at the two people glaring at him. *They* had taken the room's recliner and one visitor's chair.

"Where?" he asked.

"I'll get you another chair," Jiro said.

"Don't bother. *They're* leaving."

"Ryan, come on…."

"I'm his mother," the female half of *They* huffed, "and I have every right to be here."

"Not on Thursday." Ryan said, first looking at Jiro, then Jamie, and finally at Jamie's parents. "Thursdays are my days. Get out."

"Jesus Christ, Ryan, shut up." Jamie's voice was still so weak the demand was almost laughable.

"How dare you speak to my wife—"

"You too, Dad," Jamie said. "All of you, just shut up for a minute, okay?"

Jamie's parents might be upper-crust white-bread liberals who had accepted their son's homosexuality as they had accepted his former lovers without question, but they were never going to forgive Ryan for what he'd done to their only son even if it *was* an accident – a stupid, one-in-a-million freak accident that had snapped Jamie's T1 thoracic vertebra and left him paralyzed from the waist down.

They hated him almost as much as he hated himself, but he didn't need seeing that hatred reflected back at him every time he visited, so rules had been made and a schedule written. Ryan got Tuesdays, Thursdays and all day Saturday and Jamie's parents got Sundays,

Wednesdays and Fridays. Friends could come and go as they pleased except for Monday. Mondays were reserved for tests and therapy and rest.

Today was Thursday, his day, and yet there they were.

Ryan shifted his glare to the thin, pale frame on the bed crowned in a surgical steel halo.

"I asked them to be here, Ryan," Jamie said. "They didn't want to come, but I didn't want to have to go through this more than once."

"Go through what?"

Jiro was on the move again. "Really, let me get you a chair, Ry, this won't take long, but…."

Ryan waved him back and walked to the bed, placing the bag on the sheets covering Jamie's chest. Any lower and he wouldn't have felt it.

"Pistachio baklava from the Greek bakery over on Crenshaw. Gus sends his love. He wouldn't even let me pay for these."

Jamie touched the bag with his fingers. "Thank him for me."

"I did, but I will again."

"You know he can't have pastries," Jamie's mother said.

"Maybe later." His hand moved away from the bag and took Ryan's hand. "Don't get upset, okay?"

Ryan tightened his grip. "Now you're starting to scare me. What's going on, J-man?"

"Maybe we should go," his mother, the martyr, said as she stood up. "I don't want you to get upset, honey, and it is *his* day."

"Mom…Dad, please, it'll be easier if you stayed." Ryan watched the beautiful gray eyes turn toward the foot of the bed. "Jiro… would you?"

Jiro cleared his throat and began, and somewhere halfway through Jamie's mother started to cry and Ryan's hearing must have gone because he was only hearing every other word and they didn't make any sense at all.

"What?"

Jiro stopped and looked at him and it was only then that Ryan noticed their friend had been reading from a very formal-looking sheaf of papers in his hand.

"It's what Jamie wants."

Ryan shook his head. "What is?"

"No!" Jamie's mother was on her feet, clawing the air between her and Jamie's father as she reached for his hand. "I won't listen to any more of this. It's insane! It's not going to happen, Jamie, it won't happen."

"Mom, please, sit down."

"Jamie, you're not thinking rationally." It was his father this time. "It's just the situation."

"Dad, I know what I'm doing."

"No! No you don't, you can't—"

And just like the night of the accident, the words came unglued and started floating around Ryan's head. Only this time he didn't have the luxury of being drunk, this time the alcohol couldn't be blamed for not understanding. One by one, while Jamie and Jiro and his parents all talked at once, Ryan put the words together.

Executor.

Will.

Power of attorney.

Life support.

No extraordinary measures.

DNR.

Jamie had signed a DNR – do not resuscitate – order with the hospital so that should anything happen he would not receive life support nor would extraordinary measures be taken to sustain him. And while Jamie had made him the executor of his Will, he'd given Jiro his power of attorney so neither he, nor Jamie's parents, would be responsible for seeing that his final decision was carried out.

"Stop."

They didn't hear him, so Ryan said it louder. "I said *stop*!"

And they did.

"No way, Jamie. It's not going to happen."

"That's what I've been saying," Jamie's mother said and, for once Ryan agreed with her...to a point.

Ryan shifted his weight and leaned down so he was looking into his partner's eyes. "There's no way I'm going to let Jiro have your power of attorney, pal."

"Listen to me, Ryan." Jiro closed the sheaf of papers and became a lawyer. "While it is customary, in cases like this, for the next of kin or designated loved one to be granted power of attorney, Jamie thought it would be easier if someone outside the immediate domestic unit—"

God, was that what they were? A domestic unit?

"So, what say we get married? I'll marry you right here and now and a spouse's rights have got to trump a POA, right?"

"Not legally," Jiro said, "sorry."

Jamie smiled and for the life of him Ryan couldn't remember the last time he'd seen him smile before that.

"How could you? You…you… Why couldn't it have been you?" This time Jamie's mother didn't wait for her husband. She fled the room weeping.

Jamie's father got up more slowly. Ryan leaned back to give the man room to kiss his son.

"I – I'll talk to her. We'll be by tomorrow. Good night, son."

Ryan listened to the man's slow steps echo through the corridor.

"You know that was a lousy proposal," Jamie said.

"Hey, it was my first. Now – " he looked at their friend, " – how soon can you transfer the power of attorney to me?"

"The paperwork is easy, but I seriously don't think it's the best course of action."

"Why? And please stop talking like a lawyer…just answer me as a friend, okay?"

"Okay, then as a friend let me ask this…could you do what was necessary?"

Ryan had a feeling he knew what was coming, but couldn't stop it. "Like what?"

"Like letting them turn off life support?"

There were so many things he could say…wanted to say…but they all came down to one simple word: no.

So he lied. "Yes."

Jamie smiled up at him, gray eyes brimming with crystal tears. "I don't want you to have to make that decision, Ry."

"It won't come to that, J-man." Ryan shook his head. "Look, it's only natural you'd feel this way…now…you're depressed, it's normal, but I've talked to your doctors and they say you're getting better. It'll be okay, just give it a little time and—"

"Time?" The tears in his eyes overflowed. "How much time? It'll never be okay. This is all I'm going to be from now on and time's not going to change that. I'm not the same person I was, the person you fell in love with."

"Stop it."

"I'm nothing."

Ryan grabbed Jamie's shoulders and squeezed hard enough to make them both blink.

"Can you let me go, Ry? Can you do that?"

Ryan let go of Jamie's shoulders even though he knew that wasn't what his lover was talking about.

"Look guys, I understand, and I promise I'll do whatever needs to be done…if the time ever comes."

The lie was so easy, Ryan almost believed it himself.

But it was obvious Jamie didn't.

"Ry, I appreciate this, I really do, and maybe you're right about this place and all, but if something happened that turns me into a rutabaga with no hope of ever coming back, would you be able to let me go?"

NO! "Of course I would. I hate rutabagas."

Jamie laughed and Jiro cleared his throat.

"Jamie?" Jamie nodded. "Well, in that case I informally relinquish my claim as your power of attorney. When I get back to the office I'll start all the paperwork and give you a call when it's done."

"Thanks, Jiro," Ryan said.

Jiro walked over to Jamie and leaned down, hugging him as best he could. Jamie was still smiling when their friend walked around the bed to give Ryan his share.

"The transfer shouldn't take more than a couple days." He stared into Ryan's eyes. "Are you sure about this, Ry?"

"I'm sure," he told them and this time he wasn't lying, "because nothing is going to happen."

As Jiro headed for the door, Ryan lowered the bed rail and sat down on the thin, plastic-covered mattress.

"Bye-bye," Jiro said from the doorway. "Gotta get home or Oren'll change the locks on me. We're dealing with a diaper rash issue at the moment."

Ryan smiled. "Tell Oren to wear boxers."

"Hah hah."

Ryan took Jamie's hand and kissed it.

"You're not going anywhere except home. And once you're there, everything will be okay. You'll see."

And it would be…he'd get better and stronger and the two of them would laugh and say *'Remember that time in the hospital when all you could think about was that stupid DNR?'* and throw a Power of Attorney Burning Party and Bar-B-Que.

BYOB.

Ryan smiled. As soon as Jamie got home everything would be okay.

CHAPTER TWELVE

Helen

Helen turned the page and scanned the article on reality television's newest young and beautiful media whore, and wished, for what must have been the hundredth time, she'd brought her Kindle.

You'd think one of the nation's top cardiologists would have better reading material in his waiting room beyond the latest issues of Hollywood gossip and golf magazines. Yawn.

Helen closed the magazine with a slap and glared at the large wall clock above the glass-enclosed front office. Despite the fact that she'd asked for and had been given the first appointment of the day – 8:30 – it was now 9:45.

A nurse practitioner had come to the lobby at 9:00 to tell her there'd been an emergency at the hospital and asked if she'd like to reschedule.

Helen had answered, no, she would not.

She had the time now and if that meant twiddling her thumbs and reading drivel in order to see a doctor whose credentials and internet rating put him in the top two per cent of heart specialists, so be it.

She just wanted her life back.

In the five weeks since she woke up on the beachfront sidewalk with someone's towel wadded up under her head to find her friend in hysterics and strangers snapping pictures of her with their phones, her life had become a soap opera.

A bad one.

Everyone she knew, friends – especially Kate – law partners, even her clients had begun treating her as if she'd break at any moment: walking on tiptoes, constantly asking how she felt and telling her to 'take it easy'.

AUGH!

Although it hadn't been pleasant being literally tied to a hospital bed by electronic leads, wires, tubes and IVs, as she'd told a depressingly young cardiac resident, she felt fine.

He'd smiled and told her she was lucky she'd had a myocardial infarction, a minor one, because if she hadn't they might not have discovered the extent of atherosclerosis, a hardening of three of the four arteries in her heart, until it was too late.

Whee.

But she shouldn't worry because it was something that could easily be 'managed' with a few lifestyle changes.

Avoiding fatty foods and eating a well-balanced diet low in fat and cholesterol.

Not drinking more than two alcoholic drinks a day.

Exercising a minimum of thirty minutes a day.

That sort of thing.

All of which, Helen had told him, she'd been doing.

Great! And, of course, she'd have to take medication – aspirin and Plavix® and Crestor®, oh my – for the rest of her life.

Her partners had wanted her to take at least a two-week medical leave. She reminded them of the potentially high-profile, revenue-generating case she was working on and countered with seventy-two hours plus time served. A final settlement of one hundred and twenty hours was reached and amicably agreed on by both parties.

Helen spent the five days of enforced rest searching the internet and compiling a list of top cardiac surgeons.

She had the money and enough frequent flyer miles to go anywhere in the country, but was happy to discover three of the leading specialists had offices within driving distance.

Helen made appointments in alphabetical order.

The first two, Abrams and McMannus, had more conservative approaches than she liked, taking the *'let's wait and see how the medication works'* stance, but agreed that surgery might be a good secondary option *'if it came to that'*.

Helen thanked them, deleted them from the list and hoped Dr. Franklin A. Stanton, MD, FACC, lived up to his internet hype. Stanton was one of the top interventional cardiologists who specialized in catheter-based treatment for coronary artery disease. If anyone would be willing to perform a percutaneous transluminal coronary angioplasty

– the procedure Helen found on the internet that involved inflating a tiny balloon in her coronary artery – it'd be him.

Fingers crossed.

I need my life back.

"Miss Harmon?" The receptionist peeked over the top of the curved desk that separated her from the sick and dying. "Dr. Stanton just pulled into the parking garage. He should be here in a few minutes."

"Thank you." *About bloody well time.*

Helen crossed the empty waiting room to the large picture window that looked out on a typical SoCal vista: palm trees drooping in the smoggy air above a swath of drying grass and wilting shrubs. The shrubs in this case bordered a meandering walkway that separated the cardiology wing of the medical center from the shimmering parking lot.

Yawn.

A tiny movement caught Helen's eyes and she looked down to see a small white butterfly flutter among the faded peony blooms. Delicate as a snowflake, it bobbed and weaved and dipped among the faded blossoms. Then the butterfly's wing touched an invisible line of silk and almost too fast for Helen to track, a fat black-and-yellow spider raced out and pulled the butterfly into its embrace.

"In the midst of life we are still in deep doo-doo."

"Excuse me?"

Helen turned and smiled at the man standing in the doorway.

"Something my grandfather used to say. Dr. Stanton, I presume."

The picture on his Wikipedia page didn't do him justice.

Tall, broad-shouldered and athletic by the way he moved and, according to Wikipedia, only a few years younger than herself, divorced with no children, Dr. F. Stanton would have been a contender if one of her grandfather's other sayings hadn't been, "Don't crap where you chow down."

As much as she regretted it, she would only let him fix her heart, not steal it.

Alas.

He straightened the lab coat as he crossed the room and offered his hand. Helen took it, pleased to find his grip strong, but not too strong, and the skin surprisingly soft.

"Miss Harmon." He pumped her hand once and let go. "I'm so sorry to have kept you waiting."

Helen smiled and thanked him for taking the time to see her, adding, as they walked back to his office, her hope that everything had gone all right with his earlier emergency.

"It did, thank you," he said. "Please, make yourself comfortable."

He sat after she did then picked up the copy of the file she'd given to the receptionist when she arrived.

"Well." His eyes moved back and forth across the half dozen pages like a metronome. "I assume this didn't come as a complete surprise. The file states your primary physician has been treating your hypertension for the last five years?"

He looked up to visually verify her answer.

"Yes," she said, "but with a very low dosage, which, combined with diet and exercise, should have been enough to control it. Apparently it didn't."

"No, it didn't." Dr. Stanton closed the file and placed one hand over it as if he expected it to try and get away. "It should have and in a number of cases it does, but I'm afraid medical science has yet to develop a one-size-fits-all treatment. So, how can I help you?"

It took Helen just under two minutes to tell him.

"And you feel surgery is a better option than continuing the non-invasive regimen of medication and lifestyle adjustments that you're already employing?"

"Yes."

"And why would that be?"

Helen smiled and went into summation mode. "I don't like things hanging over my head, Dr. Stanton, especially things that can kill me at any moment. I've done the research and feel a percutaneous transluminal coronary angioplasty will give me the best chance of – " *Getting my life back.* " – improving the quality and quantity of my life."

He sat back and chuckled, but Helen knew he was impressed by her answer. She wasn't showing off (much) by rattling off the procedure by name, but wanted to make sure he understood that she not only knew what she wanted, but why.

"I assume you know that even with the surgery you'll still need to be on certain medications for the rest of your life."

"Maintenance." She paused for a moment, holding his gaze. "And I know what you're going to ask next – if I'll need to be on medication after the surgery, why not wait and see how things go with a drug regimen now, right?"

"And?"

"And, it's a difference between maintenance and forestallment. It is possible that even with the new medication and dietary restrictions, I may still be back here in a few years and by then having the procedure won't be optional, but mandatory. I'll also be a few years older and possibly much sicker, so why wait?"

Dr. Stanton was studying her the same way she'd seen a jury study a defendant they knew to be guilty. Helen sat perfectly still and let him look.

"You've done your homework."

"Yes."

"Then you know the risks involved."

Helen could have rattled them off in alphabetical order if he'd asked. Allergic reaction to the dye, bleeding at the site of the catheter insertion, blood clots, cardiac arrhythmia, cardiac dysrhythmia, coronary artery rupture, death.

"Yes."

He nodded and the smallest hint of a smile touched the corners of his mouth. "Then you also know that PTCA does not cure coronary heart diseases. You could still be back here in six months."

"Or not."

"Or not. All right, you've done some research, I suspect a great deal of research…" he waited for Helen to nod, "…but that can be a two-edged sword. I don't mind when a patient or prospective patient comes to me informed, but you have to remember that the information gleaned from Wikipedia and WebMD sites may not be one hundred per cent accurate. Or current. It's that one-size-fits-all problem again."

Helen folded her hands over the purse in her lap. Inside the purse was a flash drive onto which she'd downloaded all the research materials she'd gotten from Wikipedia and WebMD sites.

"I understand," she said.

"So, let's pretend you know nothing about this thing called

percutaneous transluminal coronary angioplasty, PTCA as we call it when we don't want to overburden our already well established god-complexes, and I'll explain the procedure."

Helen allowed herself a small laugh and, as he was talking about the procedure and possible side effects, she mentally checked them off the list she'd already memorized.

If there were no complications the whole procedure took about an hour. Check.

It could be performed under local anesthesia. Check.

But he preferred that the patient be completely under. Oh, double-check that one, please.

"Now, once the catheter is in place," he said, "a small plastic tube with a balloon on the end is inserted and inflated briefly at the site of the blockage in the coronary artery. The balloon opens the blockage and, if needed, a stent is placed there to help keep the artery open. If all goes well and there are no post-operative complications you can go home within twenty-four hours. Are you with me so far?"

"Check."

"I'd want to schedule blood work and a cardiac stress test before the procedure." He flipped open a desk calendar instead of reaching for his cell phone and fumbled with a couple pages. "I'm fairly booked until...the second week in August. Why don't we schedule the tests for late July and aim for August 24th for surgery?" He looked up. "How does that sound?"

Helen took a deep breath. There, it was done. Finally. "Perfect. What day's the 24th?"

Dr. Stanton looked confused as he glanced back down at his calendar. "Thursday."

"Perfect...if you operate early enough, I'll be out of recovery and awake to watch *Grey's Anatomy*."

He laughed and it was a beautiful sound. "All right then, my nurse will give you the forms to fill out and make an appointment for the tests. But for now rest, try to relax, think good thoughts, and stop any aspirin regimen your primary put you on, okay?"

Helen promised. They walked side by side down the short hallway to the front desk and she stood there quietly as she took out her Visa card, and listened while he gave instructions on what forms, tests and dates were required on her behalf.

It took less than five minutes and then he thanked her, said he'd see her again soon and disappeared.

"All right, here are the forms." The receptionist handed Helen a manila envelope. "Fill them out and bring them with you when you come back for the tests. Let's see, we have your insurance information on the form you filled out this morning…so, all we need now is…."

Helen handed over her Visa card and the girl smiled. "Be right back."

While she waited to see how much the interview-turned-pre-surgical consultation was going to cost her insurance company (thank God she had full medical), Helen listened to the music whispering through the hidden speakers and felt….

Nothing.

She didn't feel good or bad, she wasn't overly relieved or especially worried and she most definitely was not scared. No, she wasn't scared, so, all things considered, nothing was probably the best thing she could feel.

PART THREE
AUGUST

CHAPTER THIRTEEN

Henry

"Bang! Bang-bang-bang! Bang! B-b-b...bang?"

There were tears in his eyes when he stopped the battle that had been raging all night across the valleys and hills of his rumpled blankets and looked down at the little plastic thing in his hand. He knew green, he knew hard, but he couldn't remember what it was called or who she was.

The lady sleeping in the chair.

He knew lady. He knew chair. He knew sleep.

But he didn't know what he was holding.

Or who she was.

"Bang? Bang-bang? BANG!"

The lady woke up quick-quick, her eyes going big and round.

He remembered big and round.

"What? What, Henry?"

He held out the little green plastic thing. "Bang-bang?"

And she smiled.

"Yes, that's right, Henry. Bang-bang. They're soldiers...like you were a solider."

Solider. That's what he was holding, a green plastic solider.

He remembered.

Nora watched the tears in his eyes disappear and wondered what had caused them this time. He was mostly the other one now, although she still called him Henry because it was easier and he accepted it, more or less. Hank went away on a hot day at the end of July and Nora wasn't the least bit sorry.

"I was a solider," Henry said proudly and went back to the war he'd begun playing right after dinner the night before.

"Yes, Henry, you were a soldier."

"You truly are a miracle worker, Miss Nora."

Nora turned and smiled. Dr. Cross was standing in the doorway, holding a small Burger King cup.

"Thank you, Martin, but I don't feel very miraculous."

Dr. Cross still reminded Nora of Sidney Poitier, but now she called him Martin and her secret crush had cooled.

"That's why they're called miracles," he said, walking into the room. "You don't feel them, they just happen."

"No!" Henry said, "No! Shoot you!"

Nora turned to look at her husband. His eyes were narrowed and he was pointing one of his plastic soldiers at Martin as if it were a gun. Reaching out, Nora gently lowered his arm back to the bed.

"Why don't you like Dr. Cross, Henry? He's your friend."

"N'uh-uh," Henry said, "he's bad."

"Why?"

Henry's mouth opened and closed and his eyes went wide. Then his face got hard and he started to shake, and there was nothing that Nora or Martin or all the drugs and therapy could do about it. This was the worst part of the disease, having to watch someone you loved struggle so desperately for a word he knew he wanted to say, but couldn't remember.

"Henry," Nora whispered, "it's all right. Shhhh, now."

She reached out and he swiped at her with the plastic soldier, scratching the back of her hand. As blood filled the narrow gash, Nora plucked a tissue from the box on Henry's bedside table and pressed it against the wound.

"Oh, Miss Nora." Dr. Cross hurried to her side as Henry continued stabbing the air with his toy. "Give me your hand."

"It wasn't his fault." She'd said it so often the words came easy.

"I know," Dr. Cross said, frowning as he lifted the bloodstained tissue, "I know. Look, why don't you go wash up in the ladies' room down the hall and then let one of the nurses check it out? I'll be out in a minute to talk to you."

Pressing the tissue back over the cut, Dr. Cross escorted her to the door then turned back toward Henry and smiled. "But first...."

Henry stuck out his lower lip and shook his head. "No!"

"No?" Dr. Cross asked and, winking at Nora, slowly walked back toward the bed. "But I have something for you."

Nora watched the anger fade from her husband's face. "What?"

"Something special."

Dr. Cross lifted the Burger King cup and Henry dropped the toy soldier and held out both hands, fingers outstretched and grasping.

"Strawed berry?"

Dr. Cross laughed. "That's right, strawed berry, your favorite. Right?"

"Right! Gimme!"

"Okay." Dr. Cross put the cup into Henry's hands, but didn't let go. "But only if I can take a listen first."

Nora watched Henry look from the cup to the man. "Only listen, no shots?"

Dr. Cross laughed and crossed his heart with his free hand. "Only listen, no shots. Promise."

"Okay."

The pure, innocent delight on Henry's face when Dr. Cross let go of the cup and he took his first sip of the strawed berry shake made Nora catch her breath. Dr. Cross heard her and turned, a comic scowl on his face.

"Miss Nora, what are you still doing here?" He winked. "Go on, now, I'll be along shortly."

"Yeah," Henry said between sips. "Go on."

Nora watched from the doorway for another moment and left the room without them noticing.

★   ★   ★

The last thing Nora remembered, after one of the nursing staff disinfected and bandaged her hand, was walking into the lobby and settling into one of the big wing-back chairs in the 'reading corner'.

She must have fallen asleep because she'd jumped at the sound of her name.

Dr. Cross was squatting next to her chair, a worried look on his handsome young face.

"I'm sorry, I didn't mean to scare you."

"No, you didn't, I was just – " she smiled, " – resting my eyes."

"You were sound asleep." Dr. Cross tapped the chair arm with his long fingers. "You need to go home, Miss Nora, and get some rest, and I don't mean a cat nap."

"Oh, but I rest…really. It's like when Marjorie was a baby – I sleep when he sleeps."

Dr. Cross stopped tapping the chair arm and reached into his pocket, pulling out a small tissue-wrapped object. "He wanted me to give you this."

Nora peeled back the tissue to reveal a small chocolate-chip cookie, the kind the staff gave out as snacks.

"My favorite," she lied and folded the tissue back over it before putting it in her purse. "I'll just save it for later. Did he really say to give it to me? By name?"

Dr. Cross smiled. "He told me to give the sad lady a cookie."

"So, I guess you two are friends again."

"Like this." He crossed his fingers. "Sometimes I'm even his best friend. Then on days like today, he only remembers getting shots, which is strange, because I've never given him a shot or done a blood draw. That's why doctors have nurses and interns." He looked down. "Maybe it was the white coat. It's so hard to know what sets them off."

Them. Patients, like Henry.

"You're a good man, Martin, and the finest doctor I know. I want you to know how much I appreciate everything you do for Henry."

"Thank you," he said, then reached out and laid his hand against hers. "We have to talk, Miss Nora."

Nora took a deep breath. "He's dying, isn't he?"

"You are a remarkable woman, Miss Nora…. I wish I had gotten to know you and Henry before this."

"I wish so too, but you didn't."

"No, I didn't." He patted her hand.

"So, it's time?"

"You remember we talked about what would happen when Henry reached the end stage?"

Nora nodded. If they were lucky, his brain, that had already forgotten so many things, would forget to breathe and Henry would just go to sleep and it would be over.

"I remember," she said.

"Well, I think we're just about there." Dr. Cross leaned forward over his knees and took her hand in both of his. "I'm sure you've noticed that Henry has been having trouble with his coordination, he's almost entirely dependent on a wheelchair now and even then he can't sit up without support. There are also some respiratory issues that have us concerned. Over the last few weeks, we've noticed a marked decline in Henry's appetite, which is why we've been slipping him milkshakes with nutrient powder mixed in. But even then he doesn't finish them half the time."

Henry had always been a picky eater.

"He's lost weight and muscle tone and given his already limited mobility we weren't surprised to discover he's developed pneumonia in both lungs. We will put him on IVs to keep his fluid levels up and push antibiotics, but the truth is that he's shutting down, Miss Nora. I don't think he has much time left. Are you okay?"

Am I?

Nora looked into the young man's gentle Sidney Poitier brown eyes and took a deep breath. Back when they'd first talked about it, about how the disease would end, Henry had made a joke, telling her that when it came he wanted her to make a sign with a drawing of Porky Pig and the words *"Th-th-that's all, Folks!"* to hang around his neck. Dr. Cross had shaken his head and she had smiled. And kept smiling until that night when Henry was asleep. Then she'd gone into the living room and screamed into a pillow.

Am I okay?

"Is he in pain?" Nora asked. "I mean, right now?"

"No."

"Will he be?"

"No. We can keep him comfortable."

"Then I'm okay, Martin. Just promise me that he won't be in any pain."

"I promise, Miss Nora."

"Thank you."

He squeezed her hand and stood up.

"Now, I'd like you to do me a big favor."

Nora folded her hands together. "If I can."

"You can. Go home, crawl into bed and go to sleep. I don't want to see you here until tomorrow."

"But Henry's better during the day. I need to be here."

"Miss Nora, I order you to go home."

"Dr. Cross, I refuse."

He glared down at her and she glared up at him.

"I'm not going to win this, am I?" he asked.

"No."

The sigh was long and low. "Fine, but Henry's going to be busy for a couple of hours – getting cleaned up, having breakfast, the usual morning routine...so, can I offer you my bed?"

Nora wasn't sure what sort of look she'd given him, but he suddenly burst out laughing.

"No. No, no, no, *no!* I mean...." He took a breath and started again. "There are a couple rooms set aside for staff, in case we need to spend the night or just need to catch a few Z's after lunch. I can vouch for them. Comfortable beds, TV, private baths and cleaned every morning. Would you be interested?"

Nora hadn't planned to yawn, but when he mentioned comfortable beds, her jaw unhinged all by itself.

"I'll take that as a yes. Good."

Nora rubbed her eyes, embarrassed, and watched him walk to the nurses' station where he spoke to one of the volunteer aides she didn't immediately recognize. So many volunteers. They were always young, always eager to help in the beginning and then asked to be transferred to another section of the hospital.

Alzheimer's was just too hard to be around if you didn't have to be.

Nora saw the young woman nod and smile in her direction as Dr. Cross walked away.

She was putting him to a lot of trouble. Maybe she should go home and not come back until morning, but if she went home and Henry came back and wondered where she was, or if he suddenly remembered where he was and what was happening he'd be all alone and she'd never forgive herself.

"Mrs. Rolling? Dr. Cross asked me to give you this."

Nora looked at the cup of orange juice the young volunteer was holding out to her and smiled.

"Thank you, dear. That was very nice of him."

The orange juice tasted fresh-squeezed and went down cool and easy. She was just getting up to throw the cup away when Dr. Cross came back to escort her to a room that was clean and quiet and looked familiar.

Except for a twin instead of a fully adjustable hospital bed and the lack of monitoring equipment, the room looked like Henry's, even down to the color of the walls and plastic water pitcher on the bedside table.

"What do you think, Miss Nora, will it do?"

Nora resisted the urge to sit down on the bed to see if the mattress was covered with a waterproof sheet. "It's lovely, thank you."

"You are most welcome. Extra blankets and pillows are in the cabinet if you want them." He took her hands again. "Get some sleep."

"I will, but wake me when Henry's ready."

"I will. Now, rest...doctor's orders." He touched her arm and turned to leave.

"Martin?" He stopped at the door and looked back. "Tell Henry... If he asks, tell him where I am, will you?"

"Of course. And don't worry, Miss Nora, nothing's going to happen in a couple of hours."

But he was wrong.

★   ★   ★

In the dream Nora was sitting on a dock watching Henry fish from a small boat out in the middle of a lake. Pine trees surrounded the lake and when the wind blew through them it sounded like voices whispering. Henry called her – "...s Nora?" – and held up the fish he caught and she laughed because it was a small fish and then Henry laughed too and—

"Miss Nora?"

Opening her eyes, Nora blinked and looked for the clock that should have been on her bedside table. She'd moved it to her side years ago when Henry retired and didn't want it staring at him. She'd laughed at that and….

"Miss Nora, wake up."

"I'm…." She blinked again and remembered where she was. Dr. Cross was sitting on the side of the bed. "Is Henry awake?"

And when he didn't say anything, she knew. "He's gone."

"He just went to sleep, Miss Nora. It was very peaceful. I'm so very sorry."

"Thank you, Martin. Can I see him?"

"Of course."

He took her arm and let her lean on him.

"I should have been with him."

Dr. Cross patted her arm. "Don't do that to yourself, Miss Nora. Henry wouldn't want you to."

That made her smile. "No, you're right. He wouldn't. Do you think he knew I was here?"

"Maybe," Dr. Cross said, "maybe he did."

When they were still a few feet away from the door to Henry's room, Dr. Cross laid his hand on her arm and left it there.

"Are you ready, Miss Nora?"

She nodded and they walked into the room together.

And stopped.

HENRY ROLLINS
May 20, 1936 – August 24, 2017

CHAPTER FOURTEEN

Sara

He couldn't remember when he'd stopped looking at her.

One night, as he was leaving the hospital after visiting and telling her about his day and how the nursery was all ready and waiting, Danny realized he hadn't looked at his wife once.

He hadn't planned it, it just happened.

He stopped seeing her as Sara, his wife and the mother of his soon-to-be daughter, Emily. She was just a body on a bed that he talked to but didn't look at because some part of him knew that if he didn't look at *her*, didn't see *her*, it'd be easier.

Please, God, make it easier.

Easier to forget the way the skin around her eyes had crinkled up when she laughed, easier to forget the sound of that laughter, easier to let her go.

Please, God.

Danny cleared his throat as his father got up and walked across the narrow room. He was holding a cup of vending machine coffee.

"Did you say something, Danny?"

Danny shook his head. "No, I didn't say anything."

"Oh, I thought—" He held out the cup. "Want some? Still warm."

"No. Thanks."

His father nodded and Danny noticed the stubble on his chin. Either his father hadn't shaved that morning or had decided to try and grow a beard again. There were pictures of his father as a young man sporting a very dark and close-cropped Van Dyke.

It had been a rainy Tuesday morning and he was home from school with a cold. His mom had brought in a box of loose photographs and they sat together on his bed and looked at the pictures and laughed.

God, how could he remember that but not when he stopped looking at his wife's face?

When they arrived, Sara's father had stayed in the room with him. They didn't talk and Danny had let him have the only chair. After twenty minutes Sara's father excused himself and left. His mother showed up next and then it was his father's turn to stand the deathwatch with him.

Danny knew Sara's mother wouldn't be taking a turn and he didn't blame her. No mother should have to stand by and watch as the last few minutes of her daughter's life ticked down. It was something none of them ever expected they'd have to do.

So maybe it was okay that he didn't look at her.

Their friends, those who could, had stopped by earlier in the week, putting on brave faces and light voices, and tried to hold back the tears for his sake. Sometimes it worked, sometimes it didn't and then they apologized.

Just don't look at her, he almost told them. *It makes it easier.*

Danny walked over to the chair and sat down, glancing at his watch. It was only 7:53. Dr. Palmer had come into Sara's room soon after they arrived and taken Danny aside. The plan was to deliver Emily as early as possible then transfer her from the living incubator she'd been in to a manmade one in the NICU, where she would be monitored. Dr. Palmer had joked, tried to joke about giving him a few more weeks to hit the books and study up on being a father.

A single father.

When Danny didn't laugh, Dr. Palmer began talking about the delivery. He didn't anticipate any problems. The OR was scheduled for 8:00.

When they were ready, they'd hook Sara up to a manual respirator, detach the various monitor leads and wheel her into the OR where they would reattach her to machines that would keep her body alive during the caesarean section. Then he'd be brought in, dressed in a paper gown with matching booties and cap, and given a seat at the head of the table where he would be shielded from actually seeing his daughter being born. He would sit there, listening to the doctors talk and the respirator's rhythmic breathing, holding the small digital camera he'd bought, and not look at her face.

Then, when it was over and Emily took her first breath, Sara would take her last.

And time of death could finally be called.

Danny looked up as a nurse wearing pale orange scrubs came into the room.

"All ready?"

No. "Yeah."

"It's time," the nurse said and came forward, reaching out to him. Standing, he nodded and made himself look at the woman in the bed.

But somehow it was okay.

The comatose woman only looked a little like the woman he'd loved. Whatever had made Sara special, made her real, wasn't there anymore; she was already gone.

"Okay," the nurse said, "you have to go down to labor and delivery, that's on two. Another nurse will meet you there and get you ready."

Danny left the room as two other nurses, a man and a woman, came in to get Sara ready to transport.

Jessie, whose shift he knew wasn't supposed to start until late afternoon, was standing with another nurse in the hall outside the elevator when the doors opened. He stepped out and she pulled him into a hug and he hugged back.

"You gonna be there?" he asked.

"No, sweetie, but I just wanted to see you. You hanging in?" He nodded and felt her body shiver as she took a breath. "Where's the family? Upstairs?"

Danny nodded again, not letting go.

"Okay, I'll let them know what's happening." Her arms tightened and then she pushed him away. "This is Anne, you go with her and she'll take care of you."

"'Kay. Thanks for everything, Jessie. Sara would have liked you."

He shouldn't have said that. Tears immediately formed in the older woman's eyes.

"Oh, go on, now. Shoo."

Danny turned and followed the other nurse, the one he didn't know, through a set of double doors, past the nurses' station and into a narrow locker room.

"You're probably a large, right?" When Danny nodded, the nurse pulled a pair of pale yellow disposable scrubs off one of the shelves. "Now, before you get all suited up in hospital chic, there's a bathroom just opposite. Go in and wash your hands and arms…face too, if you're feeling a little queasy. After that, use the floor button to open the door and come back here and get dressed. Try to get as much hair as you can under the bonnet and be careful when you walk in the booties, they can be slippery."

"Okay."

"I'll bring you into the delivery and be nearby if you need anything. Oh, and don't forget your camera if you have one."

Danny patted his front right pocket. "It won't be sterile."

"It'll be fine. Okay, you wash up and get dressed. I'll be back for you in a few minutes."

"Thanks."

The nurse smiled at him. "It shouldn't be long now."

"Take your time."

★   ★   ★

There was music playing in the OR, just loud enough to notice but not be distracting. Danny could hear the doctors and nurses and the steady, butterfly-fast beat of Emily's heart from the fetal monitor perfectly.

"She's strong," Dr. Palmer said from behind the sterile barrier that separated them, and Danny almost asked *which one?* "This little girl wants to get out and stretch her legs."

"Good," Danny said. "That's good."

"Ready to meet Emily?" Dr. Palmer asked, peeking at Danny over the barricade.

"Yep."

The doctor disappeared back behind the raised sheet and a moment later, Danny heard Emily's voice.

She sounded pissed.

Danny didn't think it'd be possible, but he started to laugh.

"Has a pair of lungs on her, all right," Dr. Palmer's voice continued, "and I'm not sure she's very happy with us at the moment. Okay, Dad, here she is."

Then suddenly she was there, his daughter…Emily appearing above the sheet, her bottom cradled in one of the doctor's bloody gloves, her head cradled in the other. A moment later she was handed off to a nurse to be weighed and measured and cleaned up.

"Bleeding's stopped…do you want her packed?" a voice asked softly and another voice answered, "No."

Dr. Palmer walked around to the front of the operating table and nudged Danny's foot.

"Come on, Dad, go get acquainted. We got the lights, you bring the camera."

"Yeah. Right." Danny pushed aside the filmy paper gown and dug the camera out of his pocket. It felt very small and slick and he had to wind the strap around his wrist for fear of dropping it. It'd be like him to drop the damn thing before he'd taken one shot and if he did that Sara would….

He glanced at the body on the table as he passed. Sara's head and shoulders were hidden behind the raised drape and they'd covered her body with a sheet so it could have been anyone lying there.

Any body.

Danny had an overpowering urge to take a picture for the baby book and caption it – Your Mother's Last Picture – but didn't want Sara to come back and haunt him.

"We're ready for our close-up, Mr. DeMille," said the nurse holding his naked squalling red-faced daughter. "Take a couple of shots so we can get her in the incubator."

Danny did as he was told, taking five shots of Emily in the nurse's arms, two more of her after she was wrapped, burrito-style, in a pink blanket and another couple when they covered the reddish peach fuzz on her head with a tiny pink knit cap. For the tenth shot, the nurse traded him Emily for the camera.

"Okay, smile, Daddy."

Danny tried. "Okay. She's so tiny."

"Most thirty-four-weekers are – at first – but believe it or not, she's on the big side. Your little lady came in a few ounces over five pounds."

"Five pounds?" He'd eaten chickens that were bigger than that.

"And eighteen and a half inches…big for a preemie. Believe me."

"Okay."

"Ten toes, ten fingers, Apgar was seven at one minute…and that's good."

"Current?" Dr. Palmer asked from across the room.

"Solid ten."

"She's so small."

"She'll grow," Dr. Palmer said, coming to stand next to him and make faces at his daughter. "She's a beauty."

"She looks like Sara."

Someone cleared their throat, then, except for the respirator breathing for Sara and the machine that kept her heart beating, the room was quiet. Danny realized they'd turned off the music.

"She's beautiful," the nurse who'd taken his picture said. She was holding out the camera. "Okay, Daddy, I hate to do this, but her royal coach awaits. We have to take your little princess down to the neonatal nursery now."

"In a minute," he said and turned, catching the quick nod Dr. Palmer gave to the nurse when she started to interrupt. "I want to show her to Sara."

As carefully as he could, Danny walked back across the room with Emily in his arms. It was amazing, but after just a few steps holding her seemed the most natural thing in the world. Sara had read him something about how quickly fathers can bond with their babies.

He hadn't believed her.

"You were right," he said when he got back to the operating table. They'd taken down the barrier and covered her with another blanket and she looked like Sara again.

"This is Emily," he whispered, turning the baby toward her, "our daughter. She's small but she's perfect and she's going to have red hair. I'll tell her all about you. I know you wanted Melinda as her middle name, but I'm going to name her Emily Sara. Hope you don't mind."

Emily made a little noise as Danny leaned down and kissed his wife's forehead, but she was quiet when the nurse took her from him and handed him back the camera.

"We'll stop by the waiting room so her grandparents can see her," the nurse said.

Danny nodded – "Thanks." – and watched her put his daughter, his Emily, probably to be called Emmy, into the portable incubator and wheel her out of the room. Danny watched until the doors whooshed shut behind them, then slipped the camera under the paper scrub pants and into the pocket of his jeans.

"Okay," he said, "I'm ready."

Another nurse, still masked, handed Danny the clipboard holding the release form. He'd seen it before, so he didn't have to read it. All he had to do was sign it and it would be over. Danny felt the weight of the camera, heavier now by ten pictures, against his leg as he signed and handed the clipboard back to the nurse.

She said something — *"I'm so sorry"* — then walked over and turned off the respirator and all the other machines that had kept Sara's body alive, and the absolute silence that followed hurt Danny's ears.

"It won't be long, Danny," Dr. Palmer said as he came around to the opposite side of the table. "Generally, you could take as much time as you want, but since Sara registered as an organ donor...."

"Yeah, okay," he said and stood next to the operating table until his wife's heart stopped.

Dr. Palmer said something almost in a whisper, a number, the time of death, then cleared his throat. "I'm sorry, Danny."

Danny squeezed Sara's hand and wondered if he was.

SARA JENNIFER CORTLAND
March 3, 1986 — August 24, 2017

CHAPTER FIFTEEN

Jamie

Ryan sat hunched over his splayed knees and watched from the top row of steel bleachers as the D-Bs scored another goal off the Ampu-Dudes.

"YES! YES! WHOOOOOOOO-OOOOO!"

Before the match, Ryan had worried about his ability to look interested. But any fear he'd had vanished the moment the referee tossed the ball and the first volley or steal or whatever it was called in water volleyball literally erupted in a tidal wave of froth and foam.

And Jamie was fantastic.

Except for the rare beach volleyball game Ryan had managed to coerce him into, Jamie's utter lack of interest in sports went far beyond the stereotypical gay norm. It'd been Jamie's opinion anything that required you to sweat and pant without achieving an orgasm wasn't worth the effort.

So it was with wide-eyed wonder and astonishment that Ryan watched Jamie's waterlogged transformation into something resembling a jock.

Of the six men currently thrashing around in the water for the D-Bs, Jamie was always right there in the thick of things whenever the ball was snapped, tossed, or whatever it was called.

It was an amazing thing to watch.

A whistle blew, ending the match – D-Bs taking it 17–14 – and Ryan, along with all the other spectators stood en masse cheering and applauding as the players pulled themselves from the water. That was the only thing Ryan knew about the game: a player had to get in and out of the pool without assistance. An electric sling was provided for players like Jamie, but it was up to the player to swim into it under his own power and work the controls that hoisted him out of the water.

Jamie was holding onto the side of the pool, waiting his turn at the sling, when Ryan finally made it through the crowd. He kept his eyes on Jamie because he still found it difficult to look at the Ampu-Dudes, primarily ex-military men (and boys), without staring. The Ampu-Dudes were from the local VA Hospital and bussed in every Thursday afternoon for the weekly water polo match with their archrivals, the D-Bs…aka, the Dead-Butts, paraplegics like Jamie.

"Wow-zah!" Ryan said, punching the air for emphasis. "That was some game. YES!"

Jamie repositioned himself in the water as the empty sling started down. "Thanks."

"Well, forgive me for being enthusiastic."

"There's enthusiasm," Jamie said, treading water one-armed as he straightened the sling's mesh seat, "and then there's something that makes people's ears bleed."

Ryan stepped closer to the mechanical rig that operated the sling. "So, which one of these buttons is Down?"

"Hardy-har-har." Jamie swam into the sling like a merman, dragging his useless legs behind him. Once settled, he scooped the tethered remote from the water and flipped the Up toggle. "Hey, Long-John!"

The young man with half a face and wearing a prosthetic left leg turned. "Whatcha want, Flipper?"

"Good game."

The ex-soldier, captain of the Ampu-Dudes, raised the stump of his middle finger.

"Ah, don't be like that. Tell ya what, next time we'll give you guys a handicap. You know, to level the playing field."

"I got your handicap right here," the ex-soldier said, grabbing the crotch of his wet trunks. Ryan looked away.

Jamie smiled. "Mind grabbin' my chair?"

"Whazza matter?" Grunting, the man cocked his head so his remaining eye could deliver its full withering glare. "You crippled or something?"

"As a matter of fact…." There was an icy moment of silence before Jamie and the soldier broke out laughing. Ryan still wasn't used to the supposedly good-natured banter.

"Just wait until next week."

Jamie feigned a yawn. "It's so nice to have a dream. Hey, c'mon…give me a hand."

The young man lifted his mangled left hand. "Sorry, already did. Besides, you know the rules…you gotta get in and out by yourself. If I helped you – " he leaned over and yelled loud enough for everyone in the pool area to hear, " – that would be cheating!"

Jamie winced. "Jesus, are you two related? You have the same lungs. I may be deaf by next Thursday."

"That's right, start your excuses now, bro, because we're gonna cream you guys. Okay, pal – " he thumped Jamie's arm, " – gotta go, m'lady's waiting."

While Jamie hauled himself into his wheelchair, Ryan watched the young man hurry across the room and into the arms of his beautiful and very pregnant wife.

"Guess what they say is true," Jamie said, wheeling up to Ryan. "Love most assuredly is blind."

"No, it's not…. Love sees the whole picture, not just the pieces."

"Jee-zus. Come on, let's get out of here. I have to change."

"You cold?"

"You kidding? They keep this place like a sauna. I just don't like being wet once I'm out of the water."

Jamie pulled himself higher into the chair and strapped himself in place.

"Here, let me…."

Jamie slapped his hands away. Hard. "I got it."

Ryan stepped back, nodding, smiling, making out like it was a joke, and slid his hands into the pockets of his Dockers. He knew better. He'd gone to the hospital's caregivers' clinic and read every piece of literature he'd been given on the subject of 'living with a disabled loved one'.

Jamie needed to accept his limitations and learn to live with them. And so did he.

With one final grunt, Jamie snapped the last buckle into place. "There." His face was redder than it had been during the game and he was breathing hard. Ryan shoved his hands deeper into his pockets.

"Yay, team."

Jamie ignored him as he hauled back on the wheels of his chair to make room at the sling for one of his teammates.

"Yo, Jamie! Got a minute?"

Ryan looked up to see Steve, one of the poolside referees, waving him over.

"Sure, be right there!"

Jamie made a hard left, the wheels of his chair kicking up rooster tails through the deeper puddles surrounding the pool, while Ryan followed more slowly, worried about what the chlorine was doing to his Birkenstocks.

Some things changed, some things didn't. Jamie was getting better, but he was about the same…and there was no therapy or medication for that.

Jamie and Steve, who was also a physiotherapist, were laughing when Ryan joined them and offered his hand to the referee. "Great game."

"It was. Jamie's a real shark in the water," the man said, "so I can only imagine what kind of animal he'll be on dry land."

"What?"

Jamie laughed. "Steve-O's putting together a wheelchair basketball team and wants me to be the captain."

"I thought you didn't like basketball."

Both men looked at Ryan with disdain.

"*Watching* basketball," Jamie clarified, "isn't the same as *playing* basketball."

To which *Steve-O*, the refereeing physiotherapist, added a resounding, "Right. But I'm not going to lie to you, Jamie, it's a pretty rough game."

"Hey, some days just getting up is pretty rough."

Ryan looked down at his feet. He was standing in a puddle.

"I hear you, but I have to say all of us have been pretty impressed by the progress you've made in the last few weeks."

Ryan nodded even though neither man noticed.

"I've already talked to your doctors about it." Steve paused, dangling the bait. "And they all gave you the green light, if you're willing."

Jamie's smile was blinding. "Sounds great."

Steve shifted his gaze to Ryan. "I've never seen a more natural competitor."

"You should see him at Trivial Pursuit."

Steve smiled politely then turned his attention back to Jamie in such a way that Ryan wondered if the man was gay and making a move.

"I'm scheduling the first practice for tomorrow afternoon," Steve said. "You going to be available?"

"He might not even be up by tomorrow afternoon," Ryan answered before Jamie could. "Depends on how much he drinks tonight."

Steve-O frowned.

"It's nothing, Steve," Jamie said quickly. "Ryan just put together a little *thing*, sort of a party."

"It's just a little get together in the cafeteria's banquet room," Ryan explained. "Rehab's letting us use one of the Bar-B-Ques out on the dining patio and there'll be nothing stronger than beer and wine… and a lot of soft drinks, of course. I know Jamie's on medication so I was only joking about him drinking. Really. We're just going to hang out with some friends and shoot the shit. I already cleared it with his primary and…."

When Ryan realized he was rambling, he shut his mouth so quickly his back teeth clinked.

"Sounds like fun," Steve said with as much forced enthusiasm as Ryan had ever encountered. "Maybe I'll stop by."

Ryan just smiled.

"Great. Going to change now," Jamie said, already pulling his chair away.

Ryan took up his usual position next to Jamie's chair as they headed for the exit.

"You didn't overdo it, did you?"

"What – the party? No."

Which was the absolute truth.

There were only six couples and dinner was simplicity itself: hot dogs, hamburgers and vegetable kabobs grilling on a top-of-the-line gas Bar-B-Que; bowls of chips and pre-packaged salads; boxed wine, lite beer and either bottled water, soda or lemonade for those who had lost the coin toss for designated driver. The hospital had supplied the paper plates, plastic cups, napkins and several large, pre-lined garbage cans for discards. It was decidedly not up to one of their typical parties, but it was nice and everyone, including the guest of honor, seemed happy.

Which, considering how fatalistic he'd been only a month before, was better than Ryan could have wished for.

Lifting a plastic cup, Ryan tapped a plastic knife against it to get everyone's attention.

"Yes, I know. I wanted crystal and silver, but didn't feel like giving them a kidney as a deposit." He waited for the laughter to die down. "Now, if everyone will please go inside and take a seat...the educational portion of today's program will begin."

There was a smattering of expected groans, questions as to what the hell was going on and more laughter as the group began filing back inside. Jamie brought up the rear, pumping away, a half-empty plate balanced on his legs, a cup gripped firmly between his teeth.

"Here, let me get that for—"

Ryan reached for the cup but Jamie jerked his head back and managed to slop lemonade down the front of the yellow-and-blue Hawaiian shirt he'd put on for the party.

"Sorry."

Jamie took the cup from between his teeth and handed it to Ryan. "What the hell's going on, Ry?"

"Enter, O Beloved One, and the answer shall be revealed."

Jamie kept whatever comment he might have had to himself and rolled inside. Ryan downed what lemonade remained in the cup, said a small prayer and followed.

As per arrangements he'd made with the cafeteria staff, the tables and chairs had been set up facing the room's pull-down movie screen, fanning out on either side of the laptop and stand he'd brought from home. Crossing the room, Ryan opened the laptop.

"Sit," he told everyone as he turned the computer on. "The show is about to begin. With...home movies."

Everyone groaned.

"Hush," Ryan ordered. "Come on, people, sit down and be quiet."

Paper plates and plastic cups were put on tables and the folding chairs creaked as their friends took their seats. Jamie rolled up to him. "What's going on, Ry?"

"You'll see. Are we ready?"

Mutters and mumbles answered that they were.

Jamie took the plate of food off his lap and put it on the table next to him, then began blotting the lemonade off his shirt with a napkin.

"Please try to curb your enthusiasm, sir."

Jamie continued dabbing.

"Okay, will someone turn off the lights, please, and close the blinds?"

Ryan waited until the room got as dark as it was going to get and began the PowerPoint presentation of 'Jamie's New Backyard Playground'.

The bulk of the transformation had been getting the back lawn removed and paved over, and Ryan had captured every moment of that in pictures.

There were a number of gasps, none louder than Jamie's.

"Whadda think, J-man?" Ryan asked, giving each shot a three to four second pause. "See, I had them put in raised flower beds. Or we can plant veggies. And I made sure you can reach them from your chair."

When Jamie didn't answer, Ryan looked down and saw his eyes sparkle in the light reflecting off the screen. Ryan didn't think he'd be that happy and for a moment he couldn't speak.

"Pretty sweet, don't you think?"

Jamie nodded. "Yeah."

"Then you'll *really* love this." Ryan scanned ahead a dozen shots and stopped. He'd taken the picture from the back patio, also fully accessible now, using a wide angle to show as many pieces of the strength-training equipment as Ryan's savings could afford.

Jamie licked his lips, overwhelmed, Ryan thought as he straightened. Maybe he had gone a bit overboard, but so what? Now Jamie could keep up with his physical therapy in the comfort of his own home.

"So," he asked the room as he turned off the computer, "what does everyone think?"

Ryan waited for the applause and hoots to subside and looked down. Jamie was quiet, staring at the damp napkin in his hands.

"Jamie?"

"It's…" Jamie took a ragged breath, "…beyond words. You really shouldn't have done it, Ry, I don't…." He cleared his throat and looked up. "So who's going to get me a drink…and I mean a real drink…to celebrate?"

"J-man," Ryan said, "your meds, remember?"

"How could I forget," he said, winking and giving Ryan a smile that was high, wide and handsome, the way it used to be. "But one drink won't hurt me. Ah, Oren m'man, you are truly a lifesaver. Gimme!"

Jamie took the filled to near-overflowing cup from their friend's hand and finished half of it in five massive gulps.

Coming up for air, he belched and waved at the standing ovation it got.

"Thank you, thank you, you're all too kind." He took another two swallows, mere sips compared to his first go-round, and looked up. "Ry, can I talk to you for a minute outside?"

"Sure. Want me to hold—"

Jamie finished the wine as Ryan reached for the cup.

"No need," he said and tossed the empty to the floor before rolling out onto the patio.

"I think he's just a bit overwhelmed," Oren said as he picked up the cup. "You two talk and I'll keep everyone inside."

"Thanks." Ryan gave the group a thumbs-up.

Jamie had grabbed a beer from one of the ice chests and twisted off the cap.

"Hey, we promised Steve-O you wouldn't drink."

"You promised," Jamie reminded him and took a long pull. "That must have cost a fortune."

"Only a little one."

Jamie looked at him.

"Okay, so maybe it was a middle-sized fortune. But it's okay. You need it and—"

"Yeah, I *need* it." Jamie upended the bottle and finished it. He belched again, but this time no one applauded. "Don't you understand anything?"

"Apparently not, so why don't you tell me."

Jamie lifted the bottle to his lips and seemed surprised that it was empty. Shaking his head, he tossed the empty into the cooler and pulled out a fresh one. Ryan took it forcibly from him, put it back in the cooler and slammed the lid.

"Jesus fucking Christ, Ryan, you're not my mother, stop treating me like a child!"

"Then stop acting like one."

Jamie glared up at him, but only for a minute. "Sorry. I'm…. It was just a little reality slap I wasn't expecting…but the backyard's great, Ry, all the equipment and everything. Really great."

"Look, Jamie, I just thought, you know…you always liked to exercise and I thought…. I'm sorry."

"No, it's great, really. I'm just…." He tried to laugh but it didn't quite work. "Whoa… okay, guess we know why you're not supposed to mix booze and pills, huh?"

"Guess so. Look, honey, once you get home and things get back to normal, it'll be fine."

"Yeah, when I get home." Jamie looked up at him and puffed out his cheeks.

When the silence grew too long, Ryan jerked his head toward the banquet room. "How about we get back to the party?"

"In a minute. I want to run up to my room and change." He pulled the front of his shirt away from his body. "Getting a little sticky in here."

"Gotcha," Ryan said and ruffled Jamie's hair before heading back to the party. "We'll be waiting."

"Ry?" Ryan turned. "Thanks…for everything."

Ryan blew him a kiss and walked away as Jamie wheeled his chair toward the rehabilitation building.

"Aren't you missing something?" Jiro asked as Ryan entered. "Where's our guest of honor?"

"He wanted to change." Stepping to one side, Ryan waved his arms over his head. "Everybody ready for dessert? I have it on good authority that Oren and Jiro made one of their famous ice-box lemon cakes."

"With Rachel-Sachiko's help," Jiro said to which Oren added, "She was our inspiration."

"Awwww."

Ryan smiled as he walked to the industrial-sized coffee urn the staff had set up for the party and began filling Styrofoam cups. The party was winding down and if Jamie didn't get his butt back soon he'd miss saying goodbye to everyone.

Not that anyone was going to leave without seeing him. While he manned the urn, their friends waited with cake plates and coffee cups, or both, and told him how great they thought the new backyard was and how lucky Jamie was to have someone who loved him like that.

Ryan continued to smile and nod and say he was the lucky one.

Which seemed to be the right answer.

"Ry?" Jiro said, handing him his cup for a refill. "We're going to have to go soon. Our babysitter has an evening class at Cal State Long Beach tonight."

"Oh, sure." Ryan took the cup and began filling it. "Let me go get—"

The room's entrance door slammed open and everyone in the room, including Ryan, jumped.

"Ryan!"

Steve, Jamie's physiotherapist referee, was running toward him soaking wet, his clothes plastered to the lines of his body. It would have been almost erotic, if it hadn't been for the look on his face.

"Steve, what's wr—"

"It's Jamie!"

Ryan dropped Jiro's coffee down his leg but never felt it as he took off running, following the man out into the hall and down two corridors. He didn't even realize their friends had followed until he heard Jiro's scream echo off the tiled walls.

"NO!"

Jamie was lying at the edge of the pool, pale and still and limp, while an equally wet resident pumped his chest. Ryan could see the watery outline of Jamie's wheelchair at the bottom of the deep end.

"I don't know how long he was under," Steve-O shouted. "We stopped by to check the chlorine levels for the evening's session and found him. I hit the panic button then we jumped in to get him. The crash cart should be here any minute. Tom?"

The resident breathing into Jamie's mouth sat up and shook his head.

"Move!" Ryan said and shook off Steve's hand when he tried to hold him back. "I know what to do," he told the other man, "Move."

The other man, Tom, looked at Steve then got to his feet and stepped back.

"Ryan."

"It's okay," Ryan said, "I know how to do this."

He did, they covered CPR in the caregivers' clinic he took.

Kneeling, he wrapped his right hand over his left and pumped Jamie's chest five times then stopped, tipped Jamie's head back and breathed into his lungs.

Jamie's lips were cold.

Ryan sat up and started again.

"One. Two. Three. Four. Five." *Breathe.* "One. Two. Three. Four. Five." *Breathe.* "One. Two—"

"Ryan."

"Four."

Breathe.

One. Two.

"Ryan."

Four. *Breathe.*

"Ryan, stop it."

One. Two. Three.

"Ryan." Jiro touched his shoulder. "You promised, Ryan. You promised him."

Breathe. One. Two. Three. Four.

"They're here. Ryan, the crash cart's here." Steve grabbed him and hauled him to his feet. "You have to let them work on him."

Ryan felt lightheaded and nauseous as two men in white, one pushing a gurney, the other carrying a portable defibrillator, muscled him aside and kneeled next to Jamie.

"Ryan, you have to stop them."

Blinking, Ryan felt a hand turn him around and then Jiro was standing in front of him. "What?"

"You have to stop them, Ryan," his friend said. "This isn't what he wanted."

"No, it was an accident." *It had to be an accident. Jamie wouldn't have done this on purpose. He was getting better.* "He'll make it."

"You promised him, remember? You promised to let him go."

"It was an accident."

"Ryan, he'll hate you."

"If he hates me it means he's alive."

"I'm sorry, Ryan." Jiro pushed Ryan back. "Stop, he's DNR."

Ryan saw the two men kneeling next to Jamie stop and look

up. One of the men was holding the charged paddles just above Jamie's chest.

"He's DNR?"

"Yes." Jiro's hand felt very warm against his arm. "You made him a promise."

"I can't."

"You promised him. Let him go, Ryan."

Ryan took a deep breath and squeezed his eyes shut.

"Let him go, Ryan."

JAMES ALAN COOPER, Jr.
August 5, 1988 – August 24, 2017

CHAPTER SIXTEEN

Helen

Helen came out of the bedroom on tiptoes, walked to the mirror hanging over the hall table and squinted at her reflection.

As instructed by the general surgery pre-operative instruction sheet she'd been given, Helen had to arrive at the hospital without any makeup and stay that way…at least until she was out of recovery.

Not that anyone important was going to see her. The other cardiac patients would have their own problems to worry about and, as much as she hated to admit it, Dr. Stanton was only interested in her heart.

And not in a romantic or even lustful way. Still….

A tiny tingle began in the middle of her shoulder blades and quickly grew to a maddening itch.

The medicated body wash that had come in her 'pre-op/home use' package – with overly detailed instructions on how to use it – might be wonderful at killing off 99.9 per cent of her domesticated germs, but it literally made her skin crawl.

Helen carefully opened the front door, turned and pressed her back against the edge. A little shimmy-shimmy and the itch was history.

"Ah!"

"WHAT?"

The indistinct lump that had been part of Helen's divan suddenly detached itself and stood up. Kate, who'd volunteered to drive Helen to the hospital, had come over the night before with a stack of DVDs to keep her company and get her mind off 'the thing'.

"What's wrong? Is it time to go? Where're your bags?"

Helen closed the door and walked into the living room to open the blinds opposite the divan. The sky had lightened enough that she was able to see pale breakers riding into shore.

"What time is it?"

Helen pulled her cell phone from her walking shorts and thumbed the screen. "5:03. You awake?"

Kate yawned and nodded. "Uh-huh. Coffee on?"

"You can get coffee at the hospital," Helen said as she kicked the mules under the hall table and toed her feet into the knock-off Crocs she kept for running errands. "I can't eat or drink anything, remember?"

Kate yawned again and stretched. "Do I have time to change?"

She was still wearing the oversized tee-shirt and cutoffs she'd fallen asleep in.

"No. Just drop me off at the hospital and then you can go home, shower, change, grab breakfast, whatever, and come back later. I'll be fine…. Oh, God, Kate. Stop it."

Her friend nodded. "I – I'll be okay."

"I know you will," Helen said, "but I'm going to drive."

★　　★　　★

Helen studied the IV needle that had been inserted into the vein on the back of her right hand. There was some bruising under the tape, but she couldn't feel the thin piece of hollow metal invading her body, so that was something.

They'd given her a mild sedative after she'd signed another batch of release forms, these from the anesthesiologist, and it seemed to be working perfectly. Her body felt light and easy and peaceful.

She had to remember to ask Dr. Stanton if he'd give her a prescription for them.

"Knock, knock?"

Helen pushed herself higher against the bed's thin mattress. "Come in, Kate. You get your coffee?"

Her friend walked through the narrow slit in the curtain that isolated Helen from the other pre-operatives in the surgical prep area with a stack of magazines in her arms. "I brought you something to read. Later. When you're in your room, I mean."

"All garbage and gossip?"

"Yup."

"Ah, paradise."

Kate nodded. "Love the outfit."

Helen looked down at the blue ties-in-the-front hospital gown. "Ah yes, so chic and comfy."

"Are you okay? Can I get you anything?"

"A better heart?"

She should have known better than to joke about it, but she'd been drugged so it really wasn't her fault.

"Oh, God, Helen, don't say that!" Kate sobbed. "You're going to be fine!"

One of the prep nurses popped her head into the enclosure. "Is everything okay?"

Helen nodded. "She hasn't had her coffee yet."

"No, I'm okay. Sorry," her friend told the nurse. "Sorry."

"It's all right, I understand. Sometimes this is harder on friends and family than it is on the patient."

Helen was about to argue that point when an orderly walked through the curtains.

"They're ready for you, Ms. Harmon."

The nurse and orderly pushed open the curtain divider and began getting the bed ready for transport to the operating room, and suddenly it became all too real. Helen reached out to grab her friend's hand.

"It's okay." Kate's voice was calm as their roles reversed. "It's okay. You're going to be fine."

"Of course she is," another voice said.

He rose into view like a green-clad sun in a smiley-face surgical cap and Helen wished to God she'd ignored the rules and put on makeup, maybe just mascara and blush.

"I must look awful. Good morning, Dr. Stanton." She felt Kate squeeze her hand. She squeezed back.

"How are you doing, Helen?"

"Fine."

"Do you have any questions for me?"

She thought a moment just for show and shook her head. "Can't think of anything."

"How long will it take?" Kate asked. "I'm her friend. I drove her here. I'm Kate."

She let go of Helen's hand to take his.

"Pleased to meet you, Kate, and to answer your question, the operation should only be an hour or so. When we take Ms. Harmon in, you can go back to the pre-op waiting area. Once she's out of recovery, you'll be notified and given her room number. But I have to warn you, she might not be very talkative."

"That'll be a change," her friend said and everyone, except Helen, laughed.

Then very calmly, as if he were reading a bedtime story, Dr. Stanton turned to her and went over each and every detail of the operation again – explaining, without becoming too graphic, how he intended to fix her heart and what she should expect afterward.

"But this isn't a magic wand, Ms. Harmon, you won't feel like a teenager again."

"Thank God."

He gave her a quick grin. "In fact, at first you'll feel like hell. From anywhere between twenty-four and forty-eight hours a newborn kitten with asthma could beat you in arm wrestling. You'll hurt, but we have meds for that, and you'll wonder if I left a boulder in your chest cavity. Even so that won't stop us from getting you up and walking much sooner than you think possible." He paused, letting what he'd said sink in. "It's going to take time, Helen, a great deal of time before you feel even remotely like yourself again, but you have to remember that's normal. A lot of people get frustrated during convalescence because they expect too much of themselves. Any unreasonable expectations you put on yourself will only be detrimental to your health."

"But you don't know Helen," Kate said. "She's the strongest person I know."

Dr. Stanton looked at Kate, then back to Helen and nodded. "That's good to hear, because that strength will help. Questions?"

"No," Helen answered for herself and Kate.

"Okay, then, next time I see you will be in the OR. I'll be the tall, good-looking one in the mask." He started to leave, then turned around. "But before I go...." He cleared his throat. "A new patient is about to enter the hospital when he sees two doctors searching through the flower beds. 'Excuse me,' he says, 'have you lost something?' 'No,' one of the doctors replies. 'We're doing a heart transplant on an IRS agent and need to find a suitable stone.'" He winked at them. "See you soon."

Helen smiled and looked at the ceiling as the bed rails were pulled up and snapped in place.

"Okay," the orderly said, "here we go. Mind your toes."

Kate backed up into the bunched curtain until the bed was halfway out into the main room, then reached over the rails and took Helen's hand again.

"You'll be fine," she said.

"So will you," Helen said, "as soon as you get some coffee and eat something."

Kate nodded. "Okay."

The ceiling pattern changed above her and Helen heard a click and then a whoosh as a set of automatic doors opened.

"I'm sorry, miss," the orderly said, presumably to Kate, "but this is as far as you can go. Do you know how to get back to the pre-op visitors' lounge?"

Kate's grip tightened on her hand. "Yes."

"Okay. And the cafeteria should be open now."

Kate stepped closer to the bed so Helen could see her nod as the bed moved away and the ceiling went from cream to stark white.

"Wait!"

The orderly's upside-down face hovered over hers. "Is something the matter, Miss Harmon?"

"Yes," Helen said. "Kate!"

Her friend looked down at her. "What? What is it?"

Helen took a deep breath. "If...if something happens..." *deep breath,* "...if it does...will you..." *slow, dramatic exhale,* "...take care of my cat?"

"Of course I—" Kate's eyes narrowed. "You don't have a cat."

Helen winked. "Then I guess I'll be fine."

"You bitch."

The orderly was chuckling as he pushed her through the double doors. "That wasn't very nice."

"Hey," she said as he wheeled her into the operating room, "if you can't torment your friends, who can you torment?"

★   ★   ★

Well, that wasn't so bad.

Helen didn't remember anything after the anesthesiologist told her he was making her a special cocktail and asked her to count backward from ten. Nine. Eight. Seven....

But the operation had to be over and she'd probably been asleep for hours because *Grey's Anatomy* was on a massive flat-screen and it had to be after visiting hours because Kate wasn't there.

They probably made her go home.

"Rib spreaders," one of the doctors – she couldn't tell who it was – said, and Helen watched him insert the instrument and crack open the body on the table.

The TV had great definition. She'd have to ask what model it was.

"Anything?" the doctor asked.

The sound quality was damn near perfect too; she could hear every beeping machine and foot scuff and clinking instrument.

"Still tachycardic, doctor."

"Dammit. Push epinephrine," the doctor yelled. "And someone turn off that music!"

Helen recognized the voice but couldn't place the actor.

"Anything?"

"No, still dropping." Then. "She's in v-fib."

"SHIT! Okay – get me the internal paddles."

He had to be a guest star.

"Clear!"

But whoever he was, he was a good actor.

Must be a guest star, but he sounds so familiar.

"Anything?"

The camera moved in for a close-up. "No change."

"Clear!"

Helen wished she'd woken up sooner. She hated not knowing what the story line was.

"We've got sinus rhythm," a voice said.

And a moment later another added: "She's tachycardic and her pressure's dropping. 50/30."

"Oh, no you don't," the guest-star surgeon said to the body on the table, "not today. Charge."

"Doctor, she's—"

"Clear!"

Helen leaned forward and waited, nodding when the alarm on the cardiac monitor sounded.

"She's coding."

Mumbling something under his breath, he readied the paddles. "Charge to max. Clear!"

Zap.

"Nothing."

There was another dramatic pause and Helen expected a song, something recognizable and melancholy and fitting with the plot – whatever that was – to start as the guest doctor handed the paddles to a nurse and looked down.

"I'm sorry," he said and took off his mask.

Helen recognized him.

Oh my God.

Dr. Stanton took a deep breath and looked up at the operating room clock.

"Time of death—"

The TV screen and everything else went black.

HELEN LOUISE HARMON
July 7, 1972 – August 24, 2017

"What the hell?"

Dr. Stanton looked at the anesthesiologist. "What?"

"I...I don't know, but..."

"What?"

The man looked up and shrugged. "Blood pressure's rising. I don't.... We got a normal sinus rhythm."

Dr. Stanton backed away from the table, ripping off his gloves and shouting at the nurses. "Mask! And gloves, come on...hurry."

"She's back."

Well, that's more like i—

PART FOUR
AUGUST 24, 2017

CHAPTER SEVENTEEN

Nora felt the floor tilt under her and would have fallen if he hadn't caught her.

Henry was dead. He'd died alone while she'd slept and dreamed about him fishing. Henry was dead and he died alone. Dr. Cross told her he was dead.

Henry was supposed to be dead.

"I don't—"

Henry looked up at them from the bed and ran a hand under his nose, sniffling. It looked like he'd been crying for a long time; his eyes were swollen and bloodshot.

"Where's my mama?" he asked.

Nora felt Dr. Cross's arm tighten around her. He'd muttered something low, under his breath, something Nora couldn't make out over the sudden pounding in her ears.

"But you said…." Her voice sounded muffled, lost in the rush of white noise. "You said he was…."

"I don't— Miss Nora, I swear to you I—" Dr. Cross said and began pulling her away. "Come with me now, Miss Nora."

And she almost let him.

"I want my mama," Henry whimpered in a little-boy voice, as new tears filled and overflowed his eyes. "Where's my mama?"

Nora shook off the hands holding her like a dog shaking off rain. Henry was hurting and afraid and she couldn't leave him, not like that, not when he was so afraid.

Especially since she'd never seen him afraid before.

When Dr. Cross first told them about the Alzheimer's, Nora couldn't seem to catch her breath but Henry took the news with a nod. It was later that night, after they got home and Nora crumpled into sobs, Henry just sat right down next to her and held her and told her not to fret, that God knew what He was doing and things would work out as best they could.

Henry had never been the type of man to show fear, but he was afraid now, so afraid that he'd even wet himself. Nora recognized the smell hanging in the room's cool, quiet air a full moment before she noticed the bright yellow stain beginning to seep through the sheet.

"Oh, Henry."

She took a step closer and felt Dr. Cross's hand on her arm. "Miss Nora, maybe you should wait outside while I—"

"No, he needs me." Nora patted the doctor's hand away and kept walking. "It's all right, Henry, don't worry. It was an accident. It's all right."

Henry looked at her all round-eyed and quivering-lipped. It was the same look their daughter had when she woke up from a bad dream in the middle of the night.

"Who's Henry?" he asked as a tear slipped from the corner of his left eye and followed the path of wrinkles down his leathery cheek to his chin.

She stopped and grabbed onto the bed's side rail to keep herself upright and strong. This was something new.

"Martin?"

"I don't know. He was…. Miss Nora, Henry coded. That's why I came to get—"

"Who's Henry?" Henry was still using the little-boy voice, but this time there was a touch of petulance in it and a defiant pooch to the quivering lower lip. He was getting angry, but not Hank angry; this was the anger of a frustrated child whom no one was listening to. "Who's *HENRY*!?"

It wasn't just the voice. Henry was acting like a child.

"Well, you're Henry," Dr. Cross said, moving Nora back and taking her place, putting himself between them. "And this is Nora."

Henry looked at her and frowned, his whole face pickling.

"You remember Nora," Dr. Cross prompted. "She's your wife."

Henry's eyes widened and he started to laugh. It was the light, high pitched laughter of a child.

"You're silly. You're a silly old man."

Old?

Dr. Cross looked at Nora then back at Henry. "Okay, I'm silly. Can you tell me how do you feel, Henry?"

"My name's not Henry, it's Timmy! Timothy Patrick O'Neal! My name's Timmy and I want my mama! Where's my mama?" His voice got louder and louder and high-pitched until he began sobbing. "I want my MAMA! Where's my MAMA?"

When Dr. Cross reached out, Henry pulled the bed sheet over his head and hunkered down under it.

"I WANT MY MAMA! I WANT MY MAMA! I WANT MY MAAAAAMAAAA!"

Suddenly the room was full of nurses and orderlies. Dr. Cross pulled Nora away and handed her off to a nurse as two orderlies rushed forward to bracket the bed and, speaking very softly, tried to coax Henry out from under the sheet. His terrified screams echoed off the room's pale blue walls.

"MAAAAAAAAAMAAAAAAAAA!"

"Enough!"

She hadn't shouted or screamed or even raised her voice above what her daughter called her 'Mama whisper', but everyone, including her poor, sobbing Henry, heard her.

"Miss Nora…."

"Enough," Nora repeated to the orderlies as she pulled away from the nurse.

"But, ma'am."

"Please, let him go."

Nora watched their eyes shift toward Dr. Cross, who must have nodded because they moved back. Moving slowly and making hushing sounds, she walked to the bed and pulled the sheet down off his face.

"Shh, shh now," she whispered, patting his chest. "It's okay. Everything's going to be okay. Shh."

Henry looked up at her and took her hand. His skin was warm and she recognized the feel of it against her own.

"P-p-please, where's my mama?"

"I don't know, baby, but we'll find her." She looked up. "Won't we, Martin?"

Dr. Cross nodded and motioned everyone out of the room, leaving Nora alone with the man who used to be Henry.

"I'll be right back, with…another doctor, if that's okay?"

He didn't wait for Nora's answer and that was fine with her, because she had more important things to think about at the moment. When she was sure they were alone, Nora opened her purse and gently wiped away his tears with one of the lavender-scented handkerchiefs she'd started carrying since her first visit.

When Martin had come for her, telling her Henry was dead, she thought she'd finally have to use the handkerchief for herself. But it was better this way, even if Henry was crying and confused, he was alive.

And that meant Henry *hadn't* died. No one *wakes up* after they die except the Good Lord Jesus Christ and that was only because He'd been the Son of God. Henry was only the son of Leonard and Rosalind Rollins, so he couldn't have been dead.

Martin just made a mistake, that was all.

Just a mistake.

"I want my mama," Henry said in his tiny little voice and Nora stopped wondering about what happened and smiled at him.

"Poor baby," she whispered. "Everything's going to be okay, I promise. I'll take care of you."

Henry wiped his nose on the sleeve of his pajama top.

"Do you know where my mama is? She told me to go outside because I was singing too loud and she's gonna have a baby and I think Howdy's a good name or maybe Summerfallwinterspring if it's a girl and I'm gonna be the big brother but Mama gets tired and told me to go out so I got my bike and I did and big brothers can ride in the street and…."

Henry took a deep breath, ready to continue, when Nora saw him look at the door and shrink back against the pillow, pulling the sheet back up toward his face. "I don't like them. They're scary."

Nora turned to see Dr. Cross standing in the doorway with another man: white, middle-aged and paunchy in a pale gray business suit, slightly stooped-shouldered and balding but with a kind face. The man looked at Henry and smiled.

"Make 'em go 'way," Henry told her, pulling at the sheet again as the two men entered the room.

"Miss Nora, this is Dr. Ellison. Dr. Ellison is the staff psychologist here at the hospital. I'd like him to look at—"

"No doctors!" Henry suddenly grabbed Nora's arm, pulling her to him, and she gasped before she could stop herself. She'd forgotten how strong he was.

"Miss Nora?"

"I'm fine, Martin."

"No doctors," Henry hissed, his face all but buried in her side. "Doctors give shots."

"Oh, but I'm not that kind of doctor," Dr. Ellison said, taking another step closer. He had a slight Irish or Scottish accent, Nora couldn't decide which.

"No?"

"No."

"Promise?" Henry said, and the doctor walked to the foot of the bed and made an X over the front of his suit coat.

"Promise and cross my heart, hope to kiss a duck."

Henry giggled. Nora couldn't remember the last time she'd heard him do that, or if he ever had.

"I'm Dr. Ellison. Can I talk to you for a little bit?"

Henry nodded but wouldn't let go of Nora's arm. "No shots?"

Dr. Ellison laughed softly and raised both hands. He carried a small digital recorder in one hand similar to the one Marjorie had given Henry the Christmas after he'd been diagnosed – so he could keep his memories close.

"No shots," Dr. Ellison said, "but maybe a cookie afterward...if you're good."

Henry immediately let go of Nora's arm and sat up straight in the bed she'd been told he died in, hands folded in his lap. "I'm good."

Dr. Ellison chuckled again and motioned Nora out of the way before he brought up a chair and sat down.

"Well, now," he said, turning on the recorder and placing it on the bed next to Henry, "as I already told you, my name is Dr. Ellison, so I guess I need to ask your name, right?"

"Right!" Henry lifted his chin. "My name's Timothy Patrick O'Neal...but everyone calls me Timmy."

Dr. Ellison extended his hand. "Hello, Timmy."

"Hello, Dr. Ellison."

Henry pumped the doctor's hand three times – up down, up down, up down – then folded his hands back in his lap.

"Very good. Now, Timmy, do you know where you are?"

Henry shook his head.

"You're in a hospital." Henry's eyes widened. "Do you know why?"

Henry shook his head. "Where's my mama?"

"I'm not sure, Timmy. What's your mama's name?"

"Mama."

Nora pressed the handkerchief to her lips.

"Okay, but what does your daddy call her?"

"Oh! Honey."

"Ah." Dr. Ellison turned toward Nora. "This may take a while."

Dr. Cross came up and touched Nora's arm.

"Why don't we head down to the café and get some coffee? I don't know about you, Miss Nora, but I could sure use some."

Nora nodded and followed Dr. Cross to the door where she stopped and turned around. "I'll be back in a little while, Hen— Timmy."

"'Kay."

Henry didn't look at her when he answered. He was sitting up straight and tall and giving his full attention to everything Dr. Ellison had to say.

Like a good little boy.

Dr. Cross didn't say anything as they left and walked down the hall and it was only when the two of them were alone in the elevator that Nora finally found the right words to ask.

"Why did you tell me he was dead, Martin?"

"Because he was, Miss Nora."

"Then how do you explain this?"

When the elevator doors opened, Dr. Cross stepped back and let her exit first. "I can't, Miss Nora, but I really wish I could."

Dr. Ellison couldn't answer the question either when he joined them twenty minutes later. He was, however, smiling from ear to ear.

"Your husband's amazing, Mrs. Rollins, absolutely amazing. Marty, are you sure he has Alzheimer's?"

Marty? Nora stirred the cream into her second cup of coffee and kept quiet.

"Oh, come on, Barney, you know better than to ask that. Of course he had...*has* Alzheimer's, and he coded and was pronounced and—" He glanced at Nora and quickly looked away. "Do you have any idea what's going on?"

Dr. Ellison looked down at the digital recorder in his hand and shook his head. "About his spontaneous...recovery, no, except to say that it does happen from time to time. But as for his current state of mind...." He smiled. "Well, other than repeating myself about how amazing I think he is.... Mrs. Rollins, do you know if Henry had any boyhood friends or relatives named Timmy?"

Nora set her spoon aside and looked up. "He might have. I know he doesn't have any family named Timmy, but I don't know about friends."

Dr. Ellison slipped the recorder into the inside pocket of his suit coat and leaned forward, clasping his hands together on the tabletop the same way Henry had.

"Mrs. Rollins, your husband believes he's a six-year-old boy named Timmy who is about to become a big brother and wants to name his sibling after the characters on the old *Howdy Doody* show. My God, Howdy Doody...I haven't thought about him or Buffalo Bob in decades." Clearing his throat, he looked at Nora. "I need to ask Dr. Cross a few things that might be a bit uncomfortable for you to hear, Mrs. Rollins, so if you'll excuse us."

Dr. Cross pushed away from the table, about to stand, when Nora shook her head.

"It's all right, Martin," she said. "I'd like to know too."

Dr. Cross took a small notebook from his coat pocket and opened it up. He held it in front of him the way Nora's mother used to hold her prayer book every Sunday in church – fingers splayed to hold it up and using only her thumbs to turn and hold down the pages.

"See, this is why I love you, Marty," Dr. Ellison said. "As young and computer savvy as you are, you still write things down on paper."

Nodding without looking up, Dr. Cross took a deep breath and began reading.

"The patient – " he didn't use Henry's name and Nora knew that was for her benefit " – began showing signs of respiratory distress at 15:30 and, in accordance with the DNR order, was made as comfortable as possible. I stayed with him until he stabilized, after which I ordered that he be checked every fifteen minutes and left to continue my rounds. At 16:15 I was paged back to the patient's room on a Code Blue. I arrived to find that the patient had coded and declared time of death at 16:22." Closing the notebook, he looked up. "I'm so sorry, Miss Nora."

"Thank you, Martin. But are you sure he died?"

"Yes, ma'am."

"But he's alive now."

"Yes, ma'am, he is." Dr. Cross shook his head. "I just don't know why."

"There are," Dr. Ellison said, "a number of well-documented cases of people who've come back with claims of near-death experiences."

"Yes, but those are incidents where there'd been medical intervention. That wasn't the case this time, Barney." Dr. Cross sounded angry but Nora knew it was probably like when Henry got angry, back when Hank was around – you got angry so you wouldn't sound scared. "And those so-called experiences are probably nothing more than hallucinations created by a lack of oxygen to the brain."

"Very possibly, but these people were all declared clinically dead, correct?" Dr. Ellison asked.

"Yes."

"With no outward or inward signs of life, right?"

"Yes, but...."

"And then they woke up."

Dr. Cross leaned forward, keeping his voice low. "But they didn't wake up claiming to be someone else, did they?"

"No, they didn't, but generally people who claim near-death experiences aren't suffering from Alzheimer's. I think Henry's still here." Dr. Ellison tapped a finger to his forehead.

"But why does he think he's a little boy?" Nora asked.

"Why not?" Dr. Ellison replied. "What better way to deal with an illness that reduces us to children than to become a child? Timothy Patrick O'Neal is a perfectly nice little boy of six who loves *Howdy Doody* and riding his bike and lives with his mom and dad in a yellow house in Long Beach. I even have an address because his mother taught him to memorize it in case he ever got lost. Henry never lived in Long Beach, did he?"

"No."

"Absolutely fascinating."

Nora was glad the man found it so. "But he died."

"Yes, technically. Henry died – " he shot Dr. Cross a look, " – more or less. Mrs. Rollins, when was your husband born? His full birth date – month, day, year."

"May 20th, 1936."

"Timmy's birthday, he told me, is June 10th, 1950. Does that date mean anything to you?"

"No, it doesn't. But he's...Henry's all right?"

"Well." The new doctor, Dr. Ellison, licked his lips. "*Timmy's* all right. I'm not sure how long this new identity will last, but until Henry comes back, we need to accept this Timmy persona." He smiled. "At one point he asked me why he looked different and I really didn't know what to say, so I just told him that he'd been sick for a very, very long time and that seemed all the explanation he needed. Your husband thinks he's a child, Mrs. Rollins, and children have a remarkable capacity to accept things on faith."

"I see. Now if you'll both excuse me," Nora said and stood up. "I need to get back to my husband."

Both men stood up but didn't try to stop her.

"Did you give him a cookie?" she asked Dr. Ellison.

"Cookie? Oh." Dr. Ellison smiled sheepishly. "No, I forgot... sorry."

"Don't fret, I'll get one for him."

The café's selection of cookies came down to a choice between oatmeal-raisin, sugar and something called a 'gluten-free/lactose-free honeycake' that looked like an undercooked pancake. Nora bought two sugar cookies and decided right then and there that the first thing she'd do when she got home that night was bake up a batch of chocolate-chip cookies.

Because what little boy – even a little boy in an old man's body – didn't like chocolate-chip cookies?

He was watching cartoons when she got back in the room.

"Mickey Mouse! Look at the colors!" he said, pointing, his eyes never leaving the screen. "M-I-C-K-E-Y-M-O-U-S-E! Mickey's pants are RED! He has RED pants and YELLOW shoes!"

Nora glanced at the screen and tried to remember if Mickey Mouse had been in color back in the fifties when Marjorie had been a member of the Mickey Mouse Fan Club.

"Very nice. Look what I have," she said and folded back the napkin she'd wrapped around the cookies. "Just like Dr. Ellison promised."

Henry's eyes shifted away from the television just long enough to see what it was she was holding.

"COOKIES! Gimme!"

Smiling, Nora placed the cookies into his outstretched hand and turned around the chair Dr. Ellison had been sitting in so she could watch Mickey Mouse with the little boy named Timothy Patrick O'Neal who used to be her husband, Henry.

CHAPTER EIGHTEEN

Dr. Palmer cleared his throat. "Time of death, 15:30. She's gone, Danny, I'm sorry."

Danny squeezed her hand and wondered if he was.

"I love you," he whispered.

And it squeezed back.

Danny felt every muscle in his body tighten, trapping him inside his own skin as his throat struggled to expel an involuntary gasp. If he'd been able to move, he would have grabbed the closest doctor or nurse by the front of their scrubs and shouted, *"She just moved. Did you see that? She just moved."*

But he knew that was impossible. Sara was dead, had been dead long before they turned off the machines. He knew that, so all he could do was stand there and watch her hand squeeze his again.

It wasn't possible, but this time one of the nurses saw it too.

"Oh my God. Doctor? I— She moved."

Danny shook his head. "No, she's dead."

Then she moaned and someone pulled him away.

"We have a heartbeat. It's weak, but...her blood pressure's coming up. Jesus Christ, it's 120/80. It's normal."

"Sara's dead!" he shouted and they all stopped and looked at him, then Dr. Palmer shouted for someone to get him a fresh gown and gloves and to get 'him' out of there.

Him. Danny. Widower. Emily's father.

Get *him* out of there.

One of the nurses took Danny's arm and led him away.

"But she's dead," Danny told the nurse who escorted him from the OR. "She died on the kitchen floor."

The nurse nodded and kept repeating "I know, I know," but wouldn't let Danny stop moving or turn around until she'd pushed him out the double automatic doors at the end of the surgical hall. Letting go, she held up both gloved hands as if she expected him to try to run back to the OR and took a step back as the doors began to swing shut.

"The doctor will talk to you after he—" But the doors closed before she had a chance to finish what she was going to say.

Danny stood facing the doors until an orderly asked if he needed help and he asked for directions to the NICU.

He'd forgotten to take off the disposable scrubs and hat and booties, but no one seemed to mind. It was a hospital, after all, and Sara was dead.

Sara had to be dead.

Danny found his and Sara's parents huddled in front of the NICU nursery window – tapping on the glass, making goo-goo sounds, mouthing words and gesturing to the nurse who'd wheeled Emily's incubator up to the window, and taking pictures just like every other new grandparent.

As if nothing out of the ordinary had happened, because nothing had; babies are born and people die every minute of every day.

Sara was dead.

Danny turned and left the NICU without them seeing him and went to the visitors' waiting room, where he sat in a chair in the corner that was farthest from both the wall-mounted flat-screen television and the receptionist's desk. There were others in the room besides him – families, older couples, a few bored children kicking chair legs, men and women of various ages who, like him, sat alone and waited for their names to be called.

They came and went while Danny sat and waited his turn.

It was only after his mother found him, frantic and red-faced, that he realized he hadn't told the receptionist he was there.

"My God, didn't you hear them paging you?"

Danny rubbed his eyes until they throbbed. "No. I don't think so."

"Come on, Danny, get up." She grabbed his wrist and pulled. "You have to come with me right now."

He was sure she didn't know her nails were sinking into his

wrist, but he didn't mention it because the pain helped clear his head. And when it did he knew where she was taking him.

Turn left at the main lobby then walk fifteen steps and turn left again at the coffee kiosk – nod to Stu and Belinda, the morning baristas – pass the gift shop – Open, Please Come In – turn right into the elevator bank, punch the Up button, wait, enter, listen to the soft instrumentals he'd memorized by the second week, exit, turn right…walk twenty-four steps, turn left and….

Danny stopped so quickly it caused his mother to fall against him. She grabbed at his chest to keep from falling and he heard the paper scrubs tear.

"Danny!"

"Why are we doing this, Mom?"

His mother looked up at him with tears in her eyes. "It's a miracle, Danny. Sara's alive and you need to be there."

She squeezed my hand.

Danny pulled his mother's hand away. "No, Mom, she's dead." *I felt her squeeze my hand and she moaned. I heard her…I heard….* "You heard what the doctor said, Sara died on the kitchen floor. They only kept her body alive for Emily." *She squeezed my hand.* "I read that sometimes, at the end, they make sounds or twitch, you know, but she's dead."

His mother raised her chin. "No, Danny, she's alive. They didn't tell us until they were sure, but she's back in her room and she's waking up. You have to be there when she does. It's a miracle, Danny, now come on!"

It wasn't a miracle and he knew it, and probably the doctors knew it too. Some of the pamphlets he'd been given mentioned that there were occasions when the body – not the person, just the body – wouldn't know it was dead. It might twitch or make sounds or squeeze hands, but it was dead. Sara was dead.

Danny stopped, but this time his mother seemed to expect it.

A crowd of people – doctors, nurses, maintenance personnel, men and women in business dress – were standing outside her room, jostling for position in front of the glass wall. They were talking quietly to one another, nodding and smiling. It reminded Danny of the mob of parents and grandparents gathered outside the NICU nursery window. The only thing missing was someone taking pictures.

And then the flash from a smartphone went off.

"Excuse us. Excuse us, please." His mother was addressing the crowd as she pushed through them. "This is Danny, my son... Sara's husband."

"He's here," someone said.

"It's him," another voice answered.

They turned and looked at him and all of them were *smiling*.

"What the hell's going on?"

No one answered, but, along with the pats on the back and handshakes and best wishes, Danny kept hearing two words repeated over and over again. The same two words his mother had used earlier.

A miracle.

While there was a large crowd in the corridor outside the room, there was a smaller one inside. Huddled around the bed were Sara's parents, his dad, Dr. Palmer, two ICU nurses, the anesthesiologist and another man in a white lab coat who Danny didn't recognize. Sara's mother saw him first and ran to him.

"It's a miracle, Danny, there's no other explanation for it. Emily's going to have her mommy back. Oh, God...thank you, God. It's a miracle, that's all it is, Danny. A miracle. Come on, she's awake."

"What?"

"She woke up?" his mother asked, pushing him from behind, pushing him closer. "Did you hear that, Danny? When did it happen?"

"Just a few minutes ago. Sara? Sara, Danny's here."

Dr. Palmer and his father, standing at the foot of the bed, turned and smiled at him, then stepped aside to give him room.

She was wearing a pink hospital gown and a crown of EEG leads; an IV needle was taped to the inside of her left elbow and an air mask covered the lower half of her face. Multicolored peaks and valleys moved across the black screen of the monitor above her bed, registering and recording her heartbeat and respiration and brain activity.

Sara looked up at him and blinked.

She was alive.

Danny felt the room shudder around him.

"I don't...."

"Get him a chair," Dr. Palmer said and one instantly appeared behind. "Sit down and take a couple deep breaths."

Danny collapsed into the chair and gulped down two lungfuls of air that felt so cold it burned.

"I don't know what to tell you, Danny," Dr. Palmer continued. "You were there, you know what happened. She was flat-lined and then. It's—"

"A miracle."

Dr. Palmer smiled. "I suppose that's exactly what it is. So, feel like saying hi to our miracle?"

Before he could get back on his feet and take the very short, very long walk to her side, Danny needed to ask one more question.

"She's not going to...? I mean...?"

"I'd like to tell you she's fine and will stay that way," the doctor said, "but the truth is that I don't know. While there have been cases of coma patients waking up and spontaneously breathing after the respirator is removed, Sara was.... I guess she just wasn't ready to leave.

"Physically she's fine, considering she's just gone through a Caesarean section and was bedridden for the last few months. Everything's working the way it's supposed to." Dr. Palmer nodded to the doctor Danny didn't recognize. "Danny, this is Dr. Carter. Dr. Carter's a neurologist. Would you like to continue, doctor?"

After shaking Danny's hand and congratulating him on Emily's birth, Dr. Carter nodded to the monitors above the bed.

"From the scans and her reflex responses, everything looks good... better than good. Her EEGs show a fully functioning brain, but I want you to remember that Sara was *clinically* brain dead for fourteen weeks. Even though the scans don't show any anomalies or obvious bleeds, there is some indication of memory loss, which is certainly understandable and may or may not be permanent. Without more tests, we don't know what her actual mental state is at the moment. It's very likely Sara won't be the same person you knew. Do you understand?"

Danny nodded and realized that while the doctor had been

talking to him, he'd been looking into Sara's eyes and she'd been looking back.

"We'll run a battery of tests when she's more recovered, and even then we might not know the full extent of the trauma...."

"But she's – " *Alive* " – okay. For now?"

Dr. Carter stepped back. "See for yourself."

It only took Danny two tries before he was able to stand, and by then he was even able to walk around to the side of the bed without assistance. Sara's eyes followed his slow progress to her side, but she flinched and pulled her hand away when he tried to take it.

"It's okay, Danny," Sara's father whispered. "She doesn't recognize any of us right now, but like the doctor said, it might not be permanent. All we can do is hope for the best. The important thing is she's back and that's all that matters."

Danny nodded and moved his hand away.

"Sara? It's me...Danny. Are you...? How are you feeling?"

Sara's eyes darted away and back, then her hand moved cautiously to her belly and she grimaced.

"Are you in pain?" he asked and she nodded. "Dr. Palmer?"

But the doctor was already at the bedside, opposite Danny, moving slowly as he turned her face toward him. She didn't flinch at his touch or try to pull away.

"Sara, I know you're uncomfortable right now and we will get you something, but I need you to tell me how much pain you're in, okay?"

The frown between Sara's eyes deepened but she nodded.

"Good girl." Dr. Palmer nodded and one of the nurses removed the mask from Sara's face. The hard plastic had left behind a red groove pressed into her skin and it was all Danny could do to keep from trying to smooth it out. "Now, take a nice slow breath, as deeply as you can."

She took a breath and coughed, whimpering in pain. The sound was raspy and wet and jagged, but she was breathing.

Sara was breathing.

She's alive.

"I know," Dr. Palmer said, "I know it hurts, but you did very well. Okay, now tell me how bad the pain is on a scale of one to ten with ten being the most. You remember numbers, right?"

Sara gave him a look Danny remembered so well and held up both hands, ten fingers extended.

Because there were other ICU patients who weren't 'medical miracles', those gathered out in the corridor had to restrain their elation. Inside the room, there were no restrictions. Both his and Sara's mother began crying loudly, while both their fathers attempted not to and began spouting platitudes on the strength of the human spirit. Dr. Palmer and Dr. Carter puffed out their chests and congratulated each other. The only two people who didn't say anything were Danny and Sara.

"Okay, this should help a lot," Dr. Palmer said as the nurse upped the dosage on the electronic morphine drip attached to the IV in Sara's arm. Danny watched her eyes dart around the room as if trying to find someplace safe to land, and then he saw her face relax and she settled back against the pillows with a sigh. "How's the pain now?"

Sara held up three, slightly curved fingers.

"Good, now, I want you to answer me verbally this time, okay? Do you understand? Good. How do you feel, Sara?"

Her mouth opened and a sound like sandpaper against tile came out. She touched the base of her throat and looked at the doctor. *Hurts*, she mouthed.

"I bet it does, you've been on a respirator for…quite some time. Nurse, could you give her a little water on a sponge, please?" The nurse took something that looked like a small foam paintbrush from a cup of water and held it to Sara's lips. She sucked greedily but still winced when she swallowed. "Your throat will be sore for a couple of days, but we can give you an anesthetic spray to use. Would you like more?"

Sara nodded and the nurse dipped the sponge brush again and held it until Sara finished. There seemed to be less pain when she swallowed.

"I'm so sorry, baby," Danny told her. "I never wanted any of this to happen."

She looked at him without recognition, the room's overhead light turning her clear green eyes hazel.

"Sara?"

Her eyes shifted from him to Dr. Palmer.

"How do you feel?"

"B-better," she whispered and another cheer went up.

Dr. Palmer turned toward the door. "Okay, everyone, thank you for your support, but I think it's time we let the new mother get some rest."

There was a low undertone of grumbling as the hallway slowly cleared of Sara's admiring public.

"I...I don't understand." She spoke slowly, her voice so thick and husky Danny didn't recognize it. "I'm...not a...mother."

The room got very, very quiet.

"Ah," Dr. Palmer said, "no, you probably wouldn't remember that. You've been very sick for a very long time, Sara, but let me assure you, you are a mother and your little girl is perfect."

Sara tried to sit up and cried out in pain. Danny forgot and touched her arm.

"No, honey, don't, you'll hurt yourself."

She drew back in terror. "Don't touch me! I don't know you!"

"Sara?"

"Why do you keep calling me that?" Her voice was little more than a raspy whisper, but there was something else in it. Something Danny didn't recognize. "My name is not Sara."

Dr. Carter stepped closer to the bed. "What is your name?"

Sara looked at him and pulled the sheet and blanket higher against her chest. "What kind of doctor are you that you admit a patient and not know her name?"

"It's hard to explain. Please, Mrs...?"

She lifted her chin with rigid dignity and narrowed her eyes in a way that Danny had never seen before.

"My name is *Miss* Elisabeth Regina Wyman and I reside at Number 10 Gramercy Place. If you would be so kind as to notify my mother of my whereabouts, I'm sure she is desperately worried."

Sara's mother pushed the doctor aside and reached for her hand. Sara pulled back the same way she had with Danny.

"Sara! *I'm* your mother."

Sara looked at her mother with a mixture of horror and

suspicion. "You most certainly are *not* my mother! What sort of hospital is this?"

"Honey, please," Danny said, "don't get excited, you'll hurt yourself."

"How *dare* you address me in such a manner? I do not know you, sir, and I do not wish to. Doctor, if doctor you are, please send these people away."

Dr. Palmer looked as startled as the rest of them, but turned and motioned toward the door. "Perhaps it would be better if you ...gave us a few minutes alone?"

Sara's mother was sobbing against her husband as they left the room. Danny's parents left without saying a word.

Danny looked at the woman in the bed one more time and left.

It wasn't Sara.

CHAPTER NINETEEN

"You promised him. Let him go, Ryan."

Ryan took a deep breath and squeezed his eyes shut.

"Let him go."

He was panting, his arms and back quivering from fatigue, and his hands, his useless hands felt like balls of lead.

The man kneeling next to Jamie reached over to turn off the defibrillator.

"Stop," Ryan said. "Zap him."

The orderly looked at his partner. "Sir, if he's DNR...."

"I said zap him! Did you hear me?"

Jiro made the mistake of touching his arm. "Ryan, stop this."

"Shut up, Jiro." He didn't take his eyes off the man. "I have his power of attorney and I'm telling you to do it."

The orderly leaned back. "If he's DNR, sir, hospital policy states—"

"Ryan," Jiro interrupted, " he didn't want this."

Ryan kept staring at the orderly. "He does. He changed his mind. Do it."

Nodding, the orderly readied the machine while his partner tore open Jamie's shirt and applied two rubber pads on his chest.

"Charging to three hundred," the man said, placing the paddles against the pads on Jamie's chest. "Clear!"

Jiro gasped, backing away as Jamie's body lurched against the paddles and collapsed. Ryan didn't move. The first man leaned back while his partner, adjusting a stethoscope to his ears, leaned forward to listen to Jamie's chest.

He shook his head.

"Again," Ryan said.

The man with the stethoscope leaned back as his partner recharged the paddles. "Clear."

Jamie's body arced and lay still. There wasn't a sound afterward. It was so quiet Ryan could hear the water lap against the sides of the pool as the second man leaned forward to check Jamie's heart.

And nodded.

"He's back."

Before the orderlies blocked his view, Ryan saw Jamie's chest rise and then spasm as he began coughing up water.

"Easy," the man with the stethoscope said. "Take it easy. What's his name?"

Ryan opened his mouth, but he couldn't take in enough air to produce words.

"Jamie," Steve answered for him.

"Jamie?" the orderly shouted. "Jamie, can you hear me? Jamie… open your eyes. Can you open your eyes for me?"

Jamie groaned. Ryan moved closer and saw his eyelids fluttering.

"That's right, Jamie, open your eyes…come on. There, that's it. There you are. Okay, just keep breathing, you're okay."

Ryan took another step. Jamie was blinking, trying to focus.

"I'm here, Jamie," he said. "I'm here."

Jamie looked at him then closed his eyes. It'd only been for a second but Ryan saw something that didn't make sense. Jamie's eyes were gray, like a lake at twilight, but when their eyes met just now, they had looked brown.

"Okay, he's stable," the second orderly said, "let's get him up to ICU."

The orderlies picked Jamie up and put him on the gurney, covered him with a blanket and wheeled him away. Ryan followed them.

No one followed Ryan, but Jiro stopped him, briefly, as he passed.

"He really didn't want this, did he?"

"Of course he did," Ryan lied then hurried after the gurney.

He caught up with them as they were entering the ER. One of the ER doctors was standing next to the gurney, nodding as the orderlies explained the situation while simultaneously listening to Jamie's heart. Jamie was moving more now, turning his head from side to side. Ryan reached under the blanket and took his hand.

"Jamie," the doctor said, "can you hear me?"

Jamie grunted.

"Jamie, it's Ryan. You had an accident but you're okay now. Open your eyes."

Jamie wrinkled his forehead and Ryan laughed. The doctor looked at him.

"He hates getting up in the morning," he told her, then turned his full attention back to Jamie. "I know, but you have to open your eyes, baby. Come on, now, open up."

Jamie's eyelids fluttered, parted, closed, and fluttered again.

"Come on, Jamie. Open your eyes. There's a very nice lady doctor here who wants to see those big baby grays of yours. Come on."

Jamie kept trying and shaking his head.

"*Nein, nein…vo iz mein tokhter?*"

"What did he say?" the doctor asked.

Ryan stepped back. "I have no idea."

"It's Yiddish," one of the orderlies said. "He asked where his daughter is."

"Daughter?" Ryan looked down at his lover. "He doesn't have a daughter. What's going—?"

Jamie was saying something else and the orderly moved closer, motioning Ryan to be quiet.

"What? I mean, *vos?*"

Vos? "What's going on?"

The man motioned again and added a loud shush. "Say that again. I mean, oh, God, what is it? Oh, right. Jamie? Jamie, *ich farshtai nicht.* Um…*nochzogen? Yoh?*"

Jamie opened his eyes and Ryan let go of his hand and backed away.

"What's wrong with his eyes?" Ryan asked, but no one heard him. They were all listening to Jamie and the strange words he was saying in a voice Ryan didn't know. Either the near drowning had deepened Jamie's usual clear tenor to a gravely baritone or he'd done something to injure Jamie's throat when he was doing CPR.

But that didn't explain what happened to Jamie's eyes.

"His eyes are the wrong color."

"I don't know," the orderly said. "I mean, ah…*ich vais nicht,* but I will, wait. *Varten, varten.*"

The man looked at Ryan. "It's been a long time since I had to do that, but I think I got the gist of what he's asking. My grandfather was Jewish and when I was little he taught me Yiddish because it's sort of the universal language for Jews and—"

"What are you talking about?"

The man shrugged. "Sometimes when a person goes through a traumatic event they revert back to the first language they learned and—"

"Jamie's not Jewish, he's an Episcopalian from El Segundo."

Jamie reached up and touched the orderly's arm, lifting his head slightly to whisper something else that wasn't in English.

"What the hell's going on?" he asked and Jamie's chocolate-brown eyes focused on him. "And what happened to his eyes?"

"What's wrong with his eyes?" the doctor asked at the same time the orderly said, "He's still asking about Esther."

"Who's Esther?"

"His daughter. He wants to know if she got away from the men."

Ryan shook his head. "This is crazy. Jamie doesn't have a daughter and he doesn't speak Yiddish and his eyes are gray! What happened to him?"

But before anyone could answer, or try to make up something that sounded like an answer, the orderly asked Jamie another question.

And Jamie answered, "Aryeh Rosenberg."

"Who's that?" Ryan asked.

"Him." The orderly nodded down at Jamie. "That's who he says he is. Aryeh Rosenberg."

CHAPTER TWENTY

"She's back."
Well, that's more like i—

★   ★   ★

It! Pain!
"Agh!"
It was her voice, she knew it was her voice, but the pain made it echo back and forth through the darkness surrounding her. *It hurts!* The pain was like nothing she'd ever felt before, like fire burning a hole in her chest and there was nothing she could do to put it out. The pain was trying to kill her, it wanted her dead.
And the only thing she could do about it, the absolute *only* thing, was to scream into the darkness and hope someone heard her.
"AAAAAGGGGGHHHHH!"
A voice answered.
"I know, I know, shh. Are you in much pain?"
Was the voice kidding? "Aaa-HAAAAA."
The voice had a hand and it took hers. "Squeeze my hand. Come on, squeeze it."
She squeezed and the pain laughed at her. *Dumb pain.*
"Good girl." The voice's hand patted hers. "That was great. Now, can you open your eyes for me? Come on, try. Open your eyes. Come on, you can do it."
The pain tightened the darkness over her face. *Yeah, go on… try. I won't do anything.* So she tried to open her eyes, but the pain lied and burrowed deeper into her chest. *Bad, evil, dumb pain!* "Hurt."

"I know," the voice said, "I know it hurts and we'll give you something to help, but you have to open your eyes first. Come on, try."

Her eyes opened...and closed so fast she didn't actually see anything but a watery blur, but the voice seemed happy enough.

"Great, that was great. Okay, one more question, on a scale of one to ten, how bad's the pain?"

If she'd had the energy she would have shown the voice with the middle finger of her right hand.

"...hundred and five."

The voice laughed. "Okay, you can go back to sleep now."

A warm tingle rushed up her arm and into her chest and both of them – she and the pain – went to sleep.

★   ★   ★

And woke up on the subway.

The subway?

A quick look around proved it. She was on the subway and she must have gone shopping because there was a bright pink shopping bag on her lap. She didn't remember buying anything but she must have and it must have been really expensive. The silver logo on the front of the bag was very pretty, but the script was so fancy, with a lot of doodads and curlicues, she couldn't make out the name of the store, but she knew it was probably from one of the shops at the South Bay Galleria. One of the places with a French name she could never remember. They weren't the kinds of stores she and her friends usually shopped at – those bright and shiny overpriced places with their *Evita*-like salesladies who sneered and glared and followed you around like they thought you were going to steal something *(as if)* – so she had no idea why a bag like that would be in her lap....

Or what was in it.

"Why don't you take a peek?"

She felt herself blush – like she'd been caught doing something nasty – and looked up. The woman – who she would have sworn hadn't been there a moment before – was sitting on the bench seat directly across the center aisle from her, her body swaying in time with the motion of the subway car. The woman was about her mom's age, around forty, but dressed a whole lot better. Her hair and makeup and outfit were the kind of things that came in pink bags with silver logos no one could read.

"Is this yours?" she asked the woman, dipping her chin toward the bag.

"It was," the woman answered and turned to look out the window behind her.

But there was nothing to see beyond the glass but darkness. They must have been going through a tunnel and that meant she couldn't be on the Metro Green Line. She and her friends took the Metro Green down to Redondo Beach all the time but she didn't remember ever going through a tunnel before.

Maybe it wasn't the Green, but if it wasn't, what line was she on? And where were her friends? She never went on the subway without her friends, it was just too boring.

She was about to ask the fashion-plate woman where the train was going when the woman turned back and nodded at the bag.

"That was mine," the woman repeated, "but not anymore. Go ahead...look."

She looked down at the bag but shook her head, suddenly afraid because they were the only two people in the car. She'd never seen the subway that empty before.

"Where is everyone?"

"Other places." The woman's bright red lips curled into a smile. "Go on, look in the bag."

She recognized the tone; it was the same one her mom used to tell her to clean up her room. It was an order, not a request. *Do it now. Right now. This minute.*

She nodded, but her fingers only got as far as the layer of shiny incandescent tissue that peeked out the top of the bag before stopping. "I don't want to."

"You don't have a choice," the woman said.

"But what is it?"

"Mine. It was mine."

She made a face. "That doesn't make any sense."

"No, it doesn't, but open it anyway."

She was still shaking her head no when her hands moved by themselves and parted the tissue paper. When nothing jumped out at her, she dipped deeper until she felt something warm and soft and yielding.

Wool? Cotton? Silk? She sank her fingers deep into the material, if that's what it was, and felt a small tingle against her skin.

"What is it?" she asked the woman.

"Something I don't need any more. Why don't you take it out and try it on for size?"

This time there was no hesitation. Leaning forward, she set the bag on the subway car's scuffed floor then sat back, pulling the material out of the bag.

And screamed.

Maggot-pale and pulsating, the jellied mass of flesh glistened beneath the subway car's fluorescent lights. When she tried to shake it off, it tightened and oozed up her arms and over her head like in that movie about an alien blob she thought was really dumb until that moment.

She could see the woman through the translucent flesh as it devoured her.

"Tell Dr. Stanton Helen said 'goodbye'," the woman said.

★   ★   ★

Her mouth tasted like the inside of a used cat box.

God, what a dream.

Yawning, she started to turn over and bury her face into the pillow the way she always did when her mom called her – *too early* – to get ready for school and—

PAIN!

Her eyes flew open and there was only a white nothingness above her. *MOM!* Then a face that wasn't her mother's moved between her and the white nothing.

"How're you doing?"

"M–m—"

"It's okay," the face said, "your throat's going to be a little sore from intubation. I'll get you some water, but can you tell me how you feel?"

"H-h-urt." Her throat didn't just hurt, it felt on fire. "Hurt."

"Okay, we can fix that," the face said and went away. A moment later the white nothingness turned gray then black and winked out.

★   ★   ★

"Helen?"

"Hmmm?"

"Open your eyes, Helen."

"Where…?" She frowned. It was really hard to talk.

"You're still in recovery, Helen. How do you feel?"

She closed her eyes.

★   ★   ★

The pain woke her up.

"AHHHH!"

Before the echoes died, she heard the soft scuff of shoes running toward her.

"Whoa, shh…you're okay. Take it easy, shh. Slow breaths, that's right. Nice and slow. There you go."

Slowly, too slowly, the pain subsided enough for her to open her eyes.

A woman stood over her, a different woman than the one in the subway car dream. *Only a dream.* The woman in the dream had been dressed to the nines, but this one was wearing a lavender smock top that really didn't do anything for her complexion.

"Purple's not your color," she told the woman.

"I'll try to remember that. How's the pain now?"

She checked and held up one finger, the middle one. The woman laughed.

"Well, at least you still have your sense of humor. But can you really tell me how it is?"

She held up five fingers, closed her hand and opened it again. Ten.

"Thank you. Now, do you know where you are?"

She blinked her eyes and the woman came into clearer focus. The woman was wearing one of those stethoscope-y things around her neck like Billy Price wore when he played Frank Gibbs in *Our Town*...so that meant the woman was probably a nurse and she was in a....

"Hospital," she said.

The nurse smiled. "That's right. Now, can you take a deep breath for me?"

She tried and gasped in pain. The nurse was getting back at her for saying she didn't look good in purple. *The bitch.*

"OW!"

"I know, but you're doing fine."

She was going to tell her dad about the nurse and get her fired.

"Great," she said and closed her eyes.

When she opened them again a man about her father's age was looking down at her.

"Welcome back," he said and when he smiled there were wrinkles around his eyes and mouth. *Gross.* He was a doctor; she knew that because he was wearing a white coat with his name embroidered over the pocket like Doogie Howser, MD. But when she tried to read the name stitched over the pocket of his coat he leaned over and flashed a light in her eyes.

"Hey!"

"Just want to make sure you're in there."

She started to bat his hand away when the pain in her chest gave her another little reminder it was there. "Ow!"

"Still a lot of pain?" She knew a rhetorical question when she heard one so didn't bother to answer. "Here. Is that any better?"

He'd fiddled with the IV stand next to her bed as he asked and the same warm, fuzzy feeling she'd felt earlier started in her toes and quickly filled up the rest of her. She sighed.

"Oh, yeah."

"Good," the doctor said. "Feel like talking?"

She shrugged one shoulder and smiled when the pain didn't react. "'Kay."

"Do you remember anything?"

"I was on the Metro Green Line with some crazy lady and she gave me this really weird bag."

The doctor chuckled. "Sounds like you had yourself a really good analgesic dream."

"Um."

He stopped smiling and got serious. "Do you remember me talking to you the first time you woke up?"

"I woke up before?"

"Yes, and I told you what happened in the OR. Do you remember?"

She yawned. "Nah huh."

"That's okay." He took her hand and he had a good hand, big and warm and strong, like her dad's hands. "You're still in recovery, so we can monitor you. There were some complications during surgery."

Complications? Surgery? She tried to remember and remembered falling.

"What?"

"You had another heart attack while on the operating table and your heart stopped. We had to open you up and start internal cardiac massage. You were a bit stubborn and for the space of a few seconds, and *only* a few seconds, we thought we'd lost you. But your heart started beating and obviously you're okay."

Heart attack? Lost me? Open me up? "What?"

"It's okay, really."

What does he mean 'okay'? It's not okay!

"You were on oxygen the whole time and just speaking to you, I'm fairly certain you didn't suffer any mental diminution. Of course, we will continue to monitor you and—"

He kept talking and while she could hear the words, she was having a really hard time understanding what he was saying. And the pain was coming back. It made it hard to breathe, so she had to do it faster just to get in enough air.

"You...cut me...open?"

"Yes."

"And I...died?"

"Clinically, yes, but only for a few seconds. Hey, listen to me, you're starting to hyperventilate. You have to slow down your breathing. Shh, hey, slow down. Deep breaths. Come on, take it easy. You're fine."

Was he kidding? She wasn't fine and never would be again!

Her breathing got faster and without thinking, without remembering what he'd just said, she tried to sit up, to get away and the pain knocked her back. Then, before she could scream – *MOM!* – the spots between them jammed together into one big black ball and swallowed her.

★   ★   ★

It was a dream, like the one about the woman on the subway.

It had to be a dream that they cut her open and she died. *Had to be*, because if it wasn't that meant she would never ever be able to wear a bikini top or scoop neck shirt or tank top again and her friends would stare at her scar and pity her and—

It was all Mr. Byrd's fault!

If it wasn't a dream.

"Helen?"

She whimpered.

"It's okay, you're okay, but you have to stay calm. Your heart's been through a lot, you have to remember that."

She remembered. She remembered he said she died and they had to cut her open.

"Okay?" he asked and she nodded. "Good. Now, listen, I want you to open your eyes and look at me, okay?"

She opened her eyes but wouldn't look at him.

"Helen, can you look at me?"

"My name's...." Her throat hurt worse than before, but she made herself swallow. "My name's not Helen."

"It's not?"

They made a mistake. She finally looked at him. "No."

He was frowning. "What do you mean? You're not Helen?"

God, they made a mistake. They cut her open and she'd died because they thought she was someone named Helen.

The tears started again, but this time she had to struggle just to get enough air into her lungs to take little breaths.

"I want my mom."

"Um. Shh, it's okay, calm down." His mouth tried to smile but the rest of his face was still frowning. "Sometimes this happens after anesthetic. It's called retrograde amnesia, but it'll pass, just give it time and try to relax, Helen."

"I'M NOT HELEN!"

She didn't think she had enough air to scream, but she did…oh, boy, did she ever and *that* got things going. The doctor – who made a mistake and cut her open and let her die and gave her a scar and who her dad would sue forever – got up and said something to the nurse, who hurried out of the room.

"Helen! Helen, you have to calm down. You've just had major heart surgery. Helen!"

"I'm not HELEN!"

But nobody seemed to be paying attention to her. The nurse came rushing back into the room and handed something to the doctor, who did something with the IV bag hanging next to her bed and….

A warm tingle started in her arm that quickly spread up over her shoulders and down into her belly, extinguishing the pain on its way to her toes.

"Oh."

The doctor handed the something back to the nurse and turned back to her.

"How are you feeling?"

Even her throat felt better, but she just nodded.

"Good."

Her eyes closed. "Mmmm."

"Okay, you rest and we'll talk about this when you wake up."

"Mmm hmmm."

He patted her hand. "You're fine, Helen. I swear."

She nodded again. "Helen said g'bye."

His voice followed her into the darkness. "You mean good night."

Whatever.

★　　★　　★

When she opened her eyes again the room was different and the light was softer and more subdued, but it still smelled like a hospital and that meant it hadn't been a dream. They really had cut her open and scarred her for the rest of her life because they made a mistake and thought she was someone named Helen.

Her eyes began to burn, but this time the tears came quietly and her whole body felt like it was made of lead. They must have given her something to keep her quiet...so she couldn't tell on them.

But she would, she'd tell her parents and the police and... and...the school board because it was *his* fault too. If he'd only given her the part none of this would have happened.

If he'd given her the part like he was supposed to she wouldn't have had to follow him into the theater and wouldn't have...have....

She felt a tear roll down her cheek.

She couldn't remember falling or landing on the chairs below the balcony, and that was probably a really good thing. All she could remembered was the sensation of falling and not being able to stop herself and the tingling rollercoaster drop feeling in the pit of her stomach as she went over the edge just before she....

My face!

Her arm felt so heavy she could barely lift it and when she did, when her hand finally lifted off the bed someone took it and held onto it.

It was him, again, the doctor who'd made a mistake and cut her open.

"Hi again," he said. "How are you feeling?"

It was like walking into Spanish class and having to answer Senorita Ripley's question '*Qué tal hoy?*'

"*Estoy bien, gracias,*" she said. "*Y usted?*"

His eyes got big. "What?"

"Eight and a half," she said, remembering the stupid pain-by--numbers game.

He nodded. "I can up your morphine drip, but let's just wait a bit, okay? You had a bit of a problem after the anesthetic—"

"Retrograde amnesia," she said. She remembered that and the pain number game and her name and how they made a mistake, but she couldn't remember anything after she fell from the balcony.

"Right," the doctor said. "Can you tell me your name?"

"Are my mom and dad here?"

"I don't know," he said.

"I want my mom and my dad's gonna sue you."

He stood there looking down at her. "Why?"

Like he didn't know.

"Thirsty."

"Sure," he said and turned away from the bed.

Her eyelids began to droop, they felt like they were made out of concrete, but she fought to keep them open. She needed to be awake when her parents showed up. She had to explain what happened, that she fell and she was really sorry, but that it was an accident and accidents happen all the time. That's what her mom always said. It wasn't like she'd *planned* to fall over the railing or go to a hospital where they mistook her for another patient named Helen and cut her open so she'd have a scar for the rest of her life or anything.

It wasn't her fault and her dad would make sure everyone knew that.

"Here," the doctor said and held something that looked like a little blue sponge stuck to one end of a white straw up to her lips. "We'll give you ice chips if this upsets your stomach."

She sucked the water from the straw and asked for more. He dipped the sponge into the cup of water he was holding three more times before putting everything on the side table.

"Let's see if that stays down," he said. "Now, can you tell me your name?"

Jeeze, not this again. "I want to see my mom and dad. Where are they?"

"I don't know," he said. "Are they here?"

The lead covering her body turned to ice. "Why wouldn't they be here? Didn't you tell them I was here?"

No, of course they didn't because they got me mixed up with someone named Helen.

Her father wasn't just going to sue the hospital but maybe even put old Dr. Doogie in jail.

"You'd better call my parents right now and tell them I'm here!"

He nodded and called the nurse over. "Will you call Helen's parents—"

"My name's not HELEN!" She'd wanted to scream so loud his ears would bleed, but she could barely make a stage whisper.

The doctor: "All right, then what is your name?"

Finally. She lifted her chin the same way Vivien Leigh had as Miss Scarlett O'Hara.

"Christine Taylor Moore."

His face fell. She'd read about that happening, but she'd never actually seen it until that moment. It was like his skin just came loose from his skull and…slipped. His mouth fell open, which was really gross, and his eyes got all round and cow-stupid-looking. It almost made her sick to her stomach so she looked away and noticed the name on his coat pocket.

Stanton.

No wonder he'd made a mistake.

"Like son like father, huh?" *Burn!*

"What?"

"I know your *son, Blankie* Frankie, and this was all *his* fault! If he hadn't messed up I wouldn't have…." A new thought struck her and the ice covering her got even colder. "Is that why you tried to kill me?"

He turned away and said something to the nurse. She nodded and left.

"If you try anything she'll know—" she began but stopped when he held up his hand.

"I'm not going to hurt you," he said. "How did…do you know Frank Stanton?"

Her eyes tried to close again. God, she was sleepy, but he wasn't going to get away with it. Her dad would put him *and* his freak son in jail.

"I go to school with him, okay? But you can tell him not to

bother bringing me any homework, because when I get out of here I'm going to go to a dramatic arts high school in New York so I never have to see him again."

She'd hoped that would have made him run, but Frankie's dad just sat there, white-faced and bug-eyed.

"I knew a Crissy Moore a long time ago. In high school. She accused me of putting her name in the wrong place on the character list for *The Crucible*."

Her heart, the one that had stopped and he'd cut her open to start, began to pound so hard it started cracking the ice that encased her.

"She didn't think the part she was given was big enough and came to our teacher's office...his name was Mr.—"

"Byrd," she said and he nodded.

"Mr. Byrd...to talk to him. I don't know what happened, or what he said to her, but after he left she followed him and she killed herself."

No.

"She jumped off the balcony in the auditorium – "

The theater. Mr. Byrd always called it the theater. Her heart was pounding so hard.

" – and snapped her neck on a light cable."

"It was an accident."

He grabbed onto the bed rail. "This isn't possible."

The blood was beating against the inside of her ears as she looked at him, really looked. There was a resemblance, but it could have been makeup. Blankie Frankie had put on makeup and this was all just a bad joke and—

This isn't real. It's just a joke...a bad joke or a dream. Maybe I'm still dreaming.

Please let me still be dreaming.

"I want my mom...please get her."

He reached over the side rail and took her hand. The pounding of her heart was making her fingers twitch.

"Crissy, your parents moved to Oregon twenty-two years ago...after your funeral."

Crissy's heart shuddered. "But I'm not dead."

His hand tightened around hers. "I... Would you like me to call your parents?"

"What?"

"It will be a shock for them, as you can imagine, but—"

She felt her heart skip a beat when she dug her nails into the back of his hand.

"No!"

For just the flicker of a second, Crissy saw the stuttering, pimply-faced dork behind the grownup mask.

"Crissy, it's okay. Calm down. I just thought... Can you imagine how happy they'll be to see you?"

"NO! THEY WOULDN'T!" Her heart was really pounding now. "This isn't me! I'M NOT ME!"

"Okay, okay." He let go of her hand and stood up to press a button on the wall behind her. "I won't. Crissy, you have to calm down."

Bells started ringing out in the hall. They sounded like passing bells telling her she was going to be late to class. Years and years late. The sob caught her by surprise, but the tears didn't.

"Please." She squeezed her eyes shut and felt the tears ooze down her cheek. "Please don't tell them, they think I'm dead so let me be dead. Just let me be dead."

CHAPTER TWENTY-ONE

August 29

At that moment Dr. Bernard Ellison, Barney to his friends, wished he wore glasses and envied those of his medical colleagues who did. Beyond, as he always thought, giving the wearer a look of distinction, glasses provided an indispensable distraction device, much like a magician's misdirection when he was about to pull a rabbit from a hat. If he wore glasses, he could flourish them or use them to tap thoughtfully against the four manila file folders on the table in front of him and thus divert the gaze of the four men sharing the conference room's table with him.

It would have been a good icebreaker.

And given him something to do with his hands.

He wasn't Barney to them, not yet. Five days ago he didn't know them and they only knew him by virtue of his title, chief of psychiatry. If any of them had had reason to call his office to ask for a consult, they wouldn't have made the call personally or even spoken to him – that's what administrative assistants were for.

They knew him by reputation and he knew them through their patients, 'The Fab Four', as they had been labeled by the hospital grapevine – the four patients who had been declared dead by each one of the doctors sitting at the table with him, only to spontaneously revive.

And all of whom claimed, upon regaining consciousness, to be someone other than themselves.

The hospital's board of directors wanted answers.

There had been cases before of patients who had clinically died and been brought back, with or without medical assistance; but four patients who died on the same day, within hours of each other, and who, upon reviving, each exhibited a previously unidentified Cluster B personality disorder with dissociative amnesia, verged on the impossible.

Almost before that first piece of gossip made the rounds, from the ER all the way to the extended care units and back, each of the four doctors had been questioned and every piece of hospital equipment that had been used in the cases tested, retested and replaced just to be safe.

When nothing physical could be blamed the board called him to ask if he'd examine and evaluate the four patients and come up with a credible explanation.

And he had.

He spoke to them, answered their questions, and did his best to calm their fears. He showed them pictures provided by their families – *their* families – and told them who they were.

But they each said no, that's not who they were.

They gave him names.

They gave him places.

They gave him lives.

They told him who they were and he'd told the board, then offered the only explanation that fit.

The board was less than happy, but accepted it.

Now it was the doctors' turn.

Feeling their eyes move with him as he sat back, Barney took a deep breath and said a small prayer.

"A fugue state is a psychiatric disorder characterized by reversible amnesia of one's personal identity, including memories, personalities and other characteristics of individuality."

They were looking at him with unconcealed boredom. So far so good.

"Usually a fugue state is short-lived," he continued, "but it can last months or even years."

"We know what a fugue state is, Dr. Ellison," Dr. Mendoza said. "We all did our psychiatric rotations."

Barney nodded. Mendoza's patient was James Cooper, Jr., who now called himself Aryeh Rosenberg and preferred speaking Yiddish because he told Barney, "When I try to talk American '*er macht a tel fun dem*' I ruin it.'"

"After recovering from a fugue state," Barney continued, as if there'd been no interruption, "a person's memories usually return intact."

Mendoza slumped back in his chair. "So we are dealing with a fugue state, here? For all four of them?"

"No," Barney said and waited for the exasperated grumblings to stop. "As I just quantified, a fugue state implies that a person is suffering from a psychiatric disorder...."

"That is characterized by reversible amnesia of their personal identity. Yes, we know." This was from Cross, Henry Rollins' primary care physician. Henry Rollins, the Alzheimer's patient who now called himself Timothy Patrick O'Neal and wanted to name his new baby sister – if it was a girl because his mommy didn't know yet – Princess Summerfall Winterspring O'Neal.

Barney smiled. "I know and I apologize, but I wanted to say for the record – " he nodded toward the small recording camera mounted in one corner of the ceiling, " – that what we're dealing with is not a contagious fugue state."

The atmosphere of the room changed as three – but only three – men exhaled in relief. Barney noted the exception: Frank Stanton, whose patient had died a forty-two-year-old woman and 'woken up' as a sixteen-year-old girl named Crissy.

"So...." Cross again. "If it's not a fugue state, then what is it?"

Barney interlocked his fingers and lifted his hands to his face, pressing his chin against the linked index and middle fingers. It was the same thing he'd seen his grandfather do when the old man had been asked a question he didn't know the answer to.

The only trouble was that Barney had an answer.

"I'll come to that in a minute," he said without lowering his hands, "but first I need to tell you that aside from their obvious anxiety and confusion, all four patients are rational and not suffering from any psychosis—"

"Whoa!" This came from Palmer, the OB/GYN who'd delivered a baby from a comatose and *clinically* brain dead Sara Cortland only to have her wake up as a repressed and angst-ridden spinster named Elisabeth Wyman. "Forgive me for this, but are you joking? Isn't psychosis typically characterized by radical changes in someone's personality?"

Barney nodded, rubbing his chin against his knuckles.

"Well, I've known Sara Cortland for years and believe me when I tell you that her personality *has* changed."

It took some effort, but Barney lowered his hands to the tabletop.

"No, it hasn't, Dr. Palmer. Sara Cortland died on August 24th when you took her off life support." When Palmer started to argue, Barney lifted one hand and silenced him. "Henry Rollins died on the same day from recurrent aspiration pneumonia in end-stage dementia. James Cooper, Jr., committed suicide by drowning, August 24th and on that same day Helen Harmon died of an acute myocardial infarction on the operating table. Each one of your patients died."

Barney waited for the shouting to stop. It was still only three of the doctors who were loudly reminding him that their patients had not died but regained consciousness. The fourth, Dr. Stanton, sat looking down at the table and said nothing.

"You will let me know when you're done," Barney said when they stopped to take a breath. "Won't you?"

The doctors looked at each other and sat back.

"Then I may continue?" It was a low shot, but Barney had never been against using them when it mattered. "Thank you. Now, as I was saying, *your* patients died—"

When the buzz started again, Stanton finally opened his mouth.

"Let him talk."

The other three doctors looked at him, then at each other.

"Seriously, Frank?" Mendoza said, getting to his feet. "Look, I don't know what kind of psychobabble Dr. Ellison is going to try and feed us, but our patients are alive."

Barney saw Stanton shake his head, but it was so slight a movement even he wasn't sure it had actually happened.

"Sit down, Chas," Stanton said, "and let him talk."

"Look, Frank, I—"

Stanton slammed his open hand down on the table. "Let him talk!"

Mendoza sat down.

"Just let him talk."

The three doctors nodded.

"Go on, Dr. Ellison."

"Thank you," Barney said. "But first, let me put any fears about your careers to rest. What happened to your patients had nothing whatsoever to do with anything you did. That much I'm sure of and said as much to the board."

A collective sigh filled the room.

"I have an idea as to what happened," Barney continued, "but why?" He raised his hands in a shrug. "I can tell you that after speaking to the patients I contacted a friend of mine who is with the World Health Organization and asked if there had been any similar cases reported."

"An epidemic?" Stanton asked and the others straightened in their chairs.

"No," Barney said. "There's no contagion, no pathogen involved. This is not a physical disease."

"Then it's a neurological virus?" Cross asked.

Barney shook his head. "It's not a disease at all."

"But there have been more cases reported?" Palmer asked.

"Yes," Barney said, "but not officially."

"How many?" Palmer asked.

"A few. Some in the United States, some in other countries."

"And it's *not* a disease? Could it be some kind of..." Mendoza frowned, shaking his head until the thought gelled, "... *hysterical* contagion?"

Barney was impressed and smiled to let Mendoza know it. The man had obviously done some research before their meeting. Barney had written a paper on hysterical contagion while he was still in medical school.

"If they had had contact with one another that could have been a reasonable assumption, but—"

"They didn't," Cross said. "Henry was pretty much confined to long-term care."

"And Sara was...." Palmer shook his head and slumped back in his chair.

"Then what is it, Dr. Ellison?" Cross asked. "You said you had an idea."

"Well, it's actually my friend's theory," Barney admitted, "but I concur. We don't know what happens to us at the moment of death, and my friend believes that there are certain people who, at this moment, have the ability to fight it...the darkness or whatever it is that comes. This theory can explain the claims of near-death experiences some people have recounted upon being resuscitated. That's part of it. My friend also thinks that a small minority of these people are so traumatized by the experience that, upon resuscitation, they return to consciousness as someone else. Some part of them knows they died and they can't accept that so they create an entire new persona, complete with a past history, as a way to…*literally* survive what happened to them."

Sitting back, Barney studied the men's faces. There was a mixture of disbelief, skepticism and doubt, but mostly hope.

"I know how impossible this sounds, but it seems the most plausible explanation."

It was Dr. Palmer who asked the question they all must have been thinking.

"Then it wasn't anything we did?"

"No, this was not caused by human or mechanical error."

There were muttered sighs of relief, but again it was only from three of the doctors. Stanton hadn't made a sound. Barney thought he understood. Of the four, he'd been the only one performing surgery when his patient 'died'. Barney made a mental note to seek the man out after the meeting and talk to him, one on one.

"But," Cross began, "how is that possible? I mean, how do you explain the details they have? My patient sounds and acts like a little boy."

"As you know better than anyone else," Barney said – and felt a bit like a bully saying it, but thought the point needed to be driven home – "Alzheimer's patients often display childlike behavior."

Cross cocked his head. He knew exactly what Barney had done and wasn't happy about it. "Yes, they do," he said, "in a generalized fashion, but they seldom *become* a child. So how do you explain why my patient suddenly thinks he's a little boy named Timothy Patrick O'Neal?"

Barney raised his hands. "Timothy Patrick O'Neal might have been a childhood friend or a friend of his daughter's. The point is that, somewhere in his history, your patient knew this little boy and obviously the boy's history, so when he was faced with either accepting his own death or abandoning what he was and becoming someone else, he became Timmy, a little boy with a full life ahead of him." Lowering his hand, he looked from one man to the next. "Your patients are remarkable. Instead of returning to a life that ended, they created new ones and have so immersed themselves in these new personas that who they were no longer exists. Until, and if, they recover from their fugue states, your patients, for all intents and purposes, did die on August 24th."

"Why then?" Stanton said, as he finally looked up and met Barney's eyes. "What's so special about that date?"

"I don't know," Barney said.

"But it's...." Mendoza shook his head. "My patient speaks Yiddish and thinks he's a Jew who was shot in the twenties. Jamie's family isn't Jewish and his partner says that, except for a few friends, they don't know a lot of Jews."

"It's very possible it might be the same with your patient as with Dr. Cross's. Maybe he had a Jewish childhood classmate or friend whose...grandfather got shot in the 1920s and spoke Yiddish. The brain is the world's greatest depository and if the scenario I proposed happened it's very likely that information was stored in Jamie's brain." Barney shrugged. "I don't know what to tell you except to say that his Yiddish is flawless and he does have the mannerisms of a much older man...which—"

"What about Sara? She calls herself Elisabeth and keeps asking about a friend named Frances who was a suffragette," Palmer said. "Suffragette?"

"History," Barney said. "She may have read a history about a woman named Elisabeth who was a suffragette and had a friend named Frances, and her reawakening mind latched onto that. What about you, Stanton, any questions about why your patient thinks she's a teenager?"

Stanton shook his head and looked back toward the table. "No."

It was the way he said it, the tone of that one word, that set off silent alarm bells behind Barney's eyes. *There's something else. We definitely have to talk.*

Barney let himself smile. "Good. So, there you are. My conclusion is that we are dealing with a rather unique and atypical fugue state that has randomly affected four critical patients in this hospital. As for my recommendation, which I will convey to the families later today, I feel it imperative that the patients be allowed to continue in their new identities until such time as they recover from the fugue state and their memories return."

"Sounds good to me," Cross said and was the first to stand. Mendoza and Palmer followed. Stanton stayed seated. "If that's all, Dr. Ellison…."

Barney nodded and the three men left the room quickly and quietly – until they reached the corridor and shut the door.

"You believe all that?"

"I don't know, maybe, but at least we didn't do anything to cause it."

"Thank God."

"Amen to that."

"How could anyone remember Yiddish?"

If Barney had been alone he would have chuckled as their voices faded, but he wasn't alone and he doubted the man sitting to his left would have found anything funny.

"So," Barney said and waited.

It was only two heartbeats before Stanton looked up.

"Do you believe in ghosts, Dr. Ellison?"

Simultaneous answers, one glib, one straight out of his abnormal psychiatry textbook, came to mind. He used neither. "Why do you ask?"

Stanton leaned back and pulled a small silver-and-black flash drive from the pocket of his lab coat and tossed it on top of the manila file folders in front of Barney.

"And this is?" Barney asked as Stanton straightened in his chair.

"Proof that ghosts do exist, Dr. Ellison. I did a little research, too, when Crissy…after Helen…. Thank God for the internet, huh? Your friend's assumption that the patients knew the people they're…that they claim to be is reasonable, and I'm sure their families will accept it wholeheartedly, but that's not what happened."

"Oh?" There were other things Barney could have and wanted to ask, but he kept quiet and just listened.

"No." Stanton closed his eyes and began to recite. "Elisabeth Regina Wyman was killed in a suffragette riot in 1914, New York City. Timothy Patrick O'Neal died as a result of a hit-and-run accident a few days shy of his sixth birthday in 1956, Norman, Oklahoma. Aryeh David Rosenberg was murdered in his shop in 1926, New York City, Lower East Side." He opened his eyes. "Christine Taylor Moore, sixteen, died of a broken neck when she became entangled in a light cord after accidentally falling from the balcony in her high school auditorium, 1992, Hollywood, California."

"I applaud your research, Dr. Stanton," Barney said, "but this just seems to corroborate what I said about them knowing—"

"Crissy Moore went to my high school. I knew her, she used to call me Blankie Frankie...not to my face, she wouldn't have done that, but you know how popular girls are when.... I was there the day she died. I went to her funeral – hell, the whole school went to her funeral – and I've kept in touch with her family since then." He took a deep breath. "I know how this is going to sound, Dr. Ellison, and you may want to see me professionally after this, but I think that when Helen died, Crissy's soul...or spirit or ghost or whatever you want to call it, entered her body. This isn't a fugue state, it's something else. I don't know how or why but I think she and the others came back."

Barney picked up the flash drive and ran his thumb over the surface. "And this holds the information you found?"

Stanton nodded and tried to laugh, and failed miserably. "I know how this must sound."

"Maybe you don't," Barney said. "Wandering souls isn't a new idea, Dr. Stanton, and neither is reincarnation. There is a term, *Gilgul Hanefesh*, which means the transmigration of souls. According to my grandfather, who was a Kabbalistic scholar, and studied the theory of the Zohar, all souls are subject to transmigration if that soul fails to acquire the experience for which it descended from heaven. If that happens, the soul is required to inhabit another body until its mission on Earth is completed."

Stanton studied his face. "You believe me?"

"It's as viable an explanation as the one my friend offered and lends credence to something else he told me." Barney slipped the flash drive into the inside breast pocket of his coat jacket. "One of the first cases reported was from the former Soviet Union. The patient, a teenage girl, was killed when the car she was riding in hit a patch of ice and rolled. She sustained numerous injuries, including a broken neck. She died on the operating table only to wake up claiming, very loudly and in a masculine tone, that she was a political prisoner in the Janowska concentration camp."

Stanton took a deep breath. "Jesus."

"Unfortunately, her injuries were too severe and she died…again, permanently, a few minutes later. That's all the information my friend had and he only obtained that because he knew the physician who worked on the girl."

When Barney finished they sat for a moment and listened to the soft hiss of cool air whispering through the ceiling vents.

"What are you going to tell their families?" Stanton asked.

"I'm not sure yet." He could feel the small weight of the flash drive get heavier with each passing moment. "You knew her? Crissy?"

Stanton nodded and a very small smile touched his lips. "Not well, girls like her didn't hang out with guys like me, but yeah, I knew her."

"A crush?"

He nodded again.

"And you're sure it's her?"

"Yes."

Barney took a deep breath. It was impossible. Under all natural law it was impossible, things like that just didn't happen. Couldn't happen. Shouldn't happen.

But what if they did?

"What are we going to tell them, Crissy and the others?"

Barney shook his head. "I don't know. I need to talk more with them and…. " *Come on, Ellison, you're evading the question. Answer the nice doctor.* "The truth, I guess."

Stanton stood up and walked to the door. "I can't imagine it… dying and coming back after so many years. Can you?"

"Can I?" Barney asked himself after Stanton left.

He'd studied the workings of the human mind for all of his adult life and knew the truth behind mental abnormalities that had once been considered works of the devil. He'd helped numerous patients separate fact from fantasy, reality from psychosis, but could he imagine dying and coming back…and coming back to a different time in a body that was not your own?

Could he put aside all he knew and not only imagine but accept it?

Even with the facts, if facts they were, staring him in the face.

His grandfather would have believed it without question. He'd been a man who'd lived through the real horror of pogroms and the Treblinka concentration camp, yet still could find delight in telling his only grandson stories of dybbuks and spiritual possessions and ghosts that came back. The old man would not only have believed such a thing was possible but accepted it.

"Why not?" he would have said. *"Why could this not happen?"*

And he would have answered, *"Because it's not possible, zaideh."*

Was it?

The question *(Was it possible?)* kept catching him off-guard during the rest of his day and accompanied him home that night. Sitting quietly at his side, the question watched while he studied the files on the flash drive Stanton had given him and listened in when Barney again called his friend at the WHO.

The question sang him to sleep that night and was there in the morning when he phoned the hospital, requesting another meeting with the hospital's board of directors to 'discuss new findings in regards to the four fugue-state patients.'

The meeting was scheduled for nine and lasted longer than the board may have thought necessary. Other meetings and appointments were either cancelled or postponed while Barney tried to convince them that he really hadn't lost his mind or didn't need to go on an extended vacation.

When the meeting ended and he'd convinced the board, more or less, to agree to his plan of action, the four doctors were called in (Barney had been careful not to mention Stanton's name when discussing the patients' histories) and Barney explained it again.

Then, on the last Friday of August, Barney stood at the podium of one of the hospital's teaching classrooms and looked out at the bowed heads of the seven people – Mrs. Rollins, Sara Cortland's husband, parents and in-laws, and Jamie Cooper's partner – seated in chairs before him. They were the families of the 'Fab Four', and they were reading the histories of the people who currently inhabited their loved ones' bodies.

The head of the hospital's legal department sat at the small table to the left of the podium and jumped visibly when Jamie Cooper's partner slapped the file shut against his knees.

"Are you fucking nuts?"

"Language!" Mrs. Rollins, widow of Henry, scolded. Looking up from the file in her hands, she glared at him through the thick lenses of her reading glasses. "You seem like a nice young man and I know you're hurting, just like the rest of us, but you don't need to be crude."

The man seemed about to say something else, then nodded and looked away. "Sorry."

"But it *is* nuts," Sara Cortland's husband, Danny, said, taking up the cause. "It's...."

"I think," Barney said, "the word you're looking for is *unbelievable*."

"No." It was Sara's mother this time. "It's impossible. Things like this don't happen."

Barney had decided not to tell them about the other cases that had occurred worldwide. "No," he said instead, "they don't, but that is precisely what seems to have happened and there's not a lot that can be done about it except to accept these...guests and try to make the best of a very unique situation."

"Make the best...?" Sara's husband crushed the file he was holding. "My wife died and you want me to accept the thing that killed her?"

A low muttering began and Barney saw the head of legal inch his chair back...possibly for a quick getaway. Barney held up his hand for quiet.

"Please. Your loved ones weren't killed and this isn't some kind of alien invasion. They...Henry, Sara, Jamie and Helen – " Barney heard Mrs. Rollins catch her breath. The rest were silent, " – died as a result of their previous medical conditions. These.... The individuals who currently inhabit their bodies had nothing to do with their deaths. I don't have an explanation as to why it happened or how, but at the moment of your loved one's passing, their bodies were...."

"Stolen?" James's partner suggested.

Another round of mutters, much angrier now. The head of legal began gathering up his things.

"No!" Barney's shout echoed in the near-empty room. "The unoccupied bodies became receptacles and however unbelievable it may be, it happened. Whatever else you might think, I personally feel this borders on the miraculous." He swiped the air in front of him, ending any new surge of comments that might have been coming. "Think about it for a moment...four wandering souls have come back from wherever it is we go at the moment of death. This is an event that cannot be ascribed to human power or the laws of nature – and that is the definition of a miracle."

While the families sat in stunned silence and, Barney hoped, thought about it, he glanced over at the hospital's legal mind and got a furtive thumbs-up. Then Sara's mother began to cry, very softly, and Mrs. Rollins closed her file and, pulling a clean white hankie from her purse, sent it down the row, via Jamie's partner and Sara's husband, to the woman.

"Are you sure?" Jamie's father wanted to know.

"Yes," Barney said.

"But how do you know this...that they are...? How do you know?"

Barney knew the head of legal wasn't going to like what he was going to say next – it did sound a bit too much like an admission of something – but that didn't stop him.

"I don't, and that's the simple truth." Silence from the families, a soft groan from the legal eagle. "At first, I believed these were all cases of a fugue state...a form of amnesia where the person not only forgets who he or she is, but all characteristics of their personality. I'm sorry, but after some research and speaking further with the patients, I have no recourse other than to accept the facts as they present themselves. These people are exactly who they say they are."

"But what if it's a different kind of fugue state?" Jamie's partner, Ryan, held up his file like a stop sign. "Just listen to me for a minute. If it is, then he...they...might all get better. Sometimes amnesia patients remember who they are."

"If they only had amnesia, yes, but that's not the case this time."

"Why not?"

"Because Jamie and the others died." Blunt and brutal and he hated himself for doing that. "This isn't a fugue state or amnesia. The people you loved are never coming back."

"You don't know that," the man said with tears in his eyes.

"I'm afraid I do," Barney said.

"How?" Sara's husband demanded. "How can you be so sure?"

Barney glanced down at the head of legal — *"Now what are you going to do?"* — and took a deep breath. So much for not telling them.

"Because there have been other cases."

The head of legal slumped back in his seat and Barney couldn't tell if it was from relief because now it was obviously not the hospital's fault, or shock.

"Others?"

"Yes, not many, but there are other cases worldwide."

"What the *fuck's* going on?"

Mrs. Rollins pressed her lips together and looked down.

"If there are more cases," Sara's father-in-law asked, "why haven't we heard about them?"

The head of legal started to stand up, thinking his work was done, but Barney waved him back down.

"To avoid panic," he said. "Can you imagine what would happen if the populace found out that the…that certain souls have come back?"

"The zombie apocalypse just got real," Jamie's partner chuckled without humor. "Jesus."

Mrs. Rollins shushed him on that.

"They're not zombies," Barney said quickly. "They're living, breathing human beings just like you and me who are just misplaced in time. Now, can you imagine what would happen if people…if the *media* found out about them? They would not only be looked at as aberrations – "

A voice muttered something that Barney chose to ignore.

" – but there are those in our society who might see them as a threat, whether it be to their religious beliefs or how they view the world as a whole. People as individuals are wonderful, but people as a mob can destroy what they don't understand. If we reveal what happened here, it could ultimately destroy them."

Barney exhaled softly and looked at their faces. His speech was a little heavy-handed, but sometimes you had to hit hard, knowing it was the only way to leave an impression.

Mrs. Rollins raised her hand. Barney nodded at her.

"Are you sure about this, Dr. Ellison?"

"Yes."

"Then what are we supposed to do?"

"Do?" Sara's husband stood up and flung his file across the room where it fluttered like a broken and dying bird to the polished floor. "I know what I'm going to do. I don't care what you say, I'm going to sue this hospital, that's what I'm – "

"Danny!"

" – going to do."

"Danny, stop it." His mother grabbed at his hand, but he pulled away. "Sit down."

"No!" He pointed a barrel-straight finger at Barney. "Something happened and the hospital's responsible for it!"

"No," the head of the legal department said as he stood up, "we're not. Before we spoke with Dr. Ellison, the board convened an M&M conference – that stands for mortality and morbidity – to discuss what happened with the four physicians involved and the assembly found them blameless of any sort of negligence. Everything that could have been done medically for the patients had been done. The hospital cannot be held accountable."

Sara's husband sat down.

"How nice for the hospital," Jamie's partner mumbled.

"Shh, now," Mrs. Rollins said, then looked up at Barney. "What's going to happen to them?"

Barney gave the floor back to the head of legal.

"The matter has been discussed," the man said, "and if no other option presents itself then suitable accommodations will be found for them in either our long-term or assisted living facilities."

Barney thought it would be Mrs. Rollins who'd ask the next question, but it was Sara's mother who raised her hand.

"What other options are you talking about?"

"Well," the man said, cool and steady as if he'd been saying things like this throughout his tenure at the hospital, "legally these people are still members of your family although the hospital has decided, given the circumstances, to forgo billing any and all expenses that have accrued before or after August 24th." He cleared his throat when no one jumped up to give him a standing ovation. "It only seemed the right thing to do."

"Thank you," Mrs. Rollins said. "But you didn't say what the other option was."

"That you take them home."

Barney had expected another round of shouting and threats, but the cold silence was worse.

"I understand," he said, "with the exception of their outward appearance, these people are strangers to you."

"That's the truth," Jamie's partner mumbled just loud enough for the whole room to hear.

"And you're under no moral obligation to have anything to do with them, but these people are lost. Everything and everyone they knew is gone. There is nothing familiar that they can see or touch that can anchor them to what they were. With the exception of Ms. Moore, whose parents, Dr. Ellison tells me, are still alive, these people are completely and totally alone. Is there any chance that Ms. Moore's family will be coming for her?"

Barney took a deep breath. "I don't know yet."

Sara's father stood up, tall and rigid, his face ashen, the veins in his neck so taut Barney was afraid they'd burst through the skin if the man so much as moved his head.

"And you want *us* to take them in? These *things* and make them a part of our lives? Are you out of your minds?" He licked his lips. "Okay, I understand about not going public.... God knows I don't want anyone to know what happened, I couldn't stand the way people would look at me, but...." His voice broke. "Sara's dead and I can't even bury her because that thing.... That's not Sara, that's not my daughter."

"No," Barney said, "it's not Sara and it's not Helen or Henry or Jamie. I understand how you feel and no one is going to force you to do anything. It's all right. Mr. Lathrop has some papers he will ask you to sign that will grant custody of the individuals to the hospital."

On cue, the head of the legal department reached for the briefcase he'd sequestered beneath the table when he arrived and pulled out a stack of papers. Barney watched seven pairs of eyes follow the stack as if it was a shooting star.

"If we sign these, it's over? We'll never see these people again?" Mrs. Rollins asked.

"Yes," Barney answered.

"It will be like Henry died and I buried him?"

"Yes."

"Then no, I'm not going to sign." Taking another handkerchief, this one pink with an embroidered band of blue flowers, from her purse, Mrs. Rollins pressed it to her nose and stood up. "And the rest of you shouldn't either. These aren't our people, but they look like them and maybe this is God's way of giving us just a little more time with them."

Someone, maybe Jamie's partner, moaned.

"I know, but I'm just an old woman who doesn't want to let go of the man she loved. Not yet, and this way I don't have to. And I know it's not him. My Henry has gone to a better place, but there's another soul to look after now, a lost little boy who's also been given another taste of the life he lost." A tear rolled down her cheek and she quickly brushed it away. "I don't know why, maybe they were all taken too soon and that's why God did this. Maybe He brought them back so we can help them. For me, I can pretend it's Henry in that fugal state Dr. Ellison talked about because it's not going to be much different than how he was before."

Barney didn't even think about correcting her. He liked the term fugal state.

"Why do you care what happens to *them*?" Sara's mother-in-law asked.

"Because," Mrs. Rollins said, "I like to think that's what Henry would do if it was the other way around." She paused to let the words sink in before turning back to Barney. "They're not sick, are they?"

"Not in the way you might mean it," he said, "but I believe all of them should remain under observation for a few more weeks at least. Elisabeth and Crissy are post-op, Timmy is responding well to the antibiotics treating his pneumonia and Aryeh is coming along with his physical therapy."

It didn't dawn on Barney until he saw the looks on their faces that he'd been using the names the Fab Four had given him. He cleared his throat.

"They should be ready to leave by the end of next month."

"They're not sick," Mrs. Rollins repeated, "and they're not crazy, so they don't deserve to spend the rest of their lives in a hospital, do they?"

Barney felt his own eyes begin to burn. "No, they don't."

The old woman smiled at him. "I don't think so either. They're alone. If we turn our backs on them, they have no one, isn't that right?"

Barney nodded and Mrs. Rollins straightened her shoulders and took a step forward.

"Dr. Ellison, I'd like to go meet Timmy now," she said, then turned to look at the others. "Whoever these people are, they're alone and in need. Let's introduce ourselves and see if we can help them. Come on, now."

Barney watched as the woman got the others to their feet and herded them to the door, making a brief detour to pick up the file Sara's husband had thrown across the room and handing it back to him.

"I'm glad she's on our side," the head of legal said as he picked up his briefcase and filed out with them.

Barney followed and found Mrs. Rollins waiting for him in the hall.

"Can I ask you something, Dr. Ellison?"

"Of course, Mrs. Rollins."

"Why did this happen?"

He smiled. "Maybe it's like you said, Mrs. Rollins, and only God knows."

PART FIVE
SEPTEMBER

CHAPTER TWENTY-TWO
Timmy

"He's dying, Miss Nora."

Nora nodded and turned to look at the man laughing at cartoons and eating ice cream from a big plastic bowl the nurses had given him. The nurses loved him and spoiled him rotten. Only a few of the nurses knew what had happened. Both Doctors Cross and Ellison thought it best to keep it that way, but Nora didn't think it would have been a problem. The nurses and hospice workers were God's own angels on Earth and took the fact that Henry now wanted to be called Timmy and behaved like any normal almost six-year-old in their stride.

After all, it wasn't as if they hadn't seen that sort of thing before with Alzheimer's patients.

"He's just a big kid," they told her, "and really sweet...not like some of the others."

Yes, Timmy was a good little boy.

"Miss Nora, did you hear what I said?"

Nora nodded. "I heard, Martin."

"He came through the pneumonia with flying colors, and we're treating his respiratory and blood pressure issues as before, but the disease is still progressing. Alzheimer's physically changes the structure of the brain – there's no way to stop or reverse it, but you already know that. Timmy's dying. His brain is shutting down and taking his body with it. I'm so sorry."

Nora made sure her face was calm when she finally turned around.

"Henry already died, Martin, and I accept that. It's just so unfair to Timmy. He's just a baby."

"I know, but you have to remember, Timmy already died once."

"But he came back. Why would God do that only to take him away again so soon?"

When he couldn't answer, Nora reached out and squeezed his arm.

"I'm sorry, Martin, I shouldn't take it out on you. It's just…. Oh, it's just that I'm pissed off."

An explosion of laughter blew Dr. Cross's face apart. "Miss Nora!"

"Well, I am," she said and squeezed his arm again before looking away. Timmy was trying to spoon another tablespoon of ice cream into his mouth without taking his eyes off the lobby's large-screen TV. Bless the nurse who'd put the oversized bib around his neck. "Poor little thing, he gets hit by a car and when he wakes up he's stuck inside a dying old man. Where's the sense in that?"

"I don't know, Miss Nora."

"Well, maybe I do. Yes, maybe I do know why." Nodding, Nora met Dr. Cross's eyes. "I'm going to take him home."

"What? No, Miss Nora, we brought him here because…."

"Henry was here because I couldn't handle him at home anymore, but this is Timmy and Timmy is just a little boy. I think I can handle a little boy, Martin, don't you?"

"A little boy in a grown man's body…a body that's slowly breaking down. Miss Nora, be reasonable, he can't walk more than a few feet without gasping for breath."

Nora lifted her chin. Stickin' it out, was what Henry used to say. *"Oh, Lord, watch out! She's gettin' feisty now. Look at that chin, she stickin' it out, ready to fight."*

"I know that, Martin, but he can move around a little and get into bed by himself and he's fine with being in a wheelchair the rest of the time. I told him it was because he was hurt in the accident. He remembers the accident."

That was a lie and Nora hoped God would forgive her for it… and for having been pissed off at Him, but since He was God she supposed He couldn't help but forgive her. Timmy didn't remember the accident or the car that killed him, but he remembered the last day

172 • P.D. CACEK

of his life and that he was going to have a baby brother or sister and even sang Nora the *Howdy Doody* song. He knew he was in a hospital and that he'd been asleep for a long time because he was bigger – he was a very bright little boy – but the only thing he was really worried about was that his mommy was mad at him.

He wanted his mommy and when Nora told him that his mommy and daddy had gone away to have the baby and asked her to take care of him he got scared and started to cry. It broke Nora's heart.

She couldn't let him live out the rest of his life in a hospital, surrounded by strangers. Timmy deserved some happiness for whatever time he had left. Timmy deserved a home.

Her home.

And maybe that's why God chose to give Henry's body to Timmy – so she could take care of him.

"I don't think it's a good idea, Miss Nora. As feisty as you are – "

"Feisty?" She smiled at the word. If both Henry and Martin thought she was *feisty*, maybe she was.

" – you know you can't take care of him by yourself."

"Then I'll get help."

"From your daughter?"

It would have been too big a lie if she said yes to that. Marjorie wanted nothing to do with Timmy. When Nora told her what happened, she saw a side of her daughter she'd never seen before nor expected.

"Daddy's dead and you want me to…. No, I'm not going to pretend that thing is Daddy."

"No, honey, no, he's not Daddy and I'm not trying to tell you he is. Baby, your daddy's gone and I pray for his soul every night, but this poor little child is—"

"Is an abomination and he can go back to hell where he came from for all I care. How can you think I'd want to…to…even be in the same room with him?"

"No," Nora told him, "Marjorie has enough to do already, what with her own children and all. I'll get a nurse to come in, like before."

Dr. Cross took a deep breath and looked past her. "But it's not like before."

"I know that."

"Do you really think you'll be able to watch him die all over again? Timmy's only a child, but he will become what Henry was – he'll forget things and get frustrated and possibly even lash out...and in the end, like Henry, he might not even know who you are. Can you go through all that again?"

Can I?

"It's not a question of if I can," Nora said. "I'm going to and that's the end of it. Timmy needs a home for as long as he has left and I'm going to give it to him. But thank you, Martin. I know what you're trying to tell me and I know how hard it's going to be, but there's nothing else I can do. If the situation was reversed, if I'd died and some poor little child took over this body, I know Henry'd be doing the same thing."

"But why put yourself through it?"

"Because right now I'm the only one that little boy has... even if he doesn't know me that well. His family buried him almost sixty years ago. Even if his parents or siblings are alive, do you think they'd want to see him like this? Do you think they'd recognize him the way he looks now, or even believe you about what happened? His parents would be about my age, I guess – what do you think it'd do to them...or to Timmy if they saw each other? He wouldn't understand what happened and it'd scare him."

Dr. Cross rubbed his eyes but when he lowered his hands he was still looking over her shoulder.

"You're right, it would. God, I can't even imagine what it's like for him and the others."

"No one can, but I think Timmy's the luckiest of them. He's just a little boy and little boys are tough, they have to be – that's how they grow up to be men." Nora followed Dr. Cross's gaze back to Timmy. There was ice cream all down the front of him, but he was happy. "How long does he have, Martin?"

"It's no easier to say now than before, but...maybe a month, six weeks? I don't think it will be much longer than that."

"Six weeks isn't very long."

"No."

"Unless you're a little boy who doesn't have to go to school and can watch cartoons all day long and help an old lady eat the cookies she bakes."

Dr. Cross smiled and there were tears in his eyes when he looked at her. "That would be a pretty perfect six weeks to me."

And she was going to make sure of it. She was going to give Timmy Patrick O'Neal the best six weeks of his young life. Just like God planned for her to do.

Nora smiled. "Can you get me whatever papers I need to sign? I'd like to take him home tonight if I can. I had my neighbor help me move in the old daybed from the back bedroom and set it up for him in the family room, right in front of the TV."

"You already *moved* the daybed?" he asked.

"Of course I did."

Dr. Cross gave her the same look Sidney Poitier had given the Mother Superior in *Lilies of the Field* when she told him he was going to build for her a *chappal*, then nodded and walked away, defeated. He would build for her a *chappal*.

Timmy's face wore a chocolate-chip ice cream beard from his cheekbones down and he was giggling when she walked up to him.

"Look! Look!" He pointed at the television with a dripping spoon. "That silly cat."

Nora looked and saw a small mouse drop an anvil on the head of a black-and-white cat and vaguely remembered Marjorie watching the same cartoon.

"Aw, the poor kitty."

"N'uh, he's okay. He always gets up."

"Well," Nora said and sat down on the sofa next to him. She'd told another tiny lie to Dr. Cross, Timmy really hated being in his wheelchair unless he was tired. He said it hurt his butt. "I'm glad of that. Do you remember who I am, Timmy?"

He nodded but never took his eyes off the screen. "Uh-huh, you're mama's friend."

"That's right. And my name is…?"

"Mrs. Nora."

"That's right, baby. I'm your mama's friend, Mrs. Nora."

Then he hiccupped and she knew what was coming next. Timmy turned toward her with tears in his eyes.

"Where's my mama?"

Nora picked up one of the unused paper napkins off the tray and wiped his face.

"Shh, baby, shh…it's okay. Don't cry. Your mama's in the hospital having your baby brother or sister, remember?"

Timmy nodded and his tears fell on her hand like rain.

"But I want my mommy."

"I know, Timmy, I know, but once your new brother or sister is born your mommy and daddy and the baby will come get you and you'll all be together again. Okay?"

"I want her NOW!"

Two nurses and an old woman knitting in front of the big window looked up. One of the nurses started toward them, but Nora shook her head and mouthed, "It's all right," and the nurse turned away. It was her own fault; it'd been a while since she'd been around little children that she'd forgotten how selfish and demanding they could be. Little children, and sometimes sick old men, wanted what they wanted NOW and there was no two ways about it. Hank had been that way, but it was different with Timmy…Timmy was just a scared little boy who wanted a mama who would never come.

It twisted her heart into a knot and Nora had to fight the tears building in her eyes.

"Shh, now. It's okay, hush now, Timmy. You don't want to make so much noise…your mama taught you better than that, didn't she?"

It was an old trick, one she'd used on her own daughter and grandchildren, and it still worked. Timmy sniffled and wiped his nose, and a good deal of the melted ice cream covering his face, off on the sleeve of his bathrobe.

"But I really want my mommy now," Timmy said in a quiet little voice. "She's been gone so long."

Nora brushed a tear off his cheek with her thumb. *Longer than you know, baby.*

"Yes, she has, but sometimes babies don't want to be born when they're supposed to be."

He thought for a minute. "He's a bad baby, I don't like him."

"Oh, no, he's not bad, just stubborn."

"What's stubborn?"

"Stubborn? Well, stubborn means, um…" *oh Lord, help me on this one,* "…ah… stubborn means being a slowpoke. You know what a slowpoke is?"

Timmy shook his head.

"It means someone who doesn't move very fast."

"Like Tommy Turtle!"

Who? "Yes, like Tommy Turtle."

"And you!"

"Yes," Nora laughed, "like me. I'm a slowpoke. You're a very smart little boy, Timmy."

Timmy smiled from ear to ear. "You're slow like Mama's baby."

"That's right…and your mama's baby is very slow, but it doesn't know that. You see, Timmy, babies don't know about things like slow or fast or even what time is."

"They don't?" *Sniff.*

"No."

"I know what time is. Time is the numbers on a clock."

"That's right and you know because you're a big boy. Which means it will be up to you to teach the baby about time and cartoons and cookies and ice cream and—"

"*Howdy Doody!*"

Dear sweet child. "Yes, you'll have to teach the baby all about Howdy Doody. Okay?"

"Okay."

The crisis over, Timmy turned his attention back to the television and ice cream. They'd had the same conversation, more or less, every time he saw her, but it was different from Henry's repeated demands and questions. Henry had been sick, but Timmy was just a little boy who wanted his mama. That's all he was and that was what she was going to believe, because if what Dr. Cross kept telling her was true, that Timmy was suffering from the same disease that took Henry away from her, it would have been too hard even for a feisty old woman like her.

But it might not be true and she had six whole weeks before she needed to accept anything.

And anything could happen in six weeks.

"Do you like it here, Timmy?"

He shrugged. "I like TV. They let me watch TV and give me ice cream. I like ice cream."

"But what about being in the hospital? Do you like being in the hospital?"

"No." His eyes were still glued to the TV, but Nora saw him pout. "I'm not sick."

"No, but you were hurt, remember?"

A new set of tears gathered in the corners of his eyes. "Yeah... Mama's gonna be mad."

Nora wiped the tears away again and patted his cheek. "No, she's not. She's...very happy you're okay and that's why she wants me to take you home with me." He turned his head toward her. "To stay at my house and help me bake cookies and cakes until she and your daddy and the new baby come to get you."

The look in his eyes was so strong, so old, that for a moment Nora forgot Henry was dead and almost called out his name.

"My mama wants me to go to your house?"

Nora nodded. "Just for a little while," she said, "just until the baby's born."

"And we'll make cookies?"

"Yes, in fact, I was thinking about making chocolate-chip cookies tonight."

Timmy smiled. "Yeah?"

"And it would be so nice if I had someone to help me."

"I can help you."

"Then would you like to come home with me?"

Timmy nodded so hard the loose skin along Henry's jowls shook like Jell-O.

"And stay with me – until the baby comes?"

"Yeah!" Then the face she remembered so well got serious and Timmy leaned toward her, whispering. "I really don't like it here... the old people scare me."

"But I'm old, Timmy, don't I scare you?"

"No! You're nice."

Nora gave his cheek one more swipe with the napkin and stood up. "Okay, I'll go tell the doctors to pack your bags because you're coming home to live with me."

"Until my mommy and daddy come with the baby," he said. "I hope it's a brother...I want a brother so we can play and I'll show him how to throw a ball and ride a bike, but he won't go in the street because only *BIG* brothers do that and *I'M* the big brother."

Nora didn't think her shattered heart could break any more than it already had, but she was wrong.

"Of course, baby, just until your mommy and daddy come. You'll be a wonderful big brother."

CHAPTER TWENTY-THREE

Elisabeth

Danny stayed by the door, one hand holding the bouquet of pink and white carnations that his folks had brought, the other holding onto the handle of Sara's…of the small wheeled suitcase Sara's mother had packed. He was keeping quiet and out of the way.

Not that anyone noticed.

His mother and Sara's were busy filling the plastic hospital tote bag with whatever the woman had used during her stay and telling her, the woman, about the house (*Sara's parents'*) she was going to and how beautiful little Emily (*his daughter*) was. That bothered him – how they kept talking about Emily, *his* baby, his and *Sara's* baby, to the woman – and he'd asked his mom to stop. But apparently his request had gone in one ear and out the other.

Just like all the others.

He didn't want to come to the hospital to help.

He didn't want to participate in the deception.

He didn't want anything to do with her.

For all the good it did.

So he stood there, holding flowers and the suitcase handle, and listened while his mother and Sara's gushed and prattled on and showed pictures of their new grandchild to the stranger in his dead wife's body.

If he'd been a different kind of man he would have told them all to go to hell and left, just gone away.

But he wasn't that kind of man and his daughter needed him.

For her part, the woman nodded each time she was shown a picture, but kept her gaze low and only spoke when pressed. She sat prim and proper in the wheelchair a nurse had brought for her – patients couldn't leave under their own power, hospital policy – her back straight as an arrow, her feet – tucked into Sara's favorite pair of Hush Puppy sandals

– flat against the wheelchair's footrests, her hands clasped in her lap. Besides the sandals, she wore a short-sleeved white sweater Danny didn't remember and one of Sara's sundresses that he remembered too well. The dress was pale blue with little yellow flowers, and Sara had bought it when she was only two months pregnant – *'I'll need something nice and loose and cool to bring the baby home in.'*

The woman hadn't wanted to wear the dress at first, calling it indecent because it was 'so flimsy and loose' but his mother had finally convinced her it was 'what all the girls wear these days'.

It was like standing deathwatch all over again. Danny wouldn't look at her like he hadn't looked at Sara, but that was okay because no one noticed him doing that either.

"Danny?"

He blinked. "What?"

His mother was standing in front of him, smiling. "I said, let me have these and I'll put them in the car."

It took a moment for Danny to process what his mother wanted, but when he finally did, he shook his head and stepped back.

"No, it's okay, I can do it."

"I know you can," his mother said, "but I thought I'd put them in my car, to save you a trip if you needed to get back to work."

And then he understood. This way he wouldn't have to drive to Sara's parents' house, where it had been decided she'd stay.

With the baby.

Danny hadn't actually given any thought to what would happen once his daughter was able to come home because there shouldn't have been anything to think about. Emily was supposed to come home with him and Sara where they'd live happily ever after.

But since that wasn't going to happen, a decision needed to be made.

He didn't ask, but Sara's parents told him they didn't think he could...or *should* have to deal with the needs of a new baby with everything he'd just been through and everything that he still *needed* to do. He had a full-time job and, even though he'd be home nights and on weekends, Emily needed not only round-the-clock care, but also a stable home environment and routine. Why on Earth should he spend money on a day nurse when his daughter already had a full-time (nonworking) grandmother who was willing and eager to care for her?

The grandmother in question, naturally, being Sara's mother, who had the time and space and guilt/grief card, which she played with all the finesse of a Mississippi riverboat gambler.

Wasn't it only fair that Emily live with them since they had lost their only daughter?

And how fair was it for him? he'd wanted to ask.

But never did.

So, less than a week after Sara died and the imposter took her place, Emily's crib and changing table, the toy box and shelves and Sara's rocking chair were picked up and moved into his in-laws' newly painted and papered guest room.

His parents had put up a good show of disappointment, but both of them worked at opposite ends of the San Fernando Valley and since they had full access to Emily, as did he, day or night, with special weekend 'sleepover' privileges, it seemed the best solution all around.

The best solution, and that had been the same reasoning they'd used when they suggested the woman, Elisabeth, stay with them when she was released from the hospital.

Which was fine with Danny. He could make sure he wouldn't see her when he came to visit his daughter. His parents, as well as Sara's, were happy he agreed with the plan. Dr. Ellison was outright enthusiastic about it.

"I can't help but think that with all she had to endure in her past life, this time around Elisabeth has found the perfect home."

Je-SUS. Danny had almost barfed when he heard that...barfed and then punched the Great and Wonderful Dr. Ellison flat on the nose. After which he'd stand over the body and finally ask the good doctor the question that had been digging a hole into his brain since August 24th: was this 'new life' responsible for his wife's death?

Danny knew it wasn't, of course. Sara was already dead, but it'd been a nice thought.

"Yeah, okay. Thanks, Mom." Letting go of the suitcase handle, Danny reached out with his left hand. "Give me your keys and I'll put these in the trunk. I need to stretch my legs and then maybe I'll head out."

Why not? He'd already done *his* part – signed all the required release papers and insurance forms and whatever else they'd stuck under his pen for both his daughter and the woman. He could leave anytime now.

Then, after work he could go home and maybe take a little tour of the empty *Offshore Mist*-and-white nursery.

"Here ya go." His mother pulled the key ring from her purse and handed it to him. "Put the suitcase in the trunk and the flowers on the back seat. Try to prop them up if you can."

"Okay."

Danny took the keys and hooked the suitcase handle with his index finger as he turned. The suitcase wasn't heavy. There were very few things in it, new things, things that had never belonged to Sara – a small toiletry case, a half dozen or so panties that Sara would have called 'grandma drawers', an ankle-length nightgown, a brush, a mirror, and the ghost of Sara's perfume trapped in the dark blue lining.

"Danny?"

It was Sara's mother this time. He stopped just outside the door.

"You know you can come over, if you like."

He nodded. "I know, but I really should get back to the office. They've been great about my taking time off, but...."

Sara's mother nodded. "But you will come over for dinner tonight, right?"

Right, the 'special' dinner tonight where both families were supposed to gather 'round the table to get to know and welcome the woman named Elisabeth into their lives. It was a lovely gesture and one that Dr. Ellison, the doctor who'd taken charge of these...people... thought was a wonderful idea. Everyone thought it was a wonderful idea, except Danny, of course. Danny thought it was a crap idea. He didn't want to get to know the woman and he especially didn't want to welcome *her* into *his* life.

The fact that Sara's parents were taking her in and giving her a home almost made him physically ill. It was like everyone *except him* seemed to forget that the woman, Elisabeth, who'd supposedly died in 1914, didn't have a home anymore.

Not here, not now, and not in Sara's body.

Sara was dead and Danny would have given anything if the woman joined her.

"You will, won't you, Danny?"

"Yeah. Maybe. Okay."

"I'm planning to put dinner on the table around seven," Sara's mother said, "but why don't you come over early so you can have a little more time with Emily? She loves her daddy."

Danny swallowed hard and nodded, then turned and walked to the elevators. Emily wasn't even a month old. If she 'smiled' it was just because she had gas. She didn't know him any more than she knew that the woman whose body they took her from wasn't her mother.

Her *real* mother had died and Emily would never get to know her.

Danny knew life wasn't fair, but up until August 24th, he thought death might be.

When the elevator doors opened, two nurses in pediatric-cute scrubs got off and smiled, said hello and asked how things were going. Danny smiled back and gave them a thumbs-up with the hand holding the bouquet as he took their place in the elevator. He thought they might have been the nurses who took care of Emily during her first few – terrifying – days in the NICU, but he wasn't sure. He'd seen so many doctors and nurses during Sara's last days and Emily's first ones that all their faces had begun to blur together.

He'd been going back and forth to the hospital too long, first with Sara, then with Emily, but now he was finally leaving and – *knock on wood* – would never have to come back.

The only trouble was that as hard as it had been, it gave him something to do. Going back to the house to catch a couple hours of sleep or to shower and change was at least *something*. Now it was just him and the house, the empty, *messy* house because for the first few weeks after he'd watched Sara die on the operating table, it was all he could do to wake up, go to work and then head out for the hospital, where he'd gulp down dinner in the cafeteria before heading up to the NICU and put on a sterilized paper gown so he could sit down next to Emily's incubator before a nurse – maybe one of the nurses from the elevator – told him to go home and get some rest.

Sara would have screamed bloody murder if she'd seen the place, but cleaning hadn't been much of a priority and probably would continue not to be. He would have given anything to hear her scream and call him a slob. He could let it slide a few more weeks or months or whenever.

The elevator doors opened and an elderly couple entered. Danny stepped back and studied the cafeteria menu that had been posted on the wall to his right. Wait, what the hell?.... The menu was different. They'd changed Tuesday Taco Night to Thursdays. And Monday was Pizza Night? No, Fridays were Pizza Night. Fridays were *always* supposed to be Pizza Night and Thursdays were supposed to be Make Your Own Salad and Sandwich nights. He'd learned the menu by heart and there were probably a lot of people who had done the same thing. They couldn't just change things around now.

It wasn't fair.

Things, especially little things, had to stay the same or...or....

Or you could start thinking about other things and maybe even remember what it was like to watch your baby being born and to sign the release and stand there while your wife died and then take her hand to say goodbye and feel it squeeze back. If it wasn't for the little things you'd remember holding your daughter for the first time and hearing the word *miracle* repeated over and over and then having to listen to Dr. Ellison tell you the most bizarre and ludicrous story imaginable.

About how a *lost* soul had reanimated your wife's dead body.

Bullshit. Pure, unadulterated bull-fucking-shit! Not even the Syfy Channel would have shown a movie with that plotline.

So little things, like cafeteria menus, *had* to stay the same.

The elevator doors opened and the elderly couple got off. No one got on. The doors closed.

And now there was nothing else *to* do but remember.

A week after Dr. Ellison detonated that first BS bombshell, he'd asked them – the grieving family members – to attend another meeting and Danny, poor sap that he was, thought, *Okay, this is it, he's going to say it was all just a big joke – hah, hah.* It wasn't a joke, as it turned out, but it almost started out as one.

When the man whose partner had drowned and 'come back' as a Yiddish-speaking Jew saw who was going to talk to them, he'd gotten to his feet, raced across the room and tried to take a swing at the lawyer. Dr. Ellison stopped it, unfortunately, and Danny booed.

"I don't want to hear any more about our legal responsibilities to these people," the drowned man's partner said.

"Then would you rather hear how you can help get him out of your life?"

That shut everyone up.

It would take a little time, the lawyer continued, but all that needed to be done was to re-establish the individuals in question (Dr. Ellison called them *Travelers*) legally back into society.

How?

Very simply, as it turned out. The government hated a vacuum almost as much as space did. If you have a person on the planet, the person needed a name and a name needed a social security number to go with it. The four deceased had names and numbers, which technically were rendered void at the time of their deaths. The fact that each body revived with a new driver only made things a bit more complicated.

True, the Travelers could, if they so wished, continue using the body's original owner's name and social security number, but – and here Dr. Ellison jumped in – there were already indications that the Travelers were not comfortable with that scenario. All of them, even Timmy, the child inside the old man, were adamant about who they were.

Which meant legalized name changes and new social security numbers, which could only be obtained with help from them, the grieving family members. Once that was completed the Travelers could begin new lives on their own.

Have a nice day.

Danny took a deep breath and suddenly realized the elevator wasn't moving. The floor indicator showed that the car had returned to the sub-basement, its default when not in use.

See what happens when the little things change?

Danny punched the Lobby button and a few seconds later the elevator lurched upward. When the doors opened, Danny stepped out, pulling the suitcase behind him like nothing had happened.

"Oh, looks like somebody's going home!"

Danny nodded at the woman at the reception desk and kept on walking. "Yeah, *somebody* is."

★ ★ ★

"I don't know why we need a nurse," *his* mother said. "We can push the wheelchair just as easily."

"It's hospital policy," *her* mother answered. "A nurse has to do it."

"Well, let me go find one so we can get out of here. Don't you two leave without me."

"Not much chance of that."

The women laughed and Elisabeth watched *his* mother, Mrs. Cortland, turn and wave as she left the room. Mrs. Cortland had asked that she be called Judy and her husband Daniel, the same way Sara's parents asked her to call them Lillian and Bob. The informality still embarrassed her, but she said she'd try. Customs, it seemed, had changed and so must she.

Not as if she hadn't changed enough already.

"I know this will be hard for all of you to understand, but...."

Dr. Ellison, a very kind man with sad eyes, had tried to explain the unexplainable to her and the two others, without much success. She herself had shown the most immodest behavior and asked if they, all of them including the doctor himself, were inmates of an asylum – because that was the only possible conclusion she could come to.

"If you're asking if all of us are crazy and this is some kind of deluded fever dream," the doctor said, "I only wish it was as simple an explanation as that, dear lady."

A fever dream, even one unto death, would have been easier to accept. For what he told them was impossible, yet there they were, she and the others, living proof that what should have been suitable only for the pen of Mr. H.G. Wells was, in fact, true.

Although the good doctor had claimed there were other 'Travelers' (a term she came to loathe) around the world, she was one of only four, two men and two women, who had 'manifested' at this particular hospital. There were only three of them, however, who sat around the table in the oddly fashioned and brightly colored room. The fourth, they were told, was a little boy entombed within the body of an old man who was too fragile and weak to leave his bed.

Dr. Ellison had used the term 'inhabiting' instead of 'entombed', but he was only being kind. When he tried to explain what had happened to them, it was obvious to Elisabeth, and possibly the others as well, that the doctor had no idea why such a thing had occurred. He called them a minor miracle, but she knew exactly what they were and there was nothing miraculous about it. They were perversions of the natural law and God's holy ordinance.

And she'd said so.

The other female Traveler, a woman calling herself Christine, had at that moment, and perhaps because of what had been said, resorted to tears and general hysterics until such time as Dr. Ellison needed to summon a nurse to administer an injection. The effects on the woman were calming enough, but did little to stop her from weeping softly throughout the rest of their time in the meeting room.

The man in the wheelchair, whose name she still could not pronounce correctly, spoke very quickly in a guttural foreign tongue, which the doctor not only seemed to know but was able to answer in kind. Elisabeth knew only as much French and Latin as were proper for a woman in her level of society (*and time*). Nevertheless, she could tell by the tonal quality of his words that the man was pleading with the doctor for something.

Perhaps the man was asking to be told it was a mistake, that the transmigration of souls and unsanctified resurrection were impossible, *had* to be impossible, even though it seemed to be wholly and unquestionably true.

For howsoever much Elisabeth wanted to deny it, she was alive and inhabiting the body of a dead woman in a time a century beyond her own.

"Dear God."

"Did you say something, dear?"

Elisabeth looked up into Lillian's soft and gently lined face. Once the pain of the incision across her abdomen — she still could not bring herself to dwell too long upon the reason for it — had passed and she was able to stand and walk without too much discomfort, she had spent an immodest amount of time staring into mirrors at the strange face she now wore, a face that, though younger and finer of features, resembled the woman who now stood before her waiting for an answer.

"It was nothing," Elisabeth lied. "Just a prayer."

"Ah." Lillian's eyes softened. "We aren't particularly religious, but there are a number of wonderful churches in the neighborhood, and we'd be more than happy to take you to whichever service you'd like to attend. I believe there's either an Episcopal or Roman Catholic church just a few blocks from the house."

Elisabeth nodded. "Thank you, but...I think I'd rather not attend services yet."

For is it not written that the damned must not enter the House of God?

"Well, of course not until you feel up to it, dear." Lillian touched Elisabeth's cheek. "You've been through so much."

They stayed that way, the mother touching her dead daughter's cheek while the trespasser sat frozen in iniquity until Danny's mother – Judy – returned with a Negro man who was wearing what Elisabeth had come to understand were called *scrubs*.

"Apparently," Judy said, laughing, "most of the nurses were having a wheelchair race down in the cafeteria."

The Negro man offered them a sheepish grin. "We do it for the kids who are ambulatory. They come down to watch and cheer. Well, little lady," he said directly to Elisabeth, meeting her eyes until it was she who looked away, "are you ready to get out of here and rejoin the big, beautiful world?"

Elisabeth lifted her eyes cautiously. "Yes, I am. Thank you."

The Negro man gave her a wink – *the impertinence!* – as he came around to the back of the wheelchair and began pushing her from the room.

"And away we go," he said.

Yes, Elisabeth thought, *but to where?*

* * *

Home, but not hers.

Sara's childhood home.

"Well, what do you think of it?"

Elisabeth pressed her trembling fingers against her lips to keep both as still as possible. The room in front of her, the room that had been given to her, smelled of freshly cut roses and windblown linen. Her mother's house had smelled of camphor and medicinal remedies, and of damp and dread. This room, in this house, smelled of new beginnings and a life she did not deserve.

"Is it all right?" Lillian asked. There was no mistaking the worry in her tone. "We can repaint it a different color if you'd like."

Elisabeth walked slowly into the room, feeling the incision along her nether parts twitch with each step and concentrating on that instead of the color of the room. The walls were the same color as the yellow primroses on the porcelain brooch her brother had given her in another life.

She tried to keep her emotions in check, but a tear fell as she crossed the floor covered with a thick pale carpeting to brush aside a sheer white curtain from the window. The view from the second-story room looked out onto a fenced side yard filled with rosebushes and dancing butterflies. Beyond the fence was a narrow street filled with automobiles.

"The street's not always this busy," Lillian said, "but it's rush hour, you know?"

Elisabeth did not, but nodded as if she did.

"Is the room all right?"

She wiped the tear from the dead woman's cheek before turning. "This is the loveliest room I have ever seen, thank you."

Lillian's chest swelled with pride. Judy, *his* mother, cleared her throat from the doorway.

"I picked out the linens and bedspread."

Elisabeth crossed to the bed and sat down, caressing the pale yellow chenille spread. She wouldn't have been so bold as to do such a thing in her mother's house, but this wasn't her mother's house and, somehow, she felt such a showing of appreciation was expected.

"It's quite elegant, thank you."

Lillian walked into the room ahead of Judy.

"There are extra sheets and towels in the linen closet just down the hall – remember, I pointed it out to you? Good. And there are some clothes in the closet, things Danny brought over, but we can go shopping once you feel up to it."

"Yes, *all* of us can go shopping," Judy added quickly.

"Of course," Lillian said and began gesturing at objects in the room. "Now, let's see…closet, dresser, desk, bookshelf, and since I was told you've become addicted to television—" She walked over to a diminutive television set sitting atop a corner hutch. "It was Sara's from college, I hope you don't mind."

"Not at all." Elisabeth shook her head. "Thank you."

The older woman picked up the remote control device similar to the one Elisabeth had learned to use in the hospital and placed it on the small bedside table. "In case you'd like to watch in bed." Then she crossed the room to a door directly opposite the bed.

"You have your own entrance to the Jack-and-Jill bathroom and…."

"Jack and Jill?"

Lillian smiled and Judy chuckled.

"It means a shared bathroom. You share it with the room on the other side."

"Ah."

Elisabeth was still not fully comfortable with the concept of water closets taking the place of under-the-bed 'necessity' pots, but it, like the demonstrative shows of emotion and gratitude, seemed the norm. It just seemed so…inconvenient to have to rouse oneself fully from sleep in order to walk into another room to answer nature's call. The first few days in the hospital had been made much easier thanks to the bedpans that were delivered and removed at her command, but even that little luxury hadn't lasted long.

Elisabeth wasn't entirely sure she liked this new century or its ways, but she had little recourse but to live in it. Standing, she straightened the bedspread before crossing the room to follow Lillian through the Jack-and-Jill door.

The blue-and-white tiled room sparkled and smelled of crushed lemons. To her right was a *toilet* and *bathtub/shower* combination, to her left a pale blue marble countertop on which had been set two gleaming white sink bowls and glistening silver faucets. A row of milk-glass lights clung to the wall above twin oval mirrors that reflected the image of the dead woman back to Elisabeth as she walked to the closed door at the opposite end of the room.

"Sara— Elisabeth, wait, that's the…."

The warning came too late and Elisabeth opened the door onto a nursery. Sara's husband was sitting in a white wood rocking chair cradling his daughter.

He'd looked up at the sound of the door opening but he didn't look at her. His eyes swept past her face – his dead wife's face – and focused only on his mother.

"Danny!" Judy said, pushing past Elisabeth. "I thought – we thought you were going to work."

His eyes remained on his mother's face. "I was, but.... I'll go in tonight and do some catch-up, but I wanted to.... I just want to be with Emily for a little bit." He looked toward Lillian and again past Elisabeth without acknowledgment. "Is that okay?"

Lillian joined them in the room. "Of course, it is, Danny. Look, I'll have Bob move that old futon in here, you know the one, and you can stay over whenever you like. How's that?"

Danny nodded. "That'd be great. Thanks."

Then, finally, he looked at her and the look in his eyes transcended time and place. It was the same look that had been in the eyes of the man, another stranger, who'd struck her down so long ago.

Elisabeth held no illusions regarding Sara's husband: he hated her and wished her dead so he could bury his wife's body.

"Do you mind?" he asked. "Could you just go away and leave us alone?"

Elisabeth left the room, closing the door behind her.

CHAPTER TWENTY-FOUR

Aryeh

Ryan took another sip of coffee and stared at the microwave's digital timer, because if he did that, if he put all his focus on watching the blinking red numbers count down to zero, he wouldn't be tempted to look outside.

And God knew the last thing he wanted to do was look outside, because, if he did, he might very well lose whatever small chunk of his mind he had left.

If any.

So he watched and waited and sipped and when the timer beeped five times, telling him it had completed its task, Ryan set his mug down, knuckled open the microwave door, took out the quart-sized measuring cup and – carefully – poured the steaming water onto the foul-smelling dried tea that waited in the warmed cup.

You had to be careful when pouring water for tea, because you didn't want to agitate the leaves too much.

It'd only taken five weeks, but he'd become an expert in the art of tea making.

Just ask him.

He knew, for instance, that the cup – and it had to be a cup, not a mug – had to be pre-warmed, and that the foul-smelling tea was called *Oolong* and that it smelled like that because, after picking, it had been allowed to wither in the sun, which caused it to ferment slightly before it was curled and twisted.

Like he gave a shit.

When Ryan finished pouring the water, he set the measuring cup down and reset the timer for three minutes – no more, no less – three – and punched go. After forty-two seconds he got bored with watching the countdown and, picking up his mug, walked into the living room.

The place still smelled of the lemon Pledge, carpet shampoo and Lysol, which helped counteract the tea stench. He'd been cleaning almost non-stop – every night after work and all day on the weekends – since getting his new roomie.

And what a roomie he turned out to be. The outside wrapper might still say 'Twinkie', but the ingredients inside were decidedly different – one hundred per cent kosher...and straight.

Ryan realized too late that he should have been a bit more specific when he'd secretly asked God, the ultimate prankster, not to let Jamie die.

Some joke, huh, *bubbeleh*?

As roommates went, however, Aryeh Rosenberg wasn't bad. Granted, everything he cooked was either under-salted and overdone or was made from boiled buckwheat groats called kasha and smelled like raw sewage, but he was clean and quiet and tended to stay out of Ryan's sight as much as possible.

Which was as good as it was going to get, apparently.

Ryan knew Aryeh – good ol' straight, homophobic Jewish Aryeh – wasn't comfortable with the living situation any more than he was, and he sure as hell didn't have any vested interest in this new 'person', but he couldn't just throw a cripple out on the street.

Could he?

Well, he could, of course.

Jamie was dead. And Jiro had concurred with what the hospital lawyer said about legal responsibilities, regardless of the fact that Ryan was...had been authorized to act on Jamie's behalf.

But Jamie was dead, and the moment that happened Ryan's legal obligation was over and, *legally*, did not extend to the new man living inside Jamie's skin.

Jamie was dead.

It was hard to remember that with ol' Aryeh Rosenberg rolling around the house, and as soon as he became a real, living and breathing human being in the eyes of the federal government the better it would be.

And maybe then the nightmares would go away.

But until then Ryan would continue making smelly tea and

maybe even grow accustomed to hearing the sound of the guest room door lock click shut each and every night.

As if.

Ryan took another sip of coffee and looked at nothing in particular because there was nothing in particular to look at. He'd taken down the framed portrait of him and Jamie that hung over the gas log fireplace, and put all the smaller framed photographs and photo albums into boxes.

Some things – Jamie's clothes, Jamie's cologne, Jamie's CDs and DVDs – went into boxes that were taped shut and put into the storage unit the day after Jamie died. Other things, small things, he gave to friends.

Jamie was dead.

Ryan bought new towels and threw out the ones Jamie had used, bought new sheets and pillows to go with the new mattress so there wouldn't be even the faintest scent of him. Jamie was dead and Ryan kept nothing…

…except one picture.

It was small, only four by six, and set in a silver frame they'd found in an antique shop in Fort Bragg. It was the last day of their first summer vacation together. Neither of them had wanted it to end and even though they were facing an eight-hour, 536-plus-mile trip back to L.A., they'd dawdled and dragged their feet and revisited every shop and tourist trap the town had to offer.

Jamie found the frame and oohed over it for a good three minutes before a display case of antique pocket watches caught his eye. Ryan bought the frame when Jamie wasn't looking. A week later, while Jamie was at the gym, Ryan pored over their vacation photos and finally selected one he thought would look best in the frame: Jamie sitting on the rocks, his back to the camera, watching the horizon.

Ryan gave Jamie the framed picture that Christmas and he cried, then put it on the small table on his side of the bed where it had stayed ever since.

Ryan kept the picture because it could have been a picture of anyone.

Just someone looking away.

When the timer beeped Ryan walked back into the kitchen to

retrieve the perfectly steeped, foul-smelling cup of tea. He'd been told, with the utmost politeness, that tea – with honey – tasted better in tall glasses and he should think about maybe getting some, but a cup was fine.

Subtle, real subtle.

Honey he could do, but Ryan drew the line at buying new glasses or a whole new set of dishes and flatware and pots and pans so milk and meat or whatever could be kept separate.

He'd already bought enough new things.

Setting his mug down, Ryan poured the stinky tea into a cup then picked up the plastic Honey Bear from the counter, thumbed off the little yellow cap, and squeezed out a dollop. It wasn't what you'd call an exact measurement, but his houseguest hadn't complained yet, either about the amount of honey in his tea or the paper plates and plastic utensils he used at every meal.

If anything, he seemed genuinely touched by the effort Ryan had made in consideration of his dietary restrictions, and Ryan hadn't bothered to correct him or tell him it was Oren who'd come up with the idea of using disposable dinnerware after trying to explain the whole 'kosher' thing.

Kosher was one thing, but crazy was another and he could deal with crazy.

Hadn't he held a memorial for Jamie at the church his parents attended and sat there watching and listening while Jamie's extended family and their friends got up and told stories and anecdotes about Jamie, before saying their goodbyes to an empty silver urn?

Hadn't he then given the urn to Jamie's parents and told them how sorry he was, and hadn't they told him to go to hell? Hadn't he told the truth to Oren and Jiro because Oren was Jewish and could talk to his new roommate, while Jiro could help him cut a path through the legal jungle ahead of him – them.

Hadn't he already done enough crazy to make him an expert?

Finished with the preparations, Ryan put the cup, on its matching saucer and with a spoon for stirring the honey, on the tray next to the insulated coffee carafe and headed for the patio. He could hear them through the open door and it sounded like they were arguing…not that he could understand a word either of them was saying.

Dr. Ellison, who'd arrived a half hour late for his weekly Saturday afternoon session with Aryeh, was shaking his head, muttering something, either in Yiddish or Hebrew, Ryan hadn't heard enough of either language to tell which was which, that brought a momentary halt to the conversation that had been raging back and forth like bullets across a battlefield.

Then Aryeh said a word: *ah-were*, or something like that, and repeated it twice. *Ah-were, ah-were.*

Maybe he was complaining to Dr. Ellison about the quality of the paper plates Ryan was using. Maybe *ahwere* meant *cheap*.

Ryan cleared his throat to let them know he was coming and stepped out onto the patio.

It was one of those rare late-September days that made the California Tourism Council cream their collective jeans and send out squadrons of photographers to capture the event. Soft white clouds rode the bright blue sky and, for once, the gusting west wind kept the smog where it belonged, in San Bernardino and Riverside.

Autumn was coming and the light had changed from the blue-white of summer to a mellow gold that couldn't be described in words. You had to recognize it when it came and the only reason Ryan could do that was because Jamie had shown him.

Jamie had shown him so much.

They were sitting on opposite sides of the bistro table at the far end of the patio. Dr. Ellison sat facing the patio door, his briefcase at his feet and a stack of papers and a small digital recorder in front of him. Aryeh sat with his back to the door, a small silver-and-black yarmulke pinned to the top of his head, the pile of books within easy reach.

Aryeh was always reading and what he read was history. Not surprising since he had over ninety years of history to catch up on, and books, as Ryan discovered – being the brain-dead dumb ass that he apparently was – were the safest way of doing that.

And regardless of what Aryeh, Dr. Ellison or his friends thought, he *hadn't* done it on purpose, at least, not consciously. Why would he? To hurt the man who'd stolen Jamie's body?

Well, maybe…but not this way.

No, it'd been a mistake, a stupid one and he should have known better, but just a mistake.

Ryan hadn't even thought about it – history was history, what could it hurt? – it just seemed a harmless thing to do. Why read about history when you could watch it on TV?

So one night, after KFC – because chicken was more or less kosher – Ryan turned on the History Channel for his new roomie and went into the study to do some work.

In hindsight, it might have been a good idea if he'd checked the TV guide first.

Just a stupid mistake.

Aryeh watched for two full hours while a retrospective of the Holocaust and the atrocities that had been committed on his people at Dachau, Treblinka, Ravensbrück, Buchenwald and Auschwitz played out in front of him.

If he had screamed or shouted or cursed or called Ryan every name under the sun, in Hebrew and English, it might have been better for both of them. But he never made a sound, even after Ryan came in to check on him and saw what he was watching.

The last time Ryan remembered moving that fast was at the pool in the rehabilitation center. He punched the power button so hard he almost broke the remote control, and in the silence that followed he'd tried to explain, to say he was sorry, God, he was so sorry, that it was a mistake.

"Mistake, yes," Aryeh had said, then nodded and wished Ryan a *gute nacht* as he rolled the wheelchair down the hall to the guest room.

Books were easier, especially books without pictures.

"Ah, Ryan, there you are," Dr. Ellison said, turning off the digital recorder as he looked up.

Ryan set the teacup down next to the history books and lifted the carafe.

"Ready for a refill, Dr. Ellison?"

Dr. Ellison looked at the mug Ryan had set down in front of him when he first sat down. The mug was full and there was an oil slick covering the surface.

"Um, no thanks…I'm good."

"*A dank*," Aryeh said, picking up the teacup. "Thank you, Ryan."

Ryan nodded and set the carafe down on the table. It was

Aryeh's voice, the strange, low voice coming out of Jamie's mouth, that still turned him inside out.

"Aryeh said he spoke with your lawyer?"

Good ol' Jiro. "Yeah. There shouldn't be any problem getting his name legally changed, although the social security department seems to be dragging its feet a bit."

"Your lawyer gave them the letter from the hospital, didn't he?"

"Yep, but you know government bureaucracy."

Dr. Ellison sighed. "That I do, unfortunately."

"Yeah. Uh…can I get you guys anything?"

Dr. Ellison asked Aryeh.

"*Nein….* No," Aryeh said. "Thank you."

Ryan nodded, all out of pithy comments.

"Well, I should be going," Dr. Ellison said and Ryan stood there, awkwardly and silent, while the man stuffed the papers he'd brought into his briefcase and stood up.

Ryan backed away even though there was more than enough room.

"Aryeh was telling me about your pancakes," Dr. Ellison said, snapping the case shut. "He says they're delicious but he thinks you're trying to make him fat because you make them so often."

"*Vos?*"

Dr. Ellison repeated what he said in Hebrew…or Yiddish…and Aryeh looked up at Ryan and smiled, nodding his head. His hair was longer than Jamie's had been and he was growing a beard. The faint lines around the chocolate-drop eyes – *brown eyes…they make him look older* – and across the forehead that Jamie had just begun to fret over were a little deeper now, but somehow they suited him. It was the face of an older man, a man who only vaguely resembled Jamie.

"Ah…*yoh,* yes. *Meh ken lecken di finger!* Very *gut,* pond cakes very good."

Neither Ryan nor the doctor bothered to correct him.

"Yeah, well, it's one of the few things I can make well. Jamie—"

His throat tightened around the name. Ryan could think it, mentally pick at it like a scab until it bled, but the moment he said the name out loud it felt like he was strangling. Drowning…yeah, it felt like he was drowning.

He cleared his throat. "Sorry. Jamie used to say the same thing… about me trying to make him fat. Funny, isn't it?"

"Then I'm envious. The last time I tried to make pancakes they came out like hockey pucks." Briefcase in hand, Dr. Ellison walked around to the opposite side of the table and offered his hand. "I'll see you next week. *Shalom*, Aryeh."

The man shook the doctor's hand and nodded. "*Shalom*."

"Ryan, see me out, will you?"

Oh-oh, Ryan thought, *now what?* Nodding, he stepped back and let his guest go ahead of him. Behind him, and echoing off the overhang, came two distinct metallic clacks. It was the sound of the wheelchair's handbrakes being released. His houseguest was going for a little roll-about.

Ryan stopped just far enough back from the sliding glass doors that he could see out without easily being seen. The man never looked back as he rolled past the raised beds of late-summer flowers and early chrysanthemums and rusting exercise equipment.

The pond cakes were very gut.

Dr. Ellison was waiting for him by the front door, balancing the open briefcase in one hand as he shifted through the papers inside.

"Looking for your bill?"

"Funny man." The doctor looked up and winked, then handed Ryan a clear plastic folder. "Here."

Ryan hefted the file while the doctor latched the briefcase and lowered it to his side. "This is some bill, doc."

"It would be, wouldn't it? But this is something another doctor at the hospital, Dr. Stanton, put together. The original idea was to give them to the Travelers when I felt the time was right." He nodded to the folder. "That's his family's history."

"Okay."

It was obvious by the look on his face that Dr. Ellison had expected Ryan to be a bit more…something…about the information. Ryan yielded to the pressure and gave him a one-shouldered shrug.

"I'll just give you the rundown, shall I? His wife and children are gone, although it's interesting to note that his son, Leben, died just a little over a year ago." Dr. Ellison paused, eyebrows raised in expectation – and was disappointed again. He cleared his throat and continued. "Leben had six children, two of whom died in infancy, and Aryeh's youngest daughter, Esther, had four. Jaffa, the eldest girl, stayed home to take care of the mother and never married. According to census records, Aryeh had eight grandchildren, seventeen great-grandchildren, twenty-two great-great…. Well, let's just say he had a rather prolific family, some of whom are living in the L.A. area."

Now Ryan got excited.

"Great! Does he want to go live with one of them? I mean they *are* his family."

"I didn't tell him, Ryan."

"Why not?"

"Because I don't know what this will do to him."

Ryan looked down at the folder in his hand. "Did you tell the others?"

"Two of them, yes," Dr. Ellison said, his lips curling into a sad smile. "Timmy, that's the little boy, wouldn't understand, but I gave his caregiver, Mrs. Rollins, the file. We decided, she and I, that it will be better for him not to know any details."

"So why is he – " Ryan jerked his head toward the back of the house as he looked up " – so special?"

"Because Aryeh was…*is* a man who is deeply rooted in his religion and history, but now that history has been taken away and his faith challenged. He doesn't know who or what he is or where he belongs."

"He belongs with his family. Don't you think that's the best place for him?"

"Yes, but we also have to think about them, his family members. What can I say to them? – 'Hello, you don't know me, but I'm a psychiatrist and we have your great-great-grandfather's reincarnated spirit in the body of a young paraplegic. Would you like him back?' They'd dial 911 faster than you could say psychotic break."

Ryan couldn't argue with that. "Yeah, I know if anyone suddenly came up to me and told me my best friend in the world and the love of my life had died and his body had been taken over by some Jewish wandering spirit I would have called the cops."

Dr. Ellison cleared his throat. "Touché."

"So what am I supposed to do with this?"

"I know he's asked you about his family so I thought, when you think the time's right, you could show it to him."

"Why me? You're his doctor."

"Exactly, I'm his doctor, but you're the closest thing he has to a friend right now. Of course, I understand if you'd rather not."

Dr. Ellison held out his hand and Ryan felt the muscles in his arm tighten. All he had to do was hand it back and—

"No," he said, "it's okay. I'll tell him."

"You're a good man, Ryan."

"Spare me." Ryan opened the door and watched as Dr. Ellison stepped down onto the Welcome mat. "I do have one question."

"Yes?"

"What does...*ah-were* mean?"

"I'm sorry? *Ah-were?*" He shrugged.

"Yeah, I heard him say it a couple of times when you were talking."

Dr. Ellison thought a moment. "Oh, you mean *averah?*"

Ryan nodded even though the word sounded exactly the way he'd pronounced it.

"It means *sin*."

"Oh."

"Anything else? Okay, then I'll see you two next Saturday."

Ryan closed the door. Sin, huh? He didn't have to think very hard to figure out what particular Old Testament *sin* they'd been talking about – especially if Dr. Ellison had explained whose body Aryeh now occupied and what its previous orientation had been.

Ah-were, sin...he'd have to remember that one.

Standing in the entranceway, Ryan studied the folder he'd been given. All he had to do was hand it to the man and stand back. Aryeh wouldn't be able to get out of the house fast enough after that and he wouldn't have to watch the face of the man he'd loved change, a little more each day, into a stranger who only looked familiar.

It would be over.

Taking a deep breath, Ryan detoured to the study, where he tossed the folder onto his desk, and then walked back through the house to the backyard so he could ask his roomie what he'd like for dinner.

Ryan found him asleep next to the accessible vertical press. His head was tipped back and to one side and he was snoring softly while the late-afternoon breeze ruffled the bushy stubble on his chin and cheeks. Even with the beard and longer hair and his eyes closed, he looked so much like Jamie….

Jamie was dead.

"Hey!"

Aryeh jerked forward, eyelids popping open, his hands gripping the chair's armrests.

"*Vos? Vos zogt ir? Vos tut zich?*"

"Sorry," Ryan said. "I didn't mean to startle you. It's okay, everything's okay."

When Aryeh looked up he blinked his brown eyes and didn't look like Jamie anymore.

"*Yoh*, yes…me too. Sorry. I was just…."

"Sleeping?"

"Thinking, first…then I fall asleep." The edges of the beard fluffed when he smiled. "Sorry."

"That's okay. So, any idea what you'd like for dinner tonight? I was thinking…Chinese? You know, chow mein?"

"*Yoh*, Chinese. Chow mein. Chicken, please, and some of the crispies, if it's not too much trouble?"

"Fried won-tons." Maybe there was something about racial profiling after all. He never knew a Jew who didn't love Chinese. "Anything else?"

"Maybe some almond cookies and a little tea?"

"Almond cookies and green tea, okay, I'll phone in the order and have it delivered."

Aryeh frowned and looked up at the sky. Ryan did the same. There were still a couple of hours before the sun set completely and the first three stars appeared through the urban glow. This, Ryan had learned, signified the end of Shabbos, at which time Aryeh would retire to the guest room to pray and Ryan would ignore him and set the table.

He might be the Shabbos goy, another thing he'd learned, and have to turn lights on and off on Friday nights, but that was it. They'd come to an understanding early in their forced co-habitation. Pork, although Ryan was free to have as much of it as he wanted while at work or with friends, was not to come into the house. Ryan made the same condition concerning gefilte fish, although he wished now he'd included kasha.

Prayers were allowed, in private, but things like celebrating the Shabbos with candles and challah and horseradish weren't going to happen.

"I won't call until the sun sets," Ryan said and Aryeh smiled with Jamie's lips. "Because eating before that would be an *aweire*, right? A sin?"

The smile faded.

"Good word. I'm going to take a nap. You need anything before I go in?"

Aryeh shook his head. "*Nein*... No, thank you. I'm fine. Have a pleasant sleep."

Ryan turned and kept walking until he reached the master bedroom. Jamie's picture, looking away, was the first thing he saw.

Taking a deep breath, he closed the door and locked it.

CHAPTER TWENTY-FIVE

Crissy

Crissy sat facing the bank manager in as demure a poise as she could portray: back straight, but shoulders slightly forward and stooped to show meekness, chin and eyes lowered for modesty, with her hands folded in her lap, ankles crossed and knees together. She'd kept quiet during the meeting, but occasionally would sigh, to round out the characterization, while Frank Stanton, MD, explained to the assistant bank manager what exactly had happened to poor Helen Harmon.

Blankie Frankie a doctor, who would have thought it?

The story was a complete fabrication, of course, and she'd helped Frankie rehearse it at her apartment – she had her own apartment, how cool was that? – and even if she couldn't understand most of the medical terms he was using, she couldn't help but be impressed by his performance.

Who would have thought he'd turn out to be that good an actor?

Still, she was getting hungry and he'd promised to take her out to Hamburger Hamlet for lunch.

"Beyond the general weakness and decreased fine motor control," Frankie said, "the aneurysm and subsequent stroke stemming from the initial cardiac episode severely damaged those portions of Miss Harmon's frontal cortex that are responsible for memory and cognitive processes."

Crissy looked up, on cue, and saw concern in Mrs. N. Sutherland's face.

"Oh, my God. I'm *so* sorry, Miss Harmon."

"Thank you."

Crissy had made her voice go all low and thick and added a little sniffle at the end for good measure. Frankie reached over and took her hand, squeezing it gently. *Over the top, bring it down a notch.* She gave him a small nod – *message received* – and smiled bravely.

"You're very kind, considering I couldn't remember your name or any of the others when we walked in. It's just so – " *pause, two, three,* " – hard."

Mrs. Sutherland put a hand to the front of her jacket. "Oh please, don't worry about that. I'll explain it to the tellers. Now, Dr. Stanton, how can I help?"

Frankie let go of Crissy's hand and sat up, facing the woman. "Due to Miss Harmon's physical limitations, especially with her fine motor control, the signatures you have on file for her accounts and, of course, her credit and debit cards will no longer match her current abilities. Both her cards were issued from this bank, were they not?"

"Why, yes," Mrs. Sutherland said and Crissy felt her belly flutter. She'd never had a credit card before. Her parents thought she was too young to have credit cards.

"Given the circumstances, I wondered if it wouldn't be best if Miss Harmon got *new* signature cards."

The woman smiled and stood up. "I'll go get them. Do you feel up to talking to our stock consultant? I'm sure he'll have a few cards and papers for you to sign as well."

Crissy looked over and Frankie nodded for her and said it was probably best if they got as much of Ms. Harmon's finances settled as quickly as possible.

"Fine, I'll be right back with the signature cards."

Mrs. Sutherland touched Crissy's shoulder as she passed and Crissy waited until she'd left the glassed-in office before relaxing into a comfortable slump.

"I'm hungry."

"It won't be much longer, and this will save a lot of time and trouble later on."

She pouted and he pretended not to notice.

"I'm not going to get in trouble doing this, am I?"

"No," Frankie said. "Why would you?"

Crissy turned in the chair to look out the glass wall behind her. Mrs. Sutherland was all the way across the bank lobby, talking to one of the tellers.

"Because," she whispered, "I'm *not* Helen Harmon."

"But you are, Crissy. According to dental records and fingerprints you are physically Helen Louise Harmon. Dr. Ellison and the lawyer explained all this to you, remember?"

Crissy sighed. "Yeah, they explained it."

But so what, it was crazy! She'd died and came back as an old lady? Jeeeee-ZUZ. Dr. Ellison told her that he understood, but how could he? He didn't suddenly go from being sixteen to forty-two in a minute. *FORTY-TWO!* God, that was four years older than her mother and one younger than her dad, for gosh sakes. It was like going from a ten to a half.

But at least her half was loaded. Helen Harmon had *money* and Dr. Ellison, the lawyer and even Frankie said how lucky she was because of it. Yeah, lucky, but they didn't still jump every time they walked past a mirror.

Crissy slumped deeper into the chair.

"This is messed up."

"Yes, it is, but it happened and you're going to have to learn to live with it. Fortunately you're a great actress, so just think of it as playing a part."

"But I'm *old!*"

"Forty-two isn't *old.*"

Crissy gave him a look. "How old are *you?*"

"Forty, but…."

"You're *younger* than me?"

"No…well, technically, given the circumstances…."

"But you were *older* than me!"

He took a deep breath. "Inside I still am, Crissy."

"No, you're not! Inside, jeeze, that's the dumbest thing you've ever said. It doesn't matter what's inside! When did you get so dumb, Frankie? You used to be smart."

"I never realized you knew that about me. Now, about the name Frankie…." He waited until she looked at him. "I go by Frank now. Okay? Now, sit up, they're coming back."

Crissy pushed herself up as Mrs. Sutherland and a middle-aged man walked into the office.

"Okay, *Frankie*," she whispered, and then resumed her characterization of one Helen Louise Harmon, age forty-two.

★   ★   ★

Crissy poked a french fry into the mound of pepper-topped catsup on her plate and left it standing.

Frankie...*Frank* looked at her over the raised forkful of salad. "I thought you were starving."

She thought about pushing the plate with its half-eaten double cheeseburger and crisp fries away to make a point, but she *was* still hungry and even though the combo plate and thick chocolate shake was good, it just wasn't the same as she remembered.

But nothing was.

"I can't believe they closed the Hamburger Hamlet on Sunset."

"You think that's bad, wait until I show you downtown L.A. You won't believe how it's changed."

Despite everything, Crissy felt a small and pleasant surge of warmth race up from her belly to her chest. He wanted to show her downtown L.A. and even though she'd never particularly liked downtown L.A. – with its smog and crowds and homeless people and dirt and smell – she wasn't going to tell him that.

Because it was obvious that *he* wanted to be with *her*, just like in school.

Unless *he* wanted to be with *Helen Louise Harmon*.

A chill replaced the warm surge as Crissy picked up the burger and took a bite that was so big it made *Helen Harmon's* jaw crack. Frank chuckled around his own bite of lettuce and feta cheese salad.

"You know, I used to watch you and your friends eat in the cafeteria."

"Mmuuew?" She swallowed. "That's sick."

"No, nothing like that. It's just that you were so popular and pretty and talented – my God, you could act – and, well, I had quite a crush on you back then."

No kidding? Crissy lowered the burger back to the plate and pouted.

"What? Did I say something wrong?"

She shrugged to prolong his agony just a bit more.

"What? Crissy, what?"

"Why didn't you tell me you liked me back then?"

He gave her a wide smile that deepened the lines around his eyes and mouth and showed how much he'd aged since she screamed at him in Mr. Byrd's office. It almost made her wish she'd have been nicer to him back then.

Back when she was just Crissy and not some celestial science experiment gone wrong.

"It's because I was a bitch, wasn't it?"

"No. Never."

"Pa-*leeze*." Crissy began picking up french fries and shoving them in her mouth just to keep from having to look at him. "I know what I am...*was*. I was a royal B-I-T-C-H who always had to have her way. That's why I yelled at you the other day...I mean, you know, when I thought you'd messed up the character list for *The Crucible*. I mean, I knew there was no way I wouldn't get the part of Abigail unless somebody screwed up and—" She swallowed and looked up. "I keep forgetting how long ago that was for you."

"Twenty-two years."

The fries hit her stomach like a ball of concrete.

"Jeeze, it doesn't feel that long to me."

"It wouldn't. Maybe you can pretend you've been in a coma for twenty-two years, it might help. You'd be about the same age."

"Except I'm *older than you*." She popped another fry and began picking apart the top of the sesame-seedless bun. "And I wasn't in a coma. I *died*."

Saying it out loud still made her tremble.

Frank set his fork down and reached across the table to take her hand. "I'm sorry; I shouldn't have mentioned it."

Crissy moved her hand away and continued picking at the bun. "It was an accident."

"I know. You told me."

"But I know you don't believe me. You think I killed myself because I didn't get the part, don't you?"

"A lot of kids kill themselves for less reason than that."

Crissy picked the balding burger up and slammed it down against the plate. "I didn't kill myself, Frankie, it was an accident."

"Okay." He looked around nervously. "Lower your voice."

She lowered her voice. "But I mean *really!*"

"Okay, okay...I believe you."

He didn't and she was about to tell him that when she noticed the three old ladies, in matching jogging suits, staring at her from the next table.

"Rehearsing," Crissy said and the three old ladies nodded and smiled and told her to break a leg before returning to their Senior Portion Lunch Specials.

Crissy felt Helen's face blush as she looked away.

"It *was* an accident," she told him again. "I was yelling at Mr. Byrd from the balcony and I tripped and...?"

"You caught a light cable on the way down." Frank lifted his water glass and finished half of it before setting it back on the table. "It was quick."

"I don't remember. There was just a—" She took a deep breath and shrugged. "I really don't remember anything after that except waking up in the hospital."

"I'm sorry."

For the next few minutes Frank used his fork to mash the chickpeas from his salad into a paste, and she alternated between picking the bun apart and finishing the milkshake.

"You know, I see him from time to time...Mr. Byrd."

Crissy looked up. "God, he's still alive?"

And Frank laughed. "Crissy, he was in his early thirties when we were in school."

"Really? Wow." She knew that, but he just seemed so much older. "Well...good. Where do you see him?"

"I belong to a couple community theaters and—"

"*You?*"

He smiled, but she could tell the remark hurt him. Picking up the hamburger, she took another humongous bite, even though her stomach felt like it was full of rocks already.

"At's ate!"

Frank cocked his head to one side and leaned forward. "What?"

It took a few tries before Crissy managed to swallow everything in her mouth.

"I said…that's great. I just— I didn't know you acted, I mean you never were in any of the school plays."

"I'm still not. I mean I don't act." He sat back and took a sip of water. "It's hard enough to commit to rehearsal and performance schedules if you have a regular nine to five job. It'd be almost impossible for me. And I couldn't see myself leaving a cast in the lurch if I had to leave in the middle of a show because I got an emergency call from the hospital. You have a little ketchup on your cheek, by the way."

He tapped a finger against his own cheek to show her the general area as Crissy dabbed with her napkin.

"Thanks. So if you don't act, whadda you do?"

"The same things I did in high school – help with membership, rig lights, build sets…I really love building sets and I'm good at it." He held up his hands. "Not one broken finger or major cut in the last ten years. Of course, if the hospital administrator knew what I was doing she'd have a small kitten. Interventional cardiologists are supposed to be very careful about their hands." Frank looked at his hands, smiling, and lowered them to the table. "But it can be very boring being *that* careful."

Crissy nodded as if she knew that. "So…does Mr. Byrd build sets too?"

"No. You know what he used to say: 'The actor's responsibility is to act, nothing else.' So, he acts…nothing else."

"Sounds like he hasn't changed very much."

"No, not very much. Would you like to see him?"

The question came so fast she didn't have time to prepare a reaction, so he just saw her – Helen – with her mouth open.

"Mr. Byrd?"

"Yeah. He's got the lead in *On Golden Pond* at a little theater in Whittier. The show opens mid-October, if you'd like to go."

Crissy sat back and closed Helen's mouth. Mid-October was a month away and anything could happen in a month. She could get used to being forty-two or Helen's heart could finally give out.

"'Kay. Sounds like fun."

"Then it's a date."

Maybe *anything* was possible. "It's a date."

Frank called for the check and after he paid for it with a credit card (just like the brand new one she had in her wallet next to Helen Harmon's driver's license), they got up and left and talked about little things as he crossed the parking lot. How she liked her condo ("*It's so cool, I never thought I'd ever live near the ocean*") and if it bothered her living alone ("*I'm never alone! The hospital has this social worker or whatever who comes over to check on me and make sure I'm taking all those pills and Dr. Ellison comes by once a week and Kate comes over at night— Oh, did I tell you? Kate and I are friends now. It was really weird for her, you know, but she's nice and I never had an African American friend before and she's helping me, you know, learn to cook and stuff because she thinks, you know. I'm glad you guys told her, it would have been weird trying to play Helen with her. She cries sometimes, you know, when she looks at me, but it's cool.*").

"And then there's you," she said. "You're always calling and checking up on me and taking me to lunch and stuff. So I'm not really alone."

He stopped when they reached his car – a boring dark blue sedan – and touched her arm.

"Am I making you uncomfortable?"

"What?"

"It never dawned on me that my presence might bother you."

"It doesn't!"

"I mean, I *was* Helen's surgeon and, well, I don't want you to feel that my only interest is based on that."

"What was Helen like?"

Frank thought a moment. "I really don't know. She was my patient so I probably knew more about her medical history than about her personally."

"Kate says she was a strong woman who knew what she wanted out of life."

"That's good. I do know she did her homework on what her medical options were before she contacted me. She wanted to get her life back without compromise as soon as possible."

"But that didn't happen."

"No, it didn't. The surgery was a success but the patient died."

"And I came back."

He smiled. "And you came back."

"Do you still like me, Frank?"

"*What?*"

Crissy took a step forward, hands on her hips, and stared at him (through the designer sunglasses she'd found in Helen's purse) the same way she had the last day she was really Crissy Moore, inside and out. They were almost the same height now. Helen was taller than her own original five foot five, and the two-inch heels she'd found in Helen's closet almost made her eyeball to eyeball with Frank.

And that seemed to make him almost as uncomfortable as her question had.

"I asked," she repeated slowly, "if you still *liked* me? You said you had a crush on me in school, and I knew you were watching me in the cafeteria. You were always looking at me, weren't you, *Frankie*?"

He stared at her and for a minute, just a minute, he looked like the *Blankie Frankie* she knew and tormented.

"Well?"

Frankie faded and Frank came back. "God help me. I forgot how manipulative sixteen-year-old girls can be."

"Seventeen."

"Excuse me?"

"This is September, my birthday was in April…so I'm seventeen now."

They stood looking at each other for another long moment until a car trying to leave the parking lot gunned its motor, reminding them they were still standing far enough away from the car to block traffic. Frank waved to the driver then took her arm and escorted her to the sedan's passenger side door.

"Well, happy belated birthday," he said as he opened the door.

Crissy waited until he'd settled behind the wheel, seat belt in place, and turned the car on before asking. "So, are you going to get me a present?"

He turned to her and smiled. "What?"

"Well, I have missed a lot of birthdays…." Pout.

"Right. Okay, so what would you like?"

"Hmm…let me think and I'll get back to you on that."

Frank turned and slowly backed the car out. "Why do I have

the feeling I should be worried?" Crissy gave him an evil laugh. "Is there any place you'd like to go before I get back to the hospital?"

She didn't need to think about it because that's all she had been thinking about, more or less, since she 'woke up'.

"Yeah. I want to see my grave."

The car did a little lurch when he stomped on the brakes. The car behind them honked.

Frank waved, muttering, "Sorry, sorry," and sped up, taking the turn onto Beverly Boulevard with a squeal of tire rubber on asphalt.

"I don't think that's a very good idea, Crissy."

"Why not?"

"It's morbid and both you and your heart are still recovering from major surgery, remember. I shouldn't even have let you eat what you had – we'll talk about your diet later – but it was a special occasion and—"

"I want to see it."

"Crissy."

"Do you know where it is? Did you go to my…you know?"

He nodded without answering.

"Was it nice?"

"No. It was your funeral, how could it be nice?"

Crissy kept quiet until Frank took the turn onto the Hollywood Freeway.

"Please?"

Silence.

"I need to see it."

"Why?"

"To make it real."

"Fine, but afterward I'm taking you right home and you're going to rest. You hear me?"

"Yes, sir."

★   ★   ★

It was harder than she thought it would be, standing there looking down at the heart-shaped pink marble tombstone.

Christine Taylor Moore

April 20, 1976 – June 4, 1992
Beloved daughter
Forever in our hearts

She was a star that shone so brightly
she filled the world with light

Rest in Peace, little girl

It was in the middle of a row, on a small hill that looked out over the San Pedro harbor. It was a great view and she wondered if her mom and dad had looked at it during the funeral. She hoped so, she hoped they'd watched the clouds on the horizon and the boats on the water and the birds, instead of watching her coffin go in the ground.

Although the day was seasonally warm, the wind coming off the sea was cold and it made Crissy shiver.

"You okay?"

She nodded.

"We should go."

She nodded again. "You said my mom and dad moved?"

"Yes."

"The flowers." She nudged the bouquet of pink roses lying on the grave with the toe of Helen's shoe. "They're fresh."

"Not really, they're about a week old."

Why wasn't she surprised? "You put flowers on my grave?"

"I've always thought graves look lonely without flowers."

Crissy looked at the other graves. Some had flowers, some had little American flags fluttering in the breeze; most had neither and they really did look lonely.

"But...I'm back," she said. "Why are you still putting flowers here?"

"Habit, I guess."

"Thanks."

When the tears came she didn't try to stop them and neither did

Frank. It was just so strange to stand at her own grave, knowing that her body, her *real* body, was down there and probably nothing more than bones covered in rags.

"Okay, that's enough. I was afraid this might happen. Let's go."

"In a minute."

"Crissy."

"It's kinda like that old song Mr. Byrd used to sing at all the cast parties, remember?"

Frank frowned, shaking his head. "Song?"

"'It's My Party'?" She looked up at him and gave him a quivering smile. "Come on, it's my grave. Can't I cry if I want to?"

PART SIX
OCTOBER

CHAPTER TWENTY-SIX
Timmy

Nora heard them laughing in the front room and stopped rummaging through the Halloween decorations to listen. Although it was Timmy laughing, there was a low, gravelly undertone to the child's voice that sounded like Henry when they first began seeing each other. He'd been such a handsome, strapping young man, tall and straight and polite, with hands that were equally happy crushing walnut shells for her papa as they were plucking off daisy petals — *she loves me, she loves me not* — until he got the answer he wanted. *She loves me.*

Her sisters and cousins had been so jealous they chewed nails and talked trash and tried their best to put him down to her.

As if they could.

She'd fallen in love with Henry the first time she'd seen him standing big and awkward and hunched against the back wall of the school gymnasium like some misplaced shadow. For all the size and strength he showed outwardly, inside he was just a shy little boy.

Just like Timmy.

Timmy was shy only until he got to know you and then, my, oh my, that child was anything but. He laughed and enjoyed life more than anyone Nora had ever known. And talk? The child never stopped from the moment he woke up until he fell asleep.

Timmy was a lot like Henry'd been before the disease whittled him down.

Henry and Timmy, her two boys in one body; no woman could be more blessed.

"...and the duck went quack!"

Nora hadn't heard the first part of Dr. Ellison's joke – he was always telling Timmy jokes or riddles – but it must have been a good one because Timmy's shrill laughter filled the house again. He was such a happy little boy despite everything.

He couldn't walk anymore and was so weak he could barely help Nora get himself in and out of the wheelchair, but it'd been the same with Henry in those last few weeks and Nora was used to it. Timmy's appetite was still better than Henry's though, and he never tried to hit her or spoke mean to her, and, except for the few times he remembered his mama and daddy, which were getting fewer now, he was a happy little boy.

"Quack!" Timmy yelled. "The duck said QUACK!"

Nora heard Dr. Ellison chuckle and mutter something she couldn't make out, but Timmy said "Okey-dokey, Mr. Pokey!" and laughed again.

Smiling, Nora went back to sorting decorations. She hadn't seen some of them in almost forty years, maybe longer, and hadn't decorated the house for Halloween except for putting up a smiling paper witch on the front door and a carved jack-o'-lantern on the porch since Marjorie was a teenager. But she knew exactly where the box was when she went down to the basement to get it.

And it felt good to be doing it.

Even before Marjorie came along, she and Henry had always decorated the house every chance they got. There'd be paper hearts for Valentine's Day; lilies and candy dishes filled with jelly beans for Easter; flags for the Fourth of July; autumn leaves, corn stalks and pumpkins for Halloween and Thanksgiving; and a hundred twinkling lights that Henry would put all along the front of the house for Christmas while she frosted the windows and hung holly.

After Marjorie came, there were even more lights and pumpkins and paper hearts, but then she grew up and got married and had her own house to decorate. After that, a carved pumpkin and paper witch or plastic wreath on the front door was all they put up.

But the decorations never got thrown away, oh no, because there might come a time when you needed them again.

Like now.

It was going to be Timmy's last Halloween, probably his last holiday ever. Nora knew that even without Dr. Ellison or Martin telling her every time they saw her, so she was bound and determined to make it the best Halloween he ever had.

Nora pulled out the plastic Frankenstein's monster mask Henry used to wear to hand out candy. It was cracked and faded and the elastic band had disappeared years ago, taking a small piece of the monster's left temple with it. The mask had caused many a trick-or-treater to squeal and scream, but now it just looked sad and lonely.

She held it up to her face when she heard Dr. Ellison coming.

"Okay, okay, I'll ask, but don't get your hopes—" She turned around. "Yah!"

Nora lowered the mask, laughing.

"Whazza matter, Dr. Ellison?" Timmy called from the front room.

"Oh, nothing," he answered, "Missus Nora just tried to scare me to death, that's all."

"Yay!" Timmy laughed, clapping his hands. "'Cause it's a'most Halloween!"

Dr. Ellison took the mask from Nora and shook his head. "Yes, it is. It most certainly is almost Halloween."

"I'm gonna be Howdy Doody! Missus Nora's gonna make me a costume, aren't you, Missus Nora?"

"I sure am, Timmy."

"See," he yelled as though Dr. Ellison had doubted him. "Ask her, Dr. Ellison!"

"Ask me what, Dr. Ellison?"

Dr. Ellison set the mask down carefully on the table. "He'd like to know if he can stay up until ten tonight."

"That boy. He's always asking to stay up late but never can

make it past nine." Shaking her head, Nora turned toward the front room and shouted, "Dr. Ellison asked me…I'll think about it, okay?"

"Okay," he called back. "Can I have a cookie?"

"You just had a cookie."

"N'uh. Dr. Ellison ate all of them."

Nora looked back at the psychiatrist and arched an eyebrow. Dr. Ellison smiled. "They were delicious, but I only ate my share."

"I'll bring you some in a minute. You watch your programs now, and let me talk to Dr. Ellison, okay?"

"Okay."

Nora waited until she heard the television go on. He'd mastered the use of the remote control without any problem.

"You want me to get the cookies?" Dr. Ellison asked and Nora shook her head.

"He'll forget about it as soon as his cartoons are on. Here, let me move those out of the way so you can sit down."

Dr. Ellison helped stack the timeworn paper decorations while Nora shoved the bulkier items to the opposite end of the dining room table. The strips of black and orange construction paper she'd cut that morning while the hospice nurse was giving Timmy his sponge bath were in a pile at the head of the table, Henry's spot, so she could get to them after supper. They were going to make new chain garlands to replace the ones she and Marjorie had made years before.

Paper chains, Karo syrup popcorn balls, cookies and one of the *Howdy Doody* DVDs she'd bought from Amazon.com – that's what Nora had planned for them and she was anxious to get to it. They didn't have many projects left.

"My gosh," Dr. Ellison said and picked up a smiling pumpkin noisemaker. "I think I had one of these when I was a kid."

Holding it gently by its wooden handle, he gave the tin rattle a shake.

"Yep, just as loud and annoying as I remember." He set it back down on the table as carefully as if it were made of spun glass. "You've got quite a collection here."

"A bit," Nora agreed, "and it will probably take me a couple days to put them all up."

Dr. Ellison ran a finger over the Frankenstein mask.

"Why don't you sit down and I'll get us both a cup of tea. Or would you rather have coffee?"

"Nothing for me, thanks." He sat down in what had been Marjorie's chair. "But don't let me stop you from having any."

"Oh, I drink too much and Lord knows I'll be up and down all night if I have another cup this late in the afternoon." He laughed politely. "You know, he likes when you visit."

"He said that but I just thought he was being polite."

"Oh, no, he really does like you…you always bring him treats."

Dr. Ellison hung his head. "Busted."

"He tells me everything you two talk about."

"Everything?"

"Well, let's see," she said, "he tells me about the memory games and guessing games you play and how you cheat at Chinese Checkers."

"I don't cheat!"

"He says you let him win and his daddy said that cheating to lose is just as bad as cheating to win. How's he supposed to learn and get better if you let him win?"

"Ah, clever boy, I'll remember that. Anything else?"

"Only that he's very happy that you're not the kind of doctor who gives shots," Nora said. "That's very important to him."

Dr. Ellison nodded and leaned back in his chair. "Does he still ask about his family?"

"Not as much as he did. Maybe that means he's getting used to being here…children can adjust to anything. I remember once when Marjorie was in second grade and they had to move her and a couple of other students to a new class because…well, I can't remember why they had to, maybe the old class was too crowded or something, but she hated it! She loved her old teacher and all her friends were in the old room. It just about broke my heart to see her so upset. She cried for a whole week and then she got used to it and couldn't have been happier. I think children can handle change better than adults."

"I think so too, but it's a little different in Timmy's case."

"Because of the Alzheimer's."

"Partially, that's true, the disease is compromising his memory, but it's more than that. He thinks his parents gave him away because he got hurt."

"Oh, that poor child." Nora felt tears come to her eyes. "What can I do?"

"I don't know if there's anything either of us can do. I've talked to him about it and reinforced what you've told him – that his parents are at the hospital with the new baby and will come for him as soon as they can – but I think there's a part of him that knows we're lying. It's very hard to tell what a typical child knows or doesn't know and it's a hundred times harder in Timmy's case. His cognitive functions are impaired and deteriorating. All we can do is keep telling him his parents love him and will come back for him."

Nora shook her head and felt a tear fall. Dear God, maybe, at the end, his parents would come for him, but until then there was nothing she could do for the little boy inside Henry except lie to him.

"It's not right," she whispered. "It's just not right."

"No, it's not, but overall he's happy and an absolute joy to be around, especially compared to some others I have to deal with."

"You mean the other three...Travelers?"

"Oh, no, no...I meant in my private practice. Sorry. The other three are doing fine and have adjusted to their new lives with varying degrees of ease."

Nora nodded and dabbed at her eyes with one of the many tissues she kept in the pocket of her cardigan. Timmy's nose always seemed to be running and he never remembered to wipe it.

She sniffed and put the damp tissue back into her pocket. "That's good to hear. They deserve to be happy."

"Happiness is a relative term, but they're coping as well as can be expected." Dr. Ellison folded his hands on the tabletop and leaned over them. "You don't have to worry about them."

"I'm not. It's just that they're lost and alone, like Timmy." She took a deep breath and used the sleeve of her sweater to polish her fingerprints off the table edge. "I've never been able to pass a stray cat or dog without wanting to take it in and care for it, and I guess that's the way I feel about these poor souls."

Dr. Ellison smiled. "That's because you're a natural mother, but I promise they're doing well. Maybe not as well as Timmy in there, but how can anyone hope to compete with this?"

"This?"

"You've created a childhood fantasyland here, Mrs. Rollins. No school, no homework, all the TV and comic books he wants... plus fresh-baked cookies on demand. I tell you, I'm more than a little jealous of him."

Nora laughed out loud. "Oh, now, it's not that much. I used to do the same for Marjorie when she was home sick from school. You have children, Dr. Ellison?"

"No. My wife and I wanted children but it never happened."

"You're still a young man, there's time."

"I'll take that as a compliment," he said and changed the subject. "Mrs. Rollins, I think it might be best if Timmy went back into the hospital."

"No. And I'll tell you the same thing I told Martin...Dr. Cross. Timmy's been through enough, more than any poor child should, and he deserves to be at peace now. Especially now. I won't put him in some sterile, soulless room to breathe his last. I won't do that, not again. I let Henry die that way but I won't let it happen to Timmy. He likes it here, Dr. Ellison, and he's happy here and here is where he's going to stay."

"Dr. Cross told me you were feisty."

Nora raised her chin. "I'm beginning to like that word."

"All right," he said, "you win, but it's not going to be easy."

"There's where you're wrong, Dr. Ellison. Dying is the easiest thing we ever get to do. It's staying behind that's hard."

"That it is, Mrs. Rollins. Well, I'd better be going. Thank you for the cookies and insight." Dr. Ellison stood up and pushed his chair back under the table, as Nora got to her feet and followed him back into the living room where he waved at Timmy. "Okay, pardner, be seein' ya next week."

"Same time, same station!" Timmy yelled back and clapped his hands.

"You got it."

"Missus Nora…can I have a cookie?"

Dr. Ellison looked at Nora and laughed. "And some things he never forgets. You go ahead, I'll let myself out. Goodbye, Mrs. Rollins."

"Goodbye, Dr. Ellison."

★   ★   ★

Three days later the living room looked like the front room of a very friendly haunted house.

Nora had found some old sheer curtains in the back of the linen closet and taken a pair of scissors to them, shredding them as they hung in the windows. With the help of the hospice nurse and under Timmy's instruction, a parade of smiling jack-o'-lanterns, cackling witches and dancing skeletons had been taped on every wall and around the doorway. Black plastic bats and tissue-paper ghosts flew from the blades of the ceiling fan.

A large, uncarved pumpkin sat on a pile of newspaper on the small table next to the hospital bed. They were going to carve it, her and Timmy, when he felt stronger, and then, maybe, they'd work on the paper chain garland they'd started but probably would never finish.

He was always tired now, sleeping most of the day, even when he woke up late. The hospice nurse told Nora that it was a normal part of the end process and that she shouldn't worry. Nora told her she wasn't worried at all.

He woke up around three and asked for cookies and milk and ate two before falling back to sleep. He was still asleep when Nora put the strips of black and orange paper and rolls of masking tape back into the plastic bin and lifted out the unfinished chain. It was still only a few feet long, but was long enough to drape around the pumpkin when she put it out on Halloween night.

And maybe she wouldn't even carve it this year; maybe she'd just leave it whole so it would last longer. When Marjorie was little she always cried the morning after Halloween when they threw away the withered and candle-cooked pumpkin. She never understood why they wouldn't let her keep it.

"Because there's a time for things, baby, and it's just the pumpkin's time to go."

Just like it was getting to be Timmy's time.

"Mama?"

Nora brought the chain with her, shuffling her feet against the floor so she wouldn't stumble over anything before she was able to turn on the lamp next to her chair.

"No, baby," she said when they could both see each other, "it's just me, just silly old Missus Nora."

"Oh."

"I was just going to wake you up, baby, because I've got some wonderful news for you." Only his eyes moved, flickered toward her. "Your mama and daddy just called and told me you have a brand new baby…sister."

"Sumfaawinsprig," he said so softly that Nora had to lean down to hear.

"That's right, little Summerfall Winterspring. You're a big brother, Timmy."

"Big."

"Yes, you are, and you know what that means?" He just looked at her. "It means your mommy and daddy and baby sister are coming to get you."

"Mama?"

"That's right, they're coming here to get you and then you'll all go home."

"Home?"

"Yes, you're going to go home."

"Home." He smiled up at her.

"That's right, baby, home. Would you like me to read to you until they come?"

Timmy smiled and closed his eyes. Nora touched his cheek. His skin was cool and dry. She pulled the blankets higher over him and sat down and put on her reading glasses. There was a small stack of library books on the end table, all due back at the end of the month. Nora picked up the one on top and opened it.

"Oh, this is your favorite, *Treasure Island*. Shall I read it?"

Timmy made a sound and Nora began reading.

It was almost midnight when the sound of his breathing changed. Nora raised her voice so he could hear her, so he knew she was there and that he wasn't alone. An hour later Timmy stopped breathing, but Nora continued to read until the night had passed and a new day began.

CHAPTER TWENTY-SEVEN

Elisabeth

Despite the warmth of the cloth against her breast, the heat rising in her face made it feel so cold to the touch that her body trembled. *Liar!* Keeping her head turned and eyes closed, lest the body she now inhabited betray her again and she see its naked reflection in the glass, Elisabeth finished swabbing the breast and covered herself with a towel before dropping the cloth into the sink.

The towel was soft, almost silken to the touch, and smelled of lavender. It was a far cry from the stiff, coarsely woven sheets that her mother had favored.

Eyes still closed, Elisabeth lowered her head and inhaled the sweet fragrance deep into her lungs, but as she did so, the towel brushed against the swollen nipple of her breast and a shiver, a tremor deeper than a chill, invaded her nether parts and made her gasp.

Elisabeth threw the towel away from her and, though her breasts still felt damp, quickly pushed them into the cumbersome *brassiere* she now wore in place of a corset. The material was not quite as soft as the bathing towel, but it provoked the same terrible secret sensation as it compressed her nipples.

The first time Elisabeth felt it was in the hospital when, still befuddled with laudanum or whatever tincture of opium the physicians had given her to battle the pain of the wound they'd inflicted upon her, the nurse had placed the babe Emily to her breast and given it to suck.

The shame was almost enough to conceal the trembling, throbbing warmth that radiated upward from betwixt her legs.

If it had not been for the babe Elisabeth would have given in to the hysterics that grew in equal measures to the terrible, *pleasurable* sensation. It was only after the babe was removed from the room, asleep and satiated, that Elisabeth gave way to her emotions.

"It's all right," Sara's mother, Lillian, had said, "a lot of new mothers are uncomfortable nursing. I'll get you a breast pump."

But I am not a mother, she'd wanted to scream. This is not my child.

Still the babe had been delivered of the body she now wore and had to be fed in those early weeks, so, twice a day, morning and afternoon, Elisabeth had been milked, first by the nurses in the hospital and now, because the mother's breast still produced milk, by her own hand, half-naked and sequestered in the Jack-and-Jill bathroom.

Opening her eyes, Elisabeth lifted the blouse she'd chosen to wear from the robe hook on the door and slipped it on. She was halfway through buttoning it in place when she stopped and, holding her breath, listened.

Was that the baby?

Every morning since becoming a part of Sara's family, she'd wakened to the soft sounds of Emily rousing herself from sleep. She had heard tales, reticently spoken, of the unearthly shrieks and howling tantrums an infant would produce upon awakening, but Sara's child, Emily, awoke only with murmurs that became a series of gentle coos and babbles, as if she were saying goodbye to the wondrous creatures that had peopled her dreams and was welcoming the bright new morning.

"What fanciful rubbish," her mother would have said if she'd dared to speak such a thought aloud. But, as she still needed to remind herself on occasion, her mother was long dead and turned to dust and, therefore, no longer a matter of consequence.

Elisabeth turned her head toward the nursery door, the fingers of her right hand motionless against the bare skin of her throat, her body already inclining forward before she remembered that the baby's father, Daniel, had taken Emily for the long Columbus Day weekend and wouldn't be returning until later that evening.

The sounds had been purely her imagination attempting to fill the inexplicable void she had felt at the child's absence.

It was such a strange fancy, almost as if she loved the child as her own.

But perhaps that was only because her body still retained its need to provide nourishment.

Nodding at the explanation, Elisabeth turned back to the bathroom's vanity mirror and finished dressing.

When she had secured the topmost button and made sure the pins holding the tight bun to the back of her head were secure, she stepped back to appraise the gray-and-mauve plaid jumper and pale lavender blouse she'd selected to wear. The colors complemented the rose-and-milk-glass complexion of the face she now wore and enhanced the color of her eyes.

For they were still her eyes even if they were now set in a younger, more beautiful face than she would ever have dared imagine for herself.

Even Frances might have been jealous of her.

And so wonderfully astonished by the strides her Suffragettes had accomplished. Closing her eyes, Elisabeth silently prayed that her beloved friend had lived long enough to at least see the Nineteenth Amendment ratified.

Frances would have made a much better *Traveler*, but she would not have wished this upon anyone else. If she had only obeyed her mother that morning so long ago and stayed at home she would have lived out her natural life, and in due course, died and been buried.

And forgotten.

And not made to suffer the indignities and…obscene sensations that the flesh she now wore was heir to.

Elisabeth could not bring herself to think of it as the *miracle* both Lillian and Daniel's mother, Judy, inferred it to be. For miracles were joyous and wondrous events for all who witness them.

And that was certainly not the case.

A true miracle would have been for Sara to come back from the abyss. It was Sara the daughter and wife and Emily's true mother they wanted, not the spirit within the animated poppet her body had become.

If self-murder was not a sin and I could be certain that my death would be final this time….

Opening her eyes to the reflection in the glass, Elisabeth tilted the head to one side and frowned. Sara had been a lovely *young* woman, but she'd worn her hair very short and though Elisabeth was allowing it to grow, it was much thicker than she was used to and almost willfully obstinate in her attempts to fashion it. Despite her best efforts, and an innumerable amount of hairpins, a number of curls consistently escaped to cascade down the sides of her face. She was told it was quite becoming, but it still somewhat irked her sense of propriety.

Giving the hair a final pat, Elisabeth picked up the jar of milk she'd siphoned that morning, but, instead of going back to her own room from which she'd descend to the kitchen, she turned and walked to the door directly opposite.

The nursery. Emily's room.

Pressing the jar of warm milk to the front of her jumper, Elisabeth stopped just short of the door and took a deep breath, imagining, even though the door was closed, that she could smell the sweet, light scent of the child – powder and soap and sun-dried linen, a smell that evoked spring even as the year was drawing to a close.

Her breasts (*Sara's breasts*), though empty, ached as she opened the door and walked into the room.

All brightness and light, it was a room she herself would have loved to occupy as a child. There were no sharp corners or unwelcoming shadows, no dark wainscoting or heavy drapes that kept out the light. Gauze curtains, ethereal as mist, moved slowly in the warm draft from the floor's furnace register. Walking to the rocking chair where, at night, she sometimes came to sit and simply watch the sleeping child in its crib, Elisabeth set it to motion.

On those nights, more so lately, she found herself having to fight a deepening urge to pick up the sleeping babe just to feel the warmth of her. It was perplexing. She wasn't Emily's mother, she wasn't anyone's mother, and therefore she had neither claim nor right to feel anything for the child.

Especially the growing sense of love.

But that was a secret Elisabeth swore she would take to the grave.

Whenever that might occur.

Stopping the motion, Elisabeth turned and left the room to Sara's ghost.

★ ★ ★

The eggs did not look like the ones Lillian made, but they were fluffy and not burned and – thanks be to God – *finally* cooked all the way through. Elisabeth was more familiar with the coddled eggs prepared by her mother's cook, so her first attempts at 'scrambling' eggs combined with her complete lack of culinary skill had resulted in either semi-coagulated soup or charred slabs that smelled of brimstone.

And were just as inedible.

She had never been taught to cook, of course, only how to select cooks. How unfortunate that particular skill was no longer essential.

Elisabeth sniffed the air cautiously – at least they smelled fine – before spooning the eggs onto a serving platter.

"I believe the eggs are done," she said, carrying the platter to the table. Bob nodded, but she'd seen the wary look in his eyes as she set the platter down.

Lillian simply smiled up at her. "They look wonderful, dear."

"But looks can be deceiving," she reminded them.

"Well," Bob said, casting all earlier tentativeness aside as he scooped eggs onto his plate with the serving spoon, "like the old saying goes: the proof of the pudding is in the taste."

Oh, dear.

He took more than his usual single scoop and Elisabeth knew it was more than his just being polite; he wanted her to succeed. Yet, both she and Lillian remained still and quiet, and perhaps Lillian was holding her breath as Elisabeth was, waiting for Bob to finish sprinkling a *salt-substitute* and pepper on the eggs and take a bite.

"Mmmm."

Elisabeth exhaled, but it was Lillian who asked, "Well?"

Bob took another forkful and winked. Lillian looked up at Elisabeth and smiled.

"That means he likes it," she explained and lifted some eggs onto her own plate, nodding in agreement when she tasted them. "And he's right, they're delicious. And much creamier than mine…what did you do differently?"

Elisabeth smiled and went to fetch the toast she'd made, a skill – thanks to the electric toasting machine – she excelled in.

"I added a quarter cup of milk and a dash of nutmeg." The

statement was met with stares from both Lillian and Bob. "It was something I saw on a cooking show on the television. Are they really all right? Not overdone?"

"No, they're perfect – really!" Bob said and took another bite. "Lil, maybe you should start watching those cooking shows."

Lillian glared at him, but since Elisabeth knew it was only in jest it was all she could do to keep from laughing.

"Then I'll go fetch the sausages and coffee pot," she said and turned away from the table.

Sausages and coffee, both of which required only the use of such modern marvels as the *microwave oven* and a *Programmable 12-Cup Combination Brew-Right and Warmer*, were two other foods Elisabeth felt most comfortable preparing.

She would not starve.

While they ate, Lillian and Bob spoke to each other and to her. It was another custom Elisabeth was having trouble getting used to, although it seemed – and was confirmed repeatedly on various television programs – that speaking while you ate was the norm.

Her mother, God rest her, had never allowed speaking at the table and thought it the height of vulgarity. If one had to have discourse when food was involved, her mother believed it was only suitable during garden parties and only if asked a direct question by the hostess.

But, as so many continually reminded her, that was then and this was now – an odd idiom, but a useful one.

Setting her fork down on the plate, Elisabeth cleared her throat. Sara's parents looked up.

"Bob, Lillian," she began, "I will never be able to express my gratitude to both of you for the kindness and understanding you have shown me in what must certainly be the darkest time of your lives."

Bob nodded and lifted his coffee cup to his lips, but not quick enough to hide the slight quiver that betrayed his feelings.

"It's been a blessing for us," Lillian said. "You've made it easier."

"Thank you, but I fear that might be very kind, but wholly untrue. I am not Sara."

Lillian's eyes moistened. Bob set down his cup and took her hand.

"No, of course you're not," he said. "We know that, Elisabeth."

"But as long as I remain here, with you, you'll not be able to mourn your daughter."

Elisabeth watched something besides tears fill Lillian's eyes. "I don't understand."

"I think it will be best if I find…other accommodations. Thanks to you, I can – "

"You can't leave."

" – provide for myself and have learned a good many skills I never had before. I can cook and – "

"Elisabeth, be sensible."

" – even use the electrified washing and drying machines. And I'm sure I will be able to find some kind of employment even with my limited—"

"*You can't leave!*"

Lillian had shaken free from her husband's hand and had gotten to her feet.

"Lillian," Elisabeth said as gently as possible, "it's time. Please try to understand I'm only considering what is best for you and Bob. And Emily. She needs—"

"You can't go, it will be like losing Sara all over again. Please, not yet, just give us a little more time."

"Maybe she's right, Lil," Bob said, taking his wife's hand again. "Maybe it would be better if she did—"

Lillian turned and left the room. There were neither hysterics nor muffled sobs echoing back through the house, only a silence that was worse than either. And they sat at the table in that silence, she and Bob, until it became too hard to bear.

"I'm truly sorry, Bob," Elisabeth said, "but I do think my presence here is doing more harm than good."

He nodded, taking up his cup again for solace and staring into it.

"Maybe." He lifted one shoulder. "I don't know. This is new ground for all of us. We knew Sara was going to die, be taken off the respirator after Emily was born. There was no hope, so when she… when you woke up it was a miracle for us as much as for you."

Elisabeth picked up her own teacup to hide behind, not daring to meet his eyes should he see the truth in them.

"But you aren't Sara and I understand how you must feel. We'll manage, but what about Emily?"

The cup trembled in Elisabeth's hand. "Emily's a baby, she doesn't know who I am."

"That's where you're wrong. She smiles every time she sees you."

"She smiles when she sees a beam of sunlight, Bob. I'm just another person for her to enchant. I'm not her mother."

"Maybe not in the usual way, but I've seen you with her. You love her as if you were her mother."

Elisabeth felt her throat tighten as she set the cup back into its saucer and stood up.

"But I am not and never will be. I had better see to the washing up. I believe that I may have used every bowl and pan in the house. Excuse me, please."

Turning, she left Bob to finish his meal. She would reintroduce the subject again at a later date, when emotions – hers included – were not running so high.

That evening when Daniel arrived with Emily an hour before supper, Elisabeth was reading in the family room, as was her habit in order to give Sara's family time alone with each other.

"Danny, talk some sense into her!"

Elisabeth put down her book, a romantic novel her mother would have banned from the house, and turned her head, listening, but all she heard were muffled voices – Lillian's for the most part, but counterpointed with Bob's deeper baritone. Of Daniel she heard very little.

It was only when Emily, her voice sweet and high, began to complain, that the voices stopped and Elisabeth put down her book.

Elisabeth found them still in the entrance hall, talking quietly now. Lillian was clutching a white tissue, a corner of which she kept touching to her eyes as Bob held her about the waist. Daniel held Emily against his shoulder, patting her back to calm her fussing.

None of them saw Elisabeth as she entered the hall, except Emily.

Squealing, the babe held out her hands to her.

"Looks like somebody's happy to see you, Elisabeth," Bob said, smiling. "She missed her mommy."

Oh, God.

234 • P.D. CACEK

A silence as thick as wool descended as they stood in the foyer of Sara's childhood home, and it was only Emily's contented cooing that proved they had not suddenly gone deaf or been transformed into wax statues.

"Oh God, Danny, I'm sorry. I didn't mean it like that."

"It's okay, Bob," Daniel said, "I know what you meant."

Of course he did. Elisabeth kept her eyes down so she wouldn't see Emily reach for her again as she walked to the staircase and began to ascend.

"If you'll excuse me," she said, "I'm afraid I won't be joining you for dinner tonight. I'm not very hungry, but please go in and have your supper."

"Danny." Lillian's voice rose behind her. "Talk to her."

"Elisabeth, look...they told me what you said this morning and I'm—"

Shaking her head, Elisabeth continued up the stairs. "There is no need, Daniel. Good night."

Emily began crying and it was that sound that accompanied Elisabeth all the way to her room. And not even closing the door and leaning back against it could diminish the sound.

It is better this way, better for all of them. Emily will grow up without confusion, and Sara's parents will be able to grieve for their child and finally lay her to rest, and Daniel...Daniel will fall in love and remarry and—

A soft knock sounded at her door, vibrating through her spine.

"Yes?"

"It's Danny...can I come in?"

It was all she could do to keep herself from correcting him – *May I come in* – as she stepped to the center of the room and turned. If nothing else, her upbringing had prepared her well for situations where she was expected to act like a lady of society, composed and serene, trained in the art of burying her emotions regardless of how she actually felt.

That training had failed her once before, when she thought her friend in danger, and she had paid the ultimate price for it.

"Yes," she called, and her voice was calm and steady, "of course you may."

He opened the door slowly and stepped into the room, closing the door behind him. It was improper, but she refrained from saying so since he stayed by the door and didn't move toward her.

"Lillian told me that you want to leave."

"Yes, I think it best."

"She told me that too, and the reason you gave her."

Elisabeth nodded.

"Is it because of me?"

"You?"

He walked past her to the bed and sat down. A similar, though less repugnant, warm sensation fluttered in the pit of her stomach.

"Yeah. I wasn't...*haven't* been very nice to you. It's just—"

"Please." She took a step closer to him. "You don't need to explain, Daniel. I know how hard this is for you and I am so sorry."

"Why are you apologizing? You haven't done anything."

"I took Sara's place."

"No, you didn't. Sara wasn't ever coming back. I know I shouldn't have, but I blamed you for that because I had to blame someone."

"I understand."

"It wasn't your fault."

"Thank you."

"I think Sara would have liked you."

Elisabeth clasped her hands in front of her and squeezed her fingers together until she could feel Sara's heartbeat in them.

"You don't have to go."

"Yes, I do."

He stood up and walked toward her. "Why?"

Why? "Dear God, I understand that society has changed but is every member of it incapable of understanding the simplest construct of communication? I am leaving because I am not Sara, I'm not your wife or Emily's mother. I am...but a living automaton, a breathing *memento mori*."

"But Emily will miss you."

Elisabeth took a deep breath.

"It is for Emily's sake most that I must leave. If I stay it will only confuse her and...and make me into something I am not. It will be better for Emily that I leave now while she is still a baby. She will easily forget me and, in time, it will be as if I was never a part of her life."

Which I never was intended to be.

"Do you want that?"

"Do I...? No, but—"

"Look, I know you're not Sara...all of us know that, but you're good with Emily. Both my mom and Lillian have told me how you take care of her, feed her when I'm not here...and how you're the first one to go to her when she cries at night."

"My room is the closest to hers," Elisabeth explained. "It is simply a matter of location."

"Oh, come on, you know that's not it." Daniel took another step closer. There was very little space between them now. If Elisabeth could have moved she would have fled the room. "You love Emily, don't you?"

"*Love* is such an easy word in this society. People love without thought or contemplation."

"Answer the question."

"It wouldn't change my decision either way."

"Answer the question."

She glared up at him. "It doesn't matter."

He glared back at her. "Answer the question."

Elisabeth felt Sara's eyes whelm with tears, but she was the one who blinked them away. "Yes."

He smiled in victory and Elisabeth wished he were closer so she could strike it from his lips.

"Yes, laughable, isn't it, that I should love the child of the man who wishes I were dead?"

The smile fell.

"Do you deny it, Daniel?"

"Yes."

"Liar."

They held each other's gaze for a moment before he looked away. "Okay, I did, but not anymore. When it first happened, well, you know better than all of us, I guess. Things happen for a reason, Elisabeth, I have to believe that or I'd go crazy. Sara was so happy when she got pregnant. All she talked about was the baby and thinking up silly names we'd never use." He laughed and the sound broke Elisabeth's heart. "She couldn't wait to be a mom, but then when that wasn't going to happen I think…I like to think that maybe she helped make sure Emily would have a mom even if it wasn't her."

Elisabeth nodded even though he wasn't looking at her.

"That is a very lovely sentiment, Daniel, but the harder truth is that when I leave, Emily will forget me and you will be free to marry again and give Emily the mother she deserves."

He stepped back, rubbing the back of his neck. "Well, yes, I suppose I can, but, you see, we're still married."

Elisabeth backed up until her spine found the doorframe.

"We most certainly are not!"

Daniel lowered his hand. "Yeah, we are…legally. You haven't changed your name yet or gotten a new social security card, so… you're still Sara Cortland on paper. And we're still married. I mean, I'm still *married* to Sara Cortland."

He slid both his hands into the back pockets of his pants and shrugged. Taking a deep breath, Elisabeth straightened her back and uttered words she never would have thought she'd be obliged to say.

"If that is the case, then divorce me."

"What?"

"Divorce me so that you will be free to marry someone else. It seems that is the most common thing to do, isn't it?"

"Well, I guess."

"Then there's no problem."

"Or…."

"Or?"

"We stay married and you move back to our…my house and be Emily's mother."

"And be your whore?" She hoped the disbelief and incredulity clearly showed on her face. "How dare you suggest—"

Daniel pulled his hands from his pockets and waved them as if he were trying to stop a runaway coach. "Wait a minute! I'm not suggesting anything like that. Look, I just want Emily to have a mother and father and you're the only mother she knows. She lived inside…that body for almost nine months and I don't want her to forget it…or the only person she thinks of as her mother. If you'll just consider this arrangement, for Emily's sake, I swear I won't touch you or bother you in any way. You'll have your own room and I'll have mine, and Emily will have the family Sara wanted for her."

Elisabeth walked to the bed and sat down on the bed. How could he suggest such a thing and not expect her to revile him for it? She was not Sara Cortland, regardless of what it said on certain government documents, and if she ever hoped to make a new life for herself as Elisabeth Wyman in some town and state where no one knew who or what she was, she had to leave.

She had to.

Daniel walked over to the bed and sat down next to her. "Please, don't cry."

"Cry?" Elisabeth would have been shocked at the audacity of such an assumption had her voice not broken on that single word. "I— I am not crying."

"But you're about to." He touched a spot beneath his right eye. "Sara's… Her cheek always got red, right here, just before she started to cry." He dropped his hand. "I'm sorry, I shouldn't have asked you something like that."

Elisabeth took a deep breath and released it so slowly that by the time the air had run out, her lungs burned.

"No," she said, "you shouldn't have."

"I'm sorry."

"My parents, when my father was alive, that is, had separate rooms. Children understand more than you think, Daniel. My brother and I knew there was no love between them."

"That must have been hard."

"It was and I think that helped make me hard and untrusting and…and terribly frightened of life. I don't want that to happen to Emily. Emily must never have reason to question that her parents are not bonded as one."

He looked confused. "Okay."

"Therefore, and in deference to your suggestion, I propose this slight modification." Her heart…Sara's heart…*their* heart began to beat so fiercely that she feared it would break through the skin. "I know this is a rather brazen and possibly shocking proposal and I know that if my own mother were alive it might possibly kill her, but I suggest that, for the sake of Emily and nothing else, we marry and live under one roof as a man and wife should."

She had no expectation of what he might say next, and so was pleased when he remained silent and only laid his hand upon hers.

Would that he had remained silent.

"That would be great," he whispered, moving closer, "but we are already married, remember?"

She pushed him away.

"No, Daniel, *we* are not, but I'm sure you can arrange something… after a moderate courtship, of course."

"Courtship?"

Elisabeth blinked her eyes slowly. "We hardly know each other, do we not?"

"Um…I guess."

"Well, perhaps a brief courtship might be advisable, considering the uniqueness of our situation. And a small, private ceremony to follow, I think."

Daniel stood up and offered her his arm, which she took.

"Sounds like a plan, although I think we're going to have to call it a renewal of vows, but don't worry, it'll be legal. And, maybe, we can even use your name, Elisabeth, and say it's… I don't know, we'll figure that out." He walked her halfway to the door and let her arm drop. "And I won't push you to do anything…you know, until you're ready. You're right about one thing, we really don't know each other, so if you're never ready to, you know, that's okay too."

Elisabeth understood what he was willing to give up for her and Emily. "Thank you, Daniel."

"You're welcome…Elisabeth."

★   ★   ★

Two weeks later, after a very abbreviated courtship and in front of a small gathering of friends and family, Daniel Allen Cortland and Sara Elisabeth Wyman Cortland renewed their marriage vows on a bright and chilly October afternoon.

Emily Sara Cortland, dressed in a burgundy velvet gown and matching bonnet, served as both flower girl and maid of honor.

CHAPTER TWENTY-EIGHT

Aryeh

"Hello?"

"Mrs. Cooper, it's Ryan, please don't hang – "

...

" – up. *Shit.*"

Ryan glared at the iPhone as if it had been responsible for the woman's rudeness before punching the redial option. He took a deep breath, the words straining against his lips like thoroughbreds waiting for the bell when the connection went through.

"LookIneedto – "

...

" – speaktoyouSHIT!"

Goddamned caller ID anyway. Whatever engi-geek thought of it should be taken out and clubbed to death with baby seals.

Ryan forgot the deep breath and took a deeper swallow of Bloody Mary, the breakfast of champions, instead, before hitting Redial. This time, after four 'rings,' his call went straight to voice mail and he wasn't surprised a bit.

"*...please leave a message after the tone. Beep.*"

Fine.

"Okay, like I said, this is Ryan and I'd like to talk to the both of *you*...not your machine. Call me or I'll keep calling until I fill up all the little electrons in your phone's memory. Promise. It's Sunday, what else I have I got to – "

– beep –

" – do?"

Ryan thumbed the phone off and tossed it onto the couch cushion before finishing his breakfast. He'd give it a few minutes to let the folks natter at each other and get it out of their system before trying again. Lord knows they'd had enough time to get over the worst of their grief – he had.

Almost.

"Yes, sir-eee bob, I'm doin' great."

Yes, he was, he was doing just fine, thank you for asking, and he lifted the empty glass in a toast to himself for being so friggin' strong. If it were an ordinary Sunday, like the ones he'd spent over the last month and a half, he'd have another shot for breakfast and maybe another for dessert and then stretch out with the Sunday funnies and laze around until it was time to drink lunch. But *this* wasn't an ordinary Sunday – he had things he *had* to do and getting drunk wasn't on the list.

Yet.

Ryan looked longingly at the empty glass before setting it down on the mosaic-glass coaster Jamie had given him two Christmases ago and picked up the phone. Redial.

One ringy-dingy. Two ringy-dingies. Three—

"We don't want to talk to you, Ryan."

"And hello to you too, Mr. Cooper."

There was a slight pause then a very soft, very disgruntled greeting. Ryan could hear Mrs. Cooper in the background, telling her husband to hang up, for God's sake just hang up on him. She sounded as if she'd had more than a one-shot breakfast herself.

"I have to go, Ryan."

"He wants to see you."

The silence that followed was so sudden and deep that for a second Ryan thought he'd gone deaf.

"Did you hear me? I said—"

"I heard you. No, it's out of the question."

"Look, I understand, but he asked me to call you. He wants to meet to ask your forgiveness."

Jamie's dad laughed at that. "What the fuck does he expect us to forgive?"

In the background: "*What's he want? What?*"

"I have to go, Ryan."

"Wait. I know how hard this is for you, but...he's a very

religious man and – I don't know why he wants you to forgive him, maybe he feels responsible for what happened."

"My son killed himself. *He* had nothing to do with it."

My son, not Jamie. "He still wants to talk to you two."

"And I want my son back, but neither of those things is going to happen, is it? I'm hanging up, Ryan."

"It'll just take a minute or two. I can drive him over this afternoon when he gets off work and—"

"STOP! We don't want to see him or talk to him or have anything to do with him. Our son's dead and gone and I'm not going to sit in the same room with a stranger who looks like him and sounds like him and—"

"He doesn't really look like Jamie that much anymore, I mean with the beard and everything, and his voice is—"

"Goodbye, Ryan. Don't call us again."

– click –

"Well, okay then," he told the phone, "can't say I didn't try. Jesus, Jamie, your folks really are...."

In pain, that's what they were; they were still in pain and probably would be for the rest of their lives. They'd lost a son and didn't want anything to do with the man who'd taken their son's physical place in the world. And who could blame them?

He felt the same way, but where Jamie's parents had had the luxury of literally being able to distance themselves from the 'situation', Ryan couldn't.

At least not until today.

Sliding the phone into his shirt pocket, Ryan stretched until he heard the muscles in his shoulders creak under the strain. He'd done way too much lifting and hauling over the past two weeks and his poor, bedraggled body was reminding him of that fact. But that was all over and after tonight, when he dropped off the last of the boxes and returned the U-Haul, he could look forward to a nice hot bath, some take-out Chinese, a little TV, and a lot of Cuervo Gold before getting into his jammies by nine.

He'd already asked for and gotten Monday off as a 'sick day' so he'd be able to sleep it (and everything else that had happened since August 24th) off. Just sleep with no one around to give him grief or ask if he was 'okay'.

Because after tonight, he was on his own.

Not that he'd need a whole lot of time to adjust to that particular state of being. Despite Aryeh's resemblance to Jamie – which grew less with each passing day – Ryan had never thought of Aryeh as anything but a temporary houseguest who needed his help in 'connecting' to the twenty-first century. They were cordial to one another but not overly friendly, respectful of each other's space and privacy, and, except for the nightly lessons in computer, cell phone and other remote device operations, generally stayed out of each other's way.

Ryan thought himself a decent teacher and Aryeh a typical student: good at the things he enjoyed, like using the CD player and microwave (he *loved* the microwave) but just hitting about average on other things, like using the computer and TV remote.

"Okay," he told himself, "time to get goin'."

The four moving boxes were sitting in the hallway and when they were gone, there'd be nothing to show that Aryeh had ever been there. And that was good, because when he was gone, the last of Jamie would be too.

It had taken some time and a lot of late nights and more than just a few thank-you bottles of wine, but Jiro had managed to machete his way through all the paperwork and legal red tape and bring forth upon this nation a man named Aryeh Rosenberg.

At which point, James Allan Cooper, Jr. was no more.

May he rest in peace.

While Jiro had done a masterful job with the whole 'name change/legal quest', neither he, nor Dr. Ellison, nor Ryan had been able to convince Aryeh that it was not only okay for him to transfer the money from Jamie's accounts into the new one bearing his name, but would save another complex round of expensive legal fees.

But he refused, loudly and in Hebrew, quoting scriptures – "Thou shalt not steal."

"It's not stealing," Ryan said, having Dr. Ellison translate – just to make sure the message got through – even though Aryeh could understand and speak English well enough when he wanted to. "It's Jamie's money."

"But not mine," Aryeh had said via Dr. Ellison because, like Ryan, he wanted to make sure *he* was understood. "I'm not Jamie."

In the end it was decided that the majority of Jamie's money would go to his family – Jiro would speak to the bank on the 'estate's' behalf, with a smaller amount of $25,000.00 going to one Aryeh Rosenberg.

With which he could start a new life.

L'chaim!

★   ★   ★

Aryeh turned when the door's electric lock buzzed and was reaching up to remove the magnifying glasses as Ryan walked up to the counter.

"Ryan," he said and a smile parted mustache from beard. The beard was filling in nicely and went a long way to disguise the face beneath. "You wait? I be finished in two shakes of a lamb's tail."

Ryan nodded and Aryeh pushed the glasses higher on his nose then turned back to the ring he'd finish in two shakes. The ring, held in metal pinchers beneath a high intensity lamp, flashed a spark of green-red-blue as Ryan leaned against the counter to watch. The lozenge-shaped diamond was about the size of the nail on his little finger and twinkled like a misplaced star with each delicate touch of the wooden-handled tool in Aryeh's hand. The man had skills Jamie's fumble-fingers could never have guessed at.

Ryan watched the repetitive motion and sparkle for a few more minutes before leaving the counter to wander the store. The guard who'd buzzed him in nodded as he passed then went back to dividing his attention between the street in front of the store and the small TV monitor that ran a constant feed from the security camera mounted over the back door. Ryan couldn't see the monitor, and he wasn't about to wander over to take a look, but he was sure that if he had, he would have seen his car. Because Aryeh had proven himself to be such a 'fine worker', the owner had given Ryan permission to park in the loading zone behind the store when dropping Aryeh off or picking him up.

This, considering the lack of on-street parking in the area and the exorbitant prices the parking garages were charging, was a blessing. True, the alley behind the store was narrow, dark, dank and smelled of piss and overheated garbage, but it had two things the mean streets of L.A. didn't: space and surveillance.

If any of the neighborhood panhandlers, bored teens, junkies or jackers so much as paused to admire the Civic's fine lines or take a leak against one of its tires, the guard would have immediately stormed into the back room and thrown his full weight against the door's steel reinforcement.

Ryan had already witnessed the guard in action twice and both times had jumped at the deafening hollow *whack* when the man hit the door.

Pershing Square and the L.A. Jewelry District might have reaped the benefits of urban renewal and the city planners' dreams of turning the City of the Angels into a slightly scaled-down version of New York, but with all its high-rise condos, glass-front Starbucks, visible police presence and four metro stations within easy (and well-lit) walking distance, downtown L.A. was still downtown L.A.

The jewelry store, one of the last remaining family-owned-and-operated in the area, couldn't hope to compete with the 'superstores' when it came to quantity of their gems and precious metals, but what they did have, as far as Ryan was concerned as he browsed the few showcases, were one-of-a-kind masterpieces that could have easily gotten them a place on Rodeo Drive.

Not that the family would ever consider moving, however.

On the drive home one evening, Aryeh had told Ryan about the store and how it had been started by the present owner's great-great-great grandfather, who'd come from Odessa with only the skill in his hands. The man had been a watchmaker and it was this, Aryeh said, that got him the job. He too had been a watchmaker – 'back then', what he called his past life – and knew how to set stones, and the owner had been impressed by this. The owner had also been very pleased that Aryeh thought $17.00 an hour was a king's ransom.

Ryan thought it best not to correct him.

Although Aryeh didn't need to work, he *had* to work. He'd never known how to do anything else. He'd always worked, and worked hard, as his father and his father's father had before him. To be a man was to work...plus he wanted to pay back the money Ryan had forced on him.

"There," Aryeh called, removing the glasses, "done. Mr. Washington? Would you come, please, to watch me put this away?"

The guard, who could probably have bench-pressed Ryan with one hand without breaking a sweat, smiled.

"It'd be my pleasure, Mr. Rosenberg."

The man had a soft, gentle voice that belied his overall dimensions. Ryan could feel the polished hardwood floor tremble with each step the man took as he crossed the room. Walking around the counter to the workbench, he stepped around Aryeh's wheelchair and bent low to admire the ring.

"You do lovely work, Mr. Rosenberg."

"Thank you. From your lips that the new bride will also think so. Now, watch, please, while I take it off the stand and put it in a box."

The guard watched up close and Ryan watched from the opposite side of the shop as Aryeh put on a pair of cotton gloves and carefully took the ring from the vise and, after a quick polish, placed it into a black velvet ring box. The box then went into some sort of safe beneath the counter – Ryan never asked about it – after which Aryeh rolled the chair out of the way.

"You saw?" he asked the guard.

"I saw. You put it in the safe."

"Good." Taking off the gloves, Aryeh set them next to the magnifying glasses and backed the chair up. "Now you please lock the safe and sign the book."

The guard smiled as he did both. "I've never known a more cautious man."

"A cautious man is a safe man," Aryeh answered. "And now, if you will excuse us, we must leave."

"All moved in?"

"Tonight, yes, I will be all moved in. Thank you for asking, Mr. Washington."

The guard walked back to his station next to the front door – going out the back door, though it was much more convenient, would have meant disabling the alarm system which was not going to happen – and Ryan waited until Aryeh had pulled his sweater and lunch tote from the lowest peg of an old-fashioned standing coat-rack before walking up to him. When the buzzer sounded, Ryan opened the door and stepped back to let Aryeh go first.

"Thank you. Good night, Mr. Washington."

"*Guten abend*," the guard said and Aryeh laughed.

"What'd he say?" Ryan asked when they were on the street.

"He said good evening. When the shop is not so busy we talk. I teach him Yiddish and he tells me the best places to eat around here. Are grits kosher?"

The chair rolled over a crack in the sidewalk. "Excuse me?"

"Grits? I'm not sure what they are, but Mr. Washington says he knows a place that makes the best grits in town."

"Oh. Grits are sort of like corn mush…but lumpy."

"Corn mush but lumpy…ah, like kasha?"

"Probably."

"Ah."

They didn't talk again until they reached Aryeh's new apartment down on Maple and Twenty-First. Dr. Ellison had suggested the place, a grand old Victorian that had been reconverted as a 'halfway house' for society's misplaced persons – and since Aryeh fit perfectly into that category, it seemed the logical place for him to live.

His room was on the first floor in what had originally been the front parlor. The bath was down the hall, which bothered Ryan but seemed perfectly natural to Aryeh. And while meals were served communal-style in the dining room directly across the hall from Aryeh's front door, there was a small L-shaped 'kitchenette' in one corner of the room that consisted of a sink, small refrigerator and hotplate in case he got hungry during the night or where he could eat if he just needed some time to be alone.

If it hadn't been for the huge bay window that looked out

onto the quaint, rundown neighborhood, the room with its twin bed, mismatched nightstand and dresser, dinette table and chair (singular) would have been as depressing as the commute which required Aryeh to rise just before dawn in order to catch the bus on Maple, transfer on Fifth for another eight blocks, then wheel across rush hour traffic to get to the shop.

A commute like that would have had Jamie screaming for mercy, but Aryeh loved riding the bus.

Go figure.

When Ryan carried in the last box from the car he found Aryeh carefully folding a brand-new, never-been-worn-by-Jamie tee-shirt into a drawer.

"This is it," Ryan said. "You're all moved in."

Aryeh closed the drawer and pulled his wheelchair around to face Ryan.

"Thank you, Ryan, I know how hard this has been for you."

Ryan set the box down on the table and shrugged. What was he going to say, *"Nah, these things happen"*?

"Look, Aryeh, I know I've been a...."

"*Varen*...wait, before you say anything. I have this."

Ryan watched Aryeh pick up a small white envelope off the top of the dresser. It would have been just as easy for him to roll the chair across the room, but no, he made Ryan come to him.

"What is it?" Ryan asked, "A thank-you note?"

"*Nein*, I found it in the shirt from the hospital I wore and...." He blushed from the eyebrows down, just like Jamie. "I didn't know what it was, so I read. I'm sorry. It is for you, from him, from Yaakov."

Ryan looked down at the envelope. Yaakov – Hebrew for James. Jamie. He took a deep breath but couldn't feel the air move into his lungs.

"God."

"*Kumt.*"

Ryan looked up.

"Come...sit and read. I go make introductions, say hello to the others. You, *bitteh*, please, sit."

Aryeh didn't move until Ryan had sat down at the table.

"I'll just be out here," he said and rolled out of the room, closing the door behind him. "Take your time."

Ryan squeezed the envelope and felt the card inside. It could have been anything, any old card or just some invitation Jamie had slipped into his pocket and forgotten to take out. It could be anything....

Dear Ryan,

I love you, please believe that and remember it because I do love you; I love you with all my heart. But I can't do this anymore.

I'm sorry.
Jamie

Four lines, three sentences.

Ryan closed the card and put it back into the envelope.

Four lines, three sentences, and not one asking Ryan to forgive him.

"Jesus."

Ryan put the envelope with Jamie's brief suicide note into the back pocket of his jeans, which seemed fitting, and walked out of the room. Aryeh was waiting for him in the dining room entrance. There was no one else around, but Ryan could hear voices and the rattling of pots coming from the kitchen at the back of the house.

"Thanks," Ryan said, walking to the front door. "Place is all yours."

"I am sorry for your loss," Aryeh called after him.

Ryan pulled the heavy door open and felt the cloying dampness in the night air against his face.

"Tell me," he asked without turning around, "is suicide a sin with your people?"

"*'Thou shalt not kill.'* It is a sin because it denies the divine gift of life and is in defiance of a man's allotted time."

"Right."

"But did not He also give man free will?" Ryan turned around.

"And who of us knows what our allotted time is?"

Ryan was getting tired of the man answering a question with a question – time to bring out the big gun.

"Okay, how about this one? Doesn't the Bible, sorry the Talmud, say it's a sin, an *averah* for a man to lie with another man?"

Aryeh shrugged. "You mean, maybe, the Torah?"

"Jesus." Ryan rubbed the heels of his hands against his eyes and when he stopped and blinked, Aryeh didn't look anything like Jamie anymore.

"Look, semantics aside, you know what we were, what *I* am, don't you?"

"Yes."

"Then, according to *your* faith, do you think Jamie's burning in hell right now because of it?"

Aryeh sat back in the wheelchair and placed his elbows on the armrests, lifting his clasped hands toward his chest.

"My faith teaches many things, but I am not a rabbi or a learned man. I am a man out of his place in the world and for some that would be a sin too, no?" He looked up at Ryan. "Should I then say what is a sin against another man? No, I cannot judge, but, from the things I have heard on the television maybe if one loves and is loved, regardless of who it is, how can that be wrong?"

It took Ryan a minute, but then he chuckled. "Well, there are a lot of other people who'll be more than happy to explain that to you."

"Yes, maybe, but do I have to listen?"

"No, you don't."

Ryan reached into his jacket pocket and held out the folded sheets of paper Dr. Ellison had given him. A part of him wondered if he would have done that if the man's last answers had been different, but it didn't matter. It was the right thing to do.

"*Vos iz?*" Aryeh squinted at the three-page list of names, addresses and phone numbers, turning them toward the energy-saving porch light.

"They're your descendants," Ryan said. "Grandchildren and great-great-great…however many grandchildren. The ones on the first page, in bold, are members of your family living nearby."

Ryan saw tears form in the eyes that weren't Jamie's and quickly looked away, nodding at the pages.

"The first one is the closest. A dentist. Name's Joel Rosowsky and he's out in Norwalk…that's not that far away."

"Rosowsky?"

Ryan nodded and backed to the divided front steps: stairs to the left, ramp to the right, handrail in the middle. He stepped down, holding the rail for support.

"Your daughter Esther's family." He took another step down. "The number's there, if you want to call and connect, although I don't know what you'll tell him. Good luck. Okay, I better be going."

"Thank you, Ryan."

Ryan nodded as he turned and hurried down the rest of the stairs. He didn't turn around again until he was at the sidewalk. Aryeh was still holding the pages in a death grip, but he looked up and smiled.

"Goodbye, Ryan…I wish you peace."

"*Shalom*, Aryeh," Ryan waved and turned away.

Goodbye, Jamie.

CHAPTER TWENTY-NINE

Crissy

"And...lights out! Great. Okay, everyone on stage for notes."

There were sounds of yawning and stretching as the cast gathered up their scripts and pencils and started moving toward the stage.

Because it was only a rehearsal, the members of the cast who hadn't been in the scene had taken seats in the house instead of waiting in the wings or downstairs in the basement's combination greenroom/costume/prop storage/dressing rooms. Most of the cast complained about the cramped quarters and poor lighting, but it seemed to Crissy that they were always complaining about one thing or another and she couldn't understand why.

Okay, so it was only a reconverted warehouse at the end of a strip mall in Long Beach – so what? It had a stage and lights and a sound booth and a box office and people paid money to see the shows they put on.

It was a *real* theater and she was part of it.

Maybe not in a major part...not yet...but that would come.

"Come on, people, on stage." The director, George, a retired electrical engineer, clapped his hands together. "Hustle, hustle."

"Hustlin' here, boss," Kevin, the high school senior who was playing young Ebenezer Scrooge, shouted and lifted himself, one-armed, onto the stage.

Someone applauded, someone else groaned.

When everyone was finally settled – Crissy found a spot and sat along the edge of the stage, legs dangling, pencil poised – George cleared his throat and picked up his notebook.

"First, let me say that you're all doing a fine job, but let's keep at those lines, people. I'd love to have full memorization by next week."

More groans filled the air, but not from her. She'd already

memorized her lines and George knew that. She'd always been a fast study, she told him, and he told her how much he appreciated it and how he wished all his actors could be more like her when it came to learning their lines.

Mr. Byrd used to tell her the same thing.

George began with notes to the various kids in the play so they, and their stage mothers, could leave first. Crissy rubbed the back of her neck and tried not to yawn – getting notes always felt like such a waste of time. She knew her lines, she knew her blocking, and she'd seen *A Christmas Carol* every year on TV since she was a kid, so what could he say that she really needed to know?

Fifteen minutes later, she found out.

"Okay...Mrs. Cratchit – Helen."

Crissy poised her pencil over her script...for show.

"First, let me say that you almost had me in tears during the Christmas Future scene when Bob is talking about Tiny Tim. The look of loss on your face is perfect... keep doing that."

There were mutters of agreement and some applause. Crissy hid her face against the teenage girl playing the Ghost of Christmas Past. The girl laughed and patted her shoulder.

"Aww, shucks, sir," Crissy said as she sat up, "it t'weren't nothin'."

George smiled. "Well, nothin' is somethin' here. But, aside from that, you're still playing Mrs. Cratchit too young."

Crissy felt the blush start just below her eyes.

"I know you have a lot of vitality and energy," George continued, "but remember...this is a woman of the late nineteenth century who's overworked and over-worried and has had too many children, one of which she knows is going to die. She's worn out, both mentally and physically, and you're playing her like a high school cheerleader."

The cast laughed and Crissy wanted to crawl into a deep hole and die.

Again.

"Not that energy on stage is a bad thing, people, but get *inside* your character and act accordingly. Helen?" Crissy looked up. "Just play your age and you'll be fine."

Crissy nodded and scribbled *TOO YOUNG!!!!!* in her script as George went on to the next set of notes.

Just play her age? What did he think she was doing? But he was right; she was still acting *too young* on stage and off.

The trouble was that she didn't know how to *act* like a forty-two-year-old woman and make it look real. Being on stage and pretending to be an adult for a couple of hours was okay, but real life didn't have scripts or a director to tell you what you were doing wrong.

Real life sucked.

The only good things about it so far were Frank and having gotten to see Mr. Miles Byrd on stage.

The theater was a little black-box set-up that had eighty seats, of which only twelve were occupied the night they went. The set was minimal, the lightning almost nonexistent, and the costumes provided by the actors themselves.

Crissy recognized the blue-knit vest Mr. Byrd wore throughout the play, although it was much more shapeless and moth-eaten than she remembered it back in high school. He called it his 'vest of leadership' and wore it to every rehearsal, even in the summer…and she would have recognized it anywhere, which was good, because she wouldn't have known the stumbling, wheezing, overacting *old* man on stage was Mr. Byrd without it.

He was awful.

Fortunately Frank hadn't asked her what she thought of the performance, so she didn't have to tell the truth. But it did give her a renewed sense of confidence – Christ, if Miles Byrd could get parts, she'd be a shoo-in.

Crissy checked every online audition notice within the Greater L.A./San Fernando Valley area and circled the ones she *knew* she could get. When Frank, her self-appointed chauffeur, wasn't available, she bummed rides with Kate or one of 'Helen's' other friends – all of whom had accepted Dr. Stanton's explanation about her temporary inability to drive.

"It's the stroke, you see. Helen will have to learn to drive all over again, just like when she was sixteen."

Right.

She'd auditioned for five shows at five theaters, giving great auditions, in her opinion, but wasn't called back before landing the role of Mrs. Cratchit.

Which she was still playing 'too young'.

George closed his notebook and looked up.

"Okay, gang, that's all the notes for tonight. This is a build weekend, so I hope to be seeing as many of you as can make it here Saturday at ten. If not...I *know* I'll be seeing all of you at Sunday's rehearsal. Call's a half hour earlier than usual for head shots. Ladies, go easy on the makeup. Gentlemen, please shave unless your character has a beard. Dark colors work best and avoid prints. What else? Oh, right – bios. ASAP people or I'll write one for you...and I promise it won't be pretty." He waited until the laughter died down. "Remember, we open on December fifth and that's only six weeks away so study, study, study those lines. Thank you all, good work and good night."

There was a dutiful round of applause and the company left the stage, stopping to collect sweaters and coats and purses before heading out into the damp autumn night.

Crissy tossed her script into her large carryall bag and grabbed her coat off the back of a chair but didn't put it on. It wasn't particularly warm in the theater, not compared to what it'd been under the stage lights, but she felt hot and prickly and irritated.

Not that anyone seemed to notice.

Back in high school, everyone, including Mr. Miles Byrd, would have seen how *irritated* she was and come over to ask if there was anything they could do.

But not here.

Crissy had gone out of her way to get to know most of the cast and they were okay, but most of them had worked with each other in other productions at other theaters and she was the 'new girl on the block'...in old girl's clothing. To the cast members she felt most drawn to, the high school kids like herself, she was just another middle-aged nonentity. To the women 'Helen's' age, most of whom had been knocking around the L.A. Basin Theater Scene since they'd been ingénues, she was an interloper with talent – a dangerous combination. To the wives of the mature actors, she was single and therefore desperate. And to the unmarried/divorced actors in the production...?

She didn't want to know what they thought of her.

"Hey, Helen?"

Speak of the devil.

Crissy pulled her carryall onto one shoulder and turned around to find Arthur Ford, the man playing Bob Cratchit, smiling at her. Tall, pale and skeletal, with crinkly red hair and pug-bulgy brown eyes, he doubled as the Ghost of Christmas Future and was a mortician in real life. 'Art imitating life' was one of his catchphrases and he always expected people to laugh at it.

It was all Crissy could do not to grimace every time he took her hand on stage.

Arthur Ford was going through an emotionally wrenching divorce from his wife of twenty-two years and made sure that every woman in the cast – especially Crissy – was aware of the pain and loneliness he was suffering.

Crissy tightened the grip on her bag and started sidestepping toward the door.

"Hey, Art…what's up?"

"First, I just wanted to add to what George said – you were great… *are* great. Really. Do you want to know how I got my voice so low when I was doing the speech about Tiny Tim? It's because I looked over at you and saw your face…you had tears in your eyes. Man, that just blew me away and I got this lump in my throat and could barely talk. It was great…I mean you were."

Crissy kept moving toward the exit. "Thanks."

"But I don't agree with George about you needing to act older."

She stopped. "Really?"

"No. I don't see why Mrs. Cratchit can't be a vibrant, you know, outgoing woman who giggles."

"I…giggle? When?"

"Huh? Oh, when, you know, Martha comes in and tells you about her day and stuff."

"I giggle."

"Yeah, and I think it's cute. I've never seen it done before but I think it adds a whole new dimension to the character."

Crissy shook her head. She had no idea she giggled.

"Hey, Helen…I was just wondering if you needed a ride home? It's still early and we could, you know, maybe stop for a drink or something on the way if you're not too tired."

"Huh? Oh, thanks, but—"

Arthur Ford backed up two steps and nodded. "Right, your boyfriend always picks you up."

My boyfriend?

"And that's really cool. But, hey, if it doesn't work out, I'm available." He laughed like it was just a joke. "Seriously though, if you'd ever like to get together to run lines and maybe work on, you know, your delivery, I can do that too."

He gave her a knowing wink and walked away to ask the light and sound tech – a girl half his age – if she needed a ride home.

Crissy left the theater shaking her head.

"Hey, Helen...over here."

Frank was parked in his usual spot in the handicap space directly in front of the stage door exit, leaning against the car's front bumper. He waved and the drops of mist on his coat sleeve glistened under the theater's security lights.

"It's raining, you know, put your coat on."

Crissy glared up at him. "Don't tell me what to do. I'm fine!"

"Okay." He stepped back and opened the passenger door for her. "How was rehearsal?"

"Fine," she said and got in. "You going to keep that open all night? Close it."

Crissy bunched the coat in her lap and slumped against the seat as he closed the door and walked around to the driver's side.

"Seat belt," he said as he got in and started the engine. "You okay?"

"Fine. Why do you always have to park in the handicapped spot? You shouldn't do that and I know where you are, so you don't have to shout like I'm deaf or anything."

Frank backed the car up slowly then gently put it in drive. "Okay, what happened?"

"*Nothing* happened. It's just that you're not supposed to park there. It's for handicapped people and you're not handicapped."

"No, but I thought it'd be easier for you to—"

"I'm not *handicapped*! How dare you say something like that?"

Frank eased the car onto Alamitos Avenue. "I'm sorry, I didn't mean to imply that you're—"

"Well, I'm not! And when are you going to teach me to drive?

You said you were going to teach me to drive so you don't have to keep picking me up."

"I like picking you up."

"Well...I just want to be able to drive myself places, that's all."

Frank nodded and turned on the windshield wipers. It was raining harder now and for a moment the only sounds that filled the car were the soft patter of rain and the *swish-swish-click* of the wipers. Frank didn't like to have music on when he drove; he said it distracted him.

He was still a dweeb.

"Well, when are you?"

"When am I what?"

SIGH. "Going to teach me to drive?"

A light caught them on Seventh.

"Crissy, we've already talked about this."

Maybe it was the way he said it or the pitch of his voice or something, but Crissy felt her face get hot. It was the rotted cherry on the puke sundae that had been her *too young, giggling* night.

"You're not my father!"

"What? Crissy, I never said I was."

"Then stop acting like it. You can't tell me what to do!"

He took a deep breath and Crissy saw his hands tighten on the steering wheel as they passed a street lamp.

"No, but as your doctor I can...."

"Lie to me and think I'll believe it?"

"What? Hold on a minute, okay?"

Flipping on the turn signal, Frank cranked the wheel hard right and cut in between a van and pickup truck. Crissy's yelp was joined by the blare of horns that continued long after Frank pulled the car into an empty space in the Vagabond Inn's parking lot.

Crissy heard a male voice shout something when Frank turned off the engine, but she wasn't about to look. She slid down in the seat.

"Now – " he turned off the engine and twisted toward her, " – what the hell is going on?"

Full frontal confrontation was never her strong suit. "Nothing."

"Nothing? Come on, you've been acting like a blister ready to pop since you got in the car. What happened? You were fine when I dropped you off. Did someone say something about your acting?"

Why did he say that?

"NO! Nothing happened! Everything's *fine*! Except I can't play *old* and I giggle."

He leaned back against the door. "Ah."

"It's not *ah*! You're lying to me."

There was enough light from the hotel sign for Crissy to see the confused look on his face. *Good.*

"About what?"

"About *everything*!"

Frank took a deep breath. "Could you be a bit more specific, please?"

"I've read those pamphlets the hospital gave me and I've looked things up on the internet – you know, WebMD – and it's been over four weeks." He shook his head. Crissy continued. "Four weeks…F-O-U-R. That's how long a person who had a heart attack shouldn't drive and it's been longer than four weeks for me, Frank."

He blinked then nodded.

"Well, yes, you're right. People who have suffered certain *types* of heart attacks can resume driving after four weeks…with permission from their doctors."

Despite the warm air blowing from the car's heater, a very cold, un-California-like chill raced up Crissy's spine. She pulled the sleeves of her coat up over her arms "You just want to keep me a prisoner, don't you? You want me to be dependent on you so everyone will think you're my boyfriend!"

"Oh. So everyone thinks I'm your boyfriend, huh?"

"DON'T CHANGE THE SUBJECT!"

"Crissy, stop yelling and calm down. Listen to me. Yes, it's been over four weeks, but your body didn't just suffer a cardiac event, okay? It needs to be taken care of and if this whole acting thing is going to get you this upset, maybe you should drop out."

"Drop out? Oh, you'd like that, wouldn't you? Then you could keep me a prisoner full-time, huh?"

"Jesus, Crissy…."

"It's not fair. It's not my body!" *Why is this happening to me?* "I shouldn't have to suffer for someone else's problem. I'm not supposed to have hamburgers or Coke or french fries or chips or anything that has too much salt on it or is too greasy or tastes good!"

"Crissy, I didn't say you can't have those things, you just can't eat like a typical teenager anymo—."

"But I *AM* a teenager!" Crissy took a deep breath. "I have to take pills for the rest of my life, you know that? And you won't let me drive or get a job."

"I didn't know you wanted to get a job."

"That's not the point! Besides, I *can't* get a job. I don't know how to *do* anything."

He reached for her. "Crissy, calm down."

"DON'T TALK TO ME LIKE I'M A CHILD!" She screamed so loud it even hurt her ears and she could feel her heart – *Helen's* heart – pounding like a drum.

"I'm sorry, but listen to me, you don't need to work. Helen's finances can—"

"Don't say that name! I hate Helen and I hate her money. Why did she have to die in the first place?"

"Maybe because if she didn't you wouldn't be here."

If he'd stopped there, if that had been the last thing he said, Crissy might have said she was sorry…but that wasn't the last thing he said.

Frank leaned forward and cocked his head. "Are you on your period?"

★   ★   ★

He'd tried to explain.

He'd tried to apologize.

He'd tried to joke her out of it.

He'd failed.

Hurricane Crissy stormed through the apartment, kicking at the piles of dirty clothes on the floor that she hadn't gotten around to picking up, slamming doors, throwing trashy YA romances and fashion magazines against the walls, and swiping the accumulated and incriminating evidence of pizza cartons, McDonald's wrappers and take-out containers off whatever piece of furniture she'd left them on. She was making a mess but *so what?* It was her place, wasn't it?

In answer to her own question, Crissy grabbed what she'd thought was an empty kung pao chicken carton off the breakfast counter and hurled it at the *Love Never Dies Bram Stoker's Dracula* poster she'd put up over the fireplace.

It wasn't empty.

When *she* moved in, the whole place was off-white with beigey-tanny carpets, beige furniture and ice-white appliances. *Boring!* There were a few paintings on the walls – all pastels and grays – a few framed photos of people she didn't know, books she would never read even if someone put a gun to her head, all carefully lined up in their built-in cases. In the white-and-chrome bathroom, the beige and tan towels were hanging neatly, and the white queen-sized bed was made. There weren't any clothes on the floor, no bananas or anything else going overripe in the empty cut-glass fruit bowl, and not so much as a glass sitting to air dry in the rack next to the sink.

If it hadn't been for the thin layer of dust on the tables and flat-screen TV Crissy would have thought she'd walked into one of those 'model' homes her mom was always dragging her to for 'fun decorating tips'.

Crissy decided Helen Louise Harmon the First had been one boring middle-aged woman without any imagination whatsoever. And she'd also decided to change all that.

Keeping the furniture, window treatments, and 'neutral' floor coverings in the kitchen and bathroom – who cared about furniture, floors and windows anyway? – Crissy had the condo repainted according to her own sense of color and to reflect the fact that she was living near the ocean.

D'oh.

Purples, lavenders and pinks covered the walls and piles of floor cushions that looked like seashells and surfboards and beach towels made the place look cozy and covered a lot of the boring carpet. There were no pictures of unicorns or sappy inspirational sunsets for her – no, ma'am – just a lot of framed movie and Broadway show posters because they made her happy.

Just like the *Dracula* poster over the mantelpiece had made her happy…before she'd splattered it with week-old fuzzy kung pao chicken.

Eeuwe.

But at least the poster was under glass, so she could clean it.

Later.

When she felt like it.

IF she felt like it.

And if she didn't?

"Who the...*fuck* cares? This is my place now!" she yelled at the poster because it was the only thing staring back at her. "I can do anything I want. And I can *eat* anything I want! Frank doesn't own me."

And to prove that to the poster, Crissy stomped her way through the clutter to the kitchen and yanked open the refrigerator door. The cans of Coors rattled in the holders, reminding her of their presence. Thus reminded, Crissy grabbed one and popped the top. She'd been so nervous when she'd bought them she almost dropped the six-pack, but the man behind the counter didn't even ask for her ID. He just took her money, thanked her, bagged the beer and told her to have a nice day.

Maybe looking forty-two had *some* advantages, after all.

Hoisting the can to her lips, Crissy took a long swallow and choked it down. Just because she *could* drink didn't make it any easier.

She bought Coors because it was the beer her father and all his friends drank. It was the only beer she was used to snitching, but it wasn't any better tasting than she remembered it.

Still – it was beer and she wasn't supposed to have any.

Crissy finished the can, grimacing after each swallow, burped, and tossed the empty into the dish-filled sink. The can bounced out and landed on the floor as Crissy thumbed open a carton and grabbed a slab of the pepperoni and sausage calzone she'd had for lunch.

The cheese was hard and the congealed grease clung to her teeth like an oil slick, but that didn't stop her from taking a second huge bite as she slammed the refrigerator door shut and....

Her heart fluttered.

Crissy set the calzone down on a Chinese take-out menu next to the coffee maker and took a deep breath.

This time her heart skipped a beat.

Then another.

And another.

And suddenly her face was hot and she got dizzy and had to sit down, right then, right there on the kitchen floor.

It was so weird. She didn't hurt, but when she tried to get up she couldn't – her legs and feet were tingling and wouldn't work right. Leaning forward, Crissy got to her hands and knees and crawled into the living room, making it all the way to the couch before her left arm cramped.

"Oh, God."

She knew what was happening; she'd read about it in the hospital pamphlets and online. Her body was having a heart attack; it was going to die and take her with it.

"No please! I'm sorry…I won't do it again. I'll eat better, I promise."

But Helen's heart didn't believe her and kept fluttering and pounding and twitching as Crissy dragged her purse off the couch and upended it onto the coffee table. Her new cell phone – with all the bells and whistles and Frank's phone number programmed into it as her emergency contact – slid off the table and into her lap.

Sobbing because she was really scared even though there wasn't any pain – except for her arm but that was good because *real* pain meant something was really wrong. *Right?*

He answered after the fourth electronic ring.

"Hey, Crissy…look, I'm sorry I said—"

"Help!"

"Crissy, what's the matter? What's wrong?"

"My heart…it—"

She started to cry because she couldn't think of how to describe the pain-not-really-pain and the cramp and tingles and dizziness and how hot her face felt. Crying was easier than explaining.

"I'm not that far away." Frank's voice got louder and softer in time with the pounding sound in her ears. "I'll be right there."

"H-h-h-hurry!"

"I am. Just try to relax, okay? Crissy? Crissy!"

Crissy nodded and lay down on the floor between the couch and coffee table.

And that's where he found her – still clutching the phone even though she'd managed to turn it off somehow – when he let himself in. He had a key and that had been one of their first real fights, the fact that he thought he should have a key to her place just because he was a doctor. But she was glad now…even though she'd probably never tell him that.

"Crissy…can you hear me?"

She felt him pick her up and carry her into the bedroom, where he put her on the bed and then got a wet washcloth from the bathroom to wipe her face. *Frank* was sweet and worried and made sure she was comfortable, but then *Dr. Stanton* showed up.

"All right, stop crying and take a deep breath," *Dr. Stanton* said and flashed a pen light into her eyes. "Now tell me where it hurts."

Crissy told him and pointed to her left arm.

"Describe the pain."

She did the best she could.

Dr. Stanton sat back down on the edge of the bed and picked up her left hand, checking her racing pulse against his watch. When he was finished he grunted and put her hand down, then reached over and squeezed her upper arm and shoulder.

"Ow!"

"Your muscles are tight. What did you do last night?"

"Nothing?"

"Crissy."

"Kate took me bowling."

Dr. Stanton took a deep breath. "Bowling. How many beers did you have tonight?"

She blinked her eyes innocently.

"Stop acting and answer the question."

"Only one."

"I saw the carnage, so let's skip the denial on this next question: besides eating like the careless little sixteen-year-old you are—"

"Seventeen."

"How much water have you been drinking?"

Crissy shrugged.

Dr. Stanton sighed. "Have you been drinking any?"

She shrugged again.

"How about your medication? Have you been taking that?"

"Yes!"

"Well, thank God for small favors," Dr. Stanton said and his voice got softer when she started to cry. "Okay, calm down. I called for an ambulance from the car. They'll be here soon and then we'll run a full series of tests at the hospital.

"Am I…going to die?"

He looked at her. "Do you want to die?"

"N–no."

"Good, then stop trying so hard to kill yourself."

"I— I'm not!"

"Yes, you are. Look, Crissy, you can't…." He took a deep breath and she could almost see him counting to ten. "Your body can't handle what you're doing to it, okay? It survived a major stroke and cardiac surgery and, unless you decide to make some pretty drastic and important lifestyle changes as of this moment, all my work will have been for nothing. Think of this as a wake-up call. You get with the program or you die. It's as simple as that."

She was so scared she couldn't cry.

"And to answer your immediate question, no, I don't think you're dying or having another attack. You're probably dehydrated and your blood pressure is undoubtedly through the roof. Most of the junk… most of the things you've been eating contain large amounts of sodium – just like it said in those pamphlets you said you read. Your arm's cramping because you went bowling and I think you might just have the worst case of indigestion known to man. At least I hope so."

"That's not very nice."

"No, it's not, but it might make you think about some things. I'll have more answers after I've run some tests and got you on IVs. Which means, miss, you will be spending the night and following few days at the hospital. Then, if everything checks out—"

"But I'm supposed to help build the set on—" He glared at her. "But I don't really need to be there."

"Good. Now, let's just take this one step at a time, shall we?" Frank turned his head toward the bedroom's double window and stood up. "I hear a siren…I'll go wave them over. You going to be okay for a minute?"

"It's not fair, Frank."

"I know."

"I'm only seventeen, Frank. I'm supposed to be seventeen."

"Crissy, stop it."

"But this isn't my body and it's sick and old. I'm trapped in here and I'll never be able to get back all the years I lost. I'm only seventeen and I'll never even date again…no guy's going to want to go out with me now."

They both heard the EMTs come in. Frank shouted at them to come back into the bedroom and then kneeled down and put his face close to hers.

"I wouldn't say no guy would want to go out with you, Crissy. I happen to know one who very much wants to go out with you."

"Art?"

"Who?"

"No one."

"Well, I don't know who this *Art* character is, but you just get better and I'll introduce you to this *other* guy. Okay?"

Crissy smiled and really hoped Frank was talking about himself.

"Okay…cross my heart."

PART SEVEN
EPILOGUE
DECEMBER 24, 2017

CHAPTER THIRTY

Bess

Gathering up the last of the gaily wrapped presents she'd hidden behind the sundries on the topmost shelf of the linen closet, Elisabeth stepped from the chair and quietly tiptoed down the hall. She allowed herself only a moment's pause at the open door of Emily's room to gaze in at the face of the sleeping child, illuminated in the band of warm yellow light from the hallway.

"God bless and keep you, little one," she whispered before continuing down the hall.

Daniel was sitting like a raja in front of the tree they'd strung with fairy lights and decorated with glittering glass ornaments. He was leaning forward, elbows resting on the knees of his flannel lounging pants, a screwdriver in hand and a frown on his face. Before him lay an assortment of gears, knobs, springs and brightly colored pieces of wood of various sizes that would, when built, become something called an 'activity center'.

Daniel's parents had bought it for Emily.

"Is it going well?" she asked as she crossed the room to place the presents under the tree.

"Oh, yeah, this is so simple *only* a child can do it." He smiled at her. "*More* presents? She's only four months old, you know."

"I do," she answered and placed a gift wrapped in blue paper with white flocked snowflakes next to one wrapped all in red, "but how do you know they're all for Emily? Mr. Claus may have left one or two for you."

Daniel set the screwdriver down and scooted on his hands and buttocks toward the tree.

"Really?" He picked up a present decorated in smiling snowmen and shook it. "Have I been a *good* boy?"

Elisabeth took the present from him and used it to tap him lightly on the head. "You have been…tolerably good, but *this* one is for Emily, from Mrs. Claus."

"Oh – Mrs. Claus." Straightening his legs, he rolled onto his belly and began pointing to one present after another. "How about this one? Is this for me? Or this one? Oh…what about that great big one back there with the reindeers?"

Elisabeth folded her robe beneath her and sat down next to him. "Don't you remember, I told you – the presents wrapped in reindeer paper are presents to Emily from Santa, the ones wrapped in paper with snowmen are presents to Emily from Mrs. Claus."

"Right. So *we're* not giving her any presents?"

Elisabeth tapped an ornament and watched her reflection dance within the bright silver ball.

"No, this year and perhaps for a few more, Emily's gifts will only come from Mr. and Mrs. Claus."

"Okay, but she's a little young to care about that now. I don't even think she'll understand what she's getting or why."

"You're probably right, but it's important to have a tradition."

"Like putting the presents out on Christmas Eve."

"That's when Santa comes, isn't it?" She handed him a small present wrapped all in green.

"Yep." He shook the gift and smiled when it rattled. "I guess my folks did the same thing, I mean, there were gifts under the tree before Christmas, but there were always new ones on Christmas morning." He looked up at her. "I know because I counted them before I went to bed."

"You see, Santa came to you as he will come to Emily."

"Is that what your parents did for you?"

Elisabeth took the present from his hand and placed it back under the tree, letting the delicate pine fronds brush against her cheek as she reached beneath the branches for the present she'd wrapped in gold paper.

"No," she said as she sat up, "my mother had no patience for fantasy in any form. Gifts were given, naturally, as the custom demanded, but in my mother's house Christmas was a time of contemplation and reflection. We'd go to church for the Christmas Eve service and exchange gifts in the morning. But Christmas Day itself was rather bleak."

Daniel took her free hand and squeezed it gently.

"That sucks."

Elisabeth was getting used to the twenty-first century's language.

"Yes, it did indeed suck. But that's not to say my brother and I didn't appreciate the gifts we received. My mother had wonderful taste, but none of the presents were ever from Santa or Mrs. Claus. A child's wonder lasts for such a short time. I want Emily to have that and cherish it and to pass it on to her own children."

The pressure on her hand grew to a warm caress. "I want that too. So…what other traditions do you have in mind?"

"Besides finishing the activity center?"

Daniel looked back at the unfinished project and made a face.

"I think…that *both* her grandfathers should help me put it together when they show up for dinner tomorrow. Okay?"

Elisabeth sighed and turned her hand so she could hold his. "Fine, but just this once and only because she is still so young. I suspect there will be a number of things *Santa* will be bringing over the next few years that will require your sole help in assembling – tricycles, doll houses, a hope chest—"

"A hope chest?"

"Another tradition," she said and held out the gold-wrapped present. "Like this one."

Daniel let go of her hand to take the gift and sat up. Smiling like a child, his eyes reflecting the twinkling lights, he shook the box gently.

"Heavy, what is it?"

"Why don't you open it and find out."

"Now?"

"My mother allowed us to open one gift on Christmas Eve…it is the one tradition of hers that I'd like to keep. Go on. Open it."

"Okay, but I'm not going to be the only one doing this." Standing up, Daniel walked to the back of the tree and pulled out a small present wrapped all in white with a silver bow. "You're not the only one who hides presents. Go on," he said, kneeling in front of her, "you first."

Elisabeth took the present and noticed her hands were trembling ever so slightly. He'd given her gifts before – some small, like new clothing and driving lessons, some beyond measure, like his hand in marriage and allowing her to be Emily's mother – but this would be their first Christmas exchange and that made it so terribly important.

Beneath the white paper was a white velvet jewel box and when she opened it, Elisabeth felt the air within her body swell to near bursting. The cameo, carved of pink coral and set in a filigreed nest of bright yellow gold, showed the side view of a woman with hair piled high and pearls gracing her long slender neck.

The woman in the cameo looked exactly as Elisabeth remembered herself.

"It's beautiful," she said. "Thank you, Daniel."

"Thank Santa Claus."

Elisabeth leaned forward and kissed his cheek. "Thank you, Santa…now, open yours."

She expected him to tear open the paper the way she'd seen children and adults do on the television commercials that had started just before Halloween, but he stopped to read the small card she'd included and that almost brought tears to her eyes.

To Daniel, Thank you for giving me back my life. Yours – Bess

"Bess?"

"Open it, please."

And while he did, she held her breath, wondering what his reaction would be. When she first found it, it seemed the perfect gift, but now she wasn't sure. If he hated it or it hurt him in some way, she'd never forgive herself.

"Oh...Bess."

He lifted the framed photograph out of the box and let the box fall, forgotten. The picture showed two young people very much in love. They stood hand in hand at the edge of the green field, looking back at the camera over their shoulders and smiling.

Elisabeth watched him touch the woman's face in the photo.

"I found it in a box of photos at your in-laws. They said they'd never gotten around to putting them into an album. I asked if I could have it."

He looked up at her. "This is the day we got engaged."

"Your mother told me. It's such a wonderful picture it needs to be set out where Emily can see it as she grows. This was her beginning as much as it was yours and Sara's. I don't know what we'll tell Emily about what happened to her mother or if she'll ever be able to understand it, but the past you and Sara shared needs to be remembered."

"It will be."

Standing, Daniel crossed the room and put the photo on the mantle, beneath which three filled stockings hung – bearing the names Emily, Daniel and Elisabeth embroidered in gold thread.

"Thank you...Bess. Bess, yeah, I like that name, it suits you. Now—" He held out his hand and waited for her to stand and take it, then led her to the sofa and motioned for her to take a seat. "One more tradition and then I'll put the activity center back in its box."

Walking to the bookcase to the right of the fireplace, he pulled out a large, thin volume, the cover of which reflected the Christmas tree's lights as he sat down.

"My dad found this and brought it over when he dropped off the activity center. Have you ever read it?"

Daniel turned the cover toward her. *The Night Before Christmas.* Elisabeth took the book and opened it. It'd been designed for children, the pages filled with colorful illustrations of a modern artist's concept of what the Victorian era looked like. The poem itself was relegated to a narrow white band down the middle of the page.

"*A Visit From St. Nicholas*. I know the poem very well, my brother read it every Christmas Eve."

"Good, then that's one tradition we have in common. My dad read it to me every Christmas Eve before I went to bed. I've never read it out loud before, but—"

Emily woke up, the sound of her still-sleepy cry whispering through the baby monitor on the end table. Daniel handed her the book and was starting to get up when Elisabeth stopped him.

"I have a bottle all ready for her. Stay here and we'll be right back."

Elisabeth hurried off, shushing the air and calling, "Mommy is coming," as she hurried to the nursery. Emily had pushed herself up onto her hands and turned her head, smiling, when Elisabeth entered the room. Using the hall light to see by, Elisabeth changed Emily's diaper then wrapped her in a knit blanket to keep away the chill.

After a momentary detour into the kitchen to warm the bottle, they came back into the living room – mother and child – and took their place on the sofa.

"Go on," Elisabeth said, placing the nipple between the baby's lips, "we're ready."

"Okay. Here we go."

As Emily drank Elisabeth listened while Daniel read the poem. He didn't sound like her brother, Benjamin, but the time and setting – though this home, *their* home was warmer in both atmosphere and spirit than her mother's house had ever been – brought back the few moments of joy Elisabeth remembered. If she and Daniel had another child, a possibility she found herself longing for, and if that child were a boy, she would ask if they could name him Benjamin.

But that was still a hope yet to come, her health permitting, and a decision they both needed to make. For now she was more than content to be Emily's mother.

"*….to his sleigh, to his team gave a whistle,*
And away they all flew like the down of a thistle.
But I heard him exclaim, 'ere he drove out of sight,
'Happy Christmas to all, and to all a good night!'"

CHAPTER THIRTY-ONE

Ryan

Ryan circled the modest, middle-income, Simi Valley split-level with attached garage cul-de-sac slowly, checking the number of the house against the one listed on the invitation. It was the same, and a moment later the GPS's annoying female voice reaffirmed that.

"You have arrived at your destination."

"Thank you, very much," Ryan muttered and turned the device off.

"Shutting down in ten seconds...ten...nine..."

Ryan put it face-down on the passenger's seat and covered it with his jacket. The electronic front-seat driver had been last year's 'Are-You-Kidding-Me?' Christmas gift from Jamie.

"You know you're always getting lost and won't ask for directions...you are such a guy sometimes."

A truer statement had never been uttered, but he never got lost anymore.

Ryan gave the house – the only one on the street that wasn't decked out in holly, a million lights and had either full-sized nativity scenes or animated non-partisan holiday displays (or both) in the front yard – another look before pulling away in search of a parking space.

He knew it wasn't going to be easy, this being Christmas Eve when visions of sugarplum martinis and other festive drinks danced in many a head, and it wasn't. When he finally found one, in the Albertsons' parking lot five blocks away, and walked back to the house (using the GPS app on his phone), he arrived twenty minutes later than the time listed on the invitation.

Please join the Rosowsky-Gerstle-Leavitt
Celebration of Lights
December 16th – 24th

Hallel and the Reading of the Torah will begin at 5p.m.
Festivities to begin at 7p.m.
Food, drink, family and friends
All are invited

An address and phone number was listed, along with Aryeh's handwritten scribble along the bottom of the card: *Ryan, if you can, please come?*

When he opened the invitation his first thought was that the mail carrier had dropped it into the wrong box, the second – quickly following the first – was that Jiro and Oren's traditional Hanukkah/Christmas/Solstice/Saturnalia party had gotten a bit more formal than in years past, but who the heck were the Rosowsky-Gerstle-Leavitts?

Then he remembered: Rosowsky was the name of the cousin or nephew or grandwhatever on the list of Aryeh's relatives. Aryeh was inviting him over to celebrate the eight days of Hanukah with him and his newfound family.

Ryan called the number on the invitation, identified himself as best he could to the woman who'd answered and said he'd try to make it…*one night*…and hung up. He marked his office calendar and then kept putting it off as the first, then second, then third, etc., nights came and went. He went to Jiro and Oren's on the sixth night and suffered through an evening spent by answering variations of the same question *"How are you doing?"* with the same lie.

"I'm fine…thanks."

Jiro had tried to get him to promise to come over and spend Christmas Eve and Christmas morning with them and the baby – *"So you won't be alone."* It was such a pure act of friendship that it was all Ryan could do not to haul off and belt Jiro right in the mouth.

But he didn't.

If they thought that spending Christmas with them and their precious little baby would help, then they didn't understand that one day out of the next 365-plus wouldn't make much of a difference. He'd still be alone the day after Christmas and the next day and all the days and weeks and months and years to follow.

He was alone and would be alone…but tonight, even though

he knew the soul inside the body was different, Ryan needed to see Jamie's face one last time.

Christmas had always been *their* holiday.

They might spend Christmas Eve with friends and Boxing Day with family, but Christmas Day was theirs and theirs alone.

"I must be out of my mind," he reassured himself as he stepped into the glow of the porch light and rang the bell.

A little boy wearing a *South Park* sweatshirt and blue yarmulke opened the door.

"Um… Hi, ah…I'm Ryan Massie – Hi – I got an invitation from Aryeh Rosenber—"

The little boy turned his head and yelled at the top of his lungs, "Uncle Ari, someone's here for you."

Uncle Ari?

A young woman hurried over instead.

"Nathan, where are your manners? Go play. I'm sorry, kids, y'know?" Smiling, she opened the door a bit wider and motioned Ryan in. "It's a bit of a madhouse, I'm afraid – the kids got tired of playing dreidel and started eating their winnings. It's sugar high central at the moment, but please…come in. I'm Rebecca Rosowsky, welcome."

They shook hands and Ryan stepped farther into the tiled entryway to let her close the door behind him. *Trapped.*

"I'm Ryan Massie. Aryeh invited me."

"Ryan, yes. Aryeh told us about you and your kindness to him. Please…come in. There's food in the dining room and the bar's out on the patio – keeps it out of sight of the little ones. We also have soft drinks in the fridge, if you'd rather. Come in, come in."

He took another step forward to show her he was moving in the right direction and held up the bottle of wine.

"I brought this – I don't know if it's any good but the man in the liquor store said it was kosher."

He handed her the bottle and she took it like it was some rare gem, holding it carefully in both hands and smiling.

"Oh, my. Baron Herzog Merlot 2009 is one of my favorites."

"Good. I didn't know there were any kosher wines besides Manischewitz."

She laughed and nodded toward the crowded living room. "We have that too. Come on, you fix yourself a plate and I'll go find Aryeh. Here you go."

She gave him a white guest yarmulke similar to the ones Oren handed out and left him to enter the lion's den by himself. Ryan stuck the yarmulke on his head and made his way through the crowd. No one stared at him, no one nudged each other as he passed and whispered, no one even seemed to notice him at all unless it was to say hello or wish him a happy Chanukah or to tell him to try the brisket which, apparently, was to die for.

And who could argue with an endorsement like that?

Standing next to a banquet-sized table that could easily have sat twelve, Ryan surveyed a spread of meats, fish – herb-baked salmon and two kinds of pickled herring – breads, platters of cheese, vegetables (more bread) and a mound of potato pancakes that would have been the envy of any East Coast delicatessen and make Oren weep outright. Since he didn't know where to begin, Ryan started with the brisket and worked his way toward the potato pancakes.

He was adding a *shmear* of sour cream to the latkes when he heard his name called.

"You Ryan?" an elderly man with a beard asked.

"Yes."

"Ari says for you to come to the kitchen. He's stuck in there."

"He's stuck?"

The man shrugged and toasted him with the red plastic cup – "*L'chaim!*" – before melting back into the crowd. Since the front of the house obviously wasn't the kitchen, Ryan popped a piece of wine-pickled herring into his mouth – *heaven!* – and zigzagged his way toward the back of the house.

"Ryan! You made it! *Kumt aher* and save me!"

Aryeh wasn't just stuck in the kitchen; he was literally trapped in a corner between a large woman in an apron and a table piled high with platters that hadn't yet made it out to the dining room.

His hair was longer and his beard had filled in completely, and he'd put on just enough weight to round off the sharp lines and ridges in his face. He didn't look like Jamie anymore, but there was still enough of a resemblance to make the pickled herring in Ryan's stomach do a flip-flop.

But it was okay…standing there in the steaming kitchen, looking at the man, it was finally okay. Jamie was gone and something opened up inside Ryan's chest and made it just a little easier to breathe.

There was a smudge of flour on Aryeh's right cheek, just above the edge of the beard, and he was wearing a flowered bib apron.

Ryan laughed out loud. "You look good. I think that's your color."

Aryeh looked down at the apron and raised his arms in a wide shrug. The silver thread on his yarmulke shimmered in the light. "What's a man to do?"

"Oh, don't listen to him," a young woman said as she crossed the room and held out her hand. "He volunteered to help. You must be Ryan…I'm Rachel Moss."

"Hi." They shook hands and she let go first. "Oh, and… *A lichtige Chanukah* – I hope I said that right."

"Perfect," Rachel said, "and Merry Christmas to you. Ari, are you going to sit there all night or go visit with your friend?"

Aryeh looked up at her. "I have a choice now?"

She looked at Ryan and rolled her eyes, then said something to Aryeh in Hebrew or Yiddish or German and pulled the apron off of him.

"Go. Talk. Enjoy," she commanded then moved the large woman aside to clear a space wide enough for the wheelchair to get through. "Get Ryan a drink…and eat something! You haven't eaten anything all night."

Aryeh shook his head. "Already she talks like a wife, huh?" *Wife?* "I haven't stopped eating in seven days and she says eat. Women are wondrous things, Ryan."

"I wouldn't know," he said under his breath as he followed Aryeh out the kitchen door.

Despite the wealth of alcoholic beverages standing in formation on the makeshift bar/picnic table, the enclosed patio was practically empty. People would come out, either from the kitchen or through the dining room's French doors, pour themselves a drink, say hello, wish them a Happy Hanukah then go back inside.

"I am happy you came," Aryeh said, rolling himself up to the table. "You like a drink?"

"Ah, no...not right now. Thanks." Aryeh nodded and backed the chair away. "I'm – I'm sorry I didn't come sooner, but—"

"*Sha.* You're here now. Thank you."

Why is he thanking me? "So...you're getting married?"

Aryeh smiled and Jamie's ghost hovered for just a moment around his eyes.

"*Yoh*, in the spring. Ryan, can I ask a favor?"

"Sure."

"Would you come and be my *shomer*? Best man, yes?"

"Your...?" *Whoa.* "Ah, I'm not Jewish."

"No, and it is not a true Jewish tradition to have such a man, best or not, but it has come to mean someone who you wish to honor. And I wish to honor you, Ryan."

"Why?"

"Because I cannot ask the man who gave me my life back, so I ask the man who loved him and who has shown me such kindness when his own heart was in such pain. You are a *mensch*, Ryan, a person of character and someone I am very proud to know. Would you consider?"

Ryan had to take three long breaths before he could get his lungs to fully inflate.

"What does a...*shomer* have to do?"

"The same as any best man – make sure the *chatan*, the groom, gets to the temple on time."

Ryan nodded and toasted Jamie's ghost as it disappeared.

"I think I can handle that."

CHAPTER THIRTY-TWO

Christine-Helene

When the president of the theater board had first asked the company how they felt about doing an extra performance on Christmas Eve, anyone who happened to be walking by might have thought a serial killer had gotten loose inside the theater. Screams, shouts and wails echoed off the rafters…and that had just been from the director. The actors just wondered, loudly, if the president and rest of the board members had lost their collective minds.

Do a show on Christmas Eve? Who would come? Not to mention that there were a few members of the cast (and crew) who might have made plans for that night.

The show's regular performance run ended with a Saturday matinee on the 23rd…with the least attendance number to date – 12, and, because of the holidays, the set strike had been postponed until the 30th so *people could be with their families.*

Crissy didn't care, of course. She and Frank were going to spend Christmas together – she'd gotten him some really cute *impractical* things – but since he was on call Christmas Eve, her only plans were to watch *It's A Wonderful Life* on TV, eat her non-salted, non-buttered air-popped popcorn, cry at the sad parts and feel sorry for herself.

"Come on, seriously…Christmas Eve? No one is going to show up and you know it."

"There's where you're wrong." The board president, a retired schoolteacher who was the living image of Eleanor Roosevelt, smiled and took a moment to look pleased with herself. "We've gotten a call from a local women's shelter saying they would love to give their clients, most of whom have *children*, people, a special Christmas Eve gift. I told them I'd have to talk to you first, but we're looking at a full house." She paused a moment before adding "A paid-in-full house."

The director stopped grumbling.

"Of course if you don't want to do it...and disappoint so many children who have already experienced so much trauma and pain...."

The board president didn't have to finish. And after a three-count pause, their director had looked at his cast, shrugged, and asked, "What do you think, gang? Can we do it?"

"Sure!" Like any of them would say no after that.

As it turned out, the Christmas Eve performance went so well and had such a wonderful audience response, that the board — all of whom had come to the show with bags of candy and 'little gifts' for the children — decided right then and there to make it a holiday tradition.

And the cast, without one exception, all volunteered to come back.

It *was* Christmas, after all...and it was nice to know she'd have another acting gig firmed up if her ambitions to become a professional actress didn't pan out.

Not that she thought that would happen.

Thanks to Frank, who'd spent six weeks teaching her to drive and the DMV examiner who'd 'retested' her after she'd gotten nervous and almost ran through a Boulevard stop, Crissy had a license and Helen's car and only a slight phobia about driving the L.A. freeway system after dark.

But she could drive and had managed to get an agent who believed in her and her monthly checks, an audition list for both Equity and non-Equity theaters and two callbacks for a television commercial: *"I don't want my kids to go to school without a good breakfast...but who has time to cook in the morning?"*

Maybe it wasn't Shakespeare, or even Ibsen, but she'd make $200.00 and get her face out into the public eye. Christine-Helene Harmon, her stage name, *was* going to have the life she wanted... even if it did come a bit later than she'd originally hoped.

Yup, things were finally looking up.

Still in costume, Crissy followed the other actors out into the house for a 'meet and greet'.

The kids, those who weren't already dozing, were really excited to be up close and personal with *real* actors and asked question after question: "Was it hard to learn your lines?" "Were you scared up there? I'd be scared." "Is that your real hair or a wig?" "Why did you draw lines on your face?" "Would Tiny Tim die if Scrooge didn't buy them the Christmas goose?" "Was that a real ghost?"

Crissy answered as best she could.

When a series of squeals followed by just as many high-pitched giggles filled the house, Crissy turned to watch Arthur, dressed as Bob Cratchit but wearing the faceless black hood of the Ghost of Christmas Future, chasing a group of laughing children around the stage. The kids were having a ball.

"You were wonderful!"

Crissy turned and smiled at the young mother. The woman, carrying a sleepy little boy of about five, had a bruise on the left side of her face that extended from her chin to her temple.

"Thank you," Crissy said and tried not to stare. "Did you have a good time?"

"Oh, yes, Brian here got a little scared when the ghosts showed up – especially the last one – but I think he liked it. Didn't you, Brian?"

Brian, the little boy, yawned then laid his head down against his mother's shoulder and closed his eyes.

"Everyone's a critic," Crissy said and the mother laughed.

"Well, *I* think it was great and I'm sure he'll be talking all about it tomorrow. I just wanted to thank you." She looked like she wanted to say something else, then shrugged. "Well, I'd better get this one to bed. Thanks again, it was great. Merry Christmas."

"Merry Christmas," Crissy answered, "and a Happier New Year."

The woman smiled, catching her meaning. "Right, you too."

I will, Crissy promised herself and watched the mother and her child join the other women heading for the door. It was getting late and Santa wouldn't come until all the children were asleep.

As the board members followed the women and children, the cast headed downstairs to change. They'd had their cast party the final night of their official run so there was no real reason to hang around.

Plus she was tired.

The only things she had to do now were to take off her makeup, hang up her costume, say goodbye and Merry Christmas to the cast and avoid Arthur.

"Hey, everybody!" It was Arthur. "Who wants to go out for a drink to celebrate?"

Crissy took a deep breath and did what any normal adult woman would do – she hid in the ladies' dressing room until he went away.

Frank was waiting for her at the stage door when she came out.

"Hiya…Christine-Helene. Have I told you how *poetic* I think your new name is? You've got a real Dr. Seuss thing going on there."

"Ha ha. But what are you doing here? I thought you were on call?"

"I was." He smiled and took her arm, pulling her off to one side to let the actors who'd played the Ghost of Christmas Past and Marley pass. "And am…I switched with Dr. Kensington – he took my slot and I'll be working his midnight to eight a.m. shift."

"Why?"

"So I could be here."

Crissy leaned back and hoped there was enough light for him to see her pout. "But we were supposed to open presents and have Christmas breakfast together."

"We still can, or we can have Christmas brunch. That way you can sleep in a bit."

"But I wanted to open presents first thing…in bed."

Frank took a deep, mournful breath. "Crissy, we already talked about this."

"I know," she said, "but I'm ready, Frank. I really am. I love you."

He pulled her into a hug, his chin tickling the top of her head when he talked.

"And I love you," he said, "and that's why we're going to wait."

He looked surprised when she stepped back, opening the front of her sweater coat. "It's because of this, isn't it? This body. It's not me and that's why you won't, isn't it?"

She expected an argument, instead she got a smile.

"No, that's not why and you know it." He closed the front of her coat. "I'm probably the first man in recorded history who can say this and be absolutely and completely truthful: I love you for what you are inside, Christine Taylor Moore. Okay?"

"Okay, so...."

"So you're still only seventeen," he whispered, then winked. "Now, do you want your Christmas Eve present or not?"

Crissy was about to squeal and say all the appropriate, silly things when the passenger side door of Frank's car opened and an old man got out. He stood there for a moment, looking at her, then opened the back passenger door and helped a woman get out. The woman was about the same age as the man, more or less, and held onto the man's hand so tight that even in the weak light Crissy could see the tips of his fingers turn pale.

They just stood there looking at her and it was starting to creep her out.

"Who are they?"

Frank wrapped his arm around her shoulders. "Don't you recognize them?"

They did look a little familiar. Crissy squinted her eyes and—

"Oh, God."

She leaned back into Frank and felt his arm tighten around her.

"It's okay, Crissy."

"They're...?"

"I had to tell them, Crissy, and, although it took some time, they understand what happened." Frank chuckled softly as her parents started walking toward them. "Well, they understand as well as any of us do. Go say hello, Crissy. They've been waiting a long time."

"But I'm not the same."

"No one is, baby. Go on."

Her parents stood in the middle of the sidewalk opposite the shelter's All Welcome sign less than two yards away from her. All she had to do was walk forward and she could touch them, but she couldn't move.

'Frank, I—"

"It's okay, Crissy...everything's going to be okay."

He gave her a little push and her body...*Helen's* body moved forward on legs that felt more rubber than flesh. Inside, the part that Frank loved couldn't tell if it was breathing or if its heart was beating or even if it was awake. It seemed so much like a dream; then, all of a sudden, her mother's arms were around her and her father's arms around them both and Crissy woke up.

And she was back, she was whole and whatever happened to her now was going to be okay.

"Merry Christmas, Crissy."

And God bless us, everyone.

CHAPTER THIRTY-THREE

Nora

"Mama, can you wake up for me?"

Nora heard another voice answer from the place on the other side of her closed eyelids but couldn't quite place it. The voice was familiar and almost sounded like Henry, but wasn't Henry.

"Oh, no, it's all right," the voice said, "I can come back later."

"No, no, it's okay; she was just awake a minute ago. Mama? Mama, open your eyes."

Nora took a deep breath and pried her eyelids apart. She was in a bright white room, but it wasn't the same one she'd just left. She'd been sitting in her living room, knitting from a ball of bright blue yarn she kept in the white birch basket by her feet and talking to Henry, while a little white boy she'd never seen before but knew was Timmy played trains on the rug between them. Henry was in his chair, holding a newspaper but not reading it; he'd wanted to talk, to apologize for the way he'd behaved back when he was sick and she'd told him it was all right, that it didn't matter.

"Don't worry about it, Henry," she'd told him and that made him smile.

"You comin'?" he asked and then Timmy looked up and he smiled too. "Yeah, you comin', Missus Nora? Nobody here makes cookies like you do."

And she laughed and told them she'd come as soon as she could.

It was good to see them both so happy.

"Mama?"

Nora blinked until her eyes focused on the here and now. She was in the hospital and Marjorie was hovering over her, looking worried and much too tired.

"You awake, Mama?"

"Seems so," Nora said and scooted herself up on the thin, crinkly pillow. "Back away, child, you're about to suffocate me."

The voice she'd heard earlier, the one that sounded like Henry but wasn't, laughed.

"Now there's the Miss Nora I know and love."

She recognized the voice now.

"Martin." Nora held out her hand and watched him hurry across the small, clean, cold room to take it. "I was hoping you'd stop by. I have a present for you."

Martin's Sidney Poitier eyes widened. "For me? But...Miss Nora, you shouldn't have."

"Oh, don't you tell me what I should and shouldn't do. I'm a crazy old woman with too much time on her hands. Marjorie, would you get Dr. Cross his gift, please?"

Nora pretended she didn't see the exchange of looks between the two just before her daughter turned away. She'd gotten good at pretending not to notice things like that since they brought her to the hospital. Pretending she didn't notice the fear in Marjorie's eyes or the pity in her friends' when they visited; pretending it didn't hurt like a million hot needles when the nurses helped her walk from the bed to the chair; pretending she believed the doctor – not Martin, but the older orthopedic surgeon who'd repaired her broken hip with steel rods – when he said she was 'doing fine'; and pretending she believed him and Marjorie and everyone else who told her she'd soon be well enough to go home.

She'd gotten good at pretending, all right.

Marjorie came back to the bed carrying a shiny green-and-red plaid gift bag. Nora had decided against using boxes this year because wrapping gifts and putting bows on them had always been something she and Henry did together.

"Mama had already started this when she...had her little accident."

Nora took the bag from her daughter's hand and rolled her eyes. "That's my daughter's way of saying when I fell off the ladder and busted up my hip. And I know, I know...that was a silly thing for an old woman to do, but I've changed that same light bulb in the hall a hundred times before and never once fell off that darn ladder. Just goes to show you, doesn't it. Well, enough of that." She lifted the gift bag. "Here you are, Martin. Merry Christmas."

Dr. Cross took the bag in one hand and carefully pried open the tissue paper with the other as if he half expected a snake to jump out at him.

"Good heavens," Nora sighed, "just open it! It's not going to bite you."

Both Marjorie and Martin laughed, but Martin stopped when he pulled out the scarf she'd knitted him.

"Miss Nora…it's beautiful."

Nora had to admit it was. She'd used a garter rib pattern for the scarf because it was not only pretty and reversible, but really showed off the yarn's mix of browns and tans and hint of pale blue.

"The color's called Driftwood and I got it over at Michael's on Hill, in case your wife asks. I was thinking about using Oceana, but it was brighter – blues and greens and aqua – and I thought it might stand out too much, you know. This is a bit more conservative."

"I don't know what to say, Miss Nora."

"Then don't say anything and wear it in good health."

"I will," he said and looped it around his neck like he was about to go out on an arctic exploration. It looked *good* on him. "You are a wonder, Miss Nora."

"That I am, and don't forget feisty," she said and he laughed. "Oh, I know a scarf's probably the most impractical thing to have in Los Angeles, but if you go up to the mountains or someplace like that it might come in handy."

"I do ski," he said.

"Well, there you go."

"She made one for all of us," Marjorie piped in, "practically everyone she knows. I think she started right after…well, back around Halloween and you wouldn't believe the trips we made to Michael's for yarn. They love her there."

"As well they should," Nora said, "I'm one of their best customers. I like making scarves because they're easy to do. So you think of that scarf as a hug from me every time you wear it."

He patted the scarf against his chest.

"That's exactly what I'll think every time I put it on." He cleared his throat. "Now…your present. It's not homemade, I'm afraid."

He pulled a small gift-wrapped box from his coat pocket and handed it to her. The wrapping, gold-embossed paper with a tiny red bow, was well done; Henry would have been pleased.

"Oh, now, Martin…you didn't have to *do* this." Nora tore open the ends and ran a shaky finger through the taped seam along the bottom. "But I'm happy you did."

"Oh – *Martin!*" Nora lifted out the spun-glass snowflake by its silver thread and watched it spin. "It's so delicate. Here, Marjorie, you take it, my hand's not as steady as it was and I'm afraid it'll fall."

"They're a lot sturdier than they look, Miss Nora," he said as Marjorie took the ornament from her and carefully put it back into its box. "We've had some on our tree for years and they're still around."

"It's lovely, Martin, thank you."

"It's something my dad did every year – gave each of us kids a special ornament to hang on the tree, so that when we grew up and moved out…and took the ornaments with us…we'd remember him. He did the same with his grandkids before he died." He smiled down at Nora and his smile was just a little sad. "See, this way, when you hang it on your tree every year, *you'll* remember *me.*"

"Oh, I don't think I'd ever forget you, Martin." She held out her hands and he took them. His skin was warm and soft against hers. "Thank you so much for everything you did for me and Henry."

She squeezed his hands, saying goodbye, and he squeezed back.

"Well, I'd best be letting you get some rest," he said and leaned down quick to give her a little peck on the cheek. "And I want to go show off my new scarf. Merry Christmas, Miss Nora."

"Merry Christmas, Martin."

He said goodbye to Marjorie and smiled back at Nora before he left. He knows, she thought to herself, and took a deep breath.

"Now, about tomorrow, Mama—"

Nora congratulated herself on keeping from groaning. Marjorie had made plans: she and her husband and the boys would come over in the afternoon with presents and holiday cookies and then, if she, Nora, felt up to it, the boys would take their granny down to the cafeteria for their holiday meal.

Doesn't that sound nice?

"Oh, Marjorie," Nora said and let herself slide down a little on the mattress to ease the ache in her hip and lower back. The pain was almost constant now, but she'd gotten used to it. "I will not make my poor grandbabies sit in a hospital cafeteria to have Christmas dinner, I will not!"

"All right, Mama, don't get upset. What if…oh, I know, I'll make dinner tonight and we can bring it here and have it in the room. How does that sound?"

Nora just looked at her daughter and let her guess how she thought that sounded.

Marjorie sighed. "Okay, then what do *you* suggest?"

Finally! "I want you and your family to wake up in the morning and open presents – you did pick up the presents I had for you and Daryl and the boys at the house, didn't you?" Marjorie nodded. "Good, and if some of the things I bought don't fit, you'll find the receipts taped to the inside of the bottom of the boxes. All right, then. I want you to open presents and eat too much and relax and maybe call me before you sit down to supper."

"Call you? Mama, tomorrow's Christmas and we're going to come see you."

Nora took a deep breath and eased down farther. She was tired but Marjorie wasn't going to give up until she got the answer she wanted. Her daughter was so much like her sometimes Nora could hear God laughing.

"All right," she said and pretended it was, "but not until later…I want the boys to get their fill of all those video gamey things I bought – and don't you look at me like that, I'm their grandmother and I'm entitled to spoil them rotten. Let them play, all right? And, call before you come over, okay? I think the nurses are planning a little party too, and I wouldn't want to ruin their plans."

"Okay, Mama, I'll call."

Marjorie leaned down to hug her and kissed her cheek on almost the same spot that Martin had kissed. The scent of her daughter's perfume – orange blossoms and jasmine and carnations – filled Nora's head.

"Oh, Marjorie, take the snowflake Dr. Cross gave me and hang it on your tree. It's too pretty to stay in a box…until next year. Will you do that?"

"All right, Mama, but next year it goes on your tree. Now, you get some rest now, okay?"

"I will," Nora promised and that was one promise she intended to keep. "Good…night, baby."

"'Night, Mama…see you tomorrow."

Nora watched the empty doorway until the sound of her daughter's footsteps faded away, and then she closed her eyes.

"Hey, lazy bones…what you doin'? We have to get goin'. "

They were standing at the foot of the bed, Henry and a smiling little boy with big brown eyes and a crooked smile. Timmy was holding Henry's hand and had on a *Howdy Doody* tee-shirt.

"Going?" Nora asked as she threw back the covers and swung her legs over the side. There was no pain and her broken hip felt all mended. "Where are we going?"

Laughing, Timmy let go of Henry's hand and darted across the room to fetch Nora's bathrobe and slippers.

"Home," Timmy said as Nora pulled on the robe. "We're all going home. Mr. Henry's making a big Christmas dinner."

Nora pretended to be shocked. "He is?"

"Turkey and all the fixin's," Henry said and offered her his arm. "Come along now."

Nora felt the last breath leave her body as she took Henry's arm and Timmy's hand, and went home.

CHAPTER THIRTY-FOUR

Dr. Bernard Ellison

He walked through halls filled with the sweet/sharp scent of lemon disinfectant and piped-in Christmas carols. Doors decorated with wreaths made by physical therapy patients and garlands of shimmering dollar store tinsel stood open, but most of the rooms were empty, their occupants downstairs in the common room having cookies and punch and watching holiday movies on the big-screen TV. There were only two closed doors on the wing, Miranda's and the 'new guy' – a young man who'd slid his motorcycle into a freeway embankment at 60 mph. Because he'd been wearing a one-piece leather body suit, most of the big pieces had stayed together, but the impact had snapped back his head, protected in its wrap-around helmet, with enough force to separate the skull from the spinal column, resulting in an atlanto-occipital dislocation.

The man had neurologically decapitated himself and his family was praying for a miracle that would never happen.

As a professional he could have told them how useless that was, but first he had to believe that himself.

"Merry Christmas! Ho, ho, ho!"

Tessa looked up from the paperback novel she was reading and smiled. "Merry Christmas, Dr. Ellison. I was hoping I'd see you before my shift ended."

"Well, I'm glad I made it before you left. And since you're my first customer…." Barney lifted the oversized Harry & David's bag onto the nurses' station. "You get first pick. I wasn't sure who was on a diet or not, so you have a choice of either truffles or dried fruits and nuts."

Tessa – tall and tan and lovely and happily married – dropped her book and dove face-first into the bag, muttering, "Decisions, decisions," before coming up with a box of truffles.

"You know you're going to spoil us," she said, prying the lid off.

"Never. And if I do, so what? Who can I spoil if not the best nursing team on earth?"

Tessa popped a truffle into her mouth and the look on her face said it all.

"You're welcome."

"Mmmm, hmm!" She swallowed and closed the box. Barney admired her self-control. "Linda said your flowers arrived this morning. I saw them when I made my ten o'clock rounds. They are absolutely gorgeous. I didn't think hothouse roses ever had much of a scent, but you can sure smell these."

Barney nodded. "Miranda thought the same thing. That's probably why she kept a rose garden. Sure saved me a lot of money on anniversary gifts, I can tell you."

And they laughed even though it was the same, or nearly the same, thing he'd said almost every day of the seven months since a drunk driver had run his wife down as she crossed the street.

It'd been a bright sunny afternoon in May, one of those rare days when people remember why they lived in California, and she'd waited until the light changed on Wilshire before crossing the street. She'd taken a late lunch to meet a friend, but wasn't hurrying back to her office, or frantic that she would be late – she owned her own travel agency – or not paying attention as the police officer who'd called him subtly insinuated.

Miranda wasn't like that.

Hadn't been like that.

The man who had run her down just hadn't noticed he was running a red light or that he was twenty miles over the speed limit or even that he'd hit someone until her body slammed into his windshield.

The police officer told Barney that he kept apologizing as they put him in the squad car, but that didn't help any more than the man's conviction and current incarceration. Miranda was gone and nothing the man or Barney could do was going to bring her back.

The only thing left was to keep a promise they'd made each other years ago but never thought they'd ever have to keep.

Barney stopped laughing first, but kept the smile on his lips. "So... big plans for tomorrow?"

Tessa smiled back. "Oh, yeah. It's my turn to make Christmas dinner and both Ted's folks and mine are going to descend on us around six. TJ's going to be making the chocolate-pecan pie this year."

TJ was Tessa's eleven-year-old son.

"I'm impressed," Barney said truthfully. "I don't remember being able to boil water at his age."

"What can I say, he takes after his mother."

They shared another brief laugh before he asked, "How's she doing?" and Tessa's face grew serious.

"About the same. Did they call you?"

Barney nodded. One of the attendings had called to let him know Miranda's breathing pattern had changed, which in 'doctor speak' meant she was dying.

But dying was an active verb. Miranda could linger for days or weeks before her lungs finally stopped and whatever was left, if anything was left of the woman he loved, would suffocate.

It was the one thing they both feared and the one thing they'd promised each other would never happen.

Barney slipped his hands into the jacket's pockets, his right hand nesting around the syringe he'd placed there before leaving his office.

Potassium chloride – just enough to keep his promise.

"Well, you take care and if I don't see you when I come out... Merry Christmas."

Tessa sat down and picked up her book. "Oh, you'll see me. Visiting hours end before I do."

Barney nodded as he turned and walked away. Miranda's room was at the far end of the hall and because it would be the last time he'd make the trip, he counted his steps. There were fifty-two from the nurses' station to the closed door of Room 618...two steps more than Miranda's age.

Barney opened the door and stepped in. A moment later he couldn't remember having walked into the room, even though he must have, because he had to turn around and take five or six steps before he reached the door again.

"Tessa! Tessa, come here!"

Barney leaned against the doorframe to hold himself up as she ran toward him. There was concern and pity on her face as if she knew what had just happened.

"Oh, Dr. Ellison…I'm so sor—"

"Do you know French?"

"What?"

"Do. You. Know. French?"

"I – um…I took a couple years in high school, but…."

"Good." Barney grabbed her arm and hauled her into the room. "Now, don't be frightened, but ask her her name."

"What? Dr. Ellison, what are you—" And then she turned and looked at the bed and let out a sound that was half gasp, half scream.

Miranda was sitting up, holding the covers up to her chest, the IV tube that was connected to the needle in her arm trembling. She was saying something, possibly the same something she'd said to Barney when he walked in, but he didn't speak French and he needed to know what that something was. It took some effort to pry Tessa's grasp off his arm and pull her to the bed, but he finally managed.

"Dr. Ellison…she's…awake."

"I know and I'll explain everything in a minute, just—"

"I need to call this in. Her doctor needs to be here!"

"In a minute – please! Tessa, what is she saying?"

"What? Um…." She turned toward the bed.

"*Ôu je suis? Ôu je suis?*"

"She's, ah, asking where she is."

Barney left Tessa standing at the foot of the bed, gape-mouthed and bug-eyed, and walked very slowly toward the woman in the bed.

"Tell her."

It took a few tries, but Tessa answered her. The woman frowned.

"*Pourquoi?*"

"Why?"

"Ask her her name."

"Oh…um…*Quel est*…ah, *votre nom?*"

The woman's eyes never left Barney's face.

"*Amandine Facet. Qui vous est?*"

"She says…what's going on? She says her name's Amandine Facet," Tessa translated, "and she wants to know what your name is. Dr. Ellison, what's going on?"

"Shhh."

Barney nodded at the woman. Her eyes were different than Miranda's. Miranda's eyes had been hazel, this woman's eyes sea-foam green.

He patted his chest. "I'm Dr. Bernard Ellison."

"*Docteur?*"

"Yes, doctor." Turning, he hurried back across the room and forcibly escorted Tessa to the door. "Get her doctor, but don't tell him anything except that she's awake. I'll...I promise, I'll explain this to both of you when he gets here. Okay? Go!"

Tessa left on a run. When he was sure she was far enough away, Barney took the syringe from his pocket and emptied the contents into the room's hand sink before dropping it into the medical waste container.

She was watching him, her green eyes wide, but she didn't seem afraid and that was important. Still, he walked back to her side very slowly and made sure he kept his voice low and reassuring.

Maybe the motorcyclist's parents were right, maybe miracles could happen after all.

"Amandine?" She nodded. "Welcome back."

FLAME TREE PRESS
FICTION WITHOUT FRONTIERS
Award-Winning Authors & Original Voices

Flame Tree Press is the trade fiction imprint of Flame Tree Publishing, focusing on excellent writing in horror and the supernatural, crime and mystery, science fiction and fantasy. Our aim is to explore beyond the boundaries of the everyday, with tales from both award-winning authors and original voices.

•

Other titles available include:

Junction by Daniel M. Bensen
Thirteen Days by Sunset Beach by Ramsey Campbell
Think Yourself Lucky by Ramsey Campbell
The Hungry Moon by Ramsey Campbell
The Haunting of Henderson Close by Catherine Cavendish
The House by the Cemetery by John Everson
The Toy Thief by D.W. Gillespie
Black Wings by Megan Hart
The Playing Card Killer by Russell James
The Siren and the Specter by Jonathan Janz
Wolf Land by Jonathan Janz
The Sorrows by Jonathan Janz
Savage Species by Jonathan Janz
The Nightmare Girl by Jonathan Janz
The Dark Game by Jonathan Janz
The Widening Gyre by Michael R. Johnston
Will Haunt You by Brian Kirk
Kosmos by Adrian Laing
The Sky Woman by J.D. Moyer
Creature by Hunter Shea
The Bad Neighbor by David Tallerman
Ten Thousand Thunders by Brian Trent
Night Shift by Robin Triggs
The Mouth of the Dark by Tim Waggoner

•

Join our mailing list for free short stories, new release details, news about our authors and special promotions:

flametreepress.com